THE WORLD'S CLASSICS

A TALE OF A TUB

AND OTHER WORKS

JONATHAN SWIFT (1667–1745) left Dublin for England in 1689, where he was secretary to Sir William Temple and taught Temple's ward Esther Johnson ('Stella'), who remained his close friend until her death in 1728. A great Anglo-Irish publicist, Swift first came to public and political attention in England with *Contests and Dissensions* (1701) and *A Tale of a Tub* (1704). He supported Harley's Tory administration in *The Conduct of the Allies* (1711), and in 1713 became Dean of St Patrick's, Dublin. When the Government fell with the death of Queen Anne the following year he retired there, emerging as a popular Irish patriot with publications such as *The Drapier's Letters* (1724) and *A Modest Proposal* (1729). His best-known work today, *Gulliver's Travels*, was published in London in 1726. He is buried in St Patrick's Cathedral, beneath the epitaph he composed himself. A master of prose style, he is also a considerable poet, excelling in ironical anti-'poetic' imagination.

ANGUS ROSS, Reader in English at the University of Sussex, writes on eighteenth-century and other literature in English and has edited texts and anthologies including *Robinson Crusoe* and *Gulliver's Travels*.

DAVID WOOLLEY commenced collecting first and early editions of Swift in Australia in 1946. During a residence of twenty years in London, he has studied the texts of Swift's verse and prose, including the extensive correspondence, from the originals in England, Ireland, and the United States. He collaborated with Angus Ross in producing *Jonathan Swift* (1984) in the Oxford Authors series.

THE WORLD'S CLASSICS

JONATHAN SWIFT

A Tale of a Tub
and Other Works

Edited with an Introduction by
ANGUS ROSS AND DAVID WOOLLEY

Oxford New York
OXFORD UNIVERSITY PRESS
1986

Oxford University Press, Walton Street, Oxford OX2 6DP
Oxford New York Toronto
Delhi Bombay Calcutta Madras Karachi
Kuala Lumpur Singapore Hong Kong Tokyo
Nairobi Dar es Salaam Cape Town
Melbourne Auckland
and associated companies in
Beirut Berlin Ibadan Nicosia

Oxford is a trade mark of Oxford University Press

British Library Cataloguing in Publication Data
Swift, Jonathan
A tale of a tub: and related pieces.—(The World's classics)
I. Title II. Ross, Angus, 1928–
III. Woolley, David
828'.509 PR3724.T3
ISBN 0–19–281689–6

Library of Congress Cataloging in Publication Data
Swift, Jonathan, 1667–1745
A tale of a tub, and related pieces.
(The World's classics)
Includes the "Battle of the books" and the "Mechanical operation of the spirit."
Bibliography: p.
I. Ross, Angus. II. Woolley, David. III. Title.
PR3724.A1 1985 823'.5 85–5072
ISBN 0–19–281689–6 (pbk.)

Printed in Great Britain by
Hazell, Watson & Viney Limited
Aylesbury, Bucks

To
Hermann Real and Heinz Vienken
and to the memory of
Irvin Ehrenpreis

CONTENTS

INTRODUCTION

THE present volume includes the contents of the volume which Swift himself first published early in 1704, namely, *A Tale of a Tub*, *A Full and True Account of the Battle of the Books*, and *A Discourse of the Mechanical Operation of the Spirit. A Fragment.* We have followed these pieces with four Additions to *A Tale*, printed sixteen years later in Holland. Appendix A gives substantial extracts from nine works, not easily available. These throw light, not just on Swift's ideas and interests, the topics of his satire, but also on his writing itself, its living tones and styles. The latter are the most bewildering, but also the most rewarding and exciting aspects of his achievement. Appendix B discusses a controversy over the authorship of *A Tale*, which began immediately after publication of the 1704 volume and which is of more than historical interest. The notion of 'authorship' is one of the areas (like 'readership') on which Swift's fertile imagination seizes in these satires.

Swift's four-shilling volume of 1704 is the masterpiece of his early life, balancing and matching *Gulliver's Travels*, the imaginative crown of his later years. It is an assemblage of writing that covers the first decade of his writing career. An imprecise tradition with a respectable pedigree pushes back the composition or sketch of part of *A Tale of a Tub*, perhaps the parable or allegory, to Swift's student days in the 1680s at Trinity College, Dublin. Most of the ostensible subject matter, and the bulk of the writing, clearly dates from the time of his employment by Sir William Temple at Moor Park (cf. Sir William Temple himself on 'chymistry' and 'critics' in 'Some Thoughts . . .', pp. 177 and 178 below). Swift also had the run of Temple's library, and it would be interesting to know more about this, especially since so much of the satire in the volume is focused on books and reading. There are indeed several references in the text of *A Tale* to the years 1696 and 1697; and in the *Apology* Swift says, 'the greatest part of the book was finished' in the former year. In consideration of the hostile reception the satire received in some quarters (see pp. 182 f.), however, he has been assumed to have exaggerated his youth when he wrote the work. His *Discourse on the Contests and Dissensions in Athens and Rome*, published in 1701, was similarly founded on his reading and thinking at Moor Park, but given a force and point by the political crisis and bitter pamphlet controversy in London in 1700–1. There are similar political touches in *A Tale*—such as its dedication to Lord Somers, who was defended in the *Contests and*

Dissensions—that may reflect some further work (or another layer of writing) in the assemblage before its publication. *The Battle of the Books* springs more obviously from Swift's life in Temple's circle at Moor Park, and the date of composition, given by 'The Bookseller to the Reader' as 1697, indicates that it is a discrete piece, finished earlier than *A Tale* itself, specifically related to a completed series of events.

A Tale of a Tub

Swift's title, like much of the writing in the text, contains several jokes working simultaneously. It makes use of both an old expression meaning a cock-and-bull story and also of the icon, to which he himself refers (p. 18), of the mariners throwing out an empty barrel to distract an inquisitive and threatening 'whale'. In all this he plays with the tone of a jocular formula in handling serious and complex ideas, and introduces the undercurrent of menace and bravado, fear and daring, into which he immerses himself in the course of the satire. In form, *A Tale* consists of a parable of the development of the Christian religion in Europe, the allegory of the Father, his will and his three sons with their coats, accompanied by a group of Digressions in which is placed a set of variations on different themes that preoccupied Swift. The whole is embellished with a comic assemblage of the kind of 'preliminaries' that swelled the Grub Street volumes pouring from the presses after the lapse of the Press Licensing Act in 1695. It ends with a manic 'Conclusion' from the modern and mercantile pen of 'The Author', exposing the talents he has acquired and boasting that he is 'by the liberty and encouragement of the press . . . grown absolute master of the occasions and opportunities'. In his later defiant and not too exculpatory *Apology*, Swift declares that 'he thought the numerous and gross corruptions in religion and learning might furnish matter for a satire'. His Christian fable develops an argument that Martin [Anglicanism] holds a moderate position between the peremptory institutionalism of Peter [Catholicism], and the anarchic, egotistical individualism of Jack [radical personal belief]. At the historical moment of *A Tale*, many English religious believers, not only heirs of the mid-seventeenth-century sectaries like the Fifth Monarchy Men, or the Ranters, or indeed the Quakers, but also the Baptists, Presbyterians, and Congregationalists, had been by the 1662 Act of Uniformity legislated into Dissenters from the Church of England by law established. Swift's brief service in 1695–6 as a Church of Ireland (Anglican) priest in a predominantly Presbyterian area at Kilroot, near Belfast, without doubt sharpened his ecclesiastical and political sensibilities. He chose to attack the force of individualistic religion as 'zeal' or 'enthusiasm', and to ascribe it to pride, that 'sufficiency' which Temple saw as the root of political dissidence and intellectual arrogance (p. 158).

The corruptions of learning flowed from the same sufficiency. They encompassed not only the scornful 'moderns' like Bentley, who hectored the 'ancients' he professed to study and attacked those, like Temple, who revered the ancient wisdom, but also all the 'edifices in the air', the elaborate intellectual structures that Swift's wide reading in Temple's library had disinterred. Swift makes a sparkling mosaic of fragments from alchemy, hermetic and occult systems, philosophical, medical, and scientific schemes. The gnostic, heretical teachers of the first two centuries of Christianity, offering secret illumination, rub shoulders in the allusive text with Paracelsus, Sendivogius, and Thomas Vaughan, offering secret knowledge of nature, with Descartes offering a programme for certain reasoning, with charismatic religious leaders like Jack of Leyden, and with military and political leaders like Alexander the Great and Louis XIV, all offering themselves at their own valuation to obedient followers. 'The Author' of *A Tale* is a practical instance of such pride and complacency, as he writes, postures, and parades his pointless ingenuity. All are types of sufficiency, and fair game for attack, ridicule, and mockery. Joined with this, however, is the freest, liveliest, and most trenchant expression of a deeply satirical temperament that Swift was ever to achieve, completely transcending the aims, interests, quarrels and preoccupations of the Temple circle, or even of his co-religionists. *A Tale of a Tub* establishes Swift with Juvenal, Rabelais, Sterne, and James Joyce as one of the great European writers in a particular mode. The text of *A Tale*, like the text of *Finnegan's Wake*, is dense and capricious, full of unsignalled references, hints, and obliquities.

The following table is offered to indicate how the piece is put together.

[PRELIMINARIES]

Treaties written by the same Author (1 page)

An Apology for the [*Tale of a Tub*] (10 pages)

[Printed here in the place traditionally given to it from the fifth edition (1710) onwards: this section was listed by Swift for independent publication, and is really a later commentary on an earlier work and its reception, not a prefatory statement: cf. 'A letter from Capt. Gulliver', which prefaces *Gulliver's Travels*.]

Dedication to Somers (3 pages)

The Bookseller [publisher] *to the Reader* (1 page)

The Epistle Dedicatory to Prince Posterity (4 pages)

The Preface (7 pages)

Section I. The Introduction (9 pages)

[DIGRESSIONS]	[PARABLE]
	Section II (10 pages) The Father, his will, his three sons, and their coats; sect of tailor-worshippers and the religion of clothing; scholastic interpretation; the eldest son takes over a lord's house, expels his children, and takes in his two brothers.
Section III. A Digression concerning Critics (7 pages)	*Section IV* (9 pages) Peter names himself; his projects; the brothers steal a copy of the will, and he kicks them out of doors.
Section V. A Digression in the Modern Kind (5 pages)	*Section VI* (5 pages) Martin [Luther] and Jack [Calvin] name themselves; their divergent behaviour in reforming their coats; Jack runs mad and founds the sect of the Aeolists.
Section VII. A Digression in Praise of Digressions (4 pages)	*Section VIII* (5 pages) The learned Aeolists and their sect.
Section IX. A Digression on Madness (10 pages)	
Section X. [*A Further Digression*] (4 pages) [Though indicated in the text as 'A Tale of a Tub' (the heading for the Parable), this is a Digression, suggesting some disturbance in the text, perhaps the loss of a section on Martin: see p. xvii.]	*Section XI* (11 pages) Jack's adventures.

The Conclusion (3 pages)

A Full and True Account of the Battle fought last Friday between the Ancient and the Modern Books in Sir James's Library

Although not published until 1704 in the volume that contained *A Tale of a Tub*, this piece was written during the closing years of the 1690s, probably not all at once, at a time when Swift's employer, Sir William Temple, had embroiled himself in the so-called Ancients and Modern Controversy. This argument (also of importance in *A Tale of a Tub*) was part of a perennial conflict but also an exchange of insults in a specific pamphlet war at the end of the seventeenth century, first in France, then in England.

There was much at that time to strengthen the self-awareness of writers and thinkers, to make them feel that they were entering a modern age, in which mathematical and scientific discoveries, economic development and geographical exploration had united to produce an intellectual and political flowering. Temple was himself in many respects an important representative of this modern self-consciousness. The impulse to publish his own *Memoirs* and *Letters*, which Swift largely transcribed for the press, and his attempt to approach comparative culture as a detached observer, are all in tune with the empirical spirit of the age. That Temple was no simple-minded believer in progress, however, is shown both in his cyclical view of history and in his belief, congenial to Swift, that the aim of history was not to accumulate information but to develop a moral philosophy. The whole-hearted devotion of some of the 'modern' writers to the self-confident acquisition of information, in the conviction that this alone led to truth, was seen by Temple as 'the sufficiency of some of the learned'. The influence of such a view is obvious in Swift's later work, not only in *A Tale of a Tub*, but at a deep level in *Gulliver's Travels*.

Temple's 'Essay upon the Ancient and Modern Learning' (see pp. 155 ff.) was occasioned partly by the general, literary *querelle* in France, represented by Perrault (see p. 222) and Fontenelle (see p. 222) as 'moderns', and on the other side by Boileau. Temple speculated on the vanished learning of the ancient East, from which he believed the Greeks and through them the Romans had drawn much. He deploys his cyclical view of history to attack modern presumption in thinking that a full and clear knowledge of a limited body of extant ancient writing would be either possible or the key to all knowledge. Looking round for examples of really ancient writing that would illustrate his own theory and which, in turning to literature, he might advance as evidence 'in favour of the ancients, that the oldest books we have are still in their kind the best', in a single paragraph out of the sixty-four of which his 'Essay' is comprised, Temple unluckily pitched on the *Fables* of Aesop and the *Epistles* of Phalaris, 'both living at the same time, which was that of Cyrus and Pythagoras [*c.* the sixth century BC]'.

In this, Temple follows an assumption which lies at the basis of ancient intellectual history, that priority means superiority. This was already being disputed in the Renaissance when scholars such as Scaliger argued that, on the contrary, priority implied crude imperfection. Further, in fixing on the *Epistles* of Phalaris, Temple was not instancing some quaint text, but exemplifying his own old-fashioned education. In the fourteenth and fifteenth centuries, various collections of 'letters', fabricated by ancient rhetoricians and attributed to Hippocrates, Plato, and other eminent men, as well as Phalaris, were much studied as improving books. The earliest printed *Phalaris* (in a Latin translation from the original Greek) appeared as early as 1471, and it proved a popular text, since by 1500 more than thirty-five versions of the collection had come from the presses of Italy, France, Germany (and one from Oxford). It had since declined in popularity.

Richard Bentley (see p. 170), the greatest classical scholar in England, had little difficulty in demonstrating that on clear textual evidence the *Epistles* were a late Greek forgery, and that the *Fables* of Aesop as they were then reproduced also contained much later material. In the process, he revolutionized the chronology of classical literature. Temple indeed mentions this judgement of the *Epistles*, but rejects it on subjective grounds of taste, indicating that he was drawn to the text as the writing of a ruler and a commander, because of his own interests as a man of affairs and a letter-writer, rather than for any more technical reason. Temple, who was no rigid enemy of modern writing, was bewildered at attacks on his polite 'Essay'. His lordly tone itself, however, was calculated to enrage professional scholars like Bentley, who habitually savaged the disengagement of the learned amateur. In 1693, an edition of Phalaris's *Epistles* was undertaken (published in 1695) ostensibly by the Honourable Charles Boyle, son of the Earl of Orrery, and an adolescent undergraduate at Christ Church, Oxford. This exercise was really carried out by Francis Atterbury and other senior members of the college, but according to custom was associated with a well-connected pupil to gain prestige for the foundation. Meantime, William Wotton (1666–1726), a young Cambridge clergyman, took the opportunity of the appearance of Temple's 'Essay' to produce *Reflections upon Ancient and Modern Learning* (1694), a diffuse but learned work evincing all the seriousness of purpose that would merit advancement in the Church (see pp. 160 ff.). Wotton's book seeks to demolish as imaginary Temple's representation of 'the mighty reservoirs and lakes of knowledge' of the pre-classical East, and to destroy Temple's cyclical theory of cultural history, which indeed could not be accommodated to orthodox theology.

There was also a political edge to the controversy, as Wotton's dedication of his book to the Earl of Nottingham indicates.

In 1697, the date given in 'The Bookseller to the Reader' as the date of composition of *The Battle of the Books*, Wotton printed a second edition of his *Reflections*, 'with large additions'; the latter included Bentley's essay *A Dissertation upon the Epistles of Phalaris, Themistocles, Socrates, Euripides and Others; and the Fables of Aesop.* The *Dissertation* proved by a magisterial examination of linguistic and other evidence that the *Epistles* were written, not by a Tyrant of the sixth century BC (see p. 124, n. 1), but at a much later date by a teacher of rhetoric. A personal note entered into the second purpose of Bentley's paper, which was to show that the 'Boyle' edition was a shoddy piece of work by incompetent High Church, Tory, Oxford dons.

Temple angrily thought of replying to Wotton. The Christ Church party in 1698 issued *Dr. Bentley's Dissertation on the Epistles of Phalaris and the Fables of Aesop, Examined by the Honourable Charles Boyle, Esq.*, a satirical and personal sally which did everything that wit could do to mock Bentley's conclusive argument. The introduction of Wotton and Bentley in the second half of *The Battle of the Books*, and of Boyle towards the end, indicates that Swift was working on that part of the piece in 1697–8. In this year, half a dozen other pamphlets were prompted by the controversy, and more in the next year, among the latter Bentley's enlarged and corrected version of his *Dissertation*, which answers in slashing style Boyle's *Examination*. In 1701, Atterbury attacked Bentley, and in the same year Swift printed Temple's *Miscellanea. The Third Part*, which contains 'Some Thoughts upon Reviewing the Essay of Ancient and Modern Learning' (see pp. 193 ff.), the answer to Wotton which he had worked on with his late employer. *The Battle of the Books* with its important mock-heroic content is Swift's satirical descant on Temple's original 'Essay' and his later 'Thoughts'.

A Discourse Concerning the Mechanical Operation of the Spirit. A Fragment.

The third and last piece that made up the miscellany volume *A Tale of a Tub* (1704), furnished like the others with its own title-page, is cast in the popular form of a 'Letter to a Friend'. The satirist adds to the rambling, 'modern' treatise of *A Tale* itself, and to the journalistically titled 'full and true account' of *The Battle of the Books*, an epistolary essay by a corresponding Fellow of the Royal Society. It attacks another modern intellectual fashion, the communication of abstruse scientific information to a society of *virtuosi*, eager to hear, and be known to hear, the latest advances in human knowledge. The title of this third piece may indeed be further intended to direct the reader's attention to a key document of modern scientific investigation, Descartes' famous *Discours de la méthode pour bien conduire la raison et chercher la vérité dans les sciences* (1637). Descartes' metaphysics, by rudely divorcing mind from matter, turned spirit or the divine force into a kind of 'mechanical spirit' brought in to keep the argument from becoming totally atheistic. *The Mechanical Operation of the Spirit* also develops Swift's attack on one of the abuses of religion, the cultivation of Enthusiasm (Greek *enthousiasmis*, from *entheos*: possessed by the god). Swift associates this false inspiration in *A Tale of a Tub* with Jack, and it is a theme suggested by Sir William Temple in an essay which Swift may have transcribed for its first printing: '... I think a clear account of enthusiasm and fascination from their natural causes, would very much deserve [esteem] from mankind in general, as well as from the commonwealth of learning: might perhaps prevent so many public disorders ...' ('Of Poetry', *Miscellanea. The Second Part*, 1690). Meric Casaubon's *Treatise concerning Enthusiasm; As it is an Effect of Nature: but is Mistaken by Many for either Divine Inspiration, or Diabolical Possession* (2nd edn., revised and enlarged, 1656), an early, cool look at ecstatic religious inspiration, is another possible source for Swift's satire.

The Mechanical Operation of the Spirit is clearly part of the complex of *A Tale of a Tub*, and particularly related to Section XI of *A Tale* itself. Swift's cousin, the Revd Thomas Swift, notes in his copy of the first edition (see p. 193), at the start of Section XI, 'The Discourse concerning Enthusiasm was designed to come in hereabouts ...', and at the 'Advertisement' prefacing *The Mechanical Operation*, 'This Treatise concerning Enthusiasm should have been printed somewhere about page 195 [p. 92], as being an essential part of Jack's character, and I think much the best ...'. Thomas further plaintively claims at the same place, against the 'Advertisement's' phrase '... the original having been sent me at a different time, and in a different hand': 'Mark that in a *Different Hand*, because the one was my hand, and I suppose, the other my cozens.' The present editors believe that sufficient good circumstantial evidence is available to make the following suggestion more than plausible. Section I of *The Mechanical Operation of the Spirit* is not as a piece of writing the equal of Section II; it may embody a first draft of a piece on Enthusiasm, incorporating contributions in some vestigial form from Thomas Swift. Section II is a reworking of this material, clearly by Jonathan, giving the strange effect in *A Discourse* as a whole of a 'treatise' that does not progress. The two sections together are slightly less than twice as long as the longest section in *A Tale*, making it too extensive to fit into the major work. Swift therefore tried again, perhaps, to supply the necessary piece on Enthusiasm, and it is this that now stands as Section XI of *A Tale*. There was probably too much good writing in the earlier pieces to abandon them completely, so Swift placed them together in the 1704 volume as a *Fragment*. The inclusion of clumsier earlier material related to discussion with Thomas Swift, as a kind of *objet trouvé*, would give point and substance to Jonathan's apparent shadow-boxing about the status of the text of the fragment in its Bookseller's 'Advertisement' (p. 126) and in the *Apology* (p. 8).

Additions to A Tale of a Tub

[a] *The History of Martin* [and] *A Digression on the nature usefulness & necessity of Wars & Quarels.*
[b] *A Project, for the universal benefit of Mankind.*
[c] *The Kingdom of Absurdities.*

The bizarre nature of the volume in which [a] and [b] appeared has been responsible for their being neglected or dismissed. There seems good reason, however, to read them both, and [c] also, as surviving parts of Swift's working drafts for *A Tale of a Tub*. The editors have raised all three to the text of the present edition in consideration of Swift's well-documented practice as an author of writing down his preliminary ideas in the form of notes, which he called 'hints', terse but grammatically complete sentences, and also of his practice as an editor, in Temple's *Miscellanea. The Third Part* (1701), of printing as substantive works two essays of his late employer in the form of such 'Heads'. Further, a reading of these *Additions* gives an insight into how the 1704 volume might have been put together, and in particular alerts us to the alluring error of reading *A Tale* reductively, as a neatly worked out structure, in defiance of the powerful impulsiveness and improvisatory sense of the text.

The History of Martin is headed *Abstract of what follows after Section IX in the Manuscript*, and indeed in the early printed editions of *A Tale*, Section X is headed 'Tale', though in fact as printed it is wholly digression. The 'Tale' proper resumes in Section XI. There is clearly a gap in the narrative: Peter is given extended treatment in Section IV and Jack in Sections VI and XI. Martin, on the other hand, assumes his separate identity when he is named in Section VI, but is almost immediately dropped, to be taken up again in only two sentences in Section XI at the end of the 'Tale'.

In *An Apology* (p. 2), Swift says of the pattern of *A Tale*, '. . . The abuses in Religion he proposed to set forth in the Allegory of the Coats and the three Brothers ... The allegory celebrates the Church of England as the most perfect of all others in discipline and doctrine.' Similarly, the writer of *A Complete Key to the Tale of a Tub* ... (1710), very likely reflecting Thomas Swift's view (see p. 193), asserts that 'The Author intended to have it very regular ... and withal so particular, that he thought not to pass by the Rise of any one single Error or its Reformation ...'. *A Tale*, as published, is not so 'regular' or 'particular'. The basic parable has been well examined by Phillip Harth (*Swift and Anglican Rationalism*, pp. 13–18), who points to the shifts in the symbolic roles of the brothers as the story proceeds. Swift first represents the primitive Christians, and then the Church of Rome assuming authority over Western Christianity, immediately followed by the breaking away of the Lutherans [Martin] and the Calvinists [Jack] from papal authority, from which in turn develop the Church of England and the Kirk of Scotland.

The first section of *The History of Martin* elaborates on the Reformation in Europe, with sardonic reference to Henry VIII (a *bête noire* of Swift's) as 'Harry Huff, Lord of Albion'. The author, as he has to, drops 'the former Martin ... to substitute in his place Lady Besses Institution [Queen Elizabeth's Church settlement]'. The second section, after *A Digression on Wars and Quarrels*, brings the story up to the moment of writing and the discomfiture of the Non-jurors in the reign of William III. It may be objected that the churchman who later wrote a sermon 'On the Martyrdom of K. Charles I' could not have written the ironical description of the Civil War: 'both sides concur to hang up the Landlord, who pretended to die a Martyr for *Martin* tho' he had been true to neither side, & was suspected by many to have a great attraction for *Peter*'. This is a Wottonian objection; the wild author of *A Tale*, who had dealt so cavalierly with the Christian mysteries and tenets such as the Trinity, is surely capable of a satirical *boutade* against the Royal Martyr, and as *An Apology* says, 'he gave a liberty to his pen, which might not suit with maturer years or graver characters ...'. Perhaps this passage, though, as well as other more general critical considerations, led to the exclusion of the piece from the final work.

A Digression on Wars and Quarrels, embedded in [a], arises naturally from the 'mighty quarrels and squabbles between *Jack* & *Martin*', just as *A Digression concerning Madness* follows Jack's association with the Aeolists in Sections VI and VIII of *A Tale* proper. The subject, as well as the mode of its treatment, was close to Swift, from his early reading in political science to *Gulliver's Travels* and later. Gulliver's celebrated exposition of the topic to his Master in the 'Voyage to the Country of the Houyhmnhmns' (*Gulliver's Travels*, Part IV, Chapter 5) nearly thirty years later employs at one point not merely an identical concept, but the very phrases to express it. 'War is an attempt to take by violence from others a part of what they have and we want' (*A Digression*): 'Sometimes our neighbours want the things which we have, or have the things which we want; and we both fight, till they take ours or give us theirs.'

A Project, for the universal benefit of Mankind [b] contains some characteristic touches found elsewhere in Swift's writing. *Terra Australis incognita*, discussed at some length in Temple's 'Essay upon the Ancient and Modern Learning', occurs three times in *A Tale*. Further, the elaborate and carefully prepared confidence trick, plausible and yet patently absurd like the Bickerstaff joke, is part of Swift's humour.

The Kingdom of Absurdities [c], first printed in 1779 as 'sketches from Swift's own hand writing', is related to the ninth of the 'Treatises writ by the same Author' (p. 1), and may be compared with a longer unfinished piece surviving in manuscript, entitled 'Of Publick Absurdityes in England'.

ACKNOWLEDGEMENTS

THE editors wish to record their particular thanks to D. D. Eddy, Cornell University Library, the Houghton Library, Harvard University, the London Library, James Woolley, and to Kenneth Craven for an opportunity of reading part of his forthcoming work on Toland, the Deists, and *A Tale of a Tub*.

NOTE ON THE TEXT

PUBLISHED in London on 10 May 1704, the text of *A Tale, The*
and *The Mechanical Operation* presumably satisfied the author, for it was frequently reprinted in his lifetime substantially as it had originally appeared. To two of these reprints it is likely that he contributed a very few corrections and revisions: the second edition (published May/June 1704), and the fifth edition (published probably in the second half of 1710), for which he wrote the *Apology* and *Notes*.

The present edition is based, in a sense eclectically, on these three authoritative editions. The text proper is that of the first edition, its errors both of words and punctuation retrieved from the carefully prepared second edition, and incorporating the mere handful of authorial revisions contributed to the fifth edition. Acceptance of the revisions is desirable, their intrinsic merit apart, to synchronize the text with the later composition (after 1705) of the *Apology* and *Notes*. And these, in turn, have been drawn from the *earlier* textual state found in the pamphlet edition dated 1711, from David Nichol Smith's unique copy now in the Bodleian Library (shelf-mark Arch.A.e.80; Teerink no. 223), with revisions from the reset *later* state of 1710.

The present edition provides a largely modernized version from these sources. The punctuation, guided by the original, seeks to release the ebb and flow of Swift's prose from the restraints of late seventeenth-century printers' conventions. Some capitalization has been retained, and virtually all of Swift's deliberate use of emphatic typography except in *The Battle of the Books*, where for some reason the level of italics (here tactfully reduced), in the manner of earlier polemics, verges on slapstick. Otherwise, editorial emendations appear within square brackets.

We have raised the four 'Additions to *A Tale of a Tub*' to the status of text. Three derive from their first printing after a lapse of nearly two decades in *Miscellaneous Works, Comical & Diverting*: By T.R.D.J.S.D. O.P.I.I. [The Hague: Thomas Johnson], 1720. They are here reprinted without modernization to convey some sense of their unfinished state. The fourth addition, 'The Kingdom of Absurdities', was printed first (probably from the holograph) by John Nichols in *A Supplement to Dr. Swift's Works. Volume the Second*, 1779, p. 367.

A narrative so full of comic incident lent itself readily to contemporary illustration. The frontispiece and seven other engraved plates from the 1710 and subsequent editions, rightly called 'flat journeywork' by ɹuthkelch, are not reproduced in the text, but the third subject may be seen on the cover. They depict consecutively the ship and the whale (p. 18), the three 'edifices in the air' (p. 25), the three brothers and the will (p. 34), Peter evicting Martin and Jack (p. 59), Jack and Martin tearing their coats (p. 65), the scene in Bedlam (p. 85), Jack upon a great horse (p. 101), and finally the battle scene in the royal library at St James's Palace (to front *The Battle of the Books*).

SELECT BIBLIOGRAPHY

BIBLIOGRAPHIES

H. Teerink, *A Bibliography of the Writings of Jonathan Swift*, 2nd edn., rev. A. H. Scouten (Philadelphia, 1963): gives full bibliographical details up to 1814 of editions of *A Tale of a Tub*, of collected works containing *A Tale*, of translations of *A Tale*, and of biography and criticism to 1895.

L. A. Landa and J. E. Tobin, *Jonathan Swift. A List of Critical Studies Published from 1895 to 1945* (New York, 1945).

J. J. Stathis, *A Bibliography of Swift Studies 1945 to 1965* (Nashville, Tenn., 1965).

R. H. Rodino, *Swift Studies 1965 to 1980. An Annotated Bibliography* (New York, 1984).

L. A. Landa, 'Swift' in A. E. Dyson (ed.), *The English Novel: Select Bibliographical Guides* (Oxford, 1974), pp. 38–41: useful annotated list.

SWIFT'S WORKS

H. J. Davis *et al.* (eds.), *The Prose Works of Jonathan Swift*, 14 vols. (Oxford, Blackwell, 1939–68), is the standard edition; vol. i is H. J. Davis (ed.), *A Tale of a Tub with Other Early Works: 1696–1707*.

Other editions with substantial information relevant to *A Tale of a Tub* and its related pieces are:

Sir H. Williams (ed.), *The Poems of Jonathan Swift*, 3 vols. (Oxford, 1937; 2nd. edn. rev., 1958); *The Journal to Stella*, 2 vols. (Oxford, 1948), fully annotated; *The Correspondence of Jonathan Swift*, 5 vols. (Oxford, 1963–5): vols. i–iii await revision; vols. iv and v partially rev. David Woolley (1972); annotated.

A. C. Guthkelch and D. Nichol Smith (eds.), *A Tale of a Tub* (Oxford, 1920; 2nd edn., rev., 1958; with corrections, 1973): in many respects still the standard edition, though scholarship in wider and related fields of politics, the history of ideas, and literary theory has made extensive revision necessary.

A. Guthkelch (ed.), *The Battle of the Books by Jonathan Swift: with Selections from the Literature of the Phalaris Controversy* (1908): contains important material not in the previous item.

H. J. Real (ed.), *Jonathan Swift: The Battle of the Books* (Berlin and New York, 1978): the most informative edition of this work, with an excellent introduction and commentary in German.

A Tale of a Tub is to be found in several selections of Swift's works, but not always with *The Battle of the Books* and *The Mechanical Operation of the Spirit*: all three are to be found in M. K. Starkman (ed.), *Gulliver's Travels and Other Writings* (Bantam Classics, New York, 1961); R. A. Greenberg and W. B. Piper (eds.), *The Writings of Jonathan Swift: Authoritative Texts, Backgrounds, Criticism* (Norton Critical Editions, N.Y. and Toronto, 1973); K. Williams (ed.), *A Tale of a Tub and* [6] *Other Satires* (Everyman's Library, 1975), with brief notes. A. Ross and D. Woolley (eds.), *Jonathan Swift* (Oxford Authors, 1984), puts the three texts in a full context of Swift's other writings in prose and verse, excluding *Gulliver*.

COMMENTARY

(a) *Biography*

I. Ehrenpreis, *Swift: the Man, his Works, and the Age*, vol. i, *Mr. Swift and his Contemporaries* [1667–99] (1962); vol. ii, *Dr. Swift* [1700–14] (1967); vol. iii, *Dean Swift* [1714–45] (1983): the most substantial modern biography of Swift, very readable and based on an unrivalled grasp of the documents as well as a subtle reading of the works; its commentary on the texts in the present volume is essential reading.

J. A. Downie, *Jonathan Swift, Political Writer* (1984): contains three sections relevant to *A Tale* etc.: 'Moor Park', 'Swift and the Church', and 'A Tale of a Tub'.

A. C. Elias, Jr., *Swift at Moor Park* (1982): contains unparalleled detail of Swift's relationship with Temple and its potential influence on the composition of *A Tale*.

(b) *General Works*

J. M. Bullitt, *Jonathan Swift and the Anatomy of Satire: A Study of Satiric Technique* (Cambridge, Mass., 1953).

H. J. Davis, *Jonathan Swift: Essays on his Satire and Other Studies* (Oxford, 1964): of particular interest to readers of the present volume are 'Literary Satire: the Author of *A Tale of a Tub*' [and in Jeffares 1969, below], 'Swift and the Pedants' and 'The Augustan Conception of History'.

D. Donoghue, *Jonathan Swift: A Critical Introduction* (Cambridge, 1969): a stimulating advanced discussion.

M. Price, *Swift's Rhetorical Art: A Study in Structure and Meaning* (New Haven, 1953).

R. Quintana, *Swift: An Introduction* (1955): a good starting point; *The Mind and Art of Jonathan Swift* (1936; 2nd edn., 1953).

E. Rosenheim, Jr., *Swift and the Satirist's Art* (Chicago, 1963): contains useful discussions on *A Tale* and *The Battle*.

P. Steele, *Jonathan Swift: Preacher and Jester* (Oxford, 1978): a lively book with perceptive scattered comments on *A Tale*; useful bibliography.

D. Ward, *Swift: An Introductory Essay* (1973).

W. A. Speck (ed.), *Swift* (Literature in Perspective Series, 1969): contains a chapter on *A Tale*.

E. Zimmerman, *Swift's Narrative Satires: Author and Authority* (1983).

Much interesting writing on Swift and his works takes the form of essays and articles, scattered through issues of periodicals and journals, and sometimes collected in anthologies. Pieces of specific interest for readers of *A Tale* etc. are noted below in section (c) of this list. Useful general compilations include:

A. N. Jeffares (ed.), *Swift: Modern Judgements* (1969).

C. T. Probyn (ed.), *The Art of Jonathan Swift* (1978).

C. J. Rawson (ed.), *The Character of Swift's Satire: A Revised Focus* (1983).

E. Tuveson (ed.), *Swift: A Collection of Critical Essays* (Twentieth-Century Views, Englewood Cliffs, N.J., 1964).

B. Vickers (ed.), *The World of Jonathan Swift: Essays for the Tercentenary* (Oxford, 1968).

K. M. Williams (ed.), *Swift: The Critical Heritage* (1970): reprints pieces and extracts 1704–1819; important for the reception of *A Tale.*

(c) *A Tale of a Tub and Related Pieces*

N. J. C. Andreasen, 'Swift's Satire on the Occult in *A Tale of A Tub*', *Texas Studies in Literature and Language*, 5 (1963–4), 410–21.

R. M. Adams, 'Jonathan Swift, Thomas Swift, and the Authorship of *A Tale of a Tub*', *Modern Philology*, 64 (1967), 198–232; qualified by Dipak Nandy, ibid., 66 (1968), 333–7.

T. L. Canavan, 'Robert Burton, Jonathan Swift, and the Tradition of Anti-Puritan Invective', *Journal of the History of Ideas*, 34, (1973), 227–42.

W. B. Carnochan, 'Swift's *Tale*: On Satire, Negation and the Uses of Irony', *Eighteenth-Century Studies*, 5 (1971), 124–44.

J. R. Clark, *Form and Frenzy in Swift's* Tale of a Tub (1970).

G. Clifford, *The Transformations of Allegory* (Concepts of Literature series, 1974).

J. R. Crider, 'Dissenting Sex: Swift's "History of Fanaticism"', *Studies in English Literature 1500–1900*, 18 (1979), 491–508: largely on *The Mechanical Operation of the Spirit.*

P. Harth, *Swift and Anglican Rationalism: The Religious Background of* A Tale of a Tub (1961).

H. D. Kelling and C. L. Preston, *A KWIC Concordance to Jonathan Swift's A Tale of a Tub, The Battle of the Books and A Discourse Concerning the Mechanical Operation of the Spirit* (Garland Publishing, N.Y., 1984).

L. A. Landa, 'Swift, the Mysteries, and Deism' (first printed in 1944; repr. in Landa, *Essays in Eighteenth-Century English Literature*, Princeton, N.J., 1980).

F. R. Leavis, 'The Irony of Swift' (first printed in 1934; repr. in Jeffares 1967, Tuveson 1964, above; and elsewhere): answered by W. Frost, 'The Irony of Swift and Gibbon: a Reply to F. R. Leavis', in *Essays in Criticism*, 17 (1967), 41–7.

R. Paulson, *Theme and Structure in Swift's* Tale of a Tub (New Haven, Conn., 1960).

P. Rogers, 'Form in *A Tale of a Tub*', *Essays in Criticism*, 22 (1972), 142–60.

A. Ross, 'The Books in the *Tale*: Swift and Reading in *A Tale of a Tub*', in H. J. Real and H. J. Vienken (eds.), *Proceedings of the First Münster Symposium on Jonathan Swift* (Munich, Fink Verlag, forthcoming).

F. N. Smith, *Language and Reality in Swift's* A Tale of a Tub (Columbus, Ohio, 1979): an important stylistic analysis.

M. K. Starkman, *Swift's Satire on Learning in* A Tale of a Tub (Princeton, N.J., 1950).

G. D. Stout, Jr., 'Satire and Self-Expression in Swift's *Tale of a Tub*' in R. F. Brissenden (ed.), *Studies in the Eighteenth Century*, 2 (Canberra and Toronto, 1973): an important caveat against unthinking discussion of 'the persona' in *A Tale.*

J. Traugott, 'A Tale of a Tub', in Rawson 1983, above: an argumentative and stimulating essay.

BACKGROUND READING

M. C. Battestin, *The Providence of Wit: Aspects of Form in Augustan Literature and the Arts* (Oxford, 1974): contains a discussion of *A Tale.*

N. O. Brown, *Life against Death: The Psychological Meaning of History* (1959): 'The Excremental Vision' repr. in Tuveson 1964, above.

Max Byrd, *Visits to Bedlam: Madness and Literature in the Eighteenth Century* (Columbia, S. Carolina, 1974): contains a discussion of *A Tale.*

M. V. DePorte, *Nightmares and Hobby Horses: Swift, Sterne, and Augustan Ideas of Madness* (San Marino, Calif., 1974): contains a discussion of *A Tale.*

P. K. Elkin, *The Augustan Defence of Satire* (Oxford, 1973).

R. C. Elliott, *The Power of Satire: Magic, Ritual, Art* (Princeton, N.J., 1960).

P. Fussell, *The Rhetorical World of Augustan Humanism: Ethics and Imagery from Swift to Burke* (Oxford, 1965).

P. J. Korshin, *Typologies in England: 1650–1820* (Princeton, N.J., 1982): diffuse and comprehensive but a good starting point for examining an important aspect of *A Tale* and *The Mechanical Operation* (which are discussed); useful bibliography.

M. C. Jacob, *The Newtonians and the English Revolution: 1689–1720* (Harvester Press, Brighton, 1976): an interesting and full account of the political and social context of the 'scientific revolution' of the late seventeenth century: useful on Wotton and Bentley.

G. Josipovici, *The World and the Book: A Study in Modern Fiction* (1971): *A Tale* as an 'anti-novel'.

A. V. Kernan, *The Plot of Satire* (New Haven, Conn., 1965).

V. Mercier, *The Irish Comic Tradition* (Oxford, 1962).

J. H. Plumb, *The Origins of Political Stability: England 1675–1725* (1976).

P. Rogers, *Grub Street: Studies in a Sub-Culture* (1972): pp. 51–65 on *The Mechanical Operation.*

A CHRONOLOGY OF *A TALE OF A TUB*

1649 Charles I executed; Commonwealth established under Cromwell; the episcopal structure of the Church of England dismantled; rule of the Saints.

1660 Charles II restored to the throne; episcopacy re-established in a triumphant Church.

1662 Royal Society incorporated by royal charter.

1667 Jonathan Swift born in Dublin, the posthumous son of an English father.

1673 Test Act passed in England, requiring communion in the Church of England as a qualification for all office-holders.

1678 Popish plot: the allegations of Titus Oates and others cause widespread hysteria and politico-religious witch-hunting.

1685 Charles II dies; accession of Roman Catholic James II.

1687 Reading of Perrault's poem *Le Siècle de Louis le Grand* at the French Academy.

1688 Perrault, *Parallèle des Anciens et des Modernes . . . Artes et Sciences: Dialogues*. Fontenelle, *Digression sur les Anciens et les Modernes*; William of Orange invades England by invitation: James II flees to France.

1689 William (and his wife) accept the Crown offered by Parliament, a political outcome causing severe problems of conscience for many Anglican churchmen: some (the 'non-jurors'), including the Archbishop of Canterbury, refuse to take new oaths of allegiance and are later deprived of their livings and dignities. James II appeals to his Roman Catholic subjects in Ireland and civil war breaks out there. Swift flees to England and enters the service of Sir William Temple at Moor Park in Surrey.

1690 Temple's 'Essay upon the Ancient and Modern Learning' published; Perrault, *Parallèle des Anciens et des Modernes* . . . , ii [Eloquence]; William III victor at the Battle of the Boyne in Ireland; James II escapes to France.

1691 Swift returns to Temple after a visit to Ireland.

1692 Perrault, *Parallèle* . . . , iii [Poetry].

1694 Swift is ordained priest in the (Anglican) Church of Ireland, at Dublin; Wotton's *Reflections upon Ancient and Modern Learning*; after some delay, Richard Bentley appointed Keeper of the Royal Library.

1695 Phalaris, *Epistolae*, ed. Boyle [with Atterbury]. Lapse of the Press Licensing Act invites great increase in political and other controversial publications. First of the anti-Catholic 'penal laws' in Ireland.

1696 After a period as a parish priest in a Presbyterian area near Belfast, Swift resumes his duties as Temple's secretary; Toland's controversial *Christianity not Mysterious*, the first important 'deist' work.

1697 Perrault, *Parallèle* . . . , iv [Astronomy, Geography, Navigation, War, Philosophy, Music, Medicine]; second edition of Wotton's *Reflections*, now including Bentley's *Dissertation upon Phalaris etc.*; Swift writes *Battle of the Books* in defence of Temple, his employer.

1698 *Dr. Bentley's Dissertation . . . Examined by the Hon. Charles Boyle, Esq.*

1699 Sir William Temple dies; Bentley's enlarged *Dissertation upon Phalaris*, 'near a thousand pages of immense erudition'.

1700 Swift presented to the vicarage of Laracor near Dublin, and a prebend in St Patrick's Cathedral; publishes Temple's *Letters* i and ii.

1701 Swift returns to England and publishes *A Discourse of the Contests and Dissensions . . . in Athens and Rome*; publishes Temple's *Miscellanea. The Third Part* (containing 'Thoughts on Reviewing the Essay upon the Ancient and Modern Learning').

1702 Swift proceeds DD at Trinity College, Dublin.

1704 Swift publishes the anonymous volume containing *A Tale of a Tub* and associated pieces; William King hastens to disown it in *Remarks*.

1705 Fourth edition of *A Tale of a Tub*. Later Swift writes *An Apology* and Notes.

1710 Fifth edition of *A Tale of a Tub*; Swift begins his career as a political writer in support of the administration of Robert Harley [later Earl of Oxford].

1712 Queen Anne refuses to give Swift the Deanery of Wells, because, Swift believed, of his authorship of *A Tale of a Tub*, 'a dang'rous treatise writ against the spleen'.

1713 The Queen refuses to make Swift a bishop, as requested by Oxford, and he is given the Deanery of St Patrick's, Dublin, in the gift of the Duke of Ormonde, Lord Lieutenant of Ireland.

1714 On the fall of Oxford and the death of the Queen (August), Swift retires to his Deanery in Dublin.

1720 *Miscellaneous Works, Comical and Diverting* by T.R.D.J.S.D.O.P.I.I. . . . [containing the *Additions* printed below, pp. 142 ff.], London [actually, The Hague].

1721 *Le Conte du Tonneau . . . Par le fameux Dr. Swift* . . ., 2 vols. (The Hague), French translation by Justus van Effen with an important 'Preface' to each volume; a manuscript of part of *Gulliver's Travels* is seen by friends.

1726 Swift arrives in London with a manuscript of *Gulliver's Travels*, published after his return to Dublin later in the year.

1742 75 years old, Swift is declared 'of unsound mind and memory' and his affairs are handed over to trustees.

1745 19 October. Swift dies in his Deanery of St Patrick's, Dublin.

A TALE OF A TUB.

Written for the Universal Improvement

OF

MANKIND.

Diu multumque desideratum.

To which is added,

An Account of a BATTLE between the Antient and Modern BOOKS in St. *James*'s Library.

ALSO

A DISCOURSE concerning the Mechanical Operation of the SPIRIT, in a LETTER to a FRIEND. A Fragment.

Basima eacabasa eanaa irraurista, diarba da caeotaba fobor camelanthi. *Iren. Lib.* I. *C.* 18.

----Juvatque novos decerpere flores,
Insignemque meo capiti petere inde coronam,
Unde prius nulli velarunt tempora Musæ. Lucr.

The Seventh EDITION: With the AUTHOR'S Apology and Explanatory Notes.
By *W. W----tt-----n*, B. D. and Others.

DUBLIN: Printed by A. RHAMES for W. SMITH at the *Hercules* in *Dame-street*, 1726.

The volume title of the second Irish edition of *A Tale*, 1726, which enumerates for the first time all items in the book. It is designated 'The Seventh EDITION' since it followed immediately upon the sixth London edition, 1724.

A TALE OF A TUB.

Written for the Universal Improvement of Mankind

Diu multumque desideratum°

Basima eacabasa eanaa irraurista, diarba da caeotaba
fobor camelanthi. *Iren. Lib.* 1. *C.* 18.°

———*Juvatque novos decerpere flores,*
Insignemque meo capiti petere inde coronam,
Unde prius nulli velarunt tempora Musæ.° Lucret.

Treatises written by the same Author, most of them mentioned in the following Discourses; which will be speedily published.

A Character of the present set of Wits *in this Island.*
A panegyrical Essay upon the Number THREE.
A Dissertation upon the principal Productions of Grub Street.
Lectures upon a Dissection of Human Nature.
A Panegyric upon the World.
An analytical Discourse upon Zeal, histori-theo-physi-logically *considered.*
A general History of Ears.
A modest Defence of the Proceedings of the Rabble *in all ages.*
A Description of the Kingdom of Absurdities.
A Voyage into England, *by a Person of Quality in* Terra Australis incognita,° *translated from the Original.*
A critical Essay upon the Art of Canting, *philosophically, physically, and musically considered.*

AN APOLOGY

For the [*Tale of a Tub.*]

If good and ill nature equally operated upon Mankind, I might have saved myself the trouble of this Apology; for it is manifest by the reception the following discourse hath met with, that those who approve it are a great majority among the men of taste; yet there have been two or three treatises written expressly against it° besides many others that have flirted at it occasionally, without one syllable having been ever published in its defence, or even quotation to its advantage that I can remember, except by the polite author of a late discourse° between a Deist and a Socinian.

Therefore, since the book seems calculated to live at least as long as our language and our taste admit no great alterations, I am content to convey some Apology along with it.

The greatest part of that book was finished above thirteen years since, 1696, *which is eight years before it was published. The author was then young, his invention at the height, and his reading fresh in his head. By the assistance of some thinking, and much conversation, he had endeavour'd to strip himself of as many real prejudices as he could; I say real ones because, under the notion of prejudices, he knew to what dangerous heights some men have proceeded. Thus prepared, he thought the numerous and gross corruptions in Religion and Learning might furnish matter for a satire that would be useful and diverting. He resolved to proceed in a manner that should be altogether new, the world having been already too long nauseated with endless repetitions upon every subject. The abuses in Religion he proposed to set forth in the Allegory of the Coats and the three Brothers, which was to make up the body of the discourse. Those in Learning he chose to introduce by way of digressions. He was then a young gentleman much in the world, and wrote to the taste of those who were like himself; therefore in order to allure them, he gave a liberty to his pen, which might not suit with maturer years or graver characters, and which he could have easily corrected with a very few blots, had he been master of his papers for a year or two before their publication.*

Not that he would have governed his judgment by the ill-placed cavils of the sour, the envious, the stupid, and the tasteless, which he mentions with disdain. He acknowledges there are several youthful sallies which, from the grave and the wise, may deserve a rebuke. But he desires to be answerable no farther than he is guilty, and that his faults may not be multiplied by the ignorant, the unnatural, and uncharitable applications of those who have neither candour to suppose good meanings, nor palate to distinguish true ones. After which he will forfeit his life if any one opinion can be fairly deduced from that book which is contrary to Religion or Morality.

Why should any clergyman of our church be angry to see the follies of fanaticism and superstition exposed, though in the most ridiculous manner; since that is perhaps the most probable way to cure them, or at least to hinder them from farther spreading? Besides, though it was not intended for their perusal, it rallies nothing but what they preach against. It contains nothing to provoke them, by the least scurrility upon their persons or their functions. It celebrates the Church of England as the most perfect of all others in discipline and doctrine; it advances no opinion they reject, nor condemns any they receive. If the clergy's resentments lay upon their hands, in my humble opinion they might have found more proper objects to employ them on: nondum tibi defuit hostis;° *I mean those heavy, illiterate scribblers, prostitute in their reputations, vicious in their lives, and ruined in their fortunes, who, to the shame of good sense as well as piety, are greedily read merely upon the strength of bold, false, impious assertions, mixed with unmannerly reflections upon the priesthood, and openly intended against all Religion; in short, full of such principles as are kindly received because they are levelled to remove those terrors that Religion tells men will be the consequence of immoral lives. Nothing like which is to be met with in this discourse, though some of them are pleased so freely to censure it. And I wish there were no other instance of what I have too frequently observed, that many of that reverend body are not always very nice in distinguishing between their enemies and their friends.*

Had the author's intentions met with a more candid interpretation from some whom out of respect he forbears to name, he might have been encouraged to an examination of books written by some of those authors above described, whose errors, ignorance, dulness and villainy, he thinks he could have detected and exposed in such a manner that the persons who are most conceived to be affected by them, would soon lay them aside and be ashamed. But he has now given over those thoughts; since the weightiest *men in the* weightiest *stations° are pleased to think it a more dangerous point to laugh at those corruptions in Religion, which they themselves must disapprove, than to endeavour pulling up those very foundations wherein all Christians have agreed.*

He thinks it no fair proceeding that any person should offer determinately to fix a name upon the author of this discourse, who hath all along concealed himself from most of his nearest friends. Yet several have gone a farther step, and pronounced another book° to have been the work of the same hand with this, which the author directly affirms to be a thorough mistake, he having as yet never so much as read that discourse; a plain instance how little truth there often is in general surmises, or in conjectures drawn from a similitude of style or way of thinking.

Letter of Enthusiasm.

Had the author written a book to expose the abuses in Law, or in Physic, he believes the learned professors in either faculty would have been so far from resenting it as to have given him thanks for his pains, especially if he had made an honourable reservation for the true practice of either science. But Religion, they tell us, ought not to be ridiculed, and they tell us truth. Yet surely the corruptions in it may; for we are taught by the tritest maxim in the world° that Religion being the best of things, its corruptions are likely to be the worst.

There is one thing which the judicious reader cannot but have observed, that some of those passages in this discourse which appear most liable to objection, are what they call parodies, where the author personates the style and manner of other writers whom he has a mind to expose. I shall produce one instance, it is in the [32]d page. Dryden, L'Estrange,° and some others I shall not name, are here levelled at, who having spent their lives in faction and apostacies and all manner of vice, pretended to be sufferers for Loyalty and Religion. So Dryden tells us in one of his prefaces° of his merits and suffering, and thanks God that he possesses his soul in patience. *In other places he talks at the same rate, and L'Estrange often uses the like style; and I believe the reader may find more persons to give that passage an application. But this is enough to direct those who may have overlooked the author's intention.*

There are three or four other passages which prejudiced or ignorant readers have drawn by great force to hint at ill meanings, as if they glanced at some tenets in religion. In answer to all which, the author solemnly protests he is entirely innocent; and never had it once in his thoughts that anything he said would in the least be capable of such interpretations, which he will engage to deduce full as fairly from the most innocent book in the world. And it will be obvious to every reader that this was not any part of his scheme or design, the abuses he notes being such as all Church of England men agree in; nor was it proper for his subject to meddle with other points than such as have been perpetually controverted since the Reformation.

To instance only in that passage about the three wooden machines mentioned in the Introduction: in the original manuscript there was a description of a fourth, which those who had the papers in their power blotted out, as having something in it of satire that I suppose they thought was too particular; and therefore they were forced to change it to the number Three, from whence some have endeavoured to squeeze out a dangerous meaning° that was never thought on. And indeed the conceit was half spoiled by changing the numbers, that of Four being much more cabalistic, and therefore better exposing the pretended virtue of Numbers, a superstition there intended to be ridiculed.

Another thing to be observed is, that there generally runs an irony through the thread of the whole book, which the men of taste will observe and distinguish, and which will render some objections that have been made, very weak and insignificant.

This Apology being chiefly intended for the satisfaction of future readers, it may be thought unnecessary to take any notice of such treatises as have been written against this ensuing discourse, which are already sunk into waste paper and oblivion after the usual fate of common answerers to books which are allowed to have any merit. They are indeed like annuals, that grow about a young tree and seem to vie with it for a summer, but fall and die with the leaves in autumn and are never heard of any more. When Dr. Eachard writ his book about the Contempt of the Clergy,° numbers of these answerers immediately started up, whose memory if he had not kept alive by his replies it would now be utterly unknown that he were ever answered at all. There is indeed an exception, when any great genius thinks it worth his while to expose a foolish piece; so we still read Marvell's Answer to Parker with pleasure, though the book it answers be sunk long ago: so the Earl of Orrery's Remarks° will be read with delight when the Dissertation he exposes will neither be sought nor found: but these are no enterprizes for common hands, nor to be hoped for above once or twice in an age. Men would be more cautious of losing their time in such an undertaking, if they did but consider that to answer a book effectually requires more pains and skill, more wit, learning, and judgment than were employed in the writing it. And the author assures those gentlemen who have given themselves that trouble with him, that his discourse is the product of the study, the observation, and the invention of several years; that he often blotted out much more than he left, and if his papers had not been a long time out of his possession, they must have still undergone more severe corrections: and do they think such a building is to be battered with dirt-pellets, however envenomed the mouths may be that discharge them? He hath seen the productions but of two answerers, one of which at first appeared as from an unknown hand,° but since avowed by a person who upon some occasions hath discovered no ill vein of humour. 'Tis a pity any *occasions should put him under a necessity of being so hasty in his productions, which otherwise might often be entertaining. But there were other reasons obvious enough for his miscarriage in this; he writ against the conviction of his talent, and entered upon one of the wrongest attempts in nature, to turn into ridicule by a week's labour a work which had cost so much time and met with so much success in ridiculing others: the manner how he has handled his* subject *I have now forgot, having just looked it over when it first came out, as others did, merely for the sake of the title.*

The other answer is from a person of a graver character,° and is made up of half invective and half annotation, in the latter of which he hath generally succeeded well enough. And the project at that time was not amiss, to draw in readers to his pamphlet, several having appeared desirous that there might be some explication of the more difficult passages. Neither can he be altogether blamed for offering at the invective part, because it is agreed on all hands that the author had given him sufficient provocation. The great objection is against his manner of treating it, very unsuitable to one of his function. It was determined by a fair majority that this answerer had in a way not to be pardoned drawn his pen against a certain great man° then alive and universally reverenced for every good quality that could possibly enter into the composition of the most accomplished person; it was observed how he was pleased, and affected to have that noble writer called his adversary; and it was a point of satire well directed, for I have been told Sir W[*illiam*] *T*[*emple*] *was sufficiently mortified at the term. All the men of wit and politeness were immediately up in arms through indignation, which prevailed over their contempt, by the consequences they apprehended from* such an example, and it grew Porsenna's case, idem trecenti juravimus.° In short, things were ripe for a general insurrection till my Lord Orrery had a little laid the spirit and settled the ferment. But his lordship being principally engaged with another antagonist,° it was thought necessary in order to quiet the minds of men, that this opposer should receive a reprimand, which partly occasioned that discourse of the Battle of the Books; and the author was further at the pains to insert one or two remarks on him in the body of the book.

This answerer has been pleased to find fault with about a dozen passages, which the author will not be at the trouble of defending further than by assuring the reader that for the greater part the reflecter is entirely mistaken, and forces interpretations which never once entered into the writer's head, nor will he is sure into that of any reader of taste and candour; he allows two or three at most, there produced, to have been delivered unwarily: for which he desires to plead the excuse offered already, of his youth, and frankness of speech, and his papers being out of his power at the time they were published.

But this answerer insists, and says what he chiefly dislikes is the design: what that was I have already told, and I believe there is not a person in England, who can understand that book, that ever imagined it to have been anything else but to expose the abuses and corruptions in Learning and Religion.

But it would be good to know what design this reflecter was serving when he concludes his pamphlet with a caution to readers to beware of thinking the author's wit was entirely his own: surely this must have had some allay of personal animosity at least mixed with the design of serving the public, by so useful a discovery; and it indeed touches the author in a tender point, who insists upon it that through the whole book he has not borrowed one single hint from any writer in the world; and he thought, of all criticisms, that would never have been one. He conceived it was never disputed to be an original, whatever faults it might have. However, this answerer produces three instances to prove this author's wit is not his own in many places. The first is, that the names of Peter, Martin and Jack, are borrowed from a Letter of the late Duke of Buckingham.° Whatever wit is contained in those three names the author is content to give it up, and desires his readers will subtract as much as they placed upon that account; at the same time protesting solemnly that he never once heard of that letter except in this passage of the answerer: so that the names were not borrowed, as he affirms, though they should happen to be the same, which however is odd enough, and what he hardly believes, that of Jack being not quite so obvious as the other two. The second instance to show the author's wit is not his own, is Peter's banter (as he calls it in his Alsatia phrase)° upon Transubstantiation, which is taken from the same Duke's conference with an Irish priest, where a cork is turned into a horse. This the author confesses to have seen about ten years after his book was writ, and a year or two after it was *published. Nay, the answerer overthrows this himself, for he allows the Tale was written in 1697, and I think that pamphlet was not printed in many years after. It was necessary that corruption should have some allegory as well as the rest, and the author invented the properest he could, without inquiring what other people had writ; and the commonest reader will find there is not the least resemblance between the two stories. The third instance is in these words: 'I have been assured, that the Battle in St. James's Library is,* mutatis mutandis, *taken out of a French book entitled* Combat des Livres,° *if I misremember not.' In which passage there are two clauses observable, 'I have been assured' and, 'if I misremember not'. I desire first to know whether, if that conjecture proves an utter falsehood, those two clauses will be a sufficient excuse for this worthy critic? The matter is a trifle; but would he venture to pronounce at this rate upon one of greater moment? I know nothing more contemptible in a writer than the character of a plagiary, which he here fixes at a venture; and this not for a passage but a whole discourse taken out from another book, only* mutatis mutandis. *The author is as much in the dark about this as the answerer, and will imitate him by an affirmation at random; that if there be a word of truth in this reflection, he is a paltry, imitating pedant and the answerer is a person of wit, manners and truth. He takes his boldness from never having seen any such treatise in his life nor heard of it before; and he is sure it is impossible for two writers of different times and countries to agree in their thoughts after such a manner that two continued discourses shall be the same, only* mutatis mutandis. *Neither will he insist upon the mistake of the title, but let the answerer and his friend° produce any book they please, he defies them to show one single particular where the judicious reader will affirm he has been obliged for the smallest hint; giving only allowance for the accidental encountering of a single thought, which he knows may sometimes happen, though he has never yet found it in that discourse, nor has heard it objected by anybody else.*

So that if ever any design was unfortunately executed, it must be that of this answerer who, when he would have it observed that the author's wit is not his own, is able to produce but three instances, two of them mere trifles, and all three manifestly false. If this be the way these gentlemen deal with the world in those criticisms where we have not leisure to defeat them, their readers had need be cautious how they rely upon their credit; and whether this proceeding can be reconciled to humanity or truth, let those who think it worth their while determine.

It is agreed this answerer would have succeeded much better if he had stuck wholly to his business as a commentator upon the Tale of a Tub, *wherein it cannot be denied that he hath been of some service to the public, and has given very fair conjectures towards clearing up some difficult passages; but it is the frequent error of those men (otherwise very commendable for their labours) to make excursions beyond their talent and their office, by pretending to point out the beauties and the faults; which is no part of their trade, which they always fail in, which the world never expected from them, nor gave them any thanks for endeavouring at. The part of Minellius or Farnaby° would have fallen in with his genius, and might have been serviceable to many readers who cannot enter into the abstruser parts of that discourse; but* optat ephippia bos piger:° *the dull, unwieldy, ill-shaped ox, would needs put on the furniture of a horse, not considering he was born to labour, to plough the ground for the sake of superior beings, and that he has neither the shape, mettle nor speed of that nobler animal he would affect to personate.*

It is another pattern of this answerer's fair dealing to give us hints that the author is dead,° and yet to lay the suspicion upon somebody, I know not who, in the country; to which can only be returned that he is absolutely mistaken in all his conjectures; and surely conjectures are at best too light a pretence to allow a man to assign a name in public. He condemns a book and consequently the author, of whom he is utterly ignorant, yet at the same time fixes, in print, what he thinks a disadvantageous character upon those who never deserved it. A man who receives a buffet in the dark may be allowed to be vexed, but it is an odd kind of revenge to go to cuffs in broad day with the first he meets with, and lay the last night's injury at his door. And thus much for this discreet, candid, pious, *and* ingenious *answerer.*

How the author came to be without his papers is a story not proper to be told and of very little use, being a private fact of which the reader would believe as little or as much as he thought good. He had, however, a blotted copy by him which he intended to have writ over with many alterations, and this the publishers° were well aware of, having put it into the bookseller's preface,° that they apprehended a surreptitious copy, which was to be altered, *&c. This though not regarded by readers, was a real truth, only the surreptitious copy was rather that which was printed; and they made all haste they could, which indeed was needless, the author not being at all prepared; but he has been told the bookseller was in much pain, having given a good sum of money for the copy.*

In the author's original copy there were not so many chasms as appear in the book, and why some of them were left, he knows not; had the publication been trusted to him, he would have made several corrections of passages against which nothing hath been ever objected. He would likewise have altered a few of those that seem with any reason to be excepted against; but to deal freely, the greatest number he should have left untouched as never suspecting it possible any wrong interpretations could be made of them.

The author observes at the end of the book there is a discourse called A Fragment, *which he more wondered to see in print than all the rest. Having been a most imperfect sketch, with the addition of a few loose hints, which he once lent a gentleman who had designed a discourse of somewhat the same subject, he never thought of it afterwards; and it was a sufficient surprise to see it pieced up together, wholly out of the method and scheme he had intended, for it was the ground work of a much larger discourse, and he was sorry to observe the materials so foolishly employed.*

There is one further objection made by those who have answered this book, as well as by some others, that Peter is frequently made to repeat oaths and curses. Every reader observes it was necessary to know that Peter did swear and curse. The oaths are not printed out, but only supposed; and the idea of an oath is not immoral like the idea of a profane or immodest speech. A man may laugh at the Popish folly of cursing people to hell, and imagine them swearing, without any crime; but lewd words or dangerous opinions though printed by halves, fill the reader's mind with ill ideas; and of these the author cannot be accused. For the judicious reader will find that the severest strokes of satire in his book are levelled against the modern custom of employing wit upon those topics, of which there is a remarkable instance in the [71]*d page as well as in several others, though perhaps once or twice expressed in too free a manner, excusable only for the reasons already alleged. Some overtures have been made by a third hand to the bookseller, for the author's altering those passages which he thought might require it; but it seems the bookseller will not hear of any such thing, being apprehensive it might spoil the sale of the book.*

The author cannot conclude this Apology without making this one reflection; that, as wit is the noblest and most useful gift of human nature, so humour is the most agreeable; and where these two enter far into the composition of any work they will render it always acceptable to the world. Now, the great part of those who have no share or taste of either, but by their pride, pedantry, and ill manners, lay themselves bare to the lashes of both, think the blow is weak because they are insensible; and where wit hath any mixture of raillery, 'tis but calling it banter and the work is done. This polite word of theirs was first borrowed from the bullies in White-Friars,° then fell among the footmen, and at last retired to the pedants, by whom it is applied as properly to the production of wit as if I should apply it to Sir Isaac Newton's mathematics. But, if this bantering as they call it be so despisable a thing, whence comes it to pass they have such a perpetual itch towards it themselves? To instance only in the answerer already mentioned, it is grievous to see him in some of his writings at every turn going out of his way to be waggish, to tell us of a cow that pricked up her tail *and in his answer to this discourse he says,* it is all a farce and a ladle*; with other passages equally shining. One may say of these* impedimenta literarum,° *that wit owes them a shame, and they cannot take wiser counsel than to keep out of harm's way, or at least, not to come till they are sure they are called.*

To conclude: with those allowances above required this book should be read;

after which the author conceives few things will remain which may not be excused in a young writer. He wrote only to the men of wit and taste, and he thinks he is not mistaken in his accounts when he says they have been all of his side, enough to give him the vanity of telling his name, wherein the world, with all its wise conjectures, is yet very much in the dark; which circumstance is no disagreeable amusement either to the public or himself.

The author is informed, that the bookseller has prevailed on several gentlemen to write some explanatory notes,° for the goodness of which he is not to answer, having never seen any of them, nor intends it, till they appear in print, when it is not unlikely he may have the pleasure to find twenty meanings which never entered into his imagination.

June 3, 1709.

POSTSCRIPT.

SINCE *the writing of this, which was about a year ago, a prostitute bookseller hath published a foolish paper° under the name of Notes on the* Tale of a Tub, *with some account of the author, and with an insolence which I suppose is punishable by law, hath presumed to assign certain names. It will be enough for the author to assure the world that the writer of that paper is utterly wrong in all his conjectures upon that affair. The author further asserts that the whole work is entirely of one hand, which every reader of judgment will easily discover. The gentleman who gave the copy° to the bookseller being a friend of the author, and using no other liberties besides that of expunging certain passages where now the chasms appear under the name of* desiderata. *But if any person will prove his claim to three lines in the whole book, let him step forth and tell his name and titles; upon which the bookseller shall have orders to prefix them to the next edition, and the claimant shall from henceforward be acknowledged the undisputed author.*

TO THE RIGHT HONOURABLE JOHN LORD SOMERS.

MY LORD,

THO' the author has written a large Dedication, yet that being addressed to a prince whom I am never likely to have the honour of being known to (a person besides, as far as I can observe, not at all regarded, or thought on by any of our present writers) and I being wholly free from that slavery which booksellers usually lie under to the caprices of authors, I think it a wise piece of presumption to inscribe these papers to your Lordship and to implore your Lordship's protection of them. God and your Lordship know their faults and their merits; for as to my own particular, I am altogether a stranger to the matter, and though everybody else should be equally ignorant, I do not fear the sale of the book at all the worse, upon that score. Your Lordship's name on the front in capital letters will at any time get off one edition, neither would I desire any other help to grow an alderman than a patent for the sole privilege of dedicating to your Lordship.

I should now, in right of a dedicator, give your Lordship a list of your own virtues and at the same time be very unwilling to offend your modesty; but chiefly I should celebrate your liberality towards men of great parts and small fortunes, and give you broad hints that I mean myself. And I was just going on in the usual method, to peruse a hundred or two of dedications, and transcribe an abstract to be applied to your Lordship; but I was diverted by a certain accident. For, upon the covers of these papers, I casually observed written in large letters the two following words, *DETUR DIGNISSIMO*; which, for aught I knew, might contain some important meaning. But it unluckily fell out that none of the authors I employ understood Latin (though I have them often in pay to translate out of that language); I was therefore compelled to have recourse to the curate of our parish, who Englished it thus, *Let it be given to the worthiest*: and his comment was, that the author meant his work should be dedicated to the sublimest genius of the age for wit, learning, judgment, eloquence, and wisdom. I called at a poet's chamber (who works for my shop) in an alley hard by, showed him the translation and desired his opinion who it was that the author could mean. He told me after some consideration, that vanity was a thing he abhorred, but by the description, he thought himself to be the person aimed at; and at the same time he very kindly offered his own assistance *gratis* towards penning a Dedication to himself. I desired him, however, to give a second guess. Why, then, said he, it must be I, or my Lord Somers. From thence I went to several other wits of my acquaintance, with no small hazard and weariness to my person, from a prodigious number of dark, winding stairs; but found them all in the same story, both of your Lordship and themselves. Now, your Lordship is to understand that this proceeding was not of my own invention; for I have somewhere heard it is a maxim that those to whom everybody allows the second place, have an undoubted title to the first.°

This infallibly convinced me that your Lordship was the person intended by the author. But being very unacquainted in the style and form of dedications, I employed those wits aforesaid to furnish me with hints and materials towards a panegyric upon your Lordship's virtues.

In two days they brought me ten sheets of paper, filled up on every side. They swore to me that they had ransacked whatever could be found in the characters of *Socrates*, *Aristides*, *Epaminondas*, *Cato*, *Tully*, *Atticus*, and other hard names which I cannot now recollect. However, I have reason to believe they imposed upon my ignorance, because when I came to read over their collections, there was not a syllable there but what I and everybody else knew as well as themselves. Therefore I grievously suspect a cheat, and that these authors of mine stole and transcribed every word from the universal report of mankind. So that I look upon myself as fifty shillings out of pocket to no manner of purpose.

If by altering the title I could make the same materials serve for another Dedication (as my betters have done) it would help to make up my loss; but I have made several persons dip here and there in those papers, and before they read three lines they have all assured me plainly that they cannot possibly be applied to any person besides your Lordship.

I expected, indeed, to have heard of your Lordship's bravery at the head of an army; of your undaunted courage in mounting a breach, or scaling a wall; or to have had your pedigree traced in a lineal descent from the House of Austria; or of your wonderful talent at dress and dancing; or your profound knowledge in algebra, metaphysics, and the oriental tongues. But to ply the world with an old beaten story of your wit, and eloquence, and learning, and wisdom, and justice, and politeness, and candour, and evenness of temper in all scenes of life; of that great discernment in discovering, and readiness in favouring deserving men; with forty other common topics; I confess I have neither conscience nor countenance to do it. Because there is no virtue, either of a public or private life, which some circumstances of your own have not often produced upon the stage of the world; and those few which, for want of occasions to exert them, might otherwise have passed unseen, or unobserved by your *friends*, your *enemies* have at length brought to light.°

'Tis true, I should be very loth the bright example of your Lordship's virtues should be lost to after-ages, both for their sake and your own; but chiefly because they will be so very necessary to adorn the history of a *late reign*.° And that is another reason why I would forbear to make a recital of them here, because I have been told by wise men that as Dedications have run for some years past, a good historian will not be apt to have recourse thither in search of characters.

There is one point, wherein I think we dedicators would do well to change our measures; I mean, instead of running on so far upon the praise of our patrons' *liberality*, to spend a word or two in admiring their *patience*. I can put no greater compliment on your Lordship's than by giving you so ample an occasion to exercise it at present; though perhaps I shall not be apt to reckon much merit to your Lordship upon that score, who having been formerly used to tedious harangues,° and sometimes to as little purpose, will be the readier to pardon this, especially when it is offered by one who is with all respect and veneration,

My Lord,

Your Lordship's most obedient,
and most faithful servant,
The Bookseller.

The BOOKSELLER to the READER.

It is now six years since these papers came first to my hands, which seems to have been about a twelvemonth after they were writ; for the author tells us in his preface° to the first treatise, that he has calculated it for the year 1697, and in *several passages of that Discourse, as well as the second, it appears they were written about that time.*

As to the author, I can give no manner of satisfaction. However, I am credibly informed that this publication is without his knowledge, for he concludes the copy is lost, having lent it to a person since dead, and being never in possession of it after. So that whether the work received his last hand, or whether he intended to fill up the defective places, is like to remain a secret.

If I should go about to tell the reader by what accident I became master of these papers, it would in this unbelieving age pass for little more than the cant or jargon of the trade. I therefore gladly spare both him and myself so unnecessary a trouble. There yet remains a difficult question, why I published them no sooner. I forbore upon two accounts. First, because I thought I had better work upon my hands; and secondly, because I was not without some hope of hearing from the author, and receiving his directions. But I have been lately alarmed with intelligence of a surreptitious copy which a certain great wit had new polished and refined, or as our present writers express themselves, fitted to the humour of the age, *as they have already done with great felicity to* Don Quixote, Boccalini,° la Bruyere, *and other authors. However, I thought it fairer dealing to offer the whole work in its naturals. If any gentleman will please to furnish me with a key in order to explain the more difficult parts, I shall very gratefully acknowledge the favour, and print it by itself.*

THE EPISTLE DEDICATORY,

TO HIS ROYAL HIGHNESS
PRINCE POSTERITY.*

SIR,

I HERE present Your Highness with the fruits of a very few leisure hours, stolen from the short intervals of a world of business and of an employment quite alien from such amusements as this; the poor production of that refuse of time, which has lain heavy upon my hands during a long prorogation of parliament, a great dearth of foreign news, and a tedious fit of rainy weather; for which and other reasons, it cannot choose extremely to deserve such a patronage as that of Your Highness, whose numberless virtues, in so few years, make the world look upon you as the future example to all princes; for although Your Highness is hardly got clear of infancy, yet has the universal learned world already resolved upon appealing to your future dictates with the lowest and most resigned submission; fate having decreed you sole arbiter of the productions of human wit, in this polite and most accomplished age. Methinks, the number of appellants were enough to shock and startle any judge, of a genius less unlimited than yours: but in order to prevent such glorious trials, the *person*° (it seems) to whose care the education of Your Highness is committed, has resolved (as I am told) to keep you in almost an universal ignorance of our studies, which it is your inherent birthright to inspect.

It is amazing to me that this *person* should have assurance, in the face of the sun, to go about persuading Your Highness that our age is almost wholly illiterate, and has hardly produced one writer upon any subject. I know very well that when Your Highness shall come to riper years, and have gone through the learning of antiquity, you will be too curious to neglect inquiring into the authors of the very age before you: and to think that this *insolent*, in the account he is preparing for your view, designs to reduce them to a number so insignificant as I am ashamed to mention, it moves my zeal and my spleen for the honour and interest of our vast

* The Citation out of Irenæus in the title-page, which seems to be all *gibberish*, is a form of initiation used anciently by the Marcosian Heretics.° W. WOTTON.

It is the usual style of decried writers to appeal to Posterity, who is here represented as a prince in his nonage, and Time as his governor; and the author begins in a way very frequent with him, by personating other writers who sometimes offer such reasons and excuses for publishing their works, as they ought chiefly to conceal and be ashamed of.

flourishing body, as well as of myself, for whom, I know by long experience, he has professed and still continues a peculiar malice.

'Tis not unlikely that when Your Highness will one day peruse what I am now writing, you may be ready to expostulate with your governor upon the credit of what I here affirm, and command him to show you some of our productions. To which he will answer (for I am well informed of his designs) by asking Your Highness, where they are? and what is become of them? and pretend it a demonstration that there never were any, because they are not then to be found. Not to be found! Who has mislaid them? Are they sunk in the abyss of things? 'Tis certain that in their own nature they were *light* enough to swim upon the surface for all eternity. Therefore the fault is in him who tied weights so heavy to their heels as to depress them to the centre. Is their very essence destroyed? Who has annihilated them? Were they drowned by *purges*, or martyred by *pipes*? Who administered them to the posteriors of —— ? But that it may no longer be a doubt with Your Highness who is to be the author of this universal ruin, I beseech you to observe that large and terrible *scythe* which your governor affects to bear continually about him. Be pleased to remark the length and strength, the sharpness and hardness, of his *nails* and *teeth*: consider his baneful, abominable *breath*, enemy to life and matter, infectious and corrupting. And then reflect whether it be possible for any mortal ink and paper of this generation to make a suitable resistance. O! that Your Highness would one day resolve to disarm this usurping *maitre de palais**° of his furious engines, and bring your empire *hors du page*.†

It were endless to recount the several methods of tyranny and destruction which your governor is pleased to practise upon this occasion. His inveterate malice is such to the writings of our age that of several thousands produced yearly from this renowned city, before the next revolution of the sun there is not one to be heard of. Unhappy infants, many of them barbarously destroyed before they have so much as learnt their *mother tongue* to beg for pity. Some he stifles in their cradles; others he frights into convulsions, whereof they suddenly die; some he flays alive; others he tears limb from limb. Great numbers are offered to Moloch,° and the rest, tainted by his breath, die of a languishing consumption.

But the concern I have most at heart, is for our corporation of *poets*, from whom I am preparing a petition to Your Highness, to be subscribed with the names of one hundred thirty six of the first rate, but whose immortal productions are never likely to reach your eyes, though each of

* Comptroller. † Out of guardianship.

them is now an humble and an earnest appellant for the laurel,° and has large comely volumes ready to show for a support to his pretensions. The *never-dying* works of these illustrious persons, your governor, sir, has devoted to unavoidable death, and Your Highness is to be made believe that our age has never arrived at the honour to produce one single poet.

We confess *Immortality* to be a great and powerful goddess, but in vain we offer up to her our devotions and our sacrifices if Your Highness's governor, who has usurped the *priesthood*, must by an unparalleled ambition and avarice, wholly intercept and devour them.

To affirm that our age is altogether unlearned, and devoid of writers in any kind, seems to be an assertion so bold and so false that I have been some time thinking the contrary may almost be proved by uncontrollable demonstration. 'Tis true indeed, that although their numbers be vast, and their productions numerous in proportion, yet are they hurried so hastily off the scene, that they escape our memory, and delude our sight. When I first thought of this address, I had prepared a copious list of *titles* to present Your Highness as an undisputed argument for what I affirm. The originals were posted fresh upon all gates and corners of streets° but, returning in a very few hours to take a review, they were all torn down, and fresh ones in their places. I inquired after them among readers and booksellers, but I inquired in vain; the *memorial of them was lost among men, their place was no more to be found*;° and I was laughed to scorn for a clown and a pedant, without all taste and refinement, little versed in the course of present affairs, and that knew nothing of what had passed in the best companies of court and town. So that I can only avow in general to Your Highness, that we *do* abound in learning and wit; but to fix upon particulars, is a task too slippery for my slender abilities. If I should venture in a windy day to affirm to Your Highness that there is a large cloud near the *horizon* in the form of a *bear*, another in the *zenith* with the head of an *ass*, a third to the westward with claws like a *dragon*, and Your Highness should in a few minutes think fit to examine the truth, 'tis certain they would all be changed in figure and position: new ones would arise, and all we could agree upon would be that clouds there were, but that I was grossly mistaken in the *zoography* and *topography* of them.°

But your governor perhaps may still insist, and put the question, What is then become of those immense bales of paper which must needs have been employed in such numbers of books? Can these also be wholly annihilate, and so of a sudden as I pretend? What shall I say in return of so invidious an objection? It ill befits the distance between Your Highness and me to send you for ocular conviction to a *jakes*, or an *oven*, to the windows of a *bawdy-house*, or to a sordid *lantern*. Books, like men their authors, have no more than one way of coming into the world, but there are ten thousand to go out of it and return no more.

I profess to Your Highness, in the integrity of my heart, that what I am going to say is literally true this minute I am writing. What revolutions may happen before it shall be ready for your perusal, I can by no means warrant. However, I beg you to accept it as a specimen of our learning, our politeness, and our wit. I do therefore affirm, upon the word of a sincere man, that there is now actually in being a certain poet called John Dryden, whose translation of Virgil° was lately printed in a large folio, well bound, and if diligent search were made, for aught I know is yet to be seen. There is another called Nahum Tate, who is ready to make oath that he has caused many reams of verse to be published, whereof both himself and his bookseller (if lawfully required) can still produce authentic copies, and therefore wonders why the world is pleased to make such a secret of it. There is a third, known by the name of Tom Durfey, a poet of a vast comprehension, an universal genius, and most profound learning. There are also one Mr. Rymer, and one Mr. Dennis, most profound critics. There is a person styled Dr. B[en]tl[e]y, who has written near a thousand pages of immense erudition, *giving a full and true account* of a certain *squabble*, of wonderful importance, between himself and a bookseller. He is a writer of infinite wit and humour; no man rallies with a better grace, and in more sprightly turns. Further, I avow to Your Highness that with these eyes I have beheld the person of William W[o]tt[o]n,° B.D., who has written a good sizeable volume against a *friend of your governor*° (from whom, alas! he must therefore look for little favour) in a most gentlemanly style, adorned with utmost politeness and civility, replete with discoveries equally valuable for their novelty and use, and embellished with *traits* of wit so poignant and so apposite, that he is a worthy yokemate to his forementioned *friend*.

Why should I go upon further particulars which might fill a volume with the just elogies of my cotemporary brethren? I shall bequeath this piece of justice to a larger work, wherein I intend to write a character of the present set of *wits* in our nation. Their persons I shall describe particularly and at length, their genius and understandings in *miniature*.

In the meantime I do here make bold to present Your Highness with a faithful abstract, drawn from the universal body of all arts and sciences, intended wholly for your service and instruction. Nor do I doubt in the least but Your Highness will peruse it as carefully, and make as considerable improvements, as *other* young *princes* have already done by the many volumes of late years written for a help to their studies.

That Your Highness may advance in wisdom and virtue, as well as years, and at last outshine all your royal ancestors, shall be the daily prayer of,

SIR,

Your Highness's

Most devoted, &c.

Decemb. 1697.

THE PREFACE.

THE wits of the present age being so very numerous and penetrating, it seems the grandees of Church and State begin to fall under horrible apprehensions lest these gentlemen, during the intervals of a long peace, should find leisure to pick holes in the weak sides of Religion and Government. To prevent which there has been much thought employed of late upon certain projects for taking off the force and edge of those formidable enquirers from canvassing and reasoning upon such delicate points. They have at length fixed upon one which will require some time as well as cost to perfect. Meanwhile, the danger hourly increasing by new levies of wits, all appointed (as there is reason to fear) with pen, ink, and paper, which may at an hour's warning be drawn out into pamphlets and other offensive weapons ready for immediate execution, it was judged of absolute necessity that some present expedient be thought on, till the main design can be brought to maturity. To this end, at a Grand Committee° some days ago, this important discovery was made by a certain curious and refined observer: that seamen have a custom when they meet a *whale*, to fling him out an empty *tub* by way of amusement, to divert him from laying violent hands upon the ship. This parable was immediately mythologised; the whale was interpreted to be Hobbes's *Leviathan*,° which tosses and plays with all schemes of Religion and Government, whereof a great many are hollow, and dry, and empty, and noisy, and wooden, and given to rotation.° This is the *Leviathan* whence the terrible wits of our age are said to borrow their weapons. The *ship* in danger is easily understood to be its old antitype, the Commonwealth.° But how to analyze the tub was a matter of difficulty; when, after long enquiry and debate, the literal meaning was preserved, and it was decreed that in order to prevent these *Leviathans* from tossing and sporting with the Commonwealth (which of itself is too apt to *fluctuate*) they should be diverted from that game by *a Tale of a Tub*. And my genius being conceived to lie not unhappily that way, I had the honour done me to be engaged in the performance.

This is the sole design in publishing the following treatise, which I hope will serve for an *interim* of some months to employ those unquiet spirits till the perfecting of that great work; into the secret of which it is reasonable the courteous reader should have some little light.

It is intended that a large Academy be erected, capable of containing nine thousand seven hundred forty and three persons, which by modest computation is reckoned to be pretty near the current number of *wits* in this island. These are to be disposed into the several schools of this academy, and there pursue those studies to which their genius most inclines them. The undertaker himself will publish his proposals with all convenient speed, to which I shall refer the curious reader for a more particular account, mentioning at present only a few of the principal schools. There is first a large *Pederastic* School, with French and Italian masters. There is also the *Spelling* School,° a very spacious building: the School of *Looking-glasses*: the School of *Swearing*: the School of *Critics*: the School of *Salivation*: the School of *Hobby-horses*: the School of *Poetry*: the School of *Tops*:* the School of *Spleen*: the School of *Gaming*: with many others too tedious to recount. No person to be admitted member into any of these schools without an attestation under two sufficient persons' hands, certifying him to be a *wit*.

But, to return. I am sufficiently instructed in the principal duty of a preface, if my genius were capable of arriving at it. Thrice have I forced my imagination to make the tour of my invention, and thrice it has returned empty, the latter having been wholly drained by the following treatise. Not so, my more successful brethren the *moderns*, who will by no means let slip a preface or dedication without some notable distinguishing stroke to surprise the reader at the entry, and kindle a wonderful expectation of what is to ensue. Such was that of a most ingenious poet who, soliciting his brain for something new, compared himself to the *hangman*, and his patron to the *patient*. This was *insigne, recens, indictum ore alio*.†° When I went through that necessary and noble course of study‡ I had the happiness to observe many such egregious touches, which I shall not injure the authors by transplanting; because I have remarked that nothing is so very tender as a *modern* piece of wit, and

* This I think the author should have omitted, it being of the very same nature with the *School of Hobby-horses*, if one may venture to censure one who is so severe a censurer of others, perhaps with too little distinction.

† Horace. Something extraordinary, new and never hit upon before.

‡ Reading Prefaces, &c.

which is apt to suffer so much in the carriage. Some things are extremely witty *today*, or *fasting*, or *in this place*, or *at eight o'clock*, or *over a bottle*, or *spoke by* Mr. What d'y'call'm, or *in a summer's morning*: any of the which, by the smallest transposal or misapplication, is utterly annihilate. Thus, *wit* has its walks and purlieus, out of which it may not stray the breadth of a hair, upon peril of being lost. The *moderns* have artfully fixed this *mercury*,° and reduced it to the circumstances of time, place, and person. Such a jest there is that will not pass out of Covent Garden, and such a one that is nowhere intelligible but at Hyde Park corner. Now, though it sometimes tenderly affects me to consider that all the towardly passages I shall deliver in the following treatise will grow quite out of date and relish with the first shifting of the present scene, yet I must need subscribe to the justice of this proceeding; because I cannot imagine why we should be at expense to furnish wit for succeeding ages, when the former have made no sort of provision for ours; wherein I speak the sentiment of the very newest, and consequently the most orthodox refiners,° as well as my own. However, being extremely solicitous that every accomplished person who has got into the taste of wit calculated for this present month of August 1697, should descend to the very *bottom* of all the *sublime* throughout this treatise, I hold fit to lay down this general maxim. Whatever reader desires to have a thorough comprehension of an author's thoughts cannot take a better method than by putting himself into the circumstances and posture of life that the writer was in upon every important passage as it flowed from his pen. For this will introduce a parity and strict correspondence of ideas between the reader and the author. Now, to assist the diligent reader in so delicate an affair as far as brevity will permit, I have recollected that the shrewdest pieces of this treatise were conceived in bed in a garret; at other times (for a reason best known to myself) I thought fit to sharpen my invention with hunger; and in general the whole work was begun, continued, and ended, under a long course of physic, and a great want of money. Now, I do affirm it will be absolutely impossible for the candid peruser to go along with me in a great many bright passages unless, upon the several difficulties emergent, he will please to capacitate and prepare himself by these directions. And this I lay down as my principal *postulatum*.

Because I have professed to be a most devoted servant of all *modern* forms, I apprehend some curious *wit* may object against me for proceeding thus far in a preface, without declaiming according to the custom against the multitude of writers, whereof the whole multitude of writers most reasonably complains. I am just come from perusing some hundreds of prefaces, wherein the authors do at the very beginning address the gentle reader concerning this enormous grievance. Of these I have preserved a few examples and shall set them down as near as my memory has been able to retain them.

One begins thus:

For a man to set up for a writer, when the press swarms with, &c.

Another:

The tax upon paper° does not lessen the number of scribblers, who daily pester, &c.

Another:

When every little would-be wit takes pen in hand, 'tis in vain to enter the lists, &c.

Another:

To observe what trash the press swarms with, &c.

Another:

Sir, It is merely in obedience to your commands that I venture into the public; for who upon a less consideration would be of a party with such a rabble of scribblers, &c.

Now, I have two words in my own defence against this objection. First, I am far from granting the number of writers a nuisance to our nation, having strenuously maintained the contrary in several parts of the following Discourse. Secondly, I do not well understand the justice of this proceeding, because I observe many of these polite prefaces to be not only from the same hand, but from those who are most voluminous in their several productions. Upon which, I shall tell the reader a short tale.

A mountebank in Leicester-Fields° *had drawn a huge assembly about him. Among the rest, a fat unwieldy fellow, half stifled in the press, would be every fit crying out, Lord! what a filthy crowd is here! Pray, good people, give way a little. Bless me! what a devil has raked this rabble together! Z—ds, what squeezing is this! Honest friend, remove your elbow. At last a weaver that stood next him could hold no longer. A plague confound you* (said he) *for an overgrown sloven; and who (in the devil's name) I wonder, helps to make up the crowd half so much as yourself? Don't you consider (with a pox) that you take up more room with that carcase than any five here? Is not the place as free for us as for you? Bring your own guts to a reasonable compass (and be d—n'd) and then I'll engage we shall have room enough for us all.*

There are certain common privileges of a writer, the benefit whereof I hope there will be no reason to doubt; particularly, that where I am not understood it shall be concluded that something very useful and profound is couched underneath; and again, that whatever word or sentence is printed in a different character shall be judged to contain something extraordinary either of *wit* or *sublime*.

As for the liberty I have thought fit to take of praising myself upon some occasions or none, I am sure it will need no excuse if a multitude of great examples be allowed sufficient authority. For it is here to be noted that *praise* was originally a pension paid by the world; but the *moderns*, finding the trouble and charge too great in collecting it, have lately bought out the *fee-simple*, since which time the right of presentation is wholly in ourselves. For this reason it is that when an author makes his own elogy, he uses a certain form to declare and insist upon his title which is commonly in these or the like words, 'I speak without vanity'; which I think plainly shows it to be a matter of right and justice. Now, I do here once for all declare that in every encounter of this nature through the following treatise, the form aforesaid is implied; which I mention to save the trouble of repeating it on so many occasions.

'Tis a great ease to my conscience that I have written so elaborate and useful a discourse without one grain of satire intermixed; which is the sole point wherein I have taken leave to dissent from the famous originals of our age and country. I have observed some satirists to use the public much at the rate that pedants do a naughty boy ready horsed for discipline: first expostulate the case, then plead the necessity of the rod from great provocations, and conclude every period with a lash. Now if I know anything of mankind, these gentlemen might very well spare their reproof and correction, for there is not through all nature another so callous and insensible a member as the *world's posteriors*, whether you apply to it the *toe* or the *birch*. Besides, most of our late satirists seem to lie under a sort of mistake, that because *nettles* have the prerogative to sting, therefore all *other weeds* must do so too. I make not this comparison out of the least design to detract from these worthy writers; for it is well known among *mythologists* that *weeds* have the pre-eminence over all other vegetables; and therefore the first *monarch* of this island, whose taste and judgment were so acute and refined, did very wisely root out the *roses* from the collar of the *Order*, and plant the *thistles* in their stead,° as the nobler flower of the two. For which reason it is conjectured by profounder antiquaries that the satirical itch, so prevalent in this part of our island, was first brought among us from beyond the Tweed. Here may it long flourish and abound. May it survive and neglect the scorn of the world with as much ease and contempt as the world is insensible to the lashes of it. May their own dulness, or that of their party, be no discouragement for the authors to proceed, but let them remember it is with *wits* as with *razors*, which are never so apt to *cut* those they are employed on as when they have *lost their edge*. Besides, those whose teeth are too rotten to bite, are best of all others, qualified to revenge that defect with their breath.

I am not like other men to envy or undervalue the talents I cannot reach; for which reason I must needs bear a true honour to this large eminent sect of our British writers. And I hope this little panegyric will not be offensive to their ears since it has the advantage of being only designed for themselves. Indeed, nature herself has taken order that fame and honour should be purchased at a better pennyworth by satire than by any other productions of the brain, the world being soonest provoked to *praise* by *lashes*, as men are to *love*. There is a problem in an ancient author, why Dedications and other bundles of flattery run all upon stale musty topics, without the smallest tincture of anything new; not only to the torment and nauseating of the Christian reader, but (if not suddenly prevented) to the universal spreading of that pestilent disease the lethargy, in this island: whereas there is very little satire which has not something in it untouched before. The defects of the former are usually imputed to the want of invention among those who are dealers in that kind, but I think with a great deal of injustice, the solution being easy and natural; for the materials of panegyric, being very few in number, have been long since exhausted. For, as health is but one thing and has been always the same, whereas diseases are by thousands, besides new and daily additions; so, all the virtues that have been ever in mankind are to be counted upon a few fingers; but his follies and vices are innumerable and time adds hourly to the heap. Now the utmost a poor poet can do is to get by heart a list of the cardinal virtues, and deal them with his utmost liberality to his hero or his patron: he may ring the changes as far as it will go, and vary his phrase till he has talked round, but the reader quickly finds it is all *pork** with a little variety of sauce. For there is no inventing terms of art beyond our ideas, and when our ideas are exhausted, terms of art must be so too.

But though the matter for panegyric were as fruitful as the topics of satire, yet would it not be hard to find out a sufficient reason why the latter will be always better received than the first. For, this being bestowed only upon one or a few persons at a time, is sure to raise envy, and consequently ill words from the rest who have no share in the blessing. But satire being levelled at all is never resented for an offence by any, since every individual person makes bold to understand it of others, and very wisely removes his particular part of the burden upon the shoulders of the world, which are broad enough and able to bear it. To this purpose I have sometimes reflected upon the difference between

* Plutarch.°

Athens and England, with respect to the point before us. In the Attic commonwealth* it was the privilege and birthright of every citizen and poet to rail aloud and in public, or to expose upon the stage by name, any person they pleased, though of the greatest figure, whether a C[l]eon, an Hyperbolus,° an Alcibiades, or a Demosthenes. But on the other side, the least reflecting word let fall against the *people* in general was immediately caught up and revenged upon the authors, however considerable for their quality or their merits. Whereas in England, it is just the reverse of all this. Here you may securely display your utmost *rhetoric* against mankind, in the face of the world; tell them, 'That all are gone astray, that there is none that doth good, no not one;° that we live in the very dregs of time; that knavery and atheism are epidemic as the pox; that honesty is fled with Astræa';° with any other commonplaces, *equally* new and eloquent, which are furnished by the *splendida bilis*.†° And when you have done, the whole audience, far from being offended, shall return you thanks as a deliverer of precious and useful truths. Nay, further, it is but to venture your lungs, and you may preach in Covent Garden° against foppery and fornication, and *something else*: against pride, and dissimulation, and bribery, at White-Hall:° you may expose rapine and injustice in the Inns of Court Chapel: and in a city° pulpit be as fierce as you please against avarice, hypocrisy, and extortion. 'Tis but a *ball* bandied to and fro, and every man carries a *racket* about him to strike it from himself among the rest of the company. But on the other side, whoever should mistake the nature of things so far as to drop but a single hint in public, how *such a one* starved half the fleet and half poisoned the rest: how *such a one*, from a true principle of *love* and *honour*, pays no debts but for *wenches* and *play*: how *such a one* has got a clap, and runs out of his estate: how Paris bribed by Juno and Venus,‡ loth to offend either party, slept out the whole cause on the bench: or, how *such an orator* makes long speeches in the senate, with much thought, little sense, and to no purpose; whoever, I say, should venture to be thus particular must expect to be imprisoned for *scandalum magnatum*, to have *challenges* sent him, to be sued for *defamation*, and to be *brought before the bar of the house.*

But I forget that I am expatiating on a subject wherein I have no concern, having neither a talent nor an inclination for satire. On the other side I am so entirely satisfied with the whole present procedure of human

* *Vide* Xenophon.°

† Spleen. *Hor.*

‡ Juno and Venus are money and a mistress, very powerful bribes to a judge, if scandal says true. I remember such reflections were cast about that time, but I cannot fix the person intended here.

things that I have been for some years preparing materials towards *A Panegyric upon the World*, to which I intended to add a second part entitled *A Modest Defence of the Proceedings of the Rabble in all Ages*.° Both these I had thoughts to publish by way of appendix to the following treatise; but finding my commonplace book fill much slower than I had reason to expect, I have chosen to defer them to another occasion. Besides, I have been unhappily prevented in that design by a certain domestic misfortune, in the particulars whereof, though it would be very seasonable and much in the *modern* way to inform the *gentle reader*, and would also be of great assistance towards extending this preface into the size now in vogue, which by rule ought to be *large* in proportion as the subsequent volume is *small*; yet I shall now dismiss our impatient reader from any further attendance at the *porch*, and having duly prepared his mind by a preliminary discourse, shall gladly introduce him to the sublime mysteries that ensue.

A TALE OF A TUB, &c.

SECT. I.

The Introduction.

WHOEVER hath an ambition to be heard in a crowd must press, and squeeze, and thrust, and climb, with indefatigable pains, till he has exalted himself to a certain degree of altitude above them. Now, in all assemblies though you wedge them ever so close, we may observe this peculiar property that over their heads there is room enough, but how to reach it is the difficult point, it being as hard to get quit of *number* as of *hell*;

*— *Evadere ad auras,*
Hoc opus, hic labor est.°

To this end, the philosopher's way in all ages has been by erecting certain *edifices in the air*.° But whatever practice and reputation these kind of structures have formerly possessed, or may still continue in, not excepting even that of Socrates when he was suspended in a basket° to help contemplation, I think with due submission they seem to labour under two inconveniences. First, that the foundations being laid too

* But to return, and view the cheerful skies;
In this the task and mighty labour lies.

high, they have been often out of *sight*, and ever out of *hearing*. Secondly, that the materials being very transitory have suffered much from inclemencies of air, especially in these north-west regions.

Therefore, towards the just performance of this great work there remain but three methods that I can think on; whereof the wisdom of our ancestors being highly sensible, has, to encourage all aspiring adventurers, thought fit to erect three wooden machines for the use of those orators who desire to talk much without interruption. These are the *pulpit*, the *ladder*°, and the *stage itinerant*. For, as to the *Bar*, though it be compounded of the same matter and designed for the same use, it cannot however be well allowed the honour of a fourth, by reason of its level or inferior situation exposing it to perpetual interruption from collaterals. Neither can the *Bench* itself, though raised to a proper eminency, put in a better claim whatever its advocates insist on. For, if they please to look into the original design of its erection and the circumstances or adjuncts subservient to that design, they will soon acknowledge the present practice exactly correspondent to the primitive institution, and both to answer the etymology of the name, which in the Phœnician tongue is a word of great signification, importing if literally interpreted, *the place of sleep*; but in common acceptation, *a seat well bolstered and cushioned for the repose of old and gouty limbs*: *senes ut in otia tuta recedant*.° Fortune being indebted to them this part of retaliation that, as formerly they have long *talked* whilst others *slept*, so now they may *sleep* as long, whilst others *talk*.

But if no other argument could occur to exclude the Bench and the Bar from the list of oratorial machines, it were sufficient that the admission of them would overthrow a number which I was resolved to establish whatever argument it might cost me; in imitation of that prudent method observed by many other philosophers and great clerks, whose chief art in division has been to grow fond of some proper mystical number which their imaginations have rendered sacred, to a degree that they force common reason to find room for it in every part of nature; reducing, including, and adjusting every *genus* and *species* within that compass, by coupling some against their wills, and banishing others at any rate. Now, among all the rest the profound number *THREE* is that which hath most employed my sublimest speculations, nor ever without wonderful delight. There is now in the press (and will be published next Term) a panegyrical essay of mine upon this number, wherein I have by most convincing proofs not only reduced the *senses* and the *elements* under its banner, but brought over several deserters from its two great rivals, *SEVEN* and *NINE*.

Now, the first of these oratorial machines, in place as well as dignity, is the *pulpit*. Of pulpits there are in this island several sorts, but I esteem only that made of timber from the *sylva Caledonia*,° which agrees very well with our climate. If it be upon its decay, 'tis the better both for conveyance of sound and for other reasons to be mentioned by and by. The degree of perfection in shape and size, I take to consist in being extremely narrow with little ornament, and, best of all, without a cover (for by ancient rule it ought to be the only uncovered *vessel* in every assembly where it is rightfully used) by which means, from its near resemblance to a pillory, it will ever have a mighty influence on human ears.°

Of *ladders* I need say nothing. 'Tis observed by foreigners themselves, to the honour of our country, that we excel all nations in our practice and understanding of this machine. The ascending orators do not only oblige their audience in the agreeable delivery, but the whole world in their *early* publication of these speeches° which I look upon as the choicest treasury of our British eloquence, and whereof, I am informed, that worthy citizen and bookseller, Mr. John Dunton, hath made a faithful and a painful collection which he shortly designs to publish in twelve volumes in folio, illustrated with copperplates. A work highly useful and curious, and altogether worthy of such a hand.

The last engine of orators is the *stage itinerant*,* erected with much sagacity *sub Jove pluvio, in triviis et quadriviis*.† It is the great seminary of the two former, and its orators are sometimes preferred to the one and sometimes to the other, in proportion to their deservings, there being a strict and perpetual intercourse between all three.

From this accurate deduction it is manifest that for obtaining attention in public, there is of necessity required a *superior position of place*. But although this point be generally granted, yet the cause is little agreed in; and it seems to me that very few philosophers have fallen into a true, natural solution of this phenomenon. The deepest account, and the most fairly digested of any I have yet met with, is this, that air being a heavy body, and therefore (according to the system of Epicurus‡) continually descending, must needs be more so when loaden and pressed down by words, which are also bodies of much weight and gravity, as it is manifest from those deep *impressions* they make and leave upon us; and therefore

* Is the *mountebank's stage*, whose orators the author determines either to the *gallows* or a *conventicle*.

† In the open air, and in streets where the greatest resort is.

‡ Lucret. Lib. 2.

must be delivered from a due altitude, or else they will neither carry a good aim nor fall down with a sufficient force.

> Corpoream quoque enim vocem constare fatendum est,
> Et sonitum, quoniam possunt impellere sensus.*
>
> LUCR. Lib. 4.

And I am the readier to favour this conjecture, from a common observation that in the several assemblies of these orators, nature itself has instructed the hearers to stand with their mouths open and erected parallel to the horizon, so as they may be intersected by a perpendicular line from the zenith to the centre of the earth. In which position, if the audience be well compact, every one carries home a share and little or nothing is lost.

I confess there is something yet more refined in the contrivance and structure of our modern theatres. For, first, the pit is sunk below the stage, with due regard to the institution above deduced; that whatever *weighty* matter shall be delivered thence (whether it be *lead* or *gold*) may fall plumb into the jaws of certain *critics* (as I think they are called) which stand ready open to devour them. Then the boxes are built round and raised to a level with the scene, in deference to the ladies, because that large portion of wit laid out in raising pruriences and protuberancies, is observed to run much upon a line and ever in a circle. The whining passions and little starved conceits are gently wafted up by their own extreme levity to the middle region, and there fix and are frozen by the frigid understandings of the inhabitants. Bombast and buffoonery, by nature lofty and light, soar highest of all and would be lost in the roof, if the prudent architect had not with much foresight contrived for them a fourth place called *the twelve-penny gallery*, and there planted a suitable colony who greedily intercept them in their passage.

Now this physico-logical scheme of oratorial receptacles or machines contains a great mystery, being a type, a sign, an emblem, a shadow, a symbol, bearing analogy to the spacious commonwealth of writers, and to those methods by which they must exalt themselves to a certain eminency above the inferior world. By the *pulpit* are adumbrated the writings of our *modern saints*° in Great Britain, as they have spiritualized and refined them from the dross and grossness of *sense* and *human reason*. The matter, as we have said, is of rotten wood, and that upon two considerations; because it is the quality of rotten wood to give *light* in the dark, and secondly, because its cavities are full of worms; which is a type

* 'Tis certain then, that *voice* that thus can wound,
Is all *material*; *body* every *sound*.

with a pair of handles,* having a respect to the two principal qualifications of the orator and the two different fates attending upon his work.

The *ladder* is an adequate symbol of *faction* and of *poetry*, to both of which so noble a number of authors are indebted for their fame. Of *faction* because† * * * * * *
* * * * * * * *
Hiatus in MS. * * * * * *
* * * * * Of *poetry*, because its orators do *perorare* with a song° and because climbing up by slow degrees, fate is sure to turn them off before they can reach within many steps of the top, and because it is a preferment attained by transferring of propriety, and a confounding of *meum* and *tuum*.

Under the *stage itinerant* are couched those productions designed for the pleasure and delight of mortal man, such as *Sixpenny-worth of Wit*, Westminster *Drolleries*, *Delightful Tales*, *Compleat Jesters*, and the like, by which the writers of and for *GRUB-STREET*° have in these latter ages so nobly triumphed over Time; have clipped his wings, pared his nails, filed his teeth, turned back his hour-glass, blunted his scythe, and drawn the hobnails out of his shoes. It is under this classis I have presumed to list my present treatise, being just come from having the honour conferred upon me to be adopted a member of that illustrious fraternity.

Now, I am not unaware how the productions of the Grub Street brotherhood have of late years fallen under many prejudices, nor how it has been the perpetual employment of two *junior* start-up societies to ridicule them and their authors as unworthy their established post in the commonwealth of wit and learning. Their own consciences will easily inform them whom I mean, nor has the world been so negligent a looker-on, as not to observe the continual efforts made by the societies of *Gresham*° and of *Will*'s‡ to edify a name and reputation upon the ruin of OURS. And this is yet a more feeling grief to us upon the regards of

* The two principal qualifications of a fanatic preacher are his inward light, and his head full of maggots; and the two different fates of his writings are to be burnt, or worm-eaten.

† Here is pretended a defect in the manuscript; and this is very frequent with our author either when he thinks he cannot say anything worth reading, or when he has no mind to enter on the subject, or when it is a matter of little moment; or perhaps to amuse his reader (whereof he is frequently very fond) or lastly, with some satirical intention.

‡ *Will*'s Coffee-House, was formerly the place where the poets usually met, which though it be yet fresh in memory, yet in some years may be forgot, and want this explanation.

tenderness as well as of justice, when we reflect on their proceedings not only as unjust, but as ungrateful, undutiful, and unnatural. For how can it be forgot by the world or themselves (to say nothing of our own records, which are full and clear in the point) that they both are seminaries not only of our *planting*, but our *watering* too? I am informed our two *rivals* have lately made an offer to enter into the lists with united forces, and challenge us to a comparison of books both as to *weight* and *number*. In return to which (with licence from our president) I humbly offer two answers. First, we say the proposal is like that which Archimedes made upon a *smaller* affair,* including an impossibility in the practice, for, where can they find scales of *capacity* enough for the first, or an arithmetician of *capacity* enough for the second? Secondly, we are ready to accept the challenge, but with this condition, that a third indifferent person be assigned, to whose impartial judgment it should be left to decide which society each book, treatise, or pamphlet, do most properly belong to. This point, God knows, is very far from being fixed at present, for we are ready to produce a catalogue of some thousands which in all common justice ought to be entitled to our fraternity, but by the revolted and newfangled writers most perfidiously ascribed to the others. Upon all which we think it very unbecoming our prudence that the determination should be remitted to the authors themselves, when our adversaries, by briguing and caballing, have caused so universal a defection from us that the greatest part of our society hath already deserted to them, and our nearest friends begin to stand aloof as if they were half ashamed to own us.

This is the utmost I am authorized to say upon so ungrateful and melancholy a subject, because we are extreme unwilling to inflame a controversy whose continuance may be so fatal to the interests of us all, desiring much rather that things be amicably composed. And we shall so far advance on our side as to be ready to receive the two *prodigals* with open arms, whenever they shall think fit to return from their *husks* and their *harlots*° (which, I think from the present course of their studies,† they most properly may be said to be engaged in) and, like an indulgent parent, continue to them our affection and our blessing.

But the greatest maim given to that general reception which the writings of our society have formerly received (next to the transitory state of all sublunary things) hath been a superficial vein among many readers of the present age, who will by no means be persuaded to inspect beyond the surface and the rind of things. Whereas, *Wisdom* is a *fox* who after

* *Viz.* About moving the earth.

† Virtuoso experiments, and modern comedies.

long hunting will at last cost you the pains to dig out. 'Tis a *cheese* which, by how much the richer, has the thicker, the homelier, and the coarser coat, and whereof, to a judicious palate, the *maggots* are the best. 'Tis a *sack-posset*, wherein the deeper you go you will find it the sweeter. *Wisdom* is a *hen* whose *cackling* we must value and consider because it is attended with an *egg*. But then lastly 'tis a *nut*, which unless you choose with judgment may cost you a tooth, and pay you with nothing but a *worm*. In consequence of these momentous truths, the Grubæan Sages have always chosen to convey their precepts and their arts shut up within the vehicles of types and fables; which having been perhaps more careful and curious in adorning than was altogether necessary, it has fared with these vehicles after the usual fate of coaches over-finely painted and gilt, that the transitory gazers have so dazzled their eyes and filled their imaginations with the outward lustre, as neither to regard nor consider the person or the parts of the owner within. A misfortune we undergo with somewhat less reluctancy because it has been common to us with Pythagoras, Æsop, Socrates,° and other of our predecessors.

However, that neither the world nor ourselves may any longer suffer by such misunderstandings, I have been prevailed on, after much importunity from my friends, to travail in a complete and laborious dissertation upon the prime productions of our society, which besides their beautiful externals for the gratification of superficial readers, have darkly and deeply couched under them the most finished and refined systems of all sciences and arts; as I do not doubt to lay open by untwisting or unwinding, and either to draw up by exantlation or display by incision.

This great work was entered upon some years ago by one of our most eminent members. He began with the *History of Reynard the Fox**° but neither lived to publish his essay nor to proceed further in so useful an attempt; which is very much to be lamented because the discovery he made and communicated with his friends is now universally received; nor do I think any of the learned will dispute that famous treatise to be a complete body of civil knowledge and the *revelation*, or rather the *apocalypse*, of all State *Arcana*. But the progress I have made is much greater, having already finished my annotations upon several dozens, from some of which I shall impart a few hints to the candid reader, as far as will be necessary to the conclusion at which I aim.

The first piece I have handled is that of *Tom Thumb*,° whose author

* The Author seems here to be mistaken, for I have seen a Latin edition of *Reynard the Fox*, above a hundred years old, which I take to be the original; for the rest, it has been thought by many people to contain some satyrical design in it.

was a Pythagorean philosopher. This dark treatise contains the whole scheme of the Metempsychosis, deducing the progress of the soul through all her stages.

The next is *Dr. Faustus*, penned by Artephius, an author *bonæ notæ* and an *adeptus*. He published it in the *nine-hundred-eighty-fourth year of his age; this writer proceeds wholly by *reincrudation*, or in the *via humida*; and the marriage between Faustus and Helen does most conspicuously dilucidate the fermenting of the *male* and *female dragon*.

Whittington and his Cat is the work of that mysterious rabbi Jehuda Hannasi, containing a defence of the *Gemara* of the Jerusalem *Mishna* and its just preference to that of Babylon, contrary to the vulgar opinion.

The Hind and Panther. This is the masterpiece of a famous writer now living,† intended for a complete abstract of sixteen thousand schoolmen from Scotus to Bellarmin.

Tommy Potts. Another piece supposed by the same hand, by way of supplement to the former.

The Wise Men of Gotham, cum appendice. This is a treatise of immense erudition, being the great original and fountain of those arguments bandied about both in France and England, for a just defence of the modern learning and wit, against the presumption, the pride, and ignorance of the ancients. This unknown author hath so exhausted the subject that a penetrating reader will easily discover whatever hath been written since upon that dispute, to be little more than repetition. An abstract of this treatise hath been lately published by a *worthy member* of our society.‡

These notices may serve to give the learned reader an idea as well as a taste of what the whole work is likely to produce; wherein I have now altogether circumscribed my thoughts and my studies, and if I can bring it to a perfection before I die, shall reckon I have well employed the poor remains of an unfortunate life.§ This, indeed, is more than I can justly expect from a quill worn to the pith in the service of the State, in *pros* and *cons* upon *Popish plots*, and *meal-tubs*,||° and *exclusion bills*, and *passive obedience*, and *addresses of lives and fortunes*, and *prerogative*, and *property*,

* He lived a thousand.

† Viz. In the year 1698.

‡ This is I suppose to be understood of Mr. W[o]tt[o]n's Discourse of Ancient and Modern Learning.

§ Here the author seems to personate L'Estrange, Dryden, and some others, who, having passed their lives in vice, faction, and falsehood, have the impudence to talk of merit and innocence and sufferings.

|| In King Charles the Second's time, there was an account of a Presbyterian plot, found in a meal-tub, which then made much noise.

and *liberty of conscience*, and *Letters to a Friend*: from an understanding and a conscience threadbare and ragged with perpetual turning; from a head broken in a hundred places by the malignants of the opposite factions; and from a body spent with poxes ill cured by trusting to bawds and surgeons who (as it afterwards appeared) were professed enemies to me and the government, and revenged their party's quarrel upon my nose and shins. Fourscore and eleven pamphlets have I writ under three reigns, and for the service of six and thirty factions. But finding the state has no further occasion for me and my ink, I retire willingly to draw it out into speculations more becoming a philospher, having, to my unspeakable comfort, passed a long life with a conscience void of offence° [towards God and towards Men].

But to return. I am assured from the reader's candour that the brief specimen I have given will easily clear all the rest of our society's productions from an aspersion grown, as it is manifest, out of envy and ignorance: that they are of little farther use or value to mankind beyond the common entertainments of their wit and their style. For these I am sure have never yet been disputed by our keenest adversaries, in both which, as well as the more profound and mystical part, I have throughout this treatise closely followed the most applauded originals. And to render all complete I have, with much thought and application of mind, so ordered that the chief title prefixed to it (I mean, that under which I design it shall pass in the common conversations of court and town) is modelled exactly after the manner peculiar to *our* society.

I confess to have been somewhat liberal in the business of titles,* having observed the humour of multiplying them to bear great vogue among certain writers whom I exceedingly reverence. And indeed it seems not unreasonable, that books, the children of the brain, should have the honour to be christened with variety of names as well as other infants of quality. Our famous Dryden has ventured to proceed a point farther, endeavouring to introduce also a multiplicity of *godfathers*†° which is an improvement of much more advantage, upon a very obvious account. 'Tis a pity this admirable invention has not been better cultivated so as to grow by this time into general imitation, when such an authority serves it for a precedent. Nor have my endeavours been wanting to second so useful an example. But it seems there is an unhappy expense usually annexed to the calling of a godfather which was clearly out of my head, as it is very reasonable to believe. Where the pinch lay, I

* The title-page in the original was so torn, that it was not possible to recover several titles which the author here speaks of.

† See Virgil translated, &c.

cannot certainly affirm; but having employed a world of thoughts and pains to split my treatise into forty sections, and having entreated forty lords of my acquaintance that they would do me the honour to stand, they all made it a matter of conscience and sent me their excuses.

SECT. II.

Once upon a time, there was a man who had three sons by one wife,* and all at a birth, neither could the midwife tell certainly which was the eldest. Their father died while they were young, and upon his deathbed, calling the lads to him, spoke thus:

'Sons, because I have purchased no estate, nor was born to any, I have long considered of some good legacies to bequeath you; and at last, with much care as well as expense, have provided each of you (here they are) a new coat.† Now, you are to understand that these coats have two virtues contained in them: one is, that with good wearing they will last you fresh and sound as long as you live: the other is that they will grow in the same proportion with your bodies, lengthening and widening of themselves so as to be always fit. Here; let me see them on you before I die. So; very well; pray, children, wear them clean and brush them often. You will find in my will‡ (here it is) full instructions in every particular concerning the wearing and management of your coats, wherein you must be very exact to avoid the penalties I have appointed for every transgression or neglect, upon which your future fortunes will entirely depend. I have also commanded in my will that you should live together in one house like brethren and friends, for then you will be sure to thrive, and not otherwise.'

Here the story says this good father died, and the three sons went all together to seek their fortunes.

I shall not trouble you with recounting what adventures they met for the first seven years,° any further than by taking notice that they carefully observed their father's will, and kept their coats in very good order, that

* By these three sons, Peter, Martin, and Jack; Popery, the Church of England, and our Protestant dissenters, are designed. W. WOTTON.

† By his *coats* which he gave his sons, the Garments of the Israelites.° W. WOTTON.
An error (with submission) of the learned commentator; for by the coats are meant the Doctrine and Faith of Christianity, by the Wisdom of the divine Founder fitted to all times, places, and circumstances. LAMBIN.°

‡ The New Testament.

they travelled through several countries, encountered a reasonable quantity of giants, and slew certain dragons.

Being now arrived at the proper age for producing themselves, they came up to town and fell in love with the ladies, but especially three who about that time were in chief reputation, the Duchess d'Argent, Madame de Grands Titres, and the Countess d'Orgueil.* On their first appearance our three adventurers met with a very bad reception, and soon with great sagacity guessing out the reason, they quickly began to improve in the good qualities of the town: they writ, and rallied, and rhymed, and sung, and said, and said nothing; they drank, and fought, and whored, and slept, and swore, and took snuff; they went to new plays on the first night, haunted the *chocolate*-houses, beat the watch, lay on bulks, and got claps; they bilked hackney-coachmen, ran in debt with shopkeepers, and lay with their wives; they killed bailiffs, kicked fiddlers down stairs, eat at Locket's,° loitered at Will's; they talked of the drawing-room and never came there; dined with lords they never saw; whispered a duchess, and spoke never a word; exposed the scrawls of their laundress for billets-doux of quality; came ever just from court and were never seen in it; attended the Levee *sub dio*; got a list of the peers by heart in one company, and with great familiarity retailed them in another. Above all, they constantly attended those Committees of Senators who are silent in the *House*, and loud in the *Coffee-House*, where they nightly adjourn to chew the cud of politics, and are encompassed with a ring of disciples who lie in wait to catch up their droppings. The three brothers had acquired forty other qualifications of the like stamp too tedious to recount, and by consequence were justly reckoned the most accomplished persons in town. But all would not suffice and the ladies aforesaid continued still inflexible. To clear up which difficulty I must, with the reader's good leave and patience, have recourse to some points of weight which the authors of that age have not sufficiently illustrated.

For about this time it happened a sect arose† whose tenets obtained and spread very far, especially in the *grande monde* and among everybody of good fashion. They worshipped a sort of *idol*‡ who, as their doctrine delivered, did daily create men by a kind of manufactory operation. This idol they placed in the highest parts of the house, on an altar erected

* Their mistresses are the Duchess d'Argent, Mademoiselle de Grands Titres, and the Countess d'Orgueil, *i.e. covetousness*, *ambition*, and *pride*; which were the three great vices that the ancient fathers inveighed against as the first corruptions of Christianity. W. Wotton.

† This is an occasional satire upon dress and fashion, in order to introduce what follows.

‡ By this *idol* is meant a tailor.

about three foot. He was shewn in the posture of a Persian emperor, sitting on a *superficies* with his legs interwoven under him. This god had a *goose* for his ensign, whence it is that some learned men pretend to deduce his original from Jupiter Capitolinus.° At his left hand beneath the altar, *Hell*° seemed to open and catch at the animals the idol was creating; to prevent which, certain of his priests hourly flung in pieces of the uninformed mass or substance, and sometimes whole limbs already enlivened, which that horrid gulf insatiably swallowed, terrible to behold. The goose was also held a subaltern divinity or *deus minorum gentium*,° before whose shrine was sacrificed that creature° whose hourly food is human gore, and who is in so great renown abroad for being the delight and favourite of the Ægyptian Cercopithecus.* Millions of these animals were cruelly slaughtered every day to appease the hunger of that consuming deity. The chief idol was also worshipped as the inventor of the *yard* and *needle*, whether as the god of seamen or on account of certain other mystical attributes, hath not been sufficiently cleared.

The worshippers of this deity had also a system of their belief which seemed to turn upon the following fundamentals. They held the universe to be a large *suit of clothes*, which *invests* everything: that the earth is invested by the air; the air is invested by the stars; and the stars are invested by the *primum mobile*.° Look on this globe of earth, you will find it to be a very complete and fashionable *dress*. What is that which some call *land*, but a fine coat faced with green? or the sea, but a waistcoat of water-tabby? Proceed to the particular works of the creation, you will find how curious *Journeyman* Nature hath been, to trim up the *vegetable* beaux; observe how sparkish a periwig adorns the head of a *beech*, and what a fine doublet of white satin is worn by the *birch*. To conclude from all, what is man himself but a *micro-coat*,† or rather a complete suit of clothes with all its trimmings? As to his body, there can be no dispute; but examine even the acquirements of his mind, you will find them all contribute in their order towards furnishing out an exact dress. To instance no more: is not religion a *cloak*, honesty a *pair of shoes* worn out in the dirt, self-love a *surtout*, vanity a *shirt*, and conscience a *pair of breeches* which, though a cover for lewdness as well as nastiness, is easily slipped down for the service of both?

These *postulata* being admitted, it will follow in due course of reasoning that those beings which the world calls improperly *suits of clothes* are in

* The Ægyptians worshipped a monkey, which animal is very fond of eating lice, styled here, creatures that feed on human gore.

† Alluding to the word *microcosm*, or a little world, as man hath been called by philosophers.

reality the most refined species of animals; or to proceed higher, that they are rational creatures, or men. For is it not manifest that they live, and move, and talk, and perform all other offices of human life? Are not beauty, and wit, and mien, and breeding, their inseparable proprieties? In short, we see nothing but them, hear nothing but them. Is it not they who walk the streets, fill up *parliament—*, *coffee—*, *play—*, *bawdy-houses*? 'Tis true indeed, that these animals which are vulgarly called *suits of clothes*, or *dresses*, do, according to certain compositions, receive different appellations. If one of them be trimmed up with a gold chain, and a red gown, and a white rod, and a great horse, it is called a *Lord Mayor*; if certain ermines and furs be placed in a certain position we style them a *Judge*; and so an apt conjunction of lawn and black satin we entitle a *Bishop*.

Others of these professors, though agreeing in the main system, were yet more refined upon certain branches of it, and held that man was an animal compounded of two *dresses*, the *natural* and the *celestial suit*, which were the body and the soul; that the soul was the outward, and the body the inward clothing; that the latter was *ex traduce*° but the former of daily creation and circumfusion. This last they proved by scripture, because *in them we live, and move, and have our being*;° as likewise by philosophy because they are *all in all*,° *and all in every part*.° Besides, said they, separate these two, and you will find the body to be only a senseless unsavoury carcass. By all which it is manifest that the outward dress must needs be the soul.

To this system of religion were tagged several subaltern doctrines which were entertained with great vogue; as particularly, the faculties of the mind were deduced by the learned among them in this manner: *embroidery* was *sheer wit*; *gold fringe* was *agreeable conversation*; *gold lace* was *repartee*; a huge long *periwig* was *humour*; and a *coat full of powder* was very good *raillery*; all which required abundance of *finesse* and *delicatesse* to manage with advantage, as well as a strict observance after times and fashions.

I have with much pains and reading collected out of ancient authors this short summary of a body of philosophy and divinity, which seems to have been composed by a vein and race° of thinking very different from any other systems either *ancient* or *modern*. And it was not merely to entertain or satisfy the reader's curiosity but rather to give him light into several circumstances of the following story; that knowing the state of dispositions and opinions in an age so remote, he may better comprehend those great events which were the issue of them. I advise therefore the courteous reader to peruse with a world of application, again and again, whatever I have written upon this matter. And so leaving these broken ends, I carefully gather up the chief thread of my story, and proceed.

These opinions therefore were so universal, as well as the practices of them, among the refined part of court and town, that our three brother-adventurers as their circumstances then stood were strangely at a loss.* For, on the one side, the three ladies they addressed themselves to (whom we have named already) were ever at the very top of the fashion, and abhorred all that were below it but the breadth of a hair. On the other side, their father's will was very precise, and it was the main precept in it with the greatest penalties annexed, not to add to, or diminish from their coats one thread without a positive command in the will. Now the coats† their father had left them were, 'tis true, of very good cloth and, besides, so neatly sewn you would swear they were all of a piece, but at the same time very plain, and with little or no ornament. And it happened that before they were a month in town, great *shoulder-knots*‡° came up. Straight, all the world was *shoulder-knots*; no approaching the ladies' *ruelles*° without the *quota* of shoulder-knots. 'That fellow,' cries one, 'has no soul; where is his shoulder-knot?' Our three brethren soon discovered their want by sad experience, meeting in their walks with forty mortifications and indignities. If they went to the playhouse, the door-keeper showed them into the twelve-penny gallery. If they called a boat, says a waterman, 'I am first sculler'.° If they stepped to the Rose° to take a bottle, the drawer would cry, 'Friend, we sell no ale.' If they went to visit a lady, a footman met them at the door with, 'Pray send up your message.' In this unhappy case they went immediately to consult their father's Will, read it over and over, but not a word of the *shoulder-knot*. What should they do? What temper° should they find? Obedience was absolutely necessary, and yet *shoulder-knots* appeared extremely requisite. After much thought one of the brothers who happened to be

* The first part of the Tale is the History of Peter; thereby Popery is exposed: everybody knows the Papists have made great additions to Christianity; that indeed is the great exception which the Church of England makes against them; accordingly Peter begins his pranks with *adding a shoulder-knot to his coat.* W. WOTTON.

† His description of the cloth of which the coat was made, has a farther meaning than the words may seem to import, 'The coats their father had left them were of very good cloth, and besides so neatly sewn, you would swear it had been all of a piece; but, at the same time, very plain with little or no ornament.' This is the distinguishing character of the Christian religion: *christiana religio absoluta et simplex* was Ammianus Marcellinus's description of it, who was himself a heathen. W. WOTTON.

‡ By this is understood the first introducing of pageantry, and unnecessary ornaments in the Church, such as were neither for convenience nor edification; as a *shoulder-knot*, in which there is neither symmetry nor use.

more book-learned than the other two, said he had found an expedient. ''Tis true,' said he, 'there is nothing here in this Will, *totidem verbis*,* making mention of *shoulder-knots*, but I dare conjecture we may find them *inclusivè*, or *totidem syllabis*.' This distinction was immediately approved by all, and so they fell again to examine the will. But their evil star had so directed the matter that the first syllable was not to be found in the whole writing. Upon which disappointment, he who found the former evasion took heart and said, 'Brothers, there is yet hopes; for though we cannot find them *totidem verbis*, nor *totidem syllabis*, I dare engage we shall make them out *tertio modo*, or *totidem literis*.' This discovery was also highly commended, upon which they fell once more to the scrutiny, and soon picked out *S,H,O,U,L,D,E,R*, when the same planet, enemy to their repose, had wonderfully contrived that a *K* was not to be found. Here was a weighty difficulty! But the distinguishing brother (for whom we shall hereafter find a name) now his hand was in, proved by a very good argument that *K* was a modern, illegitimate letter, unknown to the learned ages nor anywhere to be found in ancient manuscripts. ''Tis true,' said he, 'the word Calendæ hath in *Q.V.C.*† been sometimes writ with a *K*, but erroneously, for in the best copies, it is ever spelt with a *C*. And by consequence it was a gross mistake in our language to spell "knot" with a *K*'; but that from henceforward he would take care it should be writ with a *C*. Upon this all further difficulty vanished; *shoulder-knots* were made clearly out to be *jure paterno*,° and our three gentlemen swaggered with as large and as flaunting ones as the best.

But as human happiness is of a very short duration, so in those days were human fashions upon which it entirely depends. Shoulder-knots had their time, and we must now imagine them in their decline; for a certain lord came just from Paris with fifty yards of *gold lace* upon his coat, exactly trimmed after the court fashion of that *month*. In two days all mankind appeared closed up in bars of gold lace:‡ whoever durst peep abroad without his complement of gold lace, was as scandalous as a [eunuch], and as ill received among the women. What should our three knights do in this momentous affair? They had sufficiently strained a point already in the affair of shoulder-knots. Upon recourse to the Will

* When the Papists cannot find anything which they want in Scripture they go to *Oral Tradition*: thus Peter is introduced dissatisfied with the tedious way of looking for all the letters of any word which he has occasion for in the *Will*, when neither the constituent syllables, nor much less the whole word, were there *in terminis*. W. WOTTON.

† [Quibusdam veteribus codicibus.] Some ancient manuscripts.

‡ I cannot tell whether the author means any new innovation by this word, or whether it be only to introduce the new methods of forcing and perverting scripture.

nothing appeared there but *altum silentium.*° That of the shoulder-knots was a loose, flying, circumstantial° point; but this of gold lace seemed too considerable an alteration without better warrant. It did *aliquo modo essentiæ adhærere,*° and therefore required a positive precept. But about this time it fell out that the learned brother aforesaid had read *Aristotelis Dialectica*, and especially that wonderful piece *de Interpretatione*° which has the faculty of teaching its readers to find out a meaning in everything but itself, like commentators on the Revelations who proceed prophets without understanding a syllable of the text. 'Brothers,' said he, 'you are to be informed,* that of wills *duo sunt genera*, nuncupatory† and scriptory; that in the scriptory will here before us, there is no precept or mention about gold lace, *conceditur*: but, *si idem affirmetur de nuncupatorio, negatur.*° For brothers, if you remember, we heard a fellow say when we were boys, that he heard my father's man say, that he heard my father say, that he would advise his sons to get *gold lace* on their coats, as soon as ever they could procure money to buy it.' 'By G—! that is very true,' cries the other. 'I remember it perfectly well,' said the third. And so without more ado they got the largest gold lace in the parish, and walked about as fine as lords.

A while after there came up *all in fashion* a pretty sort of *flame-coloured satin*‡ for linings, and the mercer brought a pattern of it immediately to our three gentlemen. 'An please your worships,' said he,§ 'my Lord C[lifford] and Sir J[ohn] W[alters] had linings out of this very piece last night; it takes wonderfully, and I shall not have a remnant left enough to make my wife a pin-cushion, by tomorrow morning at ten o'clock.' Upon this, they fell again to rummage the Will, because the present case also

* The next subject of our author's wit is the *glosses* and *interpretations of scripture*, very many absurd ones of which are allowed in the most authentic books of the Church of Rome. W. WOTTON.

† By this is meant *tradition*, allowed to have equal authority with the scripture, or rather greater.

‡ This is *purgatory*, whereof he speaks more particularly hereafter, but here, only to show how scripture was perverted to prove it, which was done by giving equal authority with the *canon* to *Apocrypha*, called here a *codicil annexed*.

It is likely the author, in every one of these changes in the brothers' dresses, refers to some particular error in the Church of Rome, though it is not easy, I think, to apply them all: but by this of *flame-coloured satin* is manifestly intended *purgatory*; by *gold lace* may perhaps be understood the lofty ornaments and plate in the churches; the *shoulder-knots* and *silver fringe* are not so obvious, at least to me; but the Indian figures of men, women, and children, plainly relate to the pictures in the Romish churches, of God like an old man, of the Virgin Mary, and our Saviour as a child.

§ This shows the time the author writ, it being about fourteen years since those two persons were reckoned the fine gentlemen of the town.

required a positive precept, the lining being held by orthodox writers to be of the essence of the coat. After long search they could fix upon nothing to the matter in hand except a short advice of their father's in the Will to take care of *fire* and put out their *candles* before they went to sleep.* This, though a good deal for the purpose and helping very far towards self-conviction, yet not seeming wholly of force to establish a command; and being resolved to avoid farther scruple, as well as future occasion for scandal, says he that was the scholar, 'I remember to have read in wills of a codicil annexed,° which is indeed a part of the will, and what it contains hath equal authority with the rest. Now, I have been considering of this same will here before us, and I cannot reckon it to be complete, for want of such a codicil. I will therefore fasten one in its proper place very dexterously. I have had it by me some time; it was written by a dog-keeper° of my grandfather's,† and talks a great deal (as good luck would have it) of this very flame-coloured satin.' The project was immediately approved by the other two; an old parchment scroll was tagged on according to art, in the form of a *codicil annexed*, and the *satin* bought and worn.

Next winter a *player*, hired for the purpose by the corporation of *fringe-makers*, acted his part in a new comedy all covered with silver fringe,‡ and according to the laudable custom, gave rise to that fashion. Upon which the brothers consulting their father's Will, to their great astonishment found these words, '*Item*, I charge and command my said three sons to wear no sort of *silver fringe* upon or about their said coats,' etc., with a penalty in case of disobedience, too long here to insert. However, after some pause, the brother so often mentioned for his erudition, who was well skilled in criticisms, had found in a certain author which he said should be nameless, that the same word which in the will is called *fringe*, does also signify a *broomstick*, and doubtless ought to have the same interpretation in this paragraph. This, another of the brothers disliked because of that epithet *silver*, which could not, he humbly conceived, in propriety of speech be reasonably applied to a *broomstick*; but it was replied upon him that this epithet was understood in a *mythological* and *allegorical* sense. However, he objected again why their father should forbid them to wear a *broomstick* on their coats, a caution that seemed unnatural and impertinent; upon which he was taken up

* That is, to take care of hell, and in order to do that, to subdue and extinguish their lusts.

† I believe this refers to that part of the Apocrypha where mention is made of Tobit and his dog.

‡ This is certainly the further introducing the pomps of habit and ornament.

short, as one who spoke irreverently of a *mystery* which doubtless was very useful and significant, but ought not to be over-curiously pried into or nicely reasoned upon. And in short, their father's authority being now considerably sunk, this expedient was allowed to serve as a lawful dispensation for wearing their full proportion of silver fringe.

A while after was revived an old fashion, long antiquated, of *embroidery* with *Indian figures* of men, women, and children.* Here they had no occasion to examine the Will. They remembered but too well how their father had always abhorred this fashion; that he made several paragraphs on purpose importing his utter detestation of it, and bestowing his everlasting curse to his sons, whenever they should wear it. For all this, in a few days they appeared higher in the fashion than anybody else in town. But they solved the matter by saying that these figures were not at all the *same* with those that were formerly worn and were meant in the will. Besides, they did not wear them in that sense as forbidden by their father, but as they were a commendable custom, and of great use to the public. That these rigorous clauses in the will did therefore require some *allowance*, and a favourable intepretation, and ought to be understood *cum grano salis*.

But fashions perpetually altering in that age, the scholastic brother grew weary of searching further evasions and solving everlasting contradictions. Resolved, therefore, at all hazards to comply with the modes of the world, they concerted matters together and agreed unanimously to lock up their father's Will in a *strong box*,† brought out of Greece or Italy (I have forgot which) and trouble themselves no further to examine it, but only refer to its authority whenever they thought fit. In consequence whereof, a while after it grew a general mode to wear an infinite number of *points*, most of them tagged with silver: upon which, the scholar pronounced *ex cathedra*‡ that *points* were absolutely *jure paterno*, as they might very well remember. 'Tis true indeed, the fashion

* The images of saints, the blessed Virgin, and our Saviour as an infant.

Ibid. Images in the Church of Rome give him but too fair a handle. *The brothers remembered*, &c. The allegory here is direct. W. WOTTON.

† The Papists formerly forbade the people the use of scripture in a vulgar tongue; Peter therefore *locks up his father's will in a strong box, brought out of Greece or Italy*. Those countries are named because the New Testament is written in Greek; and the vulgar Latin, which is the authentic edition of the Bible in the Church of Rome, is in the language of old Italy. W. WOTTON.

‡ The popes, in their decretals and bulls, have given their sanction to very many gainful doctrines which are now received in the Church of Rome, that are not mentioned in scripture, and are unknown to the primitive church. Peter accordingly pronounces *ex cathedra*, that *points tagged with silver were absolutely jure paterno*, and so they wore them in great numbers. W. WOTTON.

prescribed somewhat more than were directly named in the Will; however, that they as heirs general of their father had power to make and add certain clauses for public emolument, though not deducible *totidem verbis* from the letter of the Will, or else, *multa absurda sequerentur*. This was understood for *canonical*, and therefore on the following Sunday they came to church all covered with *points*.

The learned brother, so often mentioned, was reckoned the best scholar in all that or the next street to it; insomuch as, having run something behind-hand with the world, he obtained the favour from a *certain lord*,* to receive him into his house and to teach his children. A while after the lord died, and he, by long practice upon his father's Will, found the way of contriving a *deed of conveyance* of that house to himself and his heirs; upon which he took possession, turned the young squires out, and received his brothers in their stead.†

SECT. III.

A Digression concerning Critics.

Though I have been hitherto as cautious as I could, upon all occasions most nicely to follow the rules and methods of writing laid down by the example of our illustrious *moderns*; yet has the unhappy shortncss of my memory led me into an error from which I must immediately extricate myself, before I can decently pursue my principal subject. I confess with shame it was an unpardonable omission to proceed so far as I have already done, before I had performed the due discourses expostulatory, supplicatory, or deprecatory, with my *good lords* the *critics*. Towards some atonement for this grievous neglect, I do here make humbly bold to present them with a short account of themselves and their *art*, by looking into the original and pedigree of the word as it is generally understood among us, and very briefly considering the ancient and present state thereof.

By the word *critic*, at this day so frequent in all conversations, there have sometimes been distinguished three very different species of mortal

* This was Constantine the Great, from whom the popes pretend a donation of St. Peter's patrimony, which they have never been able to produce.

† The bishops of Rome enjoyed their privileges in Rome at first by the favour of emperors, whom at last they shut out of their own capital city, and then forged a donation from Constantine the Great, the better to justify what they did. In imitation of this, Peter *having run something behind-hand in the world obtained leave of a certain lord*, &c. W. WOTTON.

men, according as I have read in *ancient books and pamphlets*. For first, by this term was understood such persons as invented or drew up rules for themselves and the world, by observing which a careful reader might be able to pronounce upon the productions of the *learned*, from his taste to a true relish of the *sublime* and the *admirable*, and divide every beauty of matter or of style from the corruption that apes it: in their common perusal of books singling out the errors and defects, the nauseous, the fulsome, the dull, and the impertinent, with the caution of a man that walks through Edinburgh streets in a morning,° who is indeed as careful as he can to watch diligently and spy out the filth in his way; not that he is curious to observe the colour and complexion of the ordure, or take its dimensions, much less to be paddling in or tasting it, but only with a design to come out as cleanly as he may. These men seem, though very erroneously, to have understood the appellation of *critic* in a literal sense; that one principal part of his office was to praise and acquit; and that a *critic* who sets up to read only for an occasion of censure and reproof, is a creature as barbarous as a *judge* who should take up a resolution to hang all men that came before him upon a trial.

Again, by the word *critic* have been meant the restorers of ancient learning from the worms, and graves, and dust of manuscripts.

Now the races of those two have been for some ages utterly extinct; and besides, to discourse any further of them would not be at all to my purpose.

The third, and noblest sort, is that of the *TRUE CRITIC*, whose original is the most ancient of all. Every *true critic* is a hero born, descending in a direct line from a celestial stem by Momus and Hybris, who begat Zoilus, who begat Tigellius,° who begat Etcætera the elder; who begat B[e]ntly, and Rym[e]r, and W[o]tton, and Perrault, and Dennis, who begat Etcætera the younger.

And these are the *critics* from whom the commonwealth of learning has in all ages received such immense benefits that the gratitude of their admirers placed their origin in Heaven, among those of Hercules, Theseus, Perseus, and other great deservers of mankind. But heroic virtue itself, hath not been exempt from the obloquy of evil tongues. For it hath been objected that those ancient heroes, famous for their combating so many giants, and dragons, and robbers, were in their own persons a greater nuisance to mankind than any of those monsters they subdued; and therefore to render their obligations more complete, when all *other* vermin were destroyed should, in conscience, have concluded with the same justice upon themselves; as Hercules most generously did,° and hath upon that score procured to himself more temples and votaries than the best of his fellows. For these reasons I suppose it is, why some have conceived it would be very expedient for the public good of learning that every *true critic*, as soon as he had finished his task assigned, should immediately deliver himself up to ratsbane, or hemp, or from some convenient altitude; and that no man's pretensions to so illustrious a character should by any means be received before that operation were performed.

Now, from this heavenly descent of *criticism*, and the close analogy it bears to *heroic virtue*, 'tis easy to assign the proper employment of a *true ancient genuine critic*;° which is to travel through this vast world of writings; to pursue and hunt those monstrous faults bred within them; to drag out the lurking errors, like Cacus from his den; to multiply them like Hydra's heads; and rake them together like Augeas's dung; or else to drive away a sort of *dangerous fowl* who have a perverse inclination to plunder the best branches of the *tree of knowledge*, like those Stymphalian birds that eat up the fruit.

These reasonings will furnish us with an adequate definition of a *true critic*: that he is *a discoverer and collector of writers' faults*, which may be further put beyond dispute by the following demonstration: That whoever will examine the writings in all kinds wherewith this ancient sect has honoured the world, shall immediately find, from the whole thread and tenor of them, that the ideas of the authors have been altogether conversant and taken up with the faults, and blemishes, and oversights, and mistakes of other writers; and let the subject treated on be whatever it will, their imaginations are so entirely possessed and replete with the defects of other pens that the very quintessence of what is bad, does of necessity distil into their own; by which means the whole appears to be nothing else but an *abstract* of the *criticisms* themselves have made.

Having thus briefly considered the original and office of a *critic*, as the word is understood in its most noble and universal acceptation, I proceed to refute the objections of those who argue from the silence and pretermission of authors; by which they pretend to prove that the very art of *criticism* as now exercised, and by me explained, is wholly *modern*; and consequently that the *critics* of Great Britain and France have no title to an original so ancient and illustrious as I have deduced. Now, if I can clearly make out on the contrary, that the most ancient writers have particularly described both the person and the office of a *true critic*, agreeable to the definition laid down by me, their grand objection from the silence of authors will fall to the ground.

I confess to have for a long time borne a part in this general error, from which I should never have acquitted myself but through the assistance of our noble *moderns* whose most edifying volumes I turn indefatigably over° night and day, for the improvement of my mind and the good of my country. These have with unwearied pains made many useful searches into the weak side of the *ancients*, and given us a comprehensive list of them.* Besides, they have proved beyond contradiction that the very finest things delivered of old, have been long since invented and brought to light by much later pens; and that the noblest discoveries those *ancients* ever made, of art or of nature, have all been produced by the transcending genius of the present age. Which clearly shows how little merit those *ancients* can justly pretend to, and takes off that blind admiration paid them by men in a corner, who have the unhappiness of conversing too little with *present things*. Reflecting maturely upon all this, and taking in the whole compass of human nature, I easily concluded that these *ancients*, highly sensible of their many imperfections, must needs have endeavoured from some passages in their works, to obviate, soften, or divert the censorious reader by *satire*, or *panegyric* upon the *true critics*, in imitation of their *masters*, the *moderns*. Now, in the *commonplaces* of both these† I was plentifully instructed by a long course of useful study in *prefaces* and *prologues*; and therefore immediately resolved to try what I could discover of either, by a diligent perusal of the most ancient writers, and especially those who treated of the earliest times. Here I found to my great surprise that although they all entered, upon occasion, into particular descriptions of the *true critic*, according as they were governed by their fears or their hopes; yet whatever they touched of that kind was with abundance of caution, adventuring no farther than *mythology* and *hieroglyphic*. This, I suppose, gave ground to superficial readers for urging the silence of authors against the antiquity of the *true critic*, though the *types* are so apposite, and the applications so necessary and natural, that it is not easy to conceive how any reader of a *modern eye* and *taste* could overlook them. I shall venture from a great number to produce a few, which I am very confident will put this question beyond dispute.

It well deserves considering that these *ancient writers*, in treating enigmatically upon this subject, have generally fixed upon the very *same hieroglyph*, varying only the story according to their affections, or their wit. For first; Pausanias is of opinion° that the perfection of writing correct was entirely owing to the institution of *critics*; and, that he can possibly mean no other than the *true critic*, is I think manifest enough from the following description. He says, *they were a race of men who delighted to nibble at the superfluities and excrescencies of books; which the*

* See Wotton *of Ancient and Modern Learning*.

† Satire and Panegyric upon Critics.

learned at length observing, took warning of their own accord, to lop the luxuriant, the rotten, the dead, the sapless, and the overgrown branches from their works. But now, all this he cunningly shades under the following allegory; *that the Nauplians in Argia learned the art of pruning their vines by observing, that when an* ASS *had browsed upon one of them, it thrived the better and bore fairer fruit*. But Herodotus,*° holding the very same *hieroglyph*, speaks much plainer and almost *in terminis*. He hath been so bold as to tax the *true critics* of ignorance and malice, telling us openly, for I think nothing can be plainer, that *in the western part of Libya, there were* ASSES *with* HORNS. Upon which relation Ctesias† yet refines,° mentioning the very same animal about India, adding, *that whereas all other* ASSES *wanted a gall, these horned ones were so redundant in that part that their flesh was not to be eaten because of its extreme bitterness*.

Now, the reason why those ancient writers treated this subject only by types and figures was, because they durst not make open attacks against a party so potent and terrible as the *critics* of those ages were, whose very voice was so dreadful, that a legion of authors would tremble and drop their pens at the sound; for so Herodotus‡ tells us expressly in another place, how *a vast army of Scythians was put to flight in a panic terror, by the braying of an* ASS. From hence it is conjectured by certain profound *philologers*, that the great awe and reverence paid to a *true critic* by the writers of Britain have been derived to us from those our Scythian ancestors.° In short, this dread was so universal that in process of time those authors who had a mind to publish their sentiments more freely, in describing the *true critics* of their several ages were forced to leave off the use of the former *hieroglyph*, as too nearly approaching the *prototype*, and invented other terms instead thereof that were more cautious and mystical. So Diodorus, speaking to the same purpose, ventures° no farther than to say that in the mountains of Helicon there grows a certain *weed*, which bears a flower of so damned a scent as to poison those who offer to smell it. Lucretius gives exactly the same relation:°

> Est etiam in magnis Heliconis montibus arbos,
> Floris odore hominem retro consueta necare.§
>
> Lib. 6.

But Ctesias,° whom we lately quoted, hath been a great deal bolder; he had been used with much severity by the *true critics* of his own age, and therefore could not forbear to leave behind him at least one deep mark of

* Lib. 4. † Vide excerpta ex eo apud Photium. ‡ Lib. 4. [129].

§ Near Helicon, and round the learned hill,
Grow trees, whose blossoms with their odour kill.

his vengeance against the whole tribe. His meaning is so near the surface that I wonder how it possibly came to be overlooked by those who deny the antiquity of the *true critics*. For, pretending to make a description of many strange animals about India, he hath set down these remarkable words: 'Among the rest,' says he, 'there is a *serpent* that wants *teeth*, and consequently cannot bite; but if its *vomit* (to which it is much addicted) happens to fall upon anything, a certain rottenness or corruption ensues. These *serpents* are generally found among the mountains where *jewels* grow, and they frequently emit a *poisonous juice*, whereof whoever drinks, that person's brains fly out of his nostrils.'

There was also among the *ancients* a sort of critic not distinguished in *specie* from the former but in growth or degree, who seem to have been only the *tyros* or *junior* scholars; yet, because of their differing employments, they are frequently mentioned as a sect by themselves. The usual exercise of these younger students was to attend constantly at theatres, and learn to spy out the *worst parts* of the play, whereof they were obliged carefully to take note and render a rational account to their tutors. Fleshed at these smaller sports, like young wolves, they grew up in time to be nimble and strong enough for hunting down large game. For it hath been observed both among ancients and moderns, that a *true critic* hath one quality in common with a *whore* and an *alderman*, never to change his title or his nature; that a *grey critic* has been certainly a *green* one, the perfections and acquirements of his age being only the improved talents of his youth; like *hemp*, which some naturalists inform us is bad for *suffocations* though taken but in the seed. I esteem the invention or at least the refinement of *prologues*, to have been owing to these younger proficients, of whom Terence makes frequent and honourable mention under the name of *malevoli*.°

Now, 'tis certain, the institution of the *true critics* was of absolute necessity to the commonwealth of learning. For all human actions seem to be divided like Themistocles and his company:° one man can *fiddle*, and another can make *a small town a great city*; and he that cannot do either one or the other deserves to be kicked out of the creation. The avoiding of which penalty has doubtless given the first birth to the nation of *critics*, and withal, an occasion for their secret detractors to report that a *true critic* is a sort of mechanic, set up with a stock and tools for his trade at as little expense as a tailor; and that there is much analogy between the utensils and abilities of both: that the tailor's *hell* is the type of a critic's *commonplace book*, and his wit and learning held forth by the *goose*; that it requires at least as many of these to the making up of one scholar, as of the others to the composition of a man;° that the valour of both is equal, and their *weapons* near of a size. Much may be said in answer to those invidious reflections, and I can positively affirm the first to be a falsehood. For on the contrary, nothing is more certain than that it requires greater layings out to be free of the *critic*'s company, than of any other you can name. For, as to be a *true beggar* it will cost the richest candidate every groat he is worth; so, before one can commence a *true critic* it will cost a man all the good qualities of his mind; which, perhaps for a less purchase, would be thought but an indifferent bargain.

Having thus amply proved the antiquity of *criticism* and described the primitive state of it, I shall now examine the present condition of this empire and show how well it agrees with its ancient self. A certain author* whose works have many ages since been entirely lost, does, in his fifth book and eighth chapter, say of *critics*, that 'their writings are the mirrors of learning.' This I understand in a literal sense, and suppose our author must mean that whoever designs to be a perfect writer must inspect into the books of *critics*, and correct his invention there as in a mirror. Now, whoever considers that the *mirrors* of the ancients were made of brass and *sine mercurio*,° may presently apply the two principal qualifications of a *true modern critic*, and consequently must needs conclude that these have always been and must be for ever the same. For *brass* is an emblem of duration, and when it is skilfully burnished will cast *reflections* from its own *superficies*, without any assistance of *mercury* from behind. All the other talents of a *critic* will not require a particular mention, being included or easily deducible to these. However, I shall conclude with three maxims which may serve both as characteristics to distinguish a *true modern critic* from a pretender, and will be also of admirable use to those worthy spirits who engage in so useful and honourable an art.

The first is that *criticism*, contrary to all other faculties of the intellect, is ever held the truest and best when it is the very *first* result of the *critic*'s mind; as fowlers reckon the first aim for the surest, and seldom fail of missing the mark if they stay for a second.

Secondly, the *true critics* are known by their talent of swarming about the noblest writers, to which they are carried merely by instinct, as a rat to the best cheese, or a wasp to the fairest fruit. So when the king is a horseback, he is sure to be the *dirtiest* person of the company, and they that make their court best, are such as *bespatter* him most.

Lastly, a *true critic* in the perusal of a book is like a *dog* at a feast, whose thoughts and stomach are wholly set upon what the guests *fling away*, and consequently is apt to *snarl* most when there are the fewest *bones*.

* A quotation after the manner of a great author. Vide Bently's *Dissertation*, &c.

Thus much, I think, is sufficient to serve by way of address to my patrons, the *true modern critics*, and may very well atone for my past silence as well as that which I am like to observe for the future. I hope I have deserved so well of their whole *body* as to meet with generous and tender usage from their *hands*. Supported by which expectation, I go on boldly to pursue those adventures already so happily begun.

SECT. IV.

A Tale of a Tub.

I have now, with much pains and study, conducted the reader to a period where he must expect to hear of great revolutions. For no sooner had our *learned brother*, so often mentioned, got a warm house of his own over his head than he began to look big, and to take mightily upon him; insomuch that unless the gentle reader, out of his great candour, will please a little to exalt his idea, I am afraid he will henceforth hardly know the *hero* of the play when he happens to meet him, his part, his dress, and his mien being so much altered.

He told his brothers he would have them to know that he was their elder, and consequently his father's sole heir; nay, a while after he would not allow them to call him *brother*, but *Mr. PETER*; and then he must be styled *Father PETER*; and sometimes, *My Lord PETER*. To support this grandeur, which he soon began to consider could not be maintained without a better *fonde* than what he was born to, after much thought he cast about at last to turn *projector* and *virtuoso*, wherein he so well succeeded that many famous discoveries, projects, and machines, which bear great vogue and practice at present in the world, are owing entirely to Lord Peter's invention. I will deduce the best account I have been able to collect of the chief amongst them, without considering much the order they came out in, because I think authors are not well agreed as to that point.

I hope, when this treatise of mine shall be translated into foreign languages (as I may without vanity affirm that the labour of collecting, the faithfulness in recounting, and the great usefulness of the matter to the public, will amply deserve that justice) that the worthy members of the several *academies* abroad, especially those of France and Italy, will favourably accept these humble offers for the advancement of universal knowledge. I do also advertise the most reverend Fathers the Eastern Missionaries, that I have, purely for their sakes, made use of such words and phrases as will best admit an easy turn into any of the oriental languages, especially the Chinese. And so I proceed with great content of mind, upon reflecting how much emolument this whole globe of the earth is likely to reap by my labours.

The first undertaking of Lord Peter was to purchase a large continent,* lately said to have been discovered in *Terra Australis Incognita.*° This tract of land he bought at a very great pennyworth from the discoverers themselves (though some pretended to doubt whether they had ever been there), and then retailed it into several cantons to certain dealers, who carried over colonies but were all shipwrecked in the voyage. Upon which Lord Peter sold the said continent to other customers *again*, and *again*, and *again*, and *again*, with the same success.

The second project I shall mention was his sovereign remedy for the *worms*,†° especially those in the *spleen.* The patient was to eat nothing after supper for three nights:‡ as soon as he went to bed he was carefully to lie on one side, and when he grew weary, to turn upon the other. He must also duly confine his two eyes to the same object, and by no means break wind at both ends together without manifest occasion. These prescriptions diligently observed, the *worms* would void insensibly by perspiration, ascending through the *brain.*

A third invention was the erecting of a *whispering-office,*§ for the public good and ease of all such as are hypochondriacal, or troubled with the colic; likewise of all eavesdroppers, physicians, midwives, small politicians, friends fallen out, repeating poets,° lovers happy or in despair, bawds, privy-councillors, pages, parasites, and buffoons: in short, of all such as are in danger of bursting with too much *wind*. An *ass*'s head was placed so conveniently that the party affected might easily with his mouth accost either of the animal's ears; which he was to apply close for a certain space, and by a fugitive faculty, peculiar to the ears of that animal, receive immediate benefit either by eructation, or expiration, or evomition.

Another very beneficial project of Lord Peter's was, an *office of*

* That is, Purgatory.

† *Penance* and *absolution* are played upon under the notion of a *sovereign remedy for the worms*, especially in the spleen, which by observing Peter's prescription would void sensibly by perspiration, ascending through the brain, &c. W. WOTTON.

‡ Here the author ridicules the penances of the Church of Rome, which may be made as easy to the sinner as he pleases, provided he will pay for them accordingly.

§ By his *whispering-office* for the relief of eavesdroppers, physicians, bawds, and privy-councillors, he ridicules auricular confession; and the priest who takes it, is described by the ass's head. W. WOTTON.

insurance for tobacco-pipes,* martyrs of the modern zeal, volumes of poetry, shadows,————and rivers: that these, nor any of these, shall receive damage by *fire*.° From whence our *friendly societies* may plainly find themselves to be only transcribers from this original, though the one and the other have been of *great* benefit to the undertakers, as well as of *equal* to the public.

Lord Peter was also held the original author of *puppets* and *raree-shows*† the great usefulness whereof being so generally known, I shall not enlarge further upon this particular.

But another discovery for which he was much renowned was his famous universal *pickle*.‡ For, having remarked how your common *pickle*,§ in use among housewives, was of no further benefit than to preserve dead flesh and certain kinds of vegetables, Peter, with great cost as well as art, had contrived a *pickle* proper for houses, gardens, towns, men, women, children, and cattle, wherein he could preserve them as sound as insects in amber. Now, this *pickle* to the taste, the smell, and the sight, appeared exactly the same with what is in common service for beef and butter and herrings (and has been often that way applied with great success); but for its many sovereign virtues, was quite a different thing. For Peter would put in a certain quantity of his *powder pimperlim-pimp*,¶° after which it never failed of success. The operation was performed by *spargefaction* in a proper time of the moon. The patient who was to be *pickled*, if it were a house, would infallibly be preserved from all spiders, rats, and weasels. If the party affected were a dog, he should be exempt from mange, and madness, and hunger. It also infallibly took away all scabs and lice, and scalled heads from children, never hindering the patient from any duty either at bed or board.

But of all Peter's rarities he most valued a certain set of *bulls*,‖ whose

* This I take to be the office of Indulgences, the gross abuses whereof first gave occasion for the Reformation.

† I believe are all the monkeries and ridiculous processions, &c., among the papists.

‡ Holy water, he calls an *universal pickle*, to preserve houses, gardens, towns, men, women, children, and cattle, wherein he could preserve them as sound as insects in amber. W. WOTTON.

§ This is easily understood to be holy water, composed of the same ingredients with many other pickles.

¶ And because holy water differs only in consecration from common water, therefore he tells us that his pickle by the powder of *pimperlim-pimp* receives new virtues, though it differs not in sight nor smell from the common pickle, which preserves beef, and butter, and herrings. W. WOTTON.

‖ The *papal bulls* are ridiculed by name, so that here we are at no loss for the author's meaning. W. WOTTON.

Ibid. Here the author has kept the name, and means the pope's Bulls, or rather his race was by great fortune preserved in a lineal descent from those that guarded the *golden fleece*. Though some who pretended to observe them curiously, doubted the breed had not been kept entirely chaste, because they had degenerated from their ancestors in some qualities, and had acquired others very extraordinary, but a foreign mixture. The bulls of Colchos° are recorded to have *brazen feet*; but whether it happened by ill pasture and running, by an allay from intervention of other parents, from stolen intrigues; whether a weakness in their progenitors had impaired the seminal virtue, or by a decline necessary through a long course of time, the originals of nature being depraved in these latter sinful ages of the world; whatever was the cause, it is certain that Lord Peter's *bulls* were extremely vitiated by the rust of time in the metal of their feet, which was now sunk into common *lead*.° However, the terrible *roaring* peculiar to their lineage, was preserved, as likewise that faculty of breathing out *fire* from their nostrils; which, notwithstanding, many of their detractors took to be a feat of art, and to be nothing so terrible as it appeared, proceeding only from their usual course of diet, which was of *squibs* and *crackers*.* However, they had two peculiar marks which extremely distinguished them from the bulls of Jason, and which I have not met together in the description of any other monster beside that in Horace—

Varias inducere plumas;

and

Atrum desinit in piscem.°

For these had *fishes' tails*, yet upon occasion could *outfly* any bird in the air. Peter put these *bulls* upon several employs. Sometimes he would set them a-*roaring* to fright *naughty boys*† and make them quiet. Sometimes he would send them out upon errands of great importance; where, it is wonderful to recount, and perhaps the cautious reader may think much to believe it, an *appetitus sensibilis*° deriving itself through the whole family from their noble ancestors, guardians of the *golden fleece*, they continued so extremely fond of *gold*, that if Peter sent them abroad though it were only upon a compliment, they would *roar*, and *spit*, and *belch*, and *piss*, and *fart*, and snivel out *fire*, and keep a perpetual coil, till you flung them a bit of *gold*; but then, *pulveris exigui jactu*,° they would grow calm and quiet as lambs. In short, whether by secret connivance or encouragement from

fulminations and excommunications of heretical princes, all signed with lead and the seal of the fisherman.

* These are the fulminations of the pope, threatening hell and damnation to those princes who offend him.

† That is, kings who incur his displeasure.

their master, or out of their own liquorish affection to gold, or both; it is certain they were no better than a sort of sturdy, swaggering beggars; and where they could not prevail to get an alms, would make women miscarry and children fall into fits, who to this day usually call sprites and hobgoblins by the name of *bull-beggars*.° They grew at last so very troublesome to the neighbourhood that some gentlemen of the *north-west*° got a parcel of right English *bull-dogs*, and baited them so terribly that they felt it ever after.

I must needs mention one more of Lord Peter's projects, which was very extraordinary and discovered him to be a master of a high reach and profound invention. Whenever it happened that any rogue of Newgate was condemned to be hanged, Peter would offer him a pardon for a certain sum of money, which when the poor caitiff had made all shifts to scrape up and send, his lordship would return a piece of paper in this form.*

'TO all mayors, sheriffs, jailors, constables, bailiffs, hangmen, &c. Whereas we are informed that A. B. remains in the hands of you, or any of you, under the sentence of death. We will and command you upon sight hereof, to let the said prisoner depart to his own habitation, whether he stands condemned for murder, sodomy, rape, sacrilege, incest, treason, blasphemy, &c., for which this shall be your sufficient warrant. And if you fail hereof, G—d d—mn you and yours to all eternity. And so we bid you heartily farewell.

Your most humble
man's man,°
EMPEROR PETER.'

The wretches trusting to this, lost their lives and money too.

I desire of those whom the *learned* among posterity will appoint for commentators upon this elaborate treatise, that they will proceed with great caution upon certain dark points wherein all who are not *verè adepti*° may be in danger to form rash and hasty conclusions, especially in some mysterious paragraphs where certain *arcana* are joined for brevity sake, which in the operation must be divided. And I am certain that future sons of art will return large thanks to my memory, for so grateful, so useful an *innuendo*.

It will be no difficult part to persuade the reader that so many worthy discoveries met with great success in the world, though I may justly

* This is a copy of a general pardon, signed *servus servorum*.

Ibid. Absolution *in articulo mortis*, and the tax *cameræ apostolicæ*,° are jested upon in Emperor Peter's letter. W. WOTTON.

assure him that I have related much the smallest number, my design having been only to single out such as will be of most benefit for public imitation, or which best served to give some idea of the reach and wit of the inventor. And therefore it need not be wondered, if by this time, Lord Peter was become exceeding rich. But alas, he had kept his brain so long and so violently upon the rack, that at last it *shook* itself and began to *turn round* for a little ease. In short, what with pride, projects, and knavery, poor Peter was grown distracted, and conceived the strangest imaginations in the world. In the height of his fits (as it is usual with those who run mad out of pride) he would call himself *God Almighty*,* and sometimes *monarch of the universe*. I have seen him (says my author) take three old *high-crowned hats*† and clap them all on his head three storey high, with a huge bunch of *keys* at his girdle,‡ and an *angling-rod* in his hand. In which guise, whoever went to take him by the hand in the way of salutation, Peter with much grace, like a well-educated spaniel, would present them with his *foot*;§ and if they refused his civility then he would raise it as high as their chops, and give them a damned kick on the mouth, which hath ever since been called a *salute*. Whoever walked by without paying him their compliments, having a wonderful strong breath he would blow their hats off into the dirt. Meantime his affairs at home went upside down, and his two brothers had a wretched time; where his first *boutade*¶ was to kick both their *wives* one morning out of doors, and his own too;‖ and in their stead, gave orders to pick up the first three strollers could be met with in the streets. A while after, he nailed up the cellar-door, and would not allow his brothers a drop of *drink* to their victuals.** Dining one day at an alderman's in the city, Peter observed him expatiating after the manner of his brethren, in the praises of his sirloin of beef. 'Beef', said the sage magistrate, 'is the king of meat; beef comprehends in it the quintessence of partridge, and quail, and venison,

* The Pope is not only allowed to be the Vicar of Christ, but by several divines is called God upon Earth, and other blasphemous titles.

† The triple crown.

Ibid. The Pope's universal monarchy, and his triple crown, and fisher's ring. W. Wotton.

‡ The keys of the Church.

§ Neither does his arrogant way of requiring men to kiss his slipper escape reflection. W. Wotton.

¶ This word properly signifies a sudden jerk, or lash of a horse, when you do not expect it.

‖ The Celibacy of the Romish clergy is struck at in Peter's beating his own and brothers' wives out of doors. W. Wotton.

** The Pope's refusing the cup to the laity, persuading them that the blood is contained in the bread, and that the bread is the real and entire body of Christ.

and pheasant, and plum-pudding, and custard.' When Peter came home, he would needs take the fancy of cooking up this doctrine into use and apply the precept, in default of a sirloin, to his brown loaf. 'Bread,' says he, 'dear brothers, is the staff of life; in which bread is contained, *inclusivè*, the quintessence of beef, mutton, veal, venison, partridge, plum-pudding, and custard. And to render all complete, there is intermingled a due quantity of water whose crudities are also corrected by yeast or barm, through which means it becomes a wholesome fermented liquor, diffused through the mass of the bread.' Upon the strength of these conclusions, next day at dinner was the brown loaf served up in all the formality of a city feast. 'Come, brothers,' said Peter, 'fall to, and spare not; here is excellent good mutton;* or hold, now my hand is in, I'll help you.' At which word, in much ceremony, with fork and knife, he carves out two good slices of the loaf and presents each on a plate to his brothers. The elder of the two, not suddenly entering into Lord Peter's conceit, began with very civil language to examine the mystery. 'My lord,' said he, 'I doubt, with great submission, there may be some mistake.' 'What,' says Peter, 'you are pleasant; come then, let us hear this jest your head is so big with.' 'None in the world, my lord, but unless I am very much deceived, your lordship was pleased a while ago to let fall a word about mutton, and I would be glad to see it with all my heart.' 'How,' said Peter, appearing in great surprise, 'I do not comprehend this at all.'—Upon which, the younger interposing to set the business aright, 'My lord,' said he, 'my brother, I suppose, is hungry, and longs for the mutton your lordship hath promised us to dinner.' 'Pray,' said Peter, 'take me along with you: either you are both mad, or disposed to be merrier than I approve of. If *you* there do not like your piece I will carve you another, though I should take that to be the choice bit of the whole shoulder.' 'What then, my lord,' replied the first 'it seems this is a shoulder of mutton all this while?' 'Pray, sir,' says Peter, 'eat your victuals and leave off your impertinence if you please, for I am not disposed to relish it at present.' But the other could not forbear, being over provoked at the affected seriousness of Peter's countenance. 'By G—, my lord,' said he, 'I can only say that to my eyes, and fingers, and teeth, and nose, it seems to be nothing but a crust of bread.' Upon which the second put in his word, 'I never saw a piece of mutton in my life so nearly resembling a slice from a twelve-penny loaf.' 'Look ye, gentlemen,' cries Peter in a rage, 'to convince you what a couple of blind, positive, ignorant, wilful

* *Transubstantiation*. Peter turns his bread into mutton, and according to the popish doctrine of concomitants, his wine too, which in his way he calls *palming his damned crusts upon the brothers for mutton*. W. Wotton.

puppies you are, I will use but this plain argument: By G—, it is true, good, natural mutton as any in Leadenhall market, and G— confound you both eternally if you offer to believe otherwise.' Such a thundering proof as this left no further room for objection. The two unbelievers began to gather and pocket up their mistake as hastily as they could. 'Why, truly,' said the first, 'upon more mature consideration'—'Ay,' says the other, interrupting him, 'now I have thought better on the thing, your lordship seems to have a great deal of reason.' 'Very well,' said Peter, 'here boy, fill me a beer-glass of claret. Here's to you both, with all my heart.' The two brethren, much delighted to see him so readily appeased, returned their most humble thanks and said they would be glad to pledge his lordship. 'That you shall,' said Peter, 'I am not a person to refuse you anything that is reasonable: wine, moderately taken, is a cordial; here is a glass apiece for you; 'tis true natural juice from the grape, none of your damned *vintners*' brewings.' Having spoke thus, he presented to each of them another large dry crust, bidding them drink it off and not be bashful, for it would do them no hurt. The two brothers after having performed the usual office in such delicate conjunctures, of staring a sufficient period at Lord Peter and each other, and finding how matters were like to go, resolved not to enter on a new dispute but let him carry the point as he pleased; for he was now got into one of his mad fits, and to argue or expostulate further would only serve to render him a hundred times more untractable.

I have chosen to relate this worthy matter in all its circumstances, because it gave a principal occasion to that great and famous *rupture** which happened about the same time among these brethren, and was never afterwards made up. But of that, I shall treat at large in another section.

However, it is certain that Lord Peter, even in his lucid intervals, was very lewdly given in his common conversation, extreme wilful and positive, and would at any time rather argue to the death than allow himself once to be in an error. Besides, he had an abominable faculty of telling huge palpable *lies* upon all occasions; and swearing not only to the truth, but cursing the whole company to Hell if they pretended to make the least scruple of believing him. One time he swore he had a *cow*† at home, which gave as much milk at a meal as would fill three thousand churches, and what was yet more extraordinary, would never turn sour.

* By this *Rupture* is meant the *Reformation*.

† The ridiculous multiplying of the Virgin Mary's *milk* among the papists, under the allegory of a *cow*, which gave as much milk at a meal as would fill three thousand churches. W. WOTTON.

Another time he was telling of an old *sign-post** that belonged to his *father*, with nails and timber enough on it to build sixteen large men-of-war. Talking one day of Chinese waggons,° which were made so light as to sail over mountains: 'Z—ds,' said Peter, 'where's the wonder of that? By G—, I saw a large house of lime and stone† travel over sea and land (granting that it stopped sometimes to bait) above two thousand German leagues.' And that which was the good of it, he would swear desperately all the while that he never told a lie in his life, and at every word, 'By G—, gentlemen, I tell you nothing but the truth, and the D—l broil them eternally that will not believe me.'

In short, Peter grew so scandalous that all the neighbourhood began in plain words to say, he was no better than a knave. And his two brothers, long weary of his ill usage, resolved at last to leave him; but first they humbly desired a copy of their father's *Will*, which had now lain by neglected time out of mind. Instead of granting this request he called them *damned sons of whores*, *rogues*, *traitors*, and the rest of the vile names he could muster up. However, while he was abroad one day upon his projects, the two youngsters watched their opportunity, made a shift to come at the *Will*‡ and took a *copia vera*, by which they presently saw how grossly they had been abused; their father having left them equal heirs, and strictly commanded that whatever they got should lie in common among them all. Pursuant to which their next enterprise was to break open the cellar-door, and get a little good *drink*§ to spirit and comfort their hearts. In copying the *Will* they had met another precept against whoring, divorce, and separate maintenance; upon which their next work¶ was to discard their concubines and send for their wives. While all this was in agitation there enters a solicitor from Newgate, desiring Lord Peter would please procure a *pardon* for a *thief* that was to be *hanged* tomorrow. But the two brothers told him he was a coxcomb to seek pardons from a fellow who deserved to be hanged much better than his client, and discovered all the method of that imposture, in the same form I delivered it a while ago, advising the solicitor to put his friend upon

* By this *sign-post* is meant the *cross* of our Blessed Saviour.

† The chapel of Loretto, which travelled from the Holy Land to Italy. He falls here only upon the ridiculous inventions of popery. The Church of Rome intended by these things to gull silly, superstitious people, and rook them of their money; the world had been too long in slavery, and our ancestors gloriously redeemed us from that yoke. The Church of Rome therefore ought to be exposed, and he deserves well of mankind that does expose it. W. WOTTON.

‡ Translated the scriptures into the vulgar tongues.

§ Administered the cup to the laity at the communion.

¶ Allowed the marriages of priests.

obtaining *a pardon from the king.** In the midst of all this clutter and revolution, in comes Peter with a file of dragoons at his heels,† and gathering from all hands what was in the wind, he and his gang, after several millions of scurrilities and curses, not very important here to repeat, by main force very fairly kicks them both out of doors,‡ and would never let them come under his roof from that day to this.

SECT. V.

A Digression in the Modern Kind.

We whom the world is pleased to honour with the title of *modern authors* should never have been able to compass our great design of an everlasting remembrance, and never-dying fame, if our endeavours had not been so highly serviceable to the general good of mankind. This, *O Universe*, is the adventurous attempt of me thy secretary;

——Quemvis perferre laborem
Suadet, et inducit noctes vigilare serenas.°

To this end I have some time since, with a world of pains and art, dissected the carcass of *human nature* and read many useful lectures upon the several parts, both *containing* and *contained*, till at last it *smelt* so strong I could preserve it no longer. Upon which, I have been at a great expense to fit up all the bones with exact contexture and in due symmetry, so that I am ready to show a complete anatomy thereof to all curious *gentlemen and others*. But not to digress further in the midst of a digression, as I have known some authors enclose digressions in one another, like a nest of boxes, I do affirm that having carefully cut up *human nature*, I have found a very strange, new, and important discovery,° that the public good of mankind is performed by two ways, *instruction* and *diversion*. And I have further proved in my said several readings (which perhaps the world may one day see, if I can prevail on any friend to steal a copy, or on certain gentlemen of my admirers to be very importunate) that as mankind is now disposed, he receives much greater advantage by being *diverted* than *instructed*; his epidemical

* Directed penitents not to trust to pardons and absolutions procured for money, but sent them to implore the mercy of God, from whence alone remission is to be obtained.

† By Peter's dragoons is meant the civil power, which those princes who were bigotted to the Romish superstition employed against the reformers.

‡ The Pope shuts all who dissent from him, out of the Church.

diseases being *fastidiosity*, *amorphy*, and *oscitation*;° whereas, in the present universal empire of wit and learning, there seems but little matter left for *instruction*. However, in compliance with a lesson of great age and authority I have attempted carrying the point in all its heights, and accordingly, throughout this divine treatise, have skilfully kneaded up both together with a layer of *utile* and a layer of *dulce*.

When I consider how exceedingly our illustrious *moderns* have eclipsed the weak glimmering lights of the *ancients* and turned them out of the road of all fashionable commerce, to a degree that our choice town wits,* of most refined accomplishments, are in grave dispute whether there have been ever any *ancients* or no° (in which point we are like to receive wonderful satisfaction from the most useful labours and lucubrations of that worthy *modern*, Dr. B[e]ntly); I say, when I consider all this I cannot but bewail that no famous *modern* hath ever yet attempted an universal system, in a small portable volume, of all things that are to be known, or believed, or imagined, or practised in life. I am, however, forced to acknowledge that such an enterprize was thought on some time ago by a great philosopher of *O. Brazile*.†° The method he proposed was by a certain curious *receipt*, a *nostrum*, which after his untimely death I found among his papers, and do here, out of my great affection to the *modern learned*, present them with it, not doubting it may one day encourage some worthy undertaker.

You take fair correct copies, well bound in calf-skin, and lettered at the back, of all modern bodies of arts and sciences whatsoever, and in what language you please. These you distil in balneo Mariæ, *infusing* quintessence of poppy Q.S.,° *together with three pints of* Lethe, *to be had from the apothecaries. You cleanse away carefully the* sordes *and* caput mortuum,° *letting all that is volatile evaporate. You preserve only the first running, which is again to be distilled seventeen times, till what remains will amount to about two drams. This you keep in a glass vial,* hermetically *sealed, for one and twenty days. Then you begin your Catholic° treatise, taking every morning fasting (first shaking the vial) three drops of this* elixir, *snuffing it strongly up your nose. It will dilate itself about the brain (where there is any) in fourteen minutes, and you immediately perceive in your head an infinite number of* abstracts, summaries, compendiums, extracts, collections, medullas, excerpta

* The learned person, here meant by our author, hath been endeavouring to annihilate so many ancient writers that, until he is pleased to stop his hand, it will be dangerous to affirm whether there have been ever any ancients in the world.

† This is an imaginary island, of kin to that which is called the *Painters' Wives Island*,° placed in some unknown part of the ocean, merely at the fancy of the map-maker.

quædams, florilegias,° *and the like, all disposed into great order, and reducible upon paper.*

I must needs own it was by the assistance of this *arcanum* that I, though otherwise *impar*, have adventured upon so daring an attempt, never achieved or undertaken before but by a certain author called Homer, in whom, though otherwise a person not without some abilities and, *for an ancient*, of a tolerable genius, I have discovered many gross errors, which are not to be forgiven his very ashes, if by chance any of them are left. For whereas we are assured he designed his work for a complete body of all knowledge,* human, divine, political, and mechanic, it is manifest he hath wholly neglected some, and been very imperfect in the rest. For first of all, as eminent a *cabalist*° as his disciples would represent him, his account of the *opus magnum*° is extremely poor and deficient; he seems to have read but very superficially either Sendivogius, Behmen, or *Anthropposophia Theomagica.*†° He is also quite mistaken about the *sphæra pyroplastica*,° a neglect not to be atoned for, and (if the reader will admit so severe a censure) *vix crederem autorem hunc, unquam audivisse ignis vocem.*° His failings are not less prominent in several parts of the *mechanics*. For, having read his writings with the utmost application usual among *modern wits*, I could never yet discover the least direction about the structure of that useful instrument, a *save-all*. For want of which, if the *moderns* had not lent their assistance, we might yet have wandered *in the dark*. But I have still behind a fault far more notorious to tax the author with; I mean, his gross ignorance‡ in the *common laws of this realm*, and in the doctrine as well as discipline of the Church of England. A defect, indeed, for which both he and all the ancients stand most justly censured by my worthy and ingenious friend Mr. W[o]tt[o]n, Bachelor of Divinity, in his incomparable treatise of *Ancient and Modern Learning:* a book never to be sufficiently valued, whether we consider the happy turns and flowings of the author's wit, the great usefulness of his sublime discoveries upon the subject of *flies* and *spittle*, or the laborious eloquence of his style. And I cannot forbear doing that author the justice of my public acknowledgments for the great *helps* and *liftings* I had out of his incomparable piece while I was penning this treatise.

* Homerus omnes res humanas poematis complexus est.—*Xenoph. in conviv.*°

† A treatise written about fifty years ago, by a Welsh gentleman of Cambridge. His name, as I remember, was Vaughan, as appears by the answer to it writ by the learned Dr. Henry More.° It is a piece of the most unintelligible *fustian*, that perhaps was ever published in any language.

‡ Mr. W[o]tt[o]n (to whom our author never gives any quarter) in his comparison of ancient and modern learning, numbers divinity, law, &c., among those parts of knowledge wherein we excel the ancients.

But, besides these omissions in Homer already mentioned, the curious reader will also observe several defects in that author's writings for which he is not altogether so accountable. For whereas every branch of knowledge has received such wonderful acquirements since his age, especially within these last three years° or thereabouts, it is almost impossible he could be so very perfect in modern discoveries as his advocates pretend. We freely acknowledge him to be the inventor of the *compass*, of *gunpowder*, and the *circulation of the blood*: but I challenge any of his admirers to show me in all his writings, a complete account of the *spleen*. Does he not also leave us wholly to seek in the art of *political wagering*?° What can be more defective and unsatisfactory than his long dissertation upon *tea*? And as to his method of *salivation without mercury*, so much celebrated of late, it is to my own knowledge and experience a thing very little to be relied on.

It was to supply such momentous defects that I have been prevailed on, after long solicitation, to take pen in hand; and I dare venture to promise the judicious reader shall find nothing neglected here that can be of use upon any emergency of life. I am confident to have included and exhausted all that human imagination can *rise* or *fall* to. Particularly, I recommend to the perusal of the learned, certain discoveries that are wholly untouched by others, whereof I shall only mention among a great many more, my *New Help [for] Smatterers*, or the *Art of being Deep-learned and Shallow-read*; *A Curious Invention about Mouse-Traps*; *An Universal Rule of Reason, or every Man his own Carver*; together with a most useful engine for *catching of owls*. All which, the judicious reader will find largely treated on, in the several parts of this discourse.

I hold myself obliged to give as much light as is possible into the beauties and excellencies of what I am writing, because it is become the fashion and humour most applauded among the first authors of this polite and learned age, when they would correct the ill nature of critical, or inform the ignorance of courteous readers. Besides, there have been several famous pieces lately published both in verse and prose, wherein if the writers had not been pleased, out of their great humanity and affection to the public, to give us a nice detail of the *sublime* and the *admirable* they contain, it is a thousand to one whether we should ever have discovered one grain of either. For my own particular, I cannot deny that whatever I have said upon this occasion had been more proper in a preface, and more agreeable to the mode which usually directs it there. But I here think fit to lay hold on that great and honourable privilege, of being the *last writer*. I claim an absolute authority in right, as the *freshest modern*, which gives me a despotic power over all authors before me. In the strength of which title I do utterly disapprove and declare against that pernicious custom of making the preface a bill of fare to the book. For I have always looked upon it as a high point of indiscretion in *monster-mongers* and other *retailers of strange sights*, to hang out a fair large picture over the door, drawn after the life with a most eloquent description underneath. This hath saved me many a threepence, for my curiosity was fully satisfied and I never offered to go in, though often invited by the urging and attending orator with his last *moving* and *standing* piece of rhetoric, 'Sir, upon my word, we are just going to begin.' Such is exactly the fate at this time of Prefaces, Epistles, Advertisements, Introductions, Prolegomenas, Apparatuses, To the Reader's. This expedient was admirable at first. Our great Dryden has long carried it as far as it would go, and with incredible success. He has often said to me in confidence that the world would have never suspected him to be so great a poet, if he had not assured them so frequently in his Prefaces that it was impossible they could either doubt or forget it. Perhaps it may be so. However, I much fear his instructions have edified out of their place, and taught men to grow wiser in certain points where he never intended they should; for it is lamentable to behold with what a lazy scorn many of the yawning readers in our age do nowadays twirl over forty or fifty pages of *preface* and *dedication* (which is the usual *modern* stint) as if it were so much Latin. Though it must be also allowed on the other hand, that a very considerable number is known to proceed *critics* and *wits* by reading nothing else.° Into which two factions, I think, all present readers may justly be divided. Now, for myself, I profess to be of the former sort; and therefore, having the *modern* inclination to expatiate upon the beauty of my own productions and display the bright parts of my discourse, I thought best to do it in the body of the work, where, as it now lies, it makes a very considerable addition to the bulk of the volume, *a circumstance by no means to be neglected by a skilful writer.*

Having thus paid my due deference and acknowledgment to an established custom of our newest authors, by *a long digression unsought for*, and *an universal censure unprovoked*, by forcing into the light, with much pains and and dexterity, my own excellencies and other men's defaults, with great justice to myself and candour to them, I now happily resume my subject, to the infinite satisfaction both of the reader and the author.

SECT. VI.

A Tale of a Tub.

We left Lord Peter in open rupture with his two brethren, both for ever discarded from his house and resigned to the wide world, with little or nothing to trust to; which are circumstances that render them proper subjects for the charity of a writer's pen to work on, scenes of misery ever affording the fairest harvest for great adventures. And in this, the world may perceive the difference between the integrity of a generous author and that of a common friend. The latter is observed to adhere close in prosperity but on the decline of fortune, to drop suddenly off. Whereas the generous author, just on the contrary, finds his hero on the dunghill, from thence by gradual steps raises him to a throne, and then immediately withdraws, expecting not so much as thanks for his pains. In imitation of which example I have placed Lord Peter in a noble house, given him a title to wear, and money to spend. There I shall leave him for some time, returning where common charity directs me, to the assistance of his two brothers at their lowest ebb. However, I shall by no means forget my character of an historian to follow the truth step by step, whatever happens or wherever it may lead me.

The two exiles, so nearly united in fortune and interest, took a lodging together, where, at their first leisure, they began to reflect on the numberless misfortunes and vexations of their life past, and could not tell on the sudden to what failure in their conduct they ought to impute them, when, after some recollection, they called to mind the copy of their father's Will which they had so happily recovered. This was immediately produced, and a firm resolution taken between them to alter whatever was already amiss, and reduce all their future measures to the strictest obedience prescribed therein. The main body of the Will (as the reader cannot easily have forgot) consisted in certain admirable rules about the wearing of their coats, in the perusal whereof the two brothers, at every period, duly comparing the doctrine with the practice, there was never seen a wider difference between two things, horrible downright transgressions of every point. Upon which they both resolved, without further delay, to fall immediately upon reducing the whole, exactly after their father's model.

But here it is good to stop the hasty reader, ever impatient to see the end of an adventure before we writers can duly prepare him for it. I am to record that these two brothers began to be distinguished at this time by certain names. One of them desired to be called *MARTIN*,* and the other took the appellation of *JACK*.† These two had lived in much friendship and agreement under the tyranny of their brother Peter, as it is the talent of fellow-sufferers to do; men in misfortune being like men in the dark, to whom all colours are the same. But when they came forward into the world and began to display themselves to each other and to the light, their complexions appeared extremely different, which the present posture of their affairs gave them sudden opportunity to discover.

But, here the severe reader may justly tax me as a writer of short memory, a deficiency to which a true *modern* cannot but, of necessity, be a little subject. Because, *memory* being an employment of the mind upon things past, is a faculty for which the learned in our illustrious age have no manner of occasion, who deal entirely with *invention*, and strike all things out of themselves, or at least by collision from each other; upon which account, we think it highly reasonable to produce our great forgetfulness as an argument unanswerable for our great wit. I ought in method to have informed the reader, about fifty pages ago, of a fancy Lord Peter took, and infused into his brothers, to wear on their coats whatever trimmings came up in fashion; never pulling off any, as they went out of the mode, but keeping on all together, which amounted in time to a medley the most antic you can possibly conceive, and this to a degree that upon the time of their falling out there was hardly a thread of the original coat to be seen, but an infinite quantity of *lace* and *ribbons*, and *fringe*, and *embroidery*, and *points* (I mean only those *tagged with silver*,‡ for the rest fell off). Now this material circumstance having been forgot in due place, as good fortune hath ordered, comes in very properly here, when the two brothers are just going to reform their vestures into the primitive state, prescribed by their father's Will.

They both unanimously entered upon this great work, looking sometimes on their coats and sometimes on the Will. Martin laid the first hand; at one twitch brought off a large handful of *points*; and with a second pull, stripped away ten dozen yards of *fringe*. But when he had gone thus far he demurred a while. He knew very well there yet remained a great deal more to be done; however, the first heat being over, his violence began to cool, and he resolved to proceed more moderately in the rest of the work; having already narrowly scaped a swingeing rent in pulling off the *points*, which being *tagged with silver* (as we have observed

* Martin Luther. † John Calvin.

‡ Points tagged with silver are those doctrines that promote the greatness and wealth of the church, which have been therefore woven deepest into the body of popery.

before) the judicious workman had, with much sagacity, double sewn to preserve them from *falling.* Resolving therefore to rid his coat of a great quantity of *gold lace*, he picked up the stitches with much caution, and diligently gleaned out all the loose threads as he went, which proved to be a work of time. Then he fell about the embroidered Indian figures of men, women, and children, against which, as you have heard in its due place, their father's testament was extremely exact and severe: these, with much dexterity and application, were after a while quite eradicated, or utterly defaced. For the rest, where he observed the embroidery to be worked so close as not to be got away without damaging the cloth, or where it served to hide or strengthen any flaw in the body of the coat contracted by the perpetual tampering of workmen upon it, he concluded the wisest course was to let it remain, resolving in no case whatsoever that the substance of the stuff should suffer injury; which he thought the best method for serving the true intent and meaning of his father's Will. And this is the nearest account I have been able to collect of Martin's proceedings upon this great revolution.

But his brother Jack, whose adventures will be so extraordinary as to furnish a great part in the remainder of this discourse, entered upon the matter with other thoughts and a quite different spirit. For the memory of Lord Peter's injuries produced a degree of hatred and spite which had a much greater share of inciting him, than any regards after his father's commands, since these appeared at best only secondary and subservient to the other. However, for this medley of humour he made a shift to find a very plausible name, honouring it with the title of *zeal*; which is perhaps the most significant word° that hath been ever yet produced in any language, as I think I have fully proved in my excellent *analytical* discourse upon that subject, wherein I have deduced a *histori-theo-physi-logical* account of *zeal*, showing how it first proceeded from a *notion* into a *word*, and thence, in a hot summer, ripened into a *tangible substance.* This work, containing three large volumes in folio, I design very shortly to publish by the *modern* way of *subscription*, not doubting but the nobility and gentry of the land will give me all possible encouragement, having already had such a taste of what I am able to perform.

I record, therefore, that brother Jack, brimful of this miraculous compound, reflecting with indignation upon Peter's tyranny, and further provoked by the despondency of Martin, prefaced his resolutions to this purpose. 'What!' said he, 'a rogue that locked up his drink, turned away our wives, cheated us of our fortunes; palmed his damned crusts upon us for mutton; and, at last, kicked us out of doors; must we be in his fashions, with a pox? A rascal, besides, that all the street cries out against.' Having thus kindled and inflamed himself as high as possible, and by consequence in a delicate temper for beginning a reformation, he set about the work immediately, and in three minutes made more dispatch than Martin had done in as many hours. For (courteous reader) you are given to understand, that *zeal* is never so highly obliged as when you set it a-*tearing*; and Jack, who doated on that quality in himself, allowed it at this time its full swinge. Thus it happened that, stripping down a parcel of *gold lace* a little too hastily, he rent the *main body* of his *coat* from top to bottom; and whereas his talent was not of the happiest in *taking up a stitch*, he knew no better way than to darn it again with *packthread* and a *skewer*. But the matter was yet infinitely worse (I record it with tears) when he proceeded to the *embroidery*: for being clumsy by nature, and of temper impatient; withal, beholding millions of stitches that required the nicest hand, and sedatest constitution, to extricate; in a great rage he tore off the whole piece, cloth and all, and flung them into the kennel, and furiously thus continuing his career: 'Ah, good brother Martin,' said he, 'do as I do, for the love of God; strip, tear, pull, rend, flay off all, that we may appear as unlike the rogue Peter as it is possible. I would not for a hundred pounds carry the least mark about me, that might give occasion to the neighbours of suspecting that I was related to such a rascal.' But Martin, who at this time happened to be extremely phlegmatic and sedate, begged his brother, of all love, not to damage his coat by any means; for he never would get such another: desired him to consider that it was not their business to form their actions by any reflection upon Peter's, but by observing the rules prescribed in their father's Will. That he should remember Peter was still their brother, whatever faults or injuries he had committed, and therefore they should, by all means, avoid such a thought as that of taking measures for good and evil, from no other rule than of opposition to him. That it was true, the testament of their good father was very exact in what related to the wearing of their *coats*; yet it was no less penal, and strict, in prescribing agreement and friendship and affection between them. And therefore, if straining a point were at all dispensible, it would certainly be so rather to the advance of unity, than increase of contradiction.

Martin had still proceeded as gravely as he began, and doubtless would have delivered an admirable lecture of morality, which might have exceedingly contributed to my reader's *repose both of body and mind* (the true ultimate end of *ethics*); but Jack was already gone a flight-shot beyond his patience. And as in scholastic disputes nothing serves to rouse the spleen of him that *opposes*, so much as a kind of pedantic affected calmness in the *respondent*; disputants being for the most part like unequal scales, where the *gravity* of one side advances the *lightness* of the other, and causes it to fly up and kick the beam; so it happened here that the *weight* of Martin's argument exalted Jack's *levity*, and made him fly out and spurn against his brother's moderation. In short, Martin's *patience* put Jack in a *rage*; but that which most afflicted him was to observe his brother's coat so well reduced into the state of innocence, while his own was either wholly rent to his shirt, or those places which had scaped his cruel clutches were still in Peter's livery. So that he looked like a drunken *beau*, half rifled by bullies; or like a fresh tenant of Newgate when he has refused the payment of *garnish*; or like a discovered *shoplifter*, left to the mercy of *Exchange-women*;° or like a *bawd* in her old velvet petticoat, resigned into the secular hands of the *mobile*. Like any or like all of these, a medley of *rags*, and *lace*, and *rents*, and *fringes*, unfortunate Jack did now appear: he would have been extremely glad to see his coat in the condition of Martin's, but infinitely gladder to find that of Martin in the same predicament with his. However, since neither of these was likely to come to pass he thought fit to lend the whole business another turn, and to dress up necessity into a virtue. Therefore, after as many of the *fox*'s arguments° as he could muster up for bringing Martin to *reason*, as he called it; or as he meant it, into his own ragged, bobtailed condition; and observing he said all to little purpose; what, alas! was left for the forlorn Jack to do, but after a million of scurrilities against his brother, to run mad with spleen, and spite, and contradiction. To be short, here began a mortal breach between these two. Jack went immediately to *new lodgings*, and in a few days it was for certain reported that he had run out of his wits. In a short time after, he appeared abroad and confirmed the report by falling into the oddest whimseys that ever a sick brain conceived.

And now the little boys in the streets began to salute him with several names. Sometimes they would call him Jack the Bald;* sometimes, Jack with a Lantern;† sometimes, Dutch Jack; ‡° sometimes, French Hugh;§ sometimes, Tom the Beggar;¶ and sometimes, Knocking Jack of the North.‖ And it was under one, or some, or all of these appellations (which I leave the learned reader to determine) that he hath given rise to the most illustrious and epidemic sect of *Æolists*,° who, with honourable

* That is, *Calvin*, from *calvus*, bald.
† All those who pretend to inward light.
‡ Jack of Leyden, who gave rise to the Anabaptists.
§ The Huguenots.
¶ The Gueuses, by which name some Protestants in Flanders were called.
‖ John Knocks, the reformer of Scotland.

commemoration, do still acknowledge the renowned *JACK* for their author and founder. Of whose original, as well as principles, I am now advancing to gratify the world with a very particular account.

— Mellæo contingens cuncta Lepore.°

SECT. VII.

A Digression in Praise of Digressions.

I have sometimes *heard* of an Iliad in a *nutshell*, but it hath been my fortune to have much oftener *seen* a *nutshell* in an Iliad. There is no doubt that human life has received most wonderful advantages from both; but to which of the two the world is chiefly indebted, I shall leave among the curious as a problem worthy of their utmost inquiry. For the invention of the latter, I think the commonwealth of learning is chiefly obliged to the great *modern* improvement of *digressions*: the late refinements in knowledge running parallel to those of diet in our nation, which among men of a judicious taste are dressed up in various compounds, consisting in *soups* and *olios*, *fricassees*, and *ragouts*.

'Tis true there is a sort of morose, detracting, ill-bred people, who pretend utterly to disrelish these polite innovations; and as to the similitude from diet, they allow the parallel but are so bold to pronounce the example itself a corruption and degeneracy of taste. They tell us that the fashion of jumbling fifty things together in a dish was at first introduced in compliance to a depraved and *debauched appetite*, as well as to a *crazy constitution*: and to see a man hunting through an *olio* after the *head* and *brains* of a *goose*, a *widgeon*, or a *woodcock*, is a sign he wants a stomach and digestion for more substantial victuals. Further, they affirm that *digressions* in a book are like *foreign troops* in a *state*, which argue the nation to want a *heart* and *hands* of its own, and often either *subdue* the *natives* or drive them into the most *unfruitful corners*.

But, after all that can be objected by these supercilious censors, 'tis manifest the society of writers would quickly be reduced to a very inconsiderable number, if men were put upon making books with the fatal confinement of delivering nothing beyond what is to the purpose. 'Tis acknowledged that were the case the same among us as with the Greeks and Romans, when learning was in its *cradle*, to be reared and fed and clothed by *invention*, it would be an easy task to fill up volumes upon particular occasions, without further expatiating from the subject than by moderate excursions, helping to advance or clear the main design. But with *knowledge* it has fared as with a numerous army encamped in a fruitful country, which for a few days maintains itself by the product of the soil it is on; till provisions being spent, they are sent to forage many a mile, among friends or enemies it matters not. Meanwhile the neighbouring fields, trampled and beaten down, become barren and dry, affording no sustenance but clouds of dust.

The whole course of things being thus entirely changed between *us* and the *ancients*, and the *moderns* wisely sensible of it, we of this age have discovered a shorter and more prudent method to become *scholars* and *wits*, without the fatigue of *reading* or of *thinking*. The most accomplished way of using books at present is two-fold; either first, to serve them as some men do *lords*, learn their *titles* exactly and then brag of their acquaintance. Or secondly, which is indeed the choicer, the profounder, and politer method, to get a thorough insight into the *index*,° by which the whole book is governed and turned, like *fishes* by the *tail*. For, to enter the palace of learning at the *great gate* requires an expense of time and forms; therefore men of much haste and little ceremony are content to get in by the *back door*. For the arts are all in a *flying* march, and therefore more easily subdued by attacking them in the *rear*. Thus physicians discover the state of the whole body by consulting only what comes from *behind*. Thus men catch knowledge by throwing their *wit* on the *posteriors* of a book, as boys do sparrows with flinging *salt* upon their *tails*. Thus human life is best understood by the wise man's rule, of *regarding the end*.° Thus are the sciences found like Hercules's oxen, by *tracing them backwards*.° Thus are *old sciences* unravelled like *old stockings*, by beginning at the *foot*.

Besides all this, the army of the sciences hath been of late, with a world of martial discipline, drawn into its *close order*, so that a view or a muster may be taken of it with abundance of expedition. For this great blessing we are wholly indebted to *systems* and *abstracts*, in which the *modern* fathers of learning, like prudent usurers, spent their sweat for the ease of us their children. For *labour* is the seed of *idleness*, and it is the peculiar happiness of our noble age to gather the *fruit*.

Now, the method of growing wise, learned, and *sublime*, having become so regular an affair, and so established in all its forms, the number of writers must needs have increased accordingly, and to a pitch that has made it of absolute necessity for them to interfere continually with each other. Besides, it is reckoned that there is not at this present a sufficient quantity of new matter left in nature to furnish and adorn any one particular subject to the extent of a volume.° This I am told by a very skilful *computer*, who hath given a full demonstration of it from rules of *arithmetic*.

This, perhaps, may be objected against by those who maintain the infinity of matter, and therefore will not allow that any *species* of it can be exhausted. For answer to which, let us examine the noblest branch of *modern* wit or invention planted and cultivated by the present age, and which of all others hath borne the most and the fairest fruit. For though some remains of it were left us by the *ancients*, yet have not any of those, as I remember, been translated or compiled into systems for *modern* use. Therefore we may affirm to our own honour, that it has, in some sort, been both invented and brought to perfection by the same hands. What I mean is that highly celebrated talent among the *modern* wits, of deducing similitudes, allusions, and applications, very surprising, agreeable, and apposite, from the *pudenda* of either sex, together with *their proper uses*. And truly, having observed how little invention bears any vogue besides what is derived into these *channels*, I have sometimes had a thought that the happy genius of our age and country was prophetically held forth by that ancient typical description of the Indian pigmies,* *whose stature did not exceed above two foot; sed quorum pudenda crassa, et ad talos usque pertingentia.*° Now, I have been very curious to inspect the late productions wherein the beauties of this kind have most prominently appeared. And although this *vein* hath bled so freely, and all endeavours have been used in the power of human breath to dilate, extend, and keep it open; like the Scythians,† *who had a custom, and an instrument, to blow up the privities of their mares, that they might yield the more milk*; yet I am under an apprehension it is near growing dry, and past all recovery, and that either some new *fonde* of wit should if possible be provided, or else that we must even be content with repetition here, as well as upon all other occasions.

This will stand as an uncontestable argument that our *modern* wits are not to reckon upon the infinity of matter for a constant supply. What remains therefore but that our last recourse must be had to large *indexes*, and little *compendiums*? *Quotations* must be plentifully gathered and booked in alphabet; to this end, though authors need be little consulted, yet *critics*, and *commentators*, and *lexicons*, carefully must. But above all, those judicious collectors of *bright parts*, and *flowers*, and *observandas*, are to be nicely dwelt on, by some called the *sieves* and *boulters* of learning, though it is left undetermined whether they dealt in *pearls* or meal, and consequently, whether we are more to value that which *passed through*, or what *stayed behind*.

By these methods, in a few weeks, there starts up many a writer capable of managing the profoundest and most universal subjects. For,

* Ctesiæ fragm. apud Photium.° † Herodot. L. 4. [2].

what though his *head* be empty provided his *commonplace book* be full, and if you will bate him but the circumstances of *method*, and *style*, and *grammar*, and *invention*; allow him but the common privileges of transcribing from others and digressing from himself as often as he shall see occasion; he will desire no more ingredients towards fitting up a treatise that shall make a very comely figure on a bookseller's shelf; there to be preserved neat and clean for a long eternity, adorned with the heraldry of its title fairly inscribed on a label; never to be thumbed or greased by students nor bound to everlasting chains of darkness in a library:° but, when the fulness of time is come, shall haply undergo the trial of purgatory in order *to ascend the sky*.

Without these allowances, how is it possible we *modern* wits should ever have an opportunity to introduce our collections, listed under so many thousand heads of a different nature; for want of which, the learned world would be deprived of infinite delight as well as instruction, and we ourselves buried beyond redress in an inglorious and undistinguished oblivion?

From such elements as these, I am alive to behold the day wherein the corporation of authors can outvie all its brethren in the *guild*. A happiness derived to us with a great many others from our Scythian ancestors, among whom the number of *pens* was so infinite that the Grecian* eloquence had no other way of expressing it, than by saying that in the regions far to the *north*, it was hardly possible for a man to travel, the very air was so replete with *feathers*.

The necessity of this digression will easily excuse the length, and I have chosen for it as proper a place as I could readily find. If the judicious reader can assign a fitter, I do here impower him to remove it into any other corner he please. And so I return with great alacrity, to pursue a more important concern.

SECT. VIII.

A Tale of a Tub.

The learned Æolists†° maintain the original cause of all things to be *wind*, from which principle this whole universe was at first produced and into which it must at last be resolved; that the same breath which had kindled and blew *up* the flame of nature, should one day blow it *out*.

Quod procul à nobis flectat fortuna gubernans.°

* Herodot. L. 4. [7 and 31]. † All pretenders to inspiration whatsoever.

This is what the *adepti* understand by their *anima mundi*;° that is to say, the *spirit*, or *breath*, or *wind* of the world; or examine the whole system by the particulars of nature, and you will find it not to be disputed. For whether you please to call the *forma informans*° of man by the name of *spiritus*, *animus*, *afflatus*, or *anima*, what are all these but several appellations for *wind*, which is the ruling *element* in every compound and into which they all resolve upon their corruption? Further, what is life itself, but as it is commonly called, the *breath* of our nostrils?° Whence it is very justly observed by naturalists that *wind* still continues of great emolument in *certain mysteries* not to be named, giving occasion for those happy epithets of *turgidus* and *inflatus*, applied either to the *emittent* or *recipient* organs.

By what I have gathered out of ancient records I find the *compass* of their doctrine took in two and thirty points, wherein it would be tedious to be very particular. However, a few of their most important precepts, deducible from it, are by no means to be omitted, among which the following maxim was of much weight: That since *wind* had the master share as well as operation in every compound, by consequence those beings must be of chief excellence wherein that *primordium* appears most prominently to abound, and therefore *man* is in the highest perfection of all created things, as having, by the great bounty of philosophers, been endued with three distinct *animas*° or *winds*, to which the sage Æolists with much liberality have added a fourth of equal necessity as well as ornament with the other three, by this *quartum principium* taking in the four corners of the world. Which gave occasion to that renowned *cabalist Bumbastus*,* of placing the body of a man in due position to the four *cardinal* points.°

In consequence of this, their next principle was that *man* brings with him into the world a peculiar portion or grain of *wind*, which may be called a *quinta essentia*, extracted from the other four. This *quintessence* is of a catholic use upon all emergencies of life, is improveable into all arts and sciences, and may be wonderfully refined as well as enlarged, by certain methods in education. This, when *blown* up to its perfection, ought not to be covetously hoarded up, stifled, or hid under a bushel, but freely communicated to mankind. Upon these reasons and others of equal weight, the wise Æolists affirm the gift of BELCHING to be the noblest act of a rational creature. To cultivate which art and render it more serviceable to mankind, they made use of several methods. At certain seasons of the year, you might behold the priests amongst them,

* This is one of the names of Paracelsus; he was called Christophorus, Theophrastus, Paracelsus, Bumbastus.

in vast numbers, with their *mouths** *gaping wide against a storm*. At other times were to be seen several hundreds linked together in a circular chain, with every man a pair of bellows applied to his neighbour's breech, by which they blew up each other to the shape and size of a *tun*; and for that reason, with great propriety of speech, did usually call their bodies, their *vessels*. When by these and the like performances they were grown sufficiently replete, they would immediately depart, and disembogue for the public good a plentiful share of their acquirements into their disciples' chaps. For we must here observe that all learning was esteemed among them to be compounded from the same principle. Because first, it is generally affirmed, or confessed, that learning *puffeth men up*;° and secondly, they proved it by the following syllogism: *Words are but wind; and learning is nothing but words*; ergo, *learning is nothing but wind*. For this reason, the philosophers among them did in their schools deliver to their pupils all their doctrines and opinions by *eructation*, wherein they had acquired a wonderful eloquence, and of incredible variety. But the great characteristic by which their chief sages were best distinguished, was a certain position of countenance, which gave undoubted intelligence to what degree or proportion the spirit agitated the inward mass. For, after certain gripings, the *wind* and vapours issuing forth, having first by their turbulence and convulsions within caused an earthquake in man's little world, distorted the mouth, bloated the cheeks, and gave the eyes a terrible kind of *relievo*. At which junctures all their *belches* were received for sacred, the sourer the better, and swallowed with infinite consolation by their meagre devotees. And to render these yet more complete, because the breath of man's life is in his nostrils, therefore the choicest, most edifying, and most enlivening *belches*, were very wisely conveyed through that vehicle° to give them a tincture as they passed.

Their gods were the four *winds*, whom they worshipped as the spirits that pervade and enliven the universe, and as those from whom alone all *inspiration* can properly be said to proceed. However, the chief of these, to whom they performed the adoration of *latria*,° was the *almighty North*, an ancient deity whom the inhabitants of Megalopolis, in Greece, had likewise in highest reverence: *omnium deorum Boream maxime celebrant.*†° This god, though endued with ubiquity, was yet supposed by the profounder Æolists to possess one peculiar habitation, or (to speak in form) a *cœlum empyræum*, wherein he was more intimately present. This was situated in a certain region well known to the ancient Greeks, by

* This is meant of those seditious preachers, who blow up the seeds of rebellion, &c.

† Pausan. L. 8.

them called Σκοτία,° or the *Land of Darkness*. And although many controversies have arisen upon that matter, yet so much is undisputed that from a region of the *like denomination* the most refined Æolists have borrowed their original, from whence, in every age, the zealous among their priesthood have brought over their choicest *inspiration*, fetching it with their own hands from the fountain-head in certain *bladders*, and disploding it among the sectaries in all nations, who did, and do, and ever will, daily gasp and pant after it.

Now, their mysteries and rites were performed in this manner. 'Tis well known among the learned that the virtuosos of former ages had a contrivance for carrying and preserving *winds* in casks or barrels, which was of great assistance upon long sea voyages, and the loss of so useful an art at present is very much to be lamented though, I know not how, with great negligence omitted by Pancirollus.*° It was an invention ascribed to Æolus himself, from whom this sect is denominated, and who, in honour of their founder's memory, have to this day preserved great numbers of those *barrels*, whereof they fix one in each of their temples, first beating out the top; into this *barrel*, upon solemn days, the priest enters, where having before duly prepared himself by the methods already described a secret funnel is also conveyed from his posteriors to the bottom of the barrel, which admits new supplies of inspiration, from a *northern* chink or cranny. Whereupon, you behold him swell immediately to the shape and size of his *vessel*. In this posture he disembogues whole tempests upon his auditory, as the spirit from beneath gives him utterance, which issuing *ex adytis* and *penetralibus*,° is not performed without much pain and gripings. And the wind in breaking forth deals with his face† as it does with that of the sea, first *blackening*, then *wrinkling*, and at last *bursting it into a foam*. It is in this guise the sacred Æolist delivers his oracular *belches* to his panting disciples; of whom some are greedily gaping after the sanctified breath, others are all the while hymning out the praises of the *winds*, and, gently wafted to and fro by their own humming, do thus represent the soft breezes of their deities appeased.

It is from this custom of the priests that some authors maintain these Æolists to have been very ancient in the world; because the delivery of their mysteries, which I have just now mentioned, appears exactly the same with that of other ancient oracles whose inspirations were owing to certain subterraneous *effluviums* of *wind*, delivered with the *same* pain to the priest and much about the *same* influence on the people. It is true

* An author who writ *De Artibus perditis* &c., of arts lost, and of arts invented.

† This is an exact description of the changes made in the face by Enthusiastic preachers.

indeed, that these were frequently managed and directed by *female* officers, whose organs were understood to be better disposed for the admission of those oracular *gusts*, as entering and passing up through a receptacle of greater capacity, and causing also a pruriency by the way, such as with due management hath been refined from a carnal into a spiritual ecstasy. And, to strengthen this profound conjecture, it is further insisted that this custom of *female* priests* is kept up still in certain refined colleges of our *modern* Æolists, who are agreed to receive their inspiration, derived through the receptacle aforesaid, like their ancestors the Sybils.

And whereas the mind of man, when he gives the spur and bridle to his thoughts, doth never stop but naturally sallies out into both extremes of high and low, of good and evil, his first flight of fancy commonly transports him to ideas of what is most perfect, finished, and exalted; till, having soared out of his own reach and sight, not well perceiving how near the frontiers of height and depth border upon each other; with the same course and wing he falls down plumb into the lowest bottom of things, like one who travels the *East* into the *West*, or like a straight line drawn by its own length into a circle. Whether a tincture of malice in our natures makes us fond of furnishing every bright idea with its reverse; or whether reason, reflecting upon the sum of things, can like the sun serve only to enlighten one half of the globe, leaving the other half by necessity under shade and darkness; or whether fancy, flying up to the imagination of what is highest and best, becomes overshot, and spent, and weary, and suddenly falls like a dead bird of paradise to the ground; or whether, after all these *metaphysical* conjectures, I have not entirely missed the true reason; the proposition however which hath stood me in so much circumstance is altogether true; that, as the most uncivilized parts of mankind have some way or other climbed up into the conception of a *God* or Supreme Power, so they have seldom forgot to provide their fears with certain ghastly notions, which instead of better have served them pretty tolerably for a *devil*. And this proceeding seems to be natural enough; for it is with men whose imaginations are lifted up very high, after the same rate as with those whose bodies are so; that, as they are delighted with the advantage of a nearer contemplation upwards, so they are equally terrified with the dismal prospect of the precipice below. Thus, in the choice of a *devil*, it hath been the usual method of mankind to single out some being, either in act or in vision, which was in most antipathy to the god they had framed. Thus also the sect of Æolists possessed themselves with a dread and horror and hatred of two malignant natures, betwixt

* Quakers, who suffer their women to preach and pray.

whom and the deities they adored, perpetual enmity was established. The first of these was the *chameleon*,* sworn foe to *inspiration*, who in scorn devoured large influences of their god without refunding the smallest blast by *eructation*. The other was a huge terrible monster called Moulinavent, who with four strong arms waged eternal battle with all their divinities, dexterously turning to avoid their blows and repay them with interest.

Thus furnished, and set out with *gods* as well as *devils*, was the renowned sect of Æolists, which makes at this day so illustrious a figure in the world, and whereof that polite nation of Laplanders are, beyond all doubt, a most authentic branch; of whom I therefore cannot without injustice here omit to make honourable mention, since they appear to be so closely allied in point of interest as well as inclinations with their brother Æolists among us, as not only to buy their *winds* by wholesale from the *same* merchants, but also to retail them after the *same* rate and method, and to customers much alike.°

Now, whether the system here delivered was wholly compiled by Jack, or as some writers believe, rather copied from the original at Delphos,° with certain additions and emendations suited to times and circumstances; I shall not absolutely determine. This I may affirm, that Jack gave it at least a new turn, and formed it into the same dress and model as it lies deduced by me.

I have long sought after this opportunity of doing justice to a society of men for whom I have a peculiar honour; and whose opinions, as well as practices, have been extremely misrepresented and traduced by the malice or ignorance of their adversaries. For I think it one of the greatest and best of human actions, to remove prejudices and place things in their truest and fairest light; which I therefore boldly undertake without any regards of my own, beside the conscience, the honour, and the thanks.

SECT. IX.

A Digression concerning the Original, the Use, and Improvement of Madness in a Commonwealth.

Nor shall it any ways detract from the just reputation of this famous sect, that its rise and institution are owing to such an author as I have described Jack to be: a person whose intellectuals were overturned, and

* I do not well understand what the Author aims at here, any more than by the terrible Monster mentioned in the following lines, called *Moulinavent*, which is the French word for a windmill.

his brain shaken out of its natural position, which we commonly suppose to be a distemper and call by the name of *madness* or *frenzy*. For, if we take a survey of the greatest actions that have been performed in the world under the influence of single men, which are *the establishment of new empires by conquest, the advance and progress of new schemes in philosophy, and the contriving, as well as the propagating, of new religions*; we shall find the authors of them all to have been persons whose natural reason hath admitted great revolutions, from their diet, their education, the prevalency of some certain temper, together with the particular influence of air and climate. Besides, there is something individual in human minds that easily kindles at the accidental approach and collision of certain circumstances, which though of paltry and mean appearance, do often flame out into the greatest emergencies of life. For great turns are not always given by strong hands, but by lucky adaption and at proper seasons; and it is of no import where the fire was kindled if the vapour has once got up into the brain. For the *upper region* of man is furnished like the *middle region* of the air; the materials are formed from causes of the widest difference, yet produce at last the same substance and effect. Mists arise from the earth, steams from dunghills, exhalations from the sea, and smoke from fire; yet all clouds are the same in composition as well as consequences, and the fumes issuing from a jakes will furnish as comely and useful a vapour as incense from an altar. Thus far, I suppose, will easily be granted me; and then it will follow that, as the face of nature never produces rain but when it is overcast and disturbed, so human understanding, seated in the brain, must be troubled and overspread by vapours ascending from the lower faculties to water the invention, and render it fruitful. Now, although these vapours (as it hath been already said) are of as various original as those of the skies, yet the crop they produce differs both in kind and degree, merely according to the soil. I will produce two instances to prove and explain what I am now advancing.

A certain great prince*° raised a mighty army, filled his coffers with infinite treasures, provided an invincible fleet, and all this without giving the least part of his design to his greatest ministers or his nearest favourites. Immediately the whole world was alarmed; the neighbouring crowns in trembling expectation towards what point the storm would burst; the small politicians everywhere forming profound conjectures. Some believed he had laid a scheme for universal monarchy; others, after much insight, determined the matter to be a project for pulling down the pope and setting up the *reformed* religion, which had once been his own.

* This was Harry the Great of France.

Some again, of a deeper sagacity, sent him into Asia to subdue the Turk and recover Palestine. In the midst of all these projects and preparations, a certain *state-surgeon** gathering the nature of the disease by these symptoms, attempted the cure, at one blow performed the operation, broke the bag, and out flew the *vapour*; nor did anything want to render it a complete remedy, only that the prince unfortunately happened to die in the performance. Now, is the reader exceeding curious to learn from whence this *vapour* took its rise, which had so long set the nations at a gaze? What secret wheel, what hidden spring, could put into motion so wonderful an engine? It was afterwards discovered that the movement of this whole machine had been directed by an absent *female* whose eyes had raised a protuberancy, and before emission, she was removed into an enemy's country. What should an unhappy prince do in such ticklish circumstances as these? He tried in vain the poet's never-failing receipt of *corpora quæque*;° for

> Idque petit corpus mens unde est saucia amore:
> Unde feritur, eo tendit, gestitque coire.° LUCR.

Having to no purpose used all peaceable endeavours, the collected part of the semen, raised and inflamed, became adust, converted to choler, turned head upon the spinal duct, and ascended to the brain. The very same principle that influences a *bully* to break the windows of a whore who has jilted him, naturally stirs up a great prince to raise mighty armies and dream of nothing but sieges, battles, and victories.

> [Cunnus] teterrima belli
> Causa —— °

The other instance† is what I have read somewhere in a very ancient author, of a mighty king,° who, for the space of above thirty years, amused himself to take and lose towns; beat armies, and be beaten; drive princes out of their dominions; fright children from their bread and butter; burn, lay waste, plunder, dragoon,° massacre subject and stranger, friend and foe, male and female. 'Tis recorded that the philosophers of each country were in grave dispute upon causes natural, moral, and political, to find out where they should assign an original solution of this *phenomenon*. At last, the *vapour* or *spirit* which animated the hero's brain, being in perpetual circulation, seized upon that region of the human body so renowned for furnishing the *zibeta occidentalis*,‡ and gathering

* Ravillac, who stabbed Henry the Great in his coach.

† This is meant of the present French king.

‡ Paracelsus, who was so famous for chemistry, tried an experiment upon human

there into a tumour, left the rest of the world for that time in peace. Of such mighty consequence it is where those exhalations fix, and of so little from whence they proceed. The same spirits which, in their superior progress, would conquer a kingdom, descending upon the *anus* conclude in a *fistula*.

Let us next examine the great introducers of new schemes in philosophy, and search till we can find from what faculty of the soul the disposition arises in mortal man, of taking it into his head to advance new systems with such an eager zeal, in things agreed on all hands impossible to be known; from what seeds this disposition springs, and to what quality of human nature these grand innovators have been indebted for their number of disciples. Because it is plain that several of the chief among them, both *ancient* and *modern*, were usually mistaken by their adversaries, and indeed by all except their own followers, to have been persons crazed, or out of their wits; having generally proceeded in the common course of their words and actions, by a method very different from the vulgar dictates of *unrefined* reason, agreeing for the most part in their several models with their present undoubted successors in the *academy* of *modern Bedlam*° (whose merits and principles I shall further examine in due place). Of this kind were *Epicurus*, *Diogenes*, *Apollonius*,° *Lucretius*, *Paracelsus*, *Des Cartes*, and others, who if they were now in the world, tied fast, and separate from their followers, would in this our undistinguishing age incur manifest danger of *phlebotomy*, and *whips*, and *chains*, and *dark chambers*, and *straw*. For what man in the natural state or course of thinking, did ever conceive it in his power to reduce the notions of all mankind exactly to the same length, and breadth, and height of his own? Yet this is the first humble and civil design of all innovators in the empire of reason. Epicurus modestly hoped that, one time or other, a certain fortuitous concourse of all men's opinions, after perpetual justlings, the sharp with the smooth, the light and the heavy, the round and the square, would by certain *clinamina*° unite in the notions of *atoms* and *void*, as these did in the originals of all things. Cartesius reckoned to see, before he died, the sentiments of all philosophers, like so many lesser stars in his *romantic* system, wrapped and drawn within his own *vortex*.° Now I would gladly be informed, how it is possible to account for such imaginations as these in particular men without recourse to my *phenomenon* of *vapours*, ascending from the lower faculties to overshadow the brain, and thence distilling into conceptions for which the

excrement to make a perfume of it; which, when he had brought to perfection, he called *zibeta occidentalis*, or *western civet*; the back parts of man (according to his division mentioned by the author, page [73]), being the *west*.

narrowness of our mother tongue has not yet assigned any other name besides that of *madness* or *phrenzy*. Let us therefore now conjecture how it comes to pass, that none of these great prescribers do ever fail providing themselves and their notions with a number of implicit disciples. And I think the reason is easy to be assigned: for there is a peculiar *string* in the harmony of human understanding which, in several individuals, is exactly of the same tuning. This, if you can dexterously screw up to its right key and then strike gently upon it, whenever you have the good fortune to light among those of the same pitch they will, by a secret necessary sympathy, strike exactly at the same time. And in this one circumstance lies all the skill or luck of the matter; for if you chance to jar the string among those who are either above or below your own height, instead of subscribing to your doctrine they will tie you fast, call you mad, and feed you with bread and water. It is therefore a point of the nicest conduct to distinguish and adapt this noble talent, with respect to the differences of persons and times. Cicero understood this very well, when writing to a friend in England with a caution, among other matters, to beware of being cheated by our *hackney-coachmen* (who it seems, in those days were as arrant rascals as they are now) has these remarkable words, *Est quod gaudeas te in ista loca venisse, ubi aliquid sapere viderere.**° For, to speak a bold truth, it is a fatal miscarriage so ill to order affairs as to pass for a *fool* in one company, when in another you might be treated as a *philosopher*. Which I desire *some certain gentlemen of my acquaintance* to lay up in their hearts as a very seasonable *innuendo*.

This, indeed, was the fatal mistake of that worthy gentleman, my most ingenious friend Mr. W[o]tt[o]n: a person, in appearance, ordained for great designs as well as performances, whether you will consider his *notions* or his *looks*. Surely no man ever advanced into the public with fitter qualifications of body and mind for the propagation of a new religion. Oh, had those happy talents, misapplied to vain philosophy, been turned into their proper channels of *dreams* and *visions*, where *distortion* of mind and countenance are of such sovereign use, the base detracting world would not then have dared to report that something is amiss, that his brain hath undergone an unlucky shake, which even his brother *modernists* themselves, like ungrates, do whisper so loud that it reaches up to the very garret I am now writing in.

Lastly, whoever pleases to look into the fountains of *enthusiasm*, from whence in all ages have eternally proceeded such fattening streams, will find the spring head to have been as *troubled* and *muddy* as the current. Of such great emolument is a tincture of this *vapour* which the world calls

* Epist. ad Fam. Trebatio.

madness, that without its help the world would not only be deprived of those two great blessings, *conquests* and *systems*, but even all mankind would unhappily be reduced to the same belief in things invisible. Now, the former *postulatum* being held, that it is of no import from what originals this *vapour* proceeds, but either in what *angles* it strikes and spreads over the understanding or upon what *species* of brain it ascends, it will be a very delicate point to cut the feather,° and divide the several reasons to a nice and curious reader, how this numerical difference in the brain can produce effects of so vast a difference from the same *vapour*, as to be the sole point of individuation between Alexander the Great, Jack of Leyden,° and Monsieur Des Cartes. The present argument is the most abstracted that ever I engaged in; it strains my faculties to their highest stretch; and I desire the reader to attend with the utmost perpensity, for I now proceed to unravel this knotty point.

There is in mankind a certain* * * * *
* * * * * * * *
Hic multa * * * * * *
desiderantur. * * * * *
* * * * And this I take to be a clear solution of the matter.

Having therefore so narrowly passed through this intricate difficulty, the reader will I am sure agree with me in the conclusion, that if the *moderns* mean by *madness*, only a disturbance or transposition of the brain by force of certain *vapours* issuing up from the lower faculties, then has this *madness* been the parent of all those mighty revolutions that have happened in *empire*, in *philosophy*, and in *religion*. For the brain, in its natural position and state of serenity, disposeth its owner to pass his life in the common forms without any thoughts of subduing multitudes to his own *power*, his *reasons*, or his *visions*; and the more he shapes his understanding by the pattern of human learning, the less he is inclined to form parties after his particular notions, because that instructs him in his private infirmities, as well as in the stubborn ignorance of the people. But when a man's fancy gets *astride* on his reason, when imagination is at cuffs with the senses, and common understanding as well as common sense, is kicked out of doors; the first proselyte he makes is himself, and when that is once compassed the difficulty is not so great in bringing over others, a strong delusion always operating from *without* as vigorously as from *within*. For cant and vision are to the ear and the eye, the same that

* Here is another defect in the manuscript; but I think the author did wisely, and that the matter which thus strained his faculties was not worth a solution; and it were well if all metaphysical cobweb problems were no otherwise answered.

tickling is to the touch. Those entertainments and pleasures we most value in life are such as *dupe* and play the wag with the senses. For, if we take an examination of what is generally understood by *happiness*, as it has respect either to the understanding or the senses, we shall find all its properties and adjuncts will herd under this short definition: that *it is a perpetual possession of being well deceived*. And first, with relation to the mind or understanding, 'tis manifest what mighty advantages fiction has over truth; and the reason is just at our elbow, because imagination can build nobler scenes and produce more wonderful revolutions than fortune or nature will be at expense to furnish. Nor is mankind so much to blame in his choice thus determining him, if we consider that the debate merely lies between *things past* and *things conceived*; and so the question is only this, whether things that have place in the *imagination* may not as properly be said to *exist* as those that are seated in the *memory*; which may be justly held in the affirmative, and very much to the advantage of the former since this is acknowledged to be the *womb* of things, and the other allowed to be no more than the *grave*. Again, if we take this definition of happiness and examine it with reference to the senses, it will be acknowledged wonderfully adapt. How fade and insipid do all objects accost us that are not conveyed in the vehicle of *delusion*! How shrunk is everything as it appears in the glass of nature! So that if it were not for the assistance of artificial *mediums*, false lights, refracted angles, varnish, and tinsel, there would be a mighty level in the felicity and enjoyments of mortal men. If this were seriously considered by the world, as I have a certain reason to suspect it hardly will, men would no longer reckon among their high points of wisdom the art of exposing weak sides and publishing infirmities; an employment, in my opinion, neither better nor worse than that of *unmasking*, which I think has never been allowed fair usage, either in the *world* or the *play-house*.

In the proportion that credulity is a more peaceful possession of the mind than curiosity; so far preferable is that wisdom which converses about the surface, to that pretended philosophy which enters into the depth of things, and then comes gravely back with the informations and discoveries that in the inside they are good for nothing. The two senses to which all objects first address themselves are the sight and the touch. These never examine further than the colour, the shape, the size, and whatever other qualities dwell, or are drawn by art, upon the outward of bodies; and then comes reason officiously, with tools for cutting, and opening, and mangling, and piercing, offering to demonstrate that they are not of the same consistence quite through. Now I take all this to be the last degree of perverting Nature, one of whose eternal laws it is, to put her best furniture forward. And therefore, in order to save the charges of all such expensive anatomy for the time to come, I do here think fit to inform the reader that in such conclusions as these, reason is certainly in the right, and that in most corporeal beings which have fallen under my cognizance, the *outside* hath been infinitely preferable to the *in*; whereof I have been further convinced from some late experiments. Last week I saw a woman *flayed*, and you will hardly believe how much it altered her person for the worse. Yesterday I ordered the carcass of a *beau* to be stripped in my presence, when we were all amazed to find so many unsuspected faults under one suit of clothes. Then I laid open his *brain*, his *heart*, and his *spleen*; but I plainly perceived at every operation that the farther we proceeded, we found the defects increase upon us in number and bulk; from all which, I justly formed this conclusion to myself. That whatever philosopher or projector can find out an art to solder and patch up the flaws and imperfections of nature will deserve much better of mankind, and teach us a more useful science than that so much in present esteem, of widening and exposing them (like him who held *anatomy* to be the ultimate end of *physic*). And he whose fortunes and dispositions have placed him in a convenient station to enjoy the fruits of this noble art; he that can with Epicurus content his ideas with the *films* and *images* that fly off upon his senses from the *superficies* of things;° such a man, truly wise, creams off Nature, leaving the sour and the dregs for philosophy and reason to lap up. This is the sublime and refined point of felicity, called *the possession of being well deceived*; the serene peaceful state, of being a fool among knaves.

But to return to *madness*. It is certain that, according to the system I have above deduced, every *species* thereof proceeds from a redundancy of *vapours*; therefore, as some kinds of *phrenzy* give double strength to the sinews, so there are of other *species* which add vigour, and life, and spirit to the brain. Now, it usually happens that these active spirits, getting possession of the brain, resemble those that haunt other waste and empty dwellings, which for want of business, either vanish and carry away a piece of the house, or else stay at home, and fling it all out of the windows. By which are mystically displayed the two principal branches of *madness*, and which some philosophers not considering so well as I, have mistook to be different in their causes, over-hastily assigning the first to deficiency, and the other to redundance.

I think it therefore manifest from what I have here advanced, that the main point of skill and address is to furnish employment for this redundancy of *vapour*, and prudently to adjust the seasons of it; by which means it may certainly become of cardinal and catholic emolument in a commonwealth. Thus one man, choosing a proper juncture, leaps into a gulf,° from thence proceeds a hero and is called the saver of his country; another achieves the same enterprise but, unluckily timing it, has left the brand of *madness* fixed as a reproach upon his memory. Upon so nice a distinction are we taught to repeat the name of Curtius with reverence and love, that of Empedocles° with hatred and contempt. Thus also it is usually conceived that the elder Brutus° only personated the *fool* and *madman* for the good of the public; but that was nothing else than a redundancy of the same *vapour* long misapplied, called by the Latins, *ingenium par negotiis*;*° or, (to translate it as nearly as I can) a sort of *phrenzy*, never in its right element till you take it up in business of the state.

Upon all which and many other reasons of equal weight, though not equally curious, I do here gladly embrace an opportunity I have long sought for, of recommending it as a very noble undertaking to Sir E[dwar]d S[eymou]r,° Sir C[hristophe]r M[usgra]ve, Sir J[oh]n B[ow]ls, J[oh]n H[o]w, Esq. and other patriots concerned, that they would move for leave to bring in a bill for appointing commissioners to inspect into Bedlam,° and the parts adjacent; who shall be empowered to *send for persons, papers, and records*, to examine into the merits and qualifications of every student and professor, to observe with utmost exactness their several dispositions and behaviour, by which means, duly distinguishing and adapting their talents, they might produce admirable instruments for the several offices in a state, [*ecclesiastical*], *civil*, and *military*, proceeding in such methods as I shall here humbly propose. And I hope the gentle reader will give some allowance to my great solicitudes in this important affair, upon account of the high esteem I have borne that honourable society whereof I had some time the happiness to be an unworthy member.

Is any student tearing his straw in piecemeal, swearing and blaspheming, biting his grate, foaming at the mouth, and emptying his piss-pot in the spectators' faces? Let the right worshipful the *commissioners of inspection* give him a regiment of dragoons, and send him into Flanders among the *rest*. Is another eternally talking, sputtering, gaping, bawling in a sound without period or article? What wonderful talents are here mislaid! Let him be furnished immediately with a green bag and papers and *threepence* in his pocket,†° and away with him to Westminster Hall. You will find a third gravely taking the dimensions of his kennel, a person of foresight and insight, though kept quite in the

* Tacit. [*Annals* vi, 39 and xvi, 18].

† A lawyer's coach-hire.

dark; for why, like Moses *ecce cornuta* erat ejus facies.*° He walks duly in one pace, entreats your penny with due gravity and ceremony, talks much of hard times, and taxes, and the whore of Babylon, bars up the wooden window of his cell constantly at eight o'clock, dreams of *fire*, and *shoplifters*, and *court-customers*, and *privileged places*. Now what a figure would all these acquirements amount to, if the owner were sent into the *city* among his brethren! Behold a fourth, in much and deep conversation with himself, biting his thumbs at proper junctures, his countenance checkered with business and design; sometimes walking very fast, with his eyes nailed to a paper that he holds in his hands; a great saver of time, somewhat thick of hearing, very short of sight, but more of memory; a man ever in haste, a great hatcher and breeder of business, and excellent at the famous art of *whispering nothing*; a huge idolator of monosyllables and procrastination, so ready to *give* his word to everybody that he never *keeps* it; one that has forgot the common *meaning* of words, but an admirable retainer of the *sound*; extremely subject to the *looseness*, for his *occasions* are perpetually *calling him away*. If you approach his grate in his familiar intervals; 'Sir,' says he, 'give me a penny and I'll sing you a song; but give me the penny first' (hence comes the common saying, and commoner practice, of parting with money for a *song*.) What a complete system of *court skill* is here described in every branch of it, and all utterly lost with wrong application! Accost the hole of another kennel, first stopping your nose, you will behold a surly, gloomy, nasty, slovenly mortal, raking in his own dung and dabbling in his urine. The best part of his diet is the reversion of his own ordure which, expiring into steams, whirls perpetually about and at last reinfunds. His complexion is of a dirty yellow with a thin scattered beard, exactly agreeable to that of his diet upon its first declination; like other insects, who having their birth and education in an excrement, from thence borrow their colour and their smell. The student of this apartment is very sparing of his words, but somewhat over-liberal of his breath. He holds his hand out ready to receive your penny, and immediately upon receipt, withdraws to his former occupations. Now, is it not amazing to think, the society of Warwick Lane° should have no more concern for the recovery of so useful a member who, if one may judge from these appearances, would become the greatest ornament to that illustrious body? Another student struts up fiercely to your teeth, puffing with his lips, half squeezing out his eyes, and very graciously holds you out his hand to kiss. The *keeper* desires you not to be afraid of this professor, for he will do you no hurt; to

* *Cornutus* is either horned or shining, and by this term Moses is described in the vulgar Latin of the Bible.

him alone is allowed the liberty of the antechamber, and the *orator* of the place° gives you to understand that this solemn person is a *tailor* run mad with pride. This considerable student is adorned with many other qualities, upon which at present I shall not further enlarge. . . . . *Hark in your ear** . . . . I am strangely mistaken if all his address, his motions, and his airs, would not then be very natural and in their proper element.

I shall not descend so minutely as to insist upon the vast number of *beaux*, *fiddlers*, *poets*, and *politicians*, that the world might recover by such a reformation. But what is more material, besides the clear gain redounding to the commonwealth by so large an acquisition of persons to employ, whose talents and acquirements, if I may be so bold to affirm it, are now buried or at least misapplied; it would be a mighty advantage accruing to the public from this inquiry, that all these would very much excel and arrive at great perfection in their several kinds; which I think is manifest from what I have already shown, and shall enforce by this one plain instance, that even I myself, the author of these momentous truths, am a person whose imaginations are hard-mouthed and exceedingly disposed to run away with his *reason*, which I have observed from long experience to be a very light rider, and easily shook off; upon which account, my friends will never trust me alone without a solemn promise to vent my speculations in this, or the like manner, for the universal benefit of human kind; which perhaps the gentle, courteous, and candid reader, brimful of that *modern* charity and tenderness usually annexed to his *office*, will be very hardly persuaded to believe.

SECT. X.

[*A Further Digression.*]

It is an unanswerable argument of a very refined age, the wonderful civilities that have passed of late years between the nation of *authors* and that of *readers*. There can hardly pop out a *play*, a *pamphlet*, or a *poem*, without a preface full of acknowledgments to the world for the general reception and applause they have given it,† which the Lord knows where, or when, or how, or from whom it received. In due deference to so laudable a custom I do here return my humble thanks to *His Majesty*, and

* I cannot conjecture what the author means here, or how this chasm could be filled, though it is capable of more than one interpretation.

† This is literally true, as we may observe in the prefaces to most plays, poems, &c.

both houses of *Parliament*; to the *Lords* of the King's Most Honourable Privy Council; to the reverend the *Judges*; to the *clergy*, and *gentry*, and *yeomanry* of this land; but in a more especial manner to my worthy brethren and friends at Will's Coffee-house, and Gresham College, and Warwick Lane, and Moorfields, and Scotland Yard, and Westminster Hall, and Guildhall;° in short, to all inhabitants and retainers whatsoever, either in court, or church, or camp, or city, or country, for their generous and universal acceptance of this divine treatise. I accept their approbation and good opinion with extreme gratitude, and, to the utmost of my poor capacity, shall take hold of all opportunities to return the obligation.

I am also happy that fate has flung me into so blessed an age for the mutual felicity of *booksellers* and *authors*, whom I may safely affirm to be at this day the two only satisfied parties in England. Ask an *author* how his last piece hath succeeded. Why, truly he thanks his stars, the world has been very favourable, and he has not the least reason to complain; and yet, by G—, he writ it in a week, at bits and starts, when he could steal an hour from his urgent affairs, as it is a hundred to one you may see further in the preface, to which he refers you, and for the rest, to the bookseller. There you go as a customer, and make the same question: he blesses his God the *thing* takes wonderfully, he is just printing a second edition, and has but three left in his shop. You beat down the *price*: 'Sir, we shall not differ'—and, in hopes of your custom another time, lets you have it as reasonable as you please, 'and pray send as many of your acquaintance as you will, I shall, upon your account, furnish them at all the same rate.'

Now, it is not well enough considered to what accidents and occasions the world is indebted for the greatest part of these noble writings which hourly start up to entertain it. If it were not for a *rainy day, a drunken vigil, a fit of the spleen, a course of physic, a sleepy Sunday, an ill run at dice, a long tailor's bill, a beggar's purse, a factious head, a hot sun, costive diet, want of books, and a just contempt of learning*—but for these events, I say, and some others too long to recite (especially *a prudent neglect of taking brimstone inwardly*) I doubt the number of *authors* and of *writings* would dwindle away to a degree most woeful to behold. To confirm this opinion, hear the words of the famous Troglodyte philosopher.° ''Tis certain' (said he) 'some grains of folly are of course annexed, as part of the composition of human nature, only the choice is left us whether we please to wear them *inlaid* or *embossed*, and we need not go very far to seek how that is usually determined, when we remember it is with human faculties as with liquors, the lightest will be ever at the top.'

There is in this famous island of Britain a certain paltry *scribbler*, very voluminous, whose character the reader cannot wholly be a stranger to.

He deals in a pernicious kind of writings called *Second Parts*, and usually passes under the name of *The Author of the First*. I easily foresee that as soon as I lay down my pen, this nimble *operator* will have stole it, and treat me as inhumanly as he hath already done Dr. B[lackmo]re,° L[estran]ge,° and many others who shall here be nameless. I therefore fly, for justice and relief, into the hands of that great *rectifier of saddles*,° and *lover of mankind*, Dr. B[en]tly, begging he will take this enormous grievance into his most *modern* consideration; and if it should so happen that the *furniture of an ass*,° in the shape of a *Second Part*, must for my sins be clapped by a mistake upon my back, that he will immediately please, in the presence of the world, to lighten me of the burden, and take it home to *his own house* till the *true beast* thinks fit to call for it.

In the meantime I do here give this public notice, that my resolutions are to circumscribe within this discourse the whole stock of matter I have been so many years providing. Since my *vein* is once opened, I am content to exhaust it all at a running for the peculiar advantage of my dear country, and for the universal benefit of mankind. Therefore, hospitably considering the number of my guests, they shall have my whole entertainment at a meal, and I scorn to set up the *leavings* in the cupboard. What the *guests* cannot eat may be given to the *poor*, and the *dogs** under the table may gnaw the *bones*. This I understand for a more generous proceeding, than to turn the company's stomach by inviting them again tomorrow to a scurvy meal of *scraps*.

If the reader fairly considers the strength of what I have advanced in the foregoing section I am convinced it will produce a wonderful revolution in his notions and opinions; and he will be abundantly better prepared to receive and to relish the concluding part of this miraculous treatise. Readers may be divided into three classes—the *superficial*, the *ignorant*, and the *learned*; and I have with much felicity fitted my pen to the genius and advantage of each. The *superficial* reader will be strangely provoked to *laughter*; which clears the breast and the lungs, is sovereign against the *spleen*, and the most innocent of all *diuretics*. The *ignorant* reader (between whom and the former the distinction is extremely nice) will find himself disposed to *stare*; which is an admirable remedy for ill eyes, serves to raise and enliven the spirits, and wonderfully helps *perspiration*. But the reader truly *learned*, chiefly for whose benefit I wake when others sleep, and sleep when others wake, will here find sufficient matter to employ his speculations for the rest of his life. It were much to be wished, and I do here humbly propose for an experiment, that every

* By dogs, the author means common injudicious critics, as he explains it himself before in his *Digression upon Critics*.

prince in Christendom will take seven of the *deepest scholars* in his dominions, and shut them up close for *seven* years in *seven* chambers, with a command to write *seven* ample commentaries on this comprehensive discourse. I shall venture to affirm that whatever difference may be found in their several conjectures, they will be all, without the least distortion, manifestly deducible from the text. Meantime it is my earnest request that so useful an undertaking may be entered upon (if their Majesties please) with all convenient speed; because I have a strong inclination, before I leave the world, to taste a blessing which we *mysterious* writers can seldom reach till we have got into our graves: whether it is that *fame*, being a fruit grafted on the body, can hardly grow and much less ripen till the *stock* is in the earth: or whether she be a bird of prey, and is lured among the rest to pursue after the scent of a *carcass*: or whether she conceives her trumpet sounds best and farthest when she stands on a *tomb*, by the advantage of a rising ground and the echo of a hollow vault.

'Tis true indeed, the republic of *dark* authors, after they once found out this excellent expedient of *dying*, have been peculiarly happy in the variety as well as extent of their reputation. For, *night* being the universal mother of things, wise philosophers hold all writings to be *fruitful*, in the proportion they are *dark*; and therefore, the *true illuminated** (that is to say, the *darkest* of all) have met with such numberless commentators, whose *scholiastic* midwifery hath delivered them of meanings that the authors themselves perhaps never conceived, and yet may very justly be allowed the lawful parents of them; the words of such writers being like seed,† which, however scattered at random, when they light upon a fruitful ground, will multiply far beyond either the hopes or imagination of the sower.

And therefore, in order to promote so useful a work I will here take leave to glance a few *innuendoes*, that may be of great assistance to those sublime spirits who shall be appointed to labour in a universal comment upon this wonderful discourse. And first,‡ I have couched a very profound mystery in the number of O's multiplied by *seven*, and divided by *nine*. Also, if a devout brother of the Rosy Cross will pray fervently for sixty three mornings with a lively faith, and then transpose certain letters and syllables according to prescription in the second and fifth section, they will certainly reveal into a full receipt of the *opus magnum*. Lastly,

* A name of the Rosicrucians.°

† Nothing is more frequent than for Commentators to force interpretations, which the authors never meant.

‡ This is what the Cabalists among the Jews have done with the Bible, and pretend to find wonderful mysteries by it.

whoever will be at the pains to calculate the whole number of each letter in this treatise, and sum up the difference exactly between the several numbers, assigning the true natural cause for every such difference, the discoveries in the product will plentifully reward his labour. But then he must beware of *Bythus* and *Sigè*,*° and be sure not to forget the qualities of *Acamoth*; *à cujus lacrymis humecta prodit substantia, à risu lucida, à tristitia solida, et à timore mobilis*;° wherein Eugenius Philalethes† hath committed an unpardonable mistake.

SECT. XI.

A Tale of a Tub.

After so wide a compass as I have wandered, I do now gladly overtake and close in with my subject, and shall henceforth hold on with it an even pace to the end of my journey, except some beautiful prospect appears within sight of my way; whereof though at present I have neither warning nor expectation, yet upon such an accident, come when it will, I shall beg my reader's favour and company, allowing me to conduct him through it along with myself. For in *writing* it is as in *travelling*: if a man is in haste to be at home (which I acknowledge to be none of my case, having never so little business as when I am there) if his *horse* be tired with long riding and ill ways or be naturally a jade, I advise him clearly to make the straightest and the commonest road, be it ever so dirty. But then surely we must own such a man to be a scurvy companion at best; he *spatters* himself and his fellow-travellers at every step; all their thoughts, and wishes, and

* I was told by an eminent divine, whom I consulted on this point, that these two barbarous words, with that of *Acamoth* and its qualities, as here set down, are quoted from Irenæus. This he discovered by searching that ancient writer for another quotation of our author, which he has placed in the title-page, and refers to the book and chapter; the curious were very inquisitive whether those barbarous words, *basima eacabasa, &c.* are really in Irenæus, and upon inquiry, 'twas found they were a sort of cant or jargon of certain heretics, and therefore very properly prefixed to such a book as this of our author.

† *Vid. Anima Magica Abscondita.*°

Ibid. To the above-mentioned treatise, called *Anthroposophia Theomagica*, there is another annexed, called *Anima Magica Abscondita*, written by the same author, Vaughan, under the name of Eugenius Philalethes, but in neither of those treatises is there any mention of *Acamoth*, or its qualities, so that this is nothing but amusement, and a ridicule of dark, unintelligible writers; only the words, *à cujus lacrymis, &c.* are, as we have said, transcribed from Irenæus, though I know not from what part. I believe one of the author's designs was to set curious men a-hunting through *indexes*, and inquiring for books out of the common road.

conversation, turn entirely upon the subject of their journey's end; and at every splash, and plunge, and stumble they heartily wish one another at the devil.

On the other side, when a traveller and his *horse* are in heart and plight, when his purse is full and the day before him, he takes the road only where it is clean or convenient; entertains his company there as agreeably as he can; but upon the first occasion carries them along with him to every delightful scene in view, whether of art, of nature, or of both; and if they chance to refuse out of stupidity or weariness, let them jog on by themselves and be d—n'd; he'll overtake them at the next town, at which arriving, he rides furiously through; the men, women, and children run out to gaze, a hundred* *noisy curs* run *barking* after him, of which if he honours the boldest with a *lash of his whip*, it is rather out of sport than revenge; but should some *sourer mongrel* dare too near an approach, he receives a *salute* on the chops by an accidental stroke from the courser's heels (nor is any ground lost by the blow) which sends him yelping and limping home.

I now proceed to sum up the singular adventures of my renowned Jack, the state of whose dispositions and fortunes the careful reader does, no doubt, most exactly remember as I last parted with them in the conclusion of a former section. Therefore, his next care must be, from two of the foregoing, to extract a scheme of notions that may best fit his understanding for a true relish of what is to ensue.

Jack had not only calculated the first revolution of his brain so prudently as to give rise to that epidemic sect of Æolists, but succeeding also into a new and strange variety of conceptions, the fruitfulness of his imagination led him into certain notions which, although in appearance very unaccountable, were not without their mysteries and their meanings, nor wanted followers to countenance and improve them. I shall therefore be extremely careful and exact in recounting such material passages of this nature as I have been able to collect, either from undoubted tradition, or indefatigable reading; and shall describe them as graphically as it is possible, and as far as notions of that height and latitude can be brought within the compass of a pen. Nor do I at all question, but they will furnish plenty of noble matter for such whose converting imaginations dispose them to reduce all things into *types*;° who can make *shadows*, no thanks to the sun, and then mould them into substances, no thanks to philosophy; whose peculiar talent lies in fixing tropes and allegories to the *letter*, and refining what is literal into figure and mystery.

* By these are meant what the author calls the *true critics*.

Jack had provided* a fair copy of his father's Will engrossed in form upon a large skin of parchment, and resolving to act the part of a most dutiful son, he became the fondest creature of it imaginable. For although, as I have often told the reader, it consisted wholly in certain plain, easy directions about the management and wearing of their coats, with legacies and penalties in case of obedience or neglect, yet he began to entertain a fancy that the matter was *deeper* and *darker*, and therefore must needs have a great deal more of mystery at the bottom. 'Gentlemen,' said he, 'I will prove this very skin of parchment to be meat, drink, and cloth, to be the philosopher's stone, and the universal medicine.' In consequence of which raptures he resolved to make use of it in the necessary, as well as the most paltry occasions of life. He had a way of working it into any shape he pleased, so that it served him for a nightcap when he went to bed, and for an umbrella in rainy weather. He would lap a piece of it about a sore toe, or when he had fits burn two inches under his nose; or if anything lay heavy on his stomach, scrape off and swallow as much of the powder as would lie on a silver penny. They were all infallible remedies. With analogy to these refinements, his common talk and conversation ran wholly in the phrase of his Will,† and he circumscribed the utmost of his eloquence within that compass, not daring to let slip a syllable without authority from thence. Once at a strange house he was suddenly taken short upon an urgent juncture, whereon it may not be allowed too particularly to dilate; and being not able to call to mind with that suddenness the occasion required, an authentic phrase for demanding the way to the back-side, he chose rather, as the more prudent course, to incur the penalty in such cases usually annexed. Neither was it possible for the united rhetoric of mankind to prevail with him to make himself clean again; because having consulted the Will upon this emergency, he met with a passage‡ near the bottom° (whether foisted in by the transcriber, is not known) which seemed to forbid it.

He made it a part of his religion never to say grace to his meat;§ nor

* The author here lashes those pretenders to purity, who place so much merit in using scripture phrases on all occasions.

† The Protestant dissenters use *scripture phrases* in their serious discourses and composures, more than the Church of England men; accordingly, Jack is introduced making *his common talk and conversation to run wholly in the phrase of his WILL.* W. WOTTON.

‡ I cannot guess the author's meaning here, which I would be very glad to know because it seems to be of importance.

§ The slovenly way of receiving the sacrament among the fanatics.

could all the world persuade him, as the common phrase is, to eat his victuals *like a Christian.**

He bore a strange kind of appetite to *snap-dragon*,† and to the livid snuffs of a burning candle, which he would catch and swallow with an agility wonderful to conceive; and by this procedure, maintained a perpetual flame in his belly, which, issuing in a glowing steam from both his eyes as well as his nostrils and his mouth, made his head appear in a dark night like the skull of an ass wherein a roguish boy hath conveyed a farthing candle, *to the terror of his Majesty's liege subjects*. Therefore, he made use of no other expedient to light himself home, but was wont to say that *a wise man was his own lantern*.

He would shut his eyes as he walked along the streets, and if he happened to bounce his head against a post, or fall into a kennel (as he seldom missed either to do one or both) he would tell the gibing prentices who looked on, that he submitted with entire resignation as to a trip, or a blow of fate, with whom he found by long experience how vain it was either to wrestle or to cuff, and whoever durst undertake to do either would be sure to come off with a swingeing fall or a bloody nose. 'It was ordained',° said he, 'some few days before the Creation, that my nose and this very post should have a rencounter, and therefore nature thought fit to send us both into the world in the same age, and to make us countrymen and fellow-citizens. Now, had my eyes been open it is very likely the business might have been a great deal worse; for how many a confounded slip is daily got by man with all his foresight about him? Besides, the eyes of the understanding see best when those of the senses are out of the way; and therefore blind men are observed to tread their steps with much more caution, and conduct, and judgment, than those who rely with too much confidence upon the virtue of the visual nerve which every little accident shakes out of order, and a drop, or a film, can wholly disconcert; like a lantern among a pack of roaring bullies when they scour the streets, exposing its owner and itself to outward kicks and buffets, which both might have escaped if the vanity of appearing would have suffered them to walk in the dark. But further, if we examine the *conduct* of these boasted lights, it will prove yet a great deal worse than their *fortune*. 'Tis true, I have broke my nose against this post because

* This is a common phrase to express eating cleanlily, and is meant for an invective against that undecent manner among some people in receiving the sacrament; so in the lines before, 'tis said, Jack *would never say Grace to his Meat*, which is to be understood of the dissenters refusing to kneel at the sacrament.

† I cannot well find the author's meaning here, unless it be the hot, untimely, blind zeal of Enthusiasts.

fortune either forgot, or did not think it convenient, to twitch me by the elbow and give me notice to avoid it. But let not this encourage either the present age, or posterity, to trust their *noses* into the keeping of their *eyes*, which may prove the fairest way of losing them for good and all. For, O ye eyes, ye blind guides, miserable guardians are ye of our frail noses; ye, I say, who fasten upon the first precipice in view, and then tow our wretched willing bodies after you to the very brink of destruction. But, alas, that brink is rotten, our feet slip, and we tumble down prone into a gulf without one hospitable shrub in the way to break the fall—a fall to which not any nose of mortal make is equal, except that of the giant Laurcalco* who was Lord of the Silver Bridge. Most properly therefore, O eyes, and with great justice may you be compared to those foolish lights which conduct men through dirt and darkness, till they fall into a deep pit or a noisome bog.'

This I have produced as a scantling of Jack's great eloquence and the force of his reasoning upon such abstruse matters.

He was, besides, a person of great design and improvement in affairs of *devotion*, having introduced a new deity who hath since met with a vast number of worshippers, by some called Babel, by others Chaos; who had an ancient temple of Gothic structure° upon Salisbury Plain, famous for its shrine and celebration by pilgrims.

When he had some roguish trick to play† he would down with his knees, up with his eyes, and fall to prayers, though in the midst of the kennel. Then it was that those who understood his pranks would be sure to get far enough out of his way; and whenever curiosity attracted strangers to laugh or to listen, he would of a sudden, with one hand, out with his *gear* and piss full in their eyes, and with the other all to-bespatter them with mud.

In winter he went always loose and unbuttoned‡ and clad as thin as possible, to let *in* the ambient heat; and in summer lapped himself close and thick to keep it *out*.

In all revolutions of government§ he would make his court for the office of *hangman* general, and in the exercise of that dignity, wherein he was very dexterous, would make use of no other *vizard*¶ than a *long prayer*.

He had a tongue so musculous and subtile that he could twist it up into

* *Vide* Don Quixote.°

† The villainies and cruelties committed by Enthusiasts and fanatics among us, were all performed under the disguise of religion and long prayers.

‡ They affect differences in habit and behaviour.

§ They are severe persecutors, and all in a form of cant and devotion.

¶ Cromwell and his confederates went, as they called it, *to seek God*, when they resolved to murder the king.

his nose and deliver a strange kind of speech° from thence. He was also the first in these kingdoms who began to improve the Spanish accomplishment of *braying*;° and having large ears, perpetually exposed and arrect, he carried his art to such a perfection, that it was a point of great difficulty to distinguish either by the view or the sound between the *original* and the *copy*.

He was troubled with a disease reverse to that called the stinging of the *tarantula*,° and would run dog-mad at the noise of *music*,* especially a *pair of bagpipes*. But he would cure himself again by taking two or three turns in Westminster Hall, or Billingsgate, or in a boarding-school, or the Royal Exchange, or a *state coffee-house*.

He was a person that *feared* no *colours*° but mortally *hated* all, and upon that account bore a cruel aversion to *painters*;† insomuch that, in his paroxysms, as he walked the streets he would have his pockets loaden with stones to pelt at the *signs*.

Having from this manner of living, frequent occasions to *wash* himself, he would often leap over head and ears into the water° though it were in the midst of the winter, but was always observed to come out again much *dirtier*, if possible, than he went in.

He was the first that ever found out the secret of contriving a *soporiferous* medicine to be conveyed in at the *ears*;‡ it was a compound of *sulphur* and *balm of Gilead*, with a little *pilgrim's salve*.°

He wore a large plaster of artificial *caustics* on his stomach, with the fervour of which he could set himself a-*groaning*, like the famous *board*° upon application of a red-hot iron.

He would stand in the turning of a street, and calling to those who passed by, would cry to one, 'Worthy sir, do me the honour of a good slap in the chaps.'§ To another, 'Honest friend, pray favour me with a handsome kick on the arse.' 'Madam, shall I entreat a small box in the ear from your ladyship's fair hands?' 'Noble captain, lend a reasonable thwack, for the love of God, with that cane of yours over these poor shoulders.' And when he had, by such earnest solicitations, made a shift to procure a basting sufficient to swell up his fancy and his sides, he

* This is to expose our dissenters' aversion to instrumental music in churches. W. WOTTON.

† They quarrel at the most innocent decency and ornament, and defaced the statues and paintings on all the churches in England.

‡ Fanatic preaching, composed either of hell and damnation, or a fulsome description of the joys of heaven; both in such a dirty, nauseous style, as to be well resembled to pilgrim's salve.

§ The fanatics have always had a way of affecting to run into persecution, and count vast merit upon every little hardship they suffer.

would return home extremely comforted, and full of terrible accounts of what he had undergone for the *public good*. 'Observe this stroke,' (said he, showing his bare shoulders) 'a plaguy janissary gave it me this very morning at seven o'clock as, with much ado, I was driving off the Great Turk. Neighbours mine, this broken head deserves a plaster; had poor Jack been tender of his noddle you would have seen the Pope, and the French king, long before this time of day among your wives and your warehouses. Dear Christians, the Great Mogul was come as far as Whitechapel, and you may thank these poor sides that he hath not (God bless us) already swallowed up man, woman, and child.'

It was highly worth observing the singular effects of that aversion* or antipathy which Jack and his brother Peter seemed, even to an affectation, to bear towards each other. Peter had lately done *some rogueries* that forced him to abscond, and he seldom ventured to stir out before night, for fear of bailiffs. Their lodgings were at the two most distant parts of the town from each other; and whenever their occasions or humours called them abroad, they would make choice of the oddest unlikely times, and most uncouth rounds they could invent, that they might be sure to avoid one another: yet, after all this, it was their perpetual fortune to meet. The reason of which is easy enough to apprehend; for the frenzy and the spleen of both having the same foundation, we may look upon them as two pair of compasses, equally extended, and the fixed foot of each remaining in the same centre; which, though moving contrary ways at first, will be sure to encounter somewhere or other in the circumference. Besides, it was among the great misfortunes of Jack to bear a huge personal resemblance with his brother Peter. Their humour and dispositions were not only the same but there was a close analogy in their shape, their size, and their mien. Insomuch, as nothing was more frequent than for a bailiff to seize Jack by the shoulders, and cry 'Mr. Peter, you are the king's prisoner.' Or, at other times, for one of Peter's nearest friends to accost Jack with open arms, 'Dear Peter, I am glad to see thee, pray send me one of your best medicines for the worms.' This we may suppose was a mortifying return of those pains and proceedings Jack had laboured in so long. And finding how directly opposite all his endeavours had answered to the sole end

* The papists and fanatics, though they appear the most averse to each other, yet bear a near resemblance in many things, as hath been observed by learned men.

Ibid. The agreement of our dissenters and the papists, in that which Bishop Stillingfleet called *the fanaticism of the Church of Rome*, is ludicrously described for several pages together, by Jack's likeness to Peter, and their being often mistaken for each other, and their frequent meeting when they least intended it. W. WOTTON.

and intention which he had proposed to himself, how could it avoid having terrible effects upon a head and heart so furnished as his? However, the poor remainders of his *coat* bore all the punishment; the orient sun never entered upon his diurnal progress without missing a piece of it. He hired a tailor to stitch up the collar so close that it was ready to choke him, and squeezed out his eyes at such a rate as one could see nothing but the white. What little was left of the main substance of the coat, he rubbed every day for two hours against a rough-cast wall in order to grind away the remnants of *lace* and *embroidery*, but at the same time went on with so much violence that he proceeded a *heathen philosopher*. Yet after all he could do of this kind, the success continued still to disappoint his expectation. For, as it is the nature of rags to bear a kind of mock resemblance to finery, there being a sort of fluttering appearance in both which is not to be distinguished at a distance, in the dark, or by short-sighted eyes; so, in those junctures it fared with Jack and his tatters that they offered to the first view a ridiculous flaunting which, assisting the resemblance in person and air, thwarted all his projects of separation, and left so near a similitude between them as frequently deceived the very disciples and followers of both.

* * * * * * * *
* * * * * * * *
Desunt non- * * * * * *
nulla. * * * * * *
* * * * * * * *
* * * * * * * *

The old Sclavonian proverb said well, that it is with *men* as with *asses*; whoever would keep them fast, must find a very good hold at their ears. Yet I think we may affirm, and it hath been verified by repeated experience, that

Effugiet tamen hæc sceleratus vincula Proteus.°

It is good, therefore, to read the maxims of our ancestors with great allowances to times and persons; for if we look into primitive records we shall find that no revolutions have been so great, or so frequent, as those of human *ears*. In former days there was a curious invention to catch and keep them, which I think we may justly reckon among the *artes perditæ*;° and how can it be otherwise when, in these latter centuries, the very species is not only diminished to a very lamentable degree but the poor remainder is also degenerated so far as to mock our skilfullest *tenure*? For, if the only slitting of one *ear* in a stag° hath been found sufficient to propagate the defect through a whole forest, why should we wonder at the greatest consequences from so many loppings and mutilations to which the *ears* of our fathers, and our own, have been of late so much exposed? 'Tis true indeed, that while this *island* of ours was under the *dominion of grace*, many endeavours were made to improve the growth of *ears*° once more among us. The proportion of largeness was not only looked upon as an ornament of the *outward* man, but as a type of grace in the *inward*. Besides, it is held by naturalists that if there be a protuberancy of parts in the *superior* region of the body, as in the *ears* and *nose*, there must be a parity also in the *inferior*; and therefore in that truly pious age, the *males* in every assembly, according as they were gifted, appeared very forward in exposing their *ears* to view, and the regions about them; because Hippocrates tells us,* that 'when the vein behind the ear happens to be cut, a man becomes a eunuch'. And the *females* were nothing backwarder in beholding and edifying by them; whereof those who had already *used the means* looked about them with great concern in hopes of conceiving a suitable offspring by such a prospect; others, who stood candidates for *benevolence*, found there a plentiful choice and were sure to fix upon such as discovered the largest *ears*, that the breed might not dwindle between them. Lastly, the devouter sisters, who looked upon all extraordinary dilatations of that member as protrusions of zeal, or spiritual excrescencies, were sure to honour every head they sat upon as if they had been *marks of grace*; but especially that of the preacher, whose *ears* were usually of the prime magnitude, which upon that account, he was very frequent and exact in exposing with all advantages to the people: in his rhetorical *paroxysms* turning sometimes to *hold forth* the one, and sometimes to *hold forth* the other; from which custom the whole operation of preaching is to this very day, among their professors, styled by the phrase of *holding forth*.

Such was the progress of the *saints* for advancing the size of that member. And it is thought the success would have been every way answerable if, in process of time, a cruel king had not arisen† who raised a bloody persecution against all *ears* above a certain standard; upon which, some were glad to hide their flourishing sprouts in a black border, others crept wholly under a periwig; some were slit, others cropped, and a great number sliced off to the stumps. But of this more hereafter in my *General History of Ears*, which I design very speedily to bestow upon the public.

From this brief survey of the falling state of *ears* in the last age, and the

* *Lib. de aëre, locis, et aquis* [50, 51].

† This was King Charles the Second, who at his restoration turned out all the dissenting teachers that would not conform.

small care had to advance their ancient growth in the present, it is manifest how little reason we can have to rely upon a hold so short, so weak, and so slippery; and that whoever desires to catch mankind fast must have recourse to some other methods. Now, he that will examine human nature with circumspection enough, may discover several *handles*, whereof the *six** senses° afford one a-piece, beside a great number that are screwed to the passions and some few rivetted to the intellect. Among these last, *curiosity* is one, and of all others affords the firmest grasp; *curiosity*, that spur in the side, that bridle in the mouth, that ring in the nose, of a lazy, an impatient, and a grunting reader. By this *handle* it is that an author should seize upon his readers; which as soon as he hath once compassed, all resistance and struggling are in vain, and they become his prisoners as close as he pleases, till weariness or dulness force him to let go his gripe.

And therefore I, the author of this miraculous treatise, having hitherto beyond expectation maintained, by the aforesaid *handle*, a firm hold upon my gentle readers, it is with great reluctance that I am at length compelled to remit my grasp, leaving them, in the perusal of what remains, to that natural *oscitancy*° inherent in the tribe. I can only assure thee, courteous reader, for both our comforts, that my concern is altogether equal to thine for my unhappiness in losing, or mislaying among my papers, the remaining part of these memoirs; which consisted of accidents, turns, and adventures, both new, agreeable, and surprising, and therefore calculated in all due points to the delicate taste of this our noble age. But, alas, with my utmost endeavours I have been able only to retain a few of the heads. Under which there was a full account, how Peter got a *protection* out of the King's Bench; and of a reconcilement† between Jack and him, upon a design they had, in a certain *rainy night* to trepan brother Martin into a *sponging-house* and there strip him to the skin. How Martin, with much ado, showed them both a fair pair of heels. How a *new warrant* came out against Peter, upon which, how Jack left him in the lurch, *stole his protection, and made use of it himself.* How Jack's tatters came into fashion in *court* and *city*; how *he got upon a great*

* Including Scaliger's.

† In the reign of King James the Second, the Presbyterians, by the king's invitation, joined with the Papists against the Church of England, and addressed him for repeal of the penal laws and Test. The king, by his dispensing power, gave liberty of conscience, which both Papists and Presbyterians made use of; but upon the Revolution, the Papists being down of course, the Presbyterians freely continued their assemblies by virtue of King James's indulgence, before they had a toleration by law. This I believe the author means by Jack's *stealing* Peter's *protection, and making use of it himself.*

horse,* *and eat custard*.† But the particulars of all these, with several others which have now slid out of my memory, are lost beyond all hopes of recovery. For which misfortune, leaving my readers to condole with each other as far as they shall find it to agree with their several constitutions, but conjuring them by all the friendship that hath passed between us, from the title-page to this, not to proceed so far as to injure their healths for an accident past remedy; I now go on to the ceremonial part of an accomplished writer and therefore, by a courtly *modern*, least of all others to be omitted.

THE CONCLUSION.

Going too long is a cause of abortion as effectual, though not so frequent, as *going too short*; and holds true especially in the *labours* of the brain. Well fare the heart of that noble Jesuit‡° who first adventured to confess in print that books must be suited to their several seasons, like dress, and diet, and diversions. And better fare our noble nation for refining upon this among other French modes. I am living fast to see the time when a *book* that misses its tide shall be neglected as the *moon* by day, or like *mackerel* a week after the season. No man hath more nicely observed our climate than the bookseller who bought the copy of this work. He knows to a tittle what subjects will best go off in a *dry year*, and which it is proper to expose foremost when the weather-glass is fallen to *much rain*. When he had seen this treatise and consulted his *almanac* upon it, he gave me to understand that he had maturely considered the two principal things, which were the *bulk* and the *subject*, and found it would never *take* but after a long vacation, and then only in case it should happen to be a hard year for turnips. Upon which I desired to know, *considering my urgent necessities*, what he thought might be acceptable this month. He looked westward and said, 'I doubt we shall have a fit of bad weather. However, if you could prepare some pretty little *banter* (*but not in verse*) or a small treatise upon the ——, it would run like wildfire. But *if it hold up*, I have already hired an author to write something against Dr. B[en]tl[e]y, which I am sure will turn to account.'

At length we agreed upon this expedient; that when a customer comes

* Sir Humphry Edwin, a Presbyterian, was some years ago [1697] Lord Mayor of London, and had the insolence to go in his formalities to a conventicle, with the ensigns of his office.

† Custard is a famous dish at a Lord Mayor's feast.

‡ Père d'Orleans.

for one of these and desires in confidence to know the author, he will tell him very privately as a friend, naming whichever of the wits shall happen to be that week in the vogue; and if Durfey's last play should be in course, I would as lieve he may be the person as Congreve. This I mention, because I am wonderfully well acquainted with the present relish of courteous readers, and have often observed with singular pleasure, that a *fly* driven from a *honey-pot* will immediately, with very good appetite, alight and finish his meal on an *excrement*.

I have one word to say upon the subject of *profound writers*, who are grown very numerous of late and I know very well the judicious world is resolved to list me in that number. I conceive therefore, as to the business of being *profound*, that it is with *writers* as with *wells*—a person with good eyes may see to the bottom of the deepest provided any *water* be there, and that often when there is nothing in the world at the bottom besides *dryness* and *dirt*, though it be but a yard and half underground it shall pass, however, for wondrous *deep*, upon no wiser a reason than because it is wondrous *dark*.

I am now trying an experiment very frequent among modern authors, which is *to write upon nothing*;° when the subject is utterly exhausted, to let the pen still move on; by some called the ghost of wit, delighting to walk after the death of its body. And to say the truth, there seems to be no part of knowledge in fewer hands than that of discerning *when to have done*. By the time that an author has writ out a book, he and his readers are become old acquaintance and grow very loth to part; so that I have sometimes known it to be in writing as in visiting, where the ceremony of taking leave has employed more time than the whole conversation before. The conclusion of a treatise resembles the conclusion of human life, which hath sometimes been compared to the end of a feast where few are satisfied to depart, *ut plenus vitæ conviva*.° For men will sit down after the fullest meal, though it be only to *doze* or to *sleep* out the rest of the day. But in this latter I differ extremely from other writers, and shall be too proud if by all my labours I can have anyways contributed to the *repose* of mankind, in times* so turbulent and unquiet as these. Neither do I think such an employment so very alien from the office of a *wit* as some would suppose. For, among a very polite nation in Greece,†° there were the same temples built and consecrated to *Sleep* and the *Muses*, between which two deities they believed the strictest friendship was established.

I have one concluding favour to request of my reader; that he will not expect to be equally diverted and informed by every line or every page of

* This was writ before the peace of Ryswick.

† Trezenii. Pausan. lib. 2.

this discourse, but give some allowance to the author's spleen and short fits or intervals of dulness, as well as his own; and lay it seriously to his conscience whether, if he were walking the streets in dirty weather or a rainy day, he would allow it fair dealing in folks at their ease from a window to critick his gait, and ridicule his dress at such a juncture.

In my disposure of employments of the brain, I have thought fit to make *invention* the *master*, and to give *method* and *reason* the office of its *lackeys*. The cause of this distribution was, from observing it my peculiar case to be often under a temptation of being *witty* upon occasion where I could be neither *wise*, nor *sound*, nor anything to the matter in hand. And I am too much a servant of the *modern* way to neglect any such opportunities, whatever pains or improprieties I may be at to introduce them. For I have observed that from a laborious collection of seven hundred thirty-eight *flowers* and *shining hints* of the best *modern* authors, digested with great reading into my book of *commonplaces*, I have not been able after five years to draw, hook, or force, into common conversation any more than a dozen. Of which dozen, the one moiety failed of success by being dropped among unsuitable company, and the other cost me so many strains, and traps, and *ambages* to introduce, that I at length resolved to give it over. Now this disappointment (to discover a secret) I must own gave me the first hint of setting up for an *author*; and I have since found, among some particular friends, that it is become a very general complaint and has produced the same effects upon many others. For I have remarked many a *towardly word* to be wholly neglected or despised in *discourse*, which has passed very smoothly, with some consideration and esteem, after its preferment and sanction in *print*. But now, since by the liberty and encouragement of the press, I am grown absolute master of the occasions and opportunities to expose the talents I have acquired, I already discover that the *issues* of my *observanda* begin to grow too large for the *receipts*. Therefore, I shall here pause a while till I find, by feeling the world's pulse and my own, that it will be of absolute necessity (for us both) to resume my pen.

A Full and True Account of the BATTEL Fought last FRIDAY, Between the *Antient* and the *Modern* BOOKS in St. JAMES's LIBRARY.

THE BOOKSELLER° TO THE READER.

THE following Discourse, as it is unquestionably of the same author, so it seems to have been written about the same time with the former; I mean the year 1697, when the famous dispute was on foot about ancient and modern learning. The controversy took its rise from an essay of Sir William Temple's upon that subject, which was answered by W. Wotton, B.D., with an Appendix by Dr. Bentley, endeavouring to destroy the credit of Æsop and Phalaris for authors, whom Sir William Temple had, in the essay before-mentioned, highly commended. In that appendix the doctor falls hard upon a new edition of Phalaris put out by the Honourable Charles Boyle, now Earl of Orrery, to which Mr. Boyle replied at large, with great learning and wit; and the doctor voluminously rejoined. In this dispute, the town highly resented to see a person of Sir William Temple's character and merits roughly used by the two reverend gentlemen aforesaid, and without any manner of provocation. At length, there appearing no end of the quarrel, our author tells us that the BOOKS in St. James's Library,° looking upon themselves as parties principally concerned, took up the controversy and came to a decisive battle. But the manuscript by the injury of fortune or weather being in several places imperfect, we cannot learn to which side the victory fell.

I must warn the reader to beware of applying to persons what is here meant only of books, in the most literal sense. So, when Virgil is mentioned, we are not to understand the person of a famous poet called by that name, but only certain sheets of paper, bound up in leather, containing in print the works of the said poet; and so of the rest.

THE PREFACE OF THE AUTHOR.

SATIRE is a sort of glass, wherein beholders do generally discover everybody's face but their own; which is the chief reason for that kind of reception it meets in the world, and that so very few are offended with it. But if it should happen otherwise, the danger is not great; and I have learned from long experience never to apprehend mischief from those understandings I have been able to provoke; for anger and fury, though they add strength to the sinews of the body, yet are found to relax those of the mind, and to render all its efforts feeble and impotent.

There is a brain that will endure but one scumming; let the owner gather it with discretion, and manage his little stock with husbandry; but of all things, let him beware of bringing it under the lash of his betters, because that will make it all bubble up into impertinence, and he will find no new supply. Wit, without knowledge, being a sort of cream, which gathers in a night to the top, and by a skilful hand may be soon whipped into froth; but once scummed away, what appears underneath will be fit for nothing but to be thrown to the hogs.

A FULL AND TRUE ACCOUNT OF THE BATTLE FOUGHT LAST FRIDAY, &c.

WHOEVER examines with due circumspection into the *_Annual Records of Time_, will find it remarked that War is the child of Pride, and Pride the daughter of Riches. The former of which assertions may be soon granted, but one cannot so easily subscribe to the latter; for Pride is nearly related to Beggary and Want, either by father or mother, and sometimes by both: and to speak naturally, it very seldom happens among men to fall out when all have enough, invasions usually travelling from north to south, that is to say, from poverty upon plenty. The most ancient and natural grounds of quarrels are lust and avarice; which, though we may allow to be brethren, or collateral branches of pride, are certainly the issues of want. For, to speak in the phrase of writers upon politics, we may observe in the Republic of Dogs° (which, in its original, seems to be an institution of the Many) that the whole state is ever in the profoundest peace after a full meal; and that civil broils arise among them when it happens for one great bone to be seized on by some leading dog, who either divides it among the few and then it falls to an oligarchy, or keeps it to himself and then it runs up to a tyranny. The same reasoning also holds place among them in those dissensions we behold upon a turgescency in any of their females. For the right of possession lying in common (it being impossible to establish a property in so delicate a case) jealousies and suspicions do so abound that the whole commonwealth of that street is reduced to a manifest state of war, of every citizen against every citizen, till some one of more courage, conduct, or fortune than the rest, seizes and enjoys the prize; upon which naturally arises plenty of

* 'Riches produceth pride; pride is war's ground, &c.' *Vide* Ephem. de Mary Clarke; opt. edit.°

heart-burning, and envy, and snarling against the happy dog. Again, if we look upon any of these republics engaged in a foreign war either of invasion or defence, we shall find the same reasoning will serve as to the grounds and occasions of each, and that poverty or want in some degree or other (whether real or in opinion, which makes no alteration in the case) has a great share as well as pride on the part of the aggressor.

Now, whoever will please to take this scheme, and either reduce or adapt it to an intellectual state or commonwealth of learning, will soon discover the first ground of disagreement between the two great parties at this time in arms, and may form just conclusions upon the merits of either cause. But the issue or events of this war are not so easy to conjecture at; for the present quarrel is so inflamed by the warm heads of either faction, and the pretensions *somewhere or other* so exorbitant, as not to admit the least overtures of accommodation. This quarrel first began (as I have heard it affirmed by an old dweller in the neighbourhood) about a small spot of ground, lying and being upon one of the two tops of the hill Parnassus; the highest and largest of which had, it seems, been time out of mind in quiet possession of certain tenants called the Ancients, and the other was held by the Moderns. But these, disliking their present station, sent certain ambassadors to the Ancients, complaining of a great nuisance; how the height of that part of Parnassus quite spoiled the prospect of theirs, especially towards the *East*;° and therefore, to avoid a war, offered them the choice of this alternative—either that the Ancients would please to remove themselves and their effects down to the lower summity, which the Moderns would graciously surrender to them, and advance in their place; or else that the said Ancients will give leave to the Moderns to come with shovels and mattocks, and level the said hill as low as they shall think it convenient. To which the Ancients made answer, how little they expected such a message as this from a colony whom they had admitted, out of their own free grace, to so near a neighbourhood. That, as to their own seat, they were aborigines of it, and therefore to talk with them of a removal or surrender, was a language they did not understand. That if the height of the hill on their side shortened the prospect of the Moderns, it was a disadvantage they could not help; but desired them to consider whether that injury (if it be any) were not largely recompensed by the shade and shelter it afforded them. That as to levelling or digging down, it was either folly or ignorance to propose it, if they did, or did not know, how that side of the hill was an entire rock, which would break their tools and hearts without any damage to itself. That they would therefore advise the Moderns rather to raise their own side of the hill than dream of pulling down that of the Ancients; to the former of which they would not only give licence, but also largely contribute. All this was rejected by the Moderns with much indignation, who still insisted upon one of the two expedients. And so this difference broke out into a long and obstinate war, maintained on the one part by resolution and by the courage of certain leaders and allies; but on the other by the greatness of their number, upon all defeats affording continual recruits. In this quarrel whole rivulets of ink have been exhausted, and the virulence of both parties enormously augmented. Now, it must here be understood that ink is the great missive weapon in all battles of the learned, which, conveyed through a sort of engine called a quill, infinite numbers of these are darted at the enemy by the valiant on each side, with equal skill and violence, as if it were an engagement of porcupines. This malignant liquor was compounded by the engineer who invented it, of two ingredients, which are gall and copperas; by its bitterness and venom to suit in some degree, as well as to foment, the genius of the combatants. And as the Grecians, after an engagement, when they could not agree about the victory, were wont to set up trophies on both sides, the beaten party being content to be at the same expense to keep itself in countenance (a laudable and ancient custom, happily revived of late in the art of war); so the learned, after a sharp and bloody dispute, do on both sides hang out their trophies too, whichever comes by the worst. These trophies have largely inscribed on them the merits of the cause, a full impartial account of such a battle, and how the victory fell clearly to the party that set them up. They are known to the world under several names, as *disputes*, *arguments*, *rejoinders*, *brief considerations*, *answers*, *replies*, *remarks*, *reflections*, *objections*, *confutations*. For a very few days they are fixed up in all public places either by themselves or their *representatives, for passengers to gaze at;° from whence the chiefest and largest are removed to certain magazines they call libraries, there to remain in a quarter purposely assigned them, and from thenceforth begin to be called Books of Controversy.

In these books is wonderfully instilled and preserved the spirit of each warrior, while he is alive; and after his death his soul transmigrates there to inform them. This at least is the more common opinion; but I believe it is with libraries as with other cemeteries, where some philosophers affirm that a certain spirit, which they call *brutum hominis*,° hovers over the monument till the body is corrupted and turns to dust or to worms, but then vanishes or dissolves. So, we may say, a restless spirit haunts over every book till dust or worms have seized upon it, which to some may

* Their title-pages.

happen in a few days, but to others, later; and therefore books of controversy, being of all others haunted by the most disorderly spirits, have always been confined in a separate lodge from the rest; and, for fear of mutual violence against each other, it was thought prudent by our ancestors to bind them to the peace with strong iron chains.° Of which invention the original occasion was this. When the works of Scotus° first came out, they were carried to a certain library and had lodgings appointed them; but this author was no sooner settled than he went to visit his master Aristotle; and there both concerted together to seize Plato by main force and turn him out from his ancient station among the divines, where he had peaceably dwelt near eight hundred years. The attempt succeeded, and the two usurpers have reigned ever since in his stead: but to maintain quiet for the future, it was decreed that all polemics of the larger size should be held fast with a chain.

By this expedient the public peace of libraries might certainly have been preserved, if a new species of controversial books had not arose of late years, instinct with a most malignant spirit, from the war above-mentioned between the learned about the higher summity of Parnassus.

When these books were first admitted into the public libraries, I remember to have said upon occasion to several persons concerned, how I was sure they would create broils wherever they came, unless a world of care were taken; and therefore I advised that the champions of each side should be coupled together or otherwise mixed, that, like the blending of contrary poisons, their malignity might be employed among themselves. And it seems I was neither an ill prophet nor an ill counsellor; for it was nothing else but the neglect of this caution which gave occasion to the terrible fight that happened on Friday last, between the ancient and modern books in the King's Library. Now, because the talk of this battle is so fresh in everybody's mouth, and the expectation of the town so great to be informed in the particulars; I, being possessed of all qualifications requisite in an historian, and retained by neither party, have resolved to comply with the urgent *importunity of my friends* by writing down a full impartial account thereof.

The guardian of the regal library, a person of great valour but chiefly renowned for his **humanity*,° had been a fierce champion for the Moderns; and, in an engagement upon Parnassus, had vowed, with his own hands, to knock down two of the Ancient chiefs° who guarded a small pass on the superior rock; but endeavouring to climb up was cruelly

* The Honourable Mr. Boyle, in the preface to his edition of Phalaris, says he was refused a manuscript by the library-keeper, '*pro solita humanitate suâ*'.

obstructed by his own unhappy weight and tendency towards his centre, a quality to which those of the Modern party are extreme subject; for, being light-headed, they have in speculation a wonderful agility, and conceive nothing too high for them to mount; but in reducing to practice, discover a mighty pressure about their posteriors and their heels. Having thus failed in his design, the disappointed champion bore a cruel rancour to the Ancients, which he resolved to gratify by showing all marks of his favour to the books of their adversaries, and lodging them in the fairest apartments; when at the same time, whatever book had the boldness to own itself for an advocate of the Ancients, was buried alive in some obscure corner, and threatened upon the least displeasure to be turned out of doors. Besides, it so happened that about this time there was a strange confusion of place among all the books in the library,° for which several reasons were assigned. Some imputed it to a great heap of learned dust, which a perverse wind blew off from a shelf of Moderns into the keeper's eyes. Others affirmed he had a humour to pick the worms out of the schoolmen, and swallow them fresh and fasting; whereof some fell upon his spleen, and some climbed up into his head, to the great perturbation of both. And lastly, others maintained that by walking much in the dark about the library, he had quite lost the situation of it out of his head; and therefore, in replacing his books, he was apt to mistake and clap Des Cartes next to Aristotle; poor Plato had got between Hobbes and the *Seven Wise Masters*,° and Virgil was hemmed in with Dryden on one side, and Withers° on the other.

Meanwhile, those books that were advocates for the Moderns chose out one from among them to make a progress through the whole library, examine the number and strength of their party, and concert their affairs. This messenger performed all things very industriously, and brought back with him a list of their forces, in all fifty thousand, consisting chiefly of light-horse, heavy-armed foot, and mercenaries;° whereof the foot were in general but sorrily armed, and worse clad; their horses large, but extremely out of case and heart; however, some few, by trading among the Ancients, had furnished themselves tolerably enough.

While things were in this ferment, discord grew extremely high; hot words passed on both sides, and ill blood was plentifully bred. Here a solitary Ancient, squeezed up among a whole shelf of Moderns, offered fairly to dispute the case, and to prove by manifest reasons, that the priority was due to them, from long possession, and in regard of their prudence, antiquity, and, above all, their great merits towards the Moderns. But these denied the premisses, and seemed very much to wonder how the Ancients could pretend to insist upon their antiquity, when it was so plain (if they went to that) that the Moderns were much the more **ancient* of the two.° As for any obligations they owed to the Ancients, they renounced them all. ''Tis true,' said they, 'we are informed some few of our party have been so mean to borrow their subsistence from you; but the rest, infinitely the greater number (and especially we French and English), were so far from stooping to so base an example that there never passed, till this very hour, six words between us. For our horses are of our own breeding, our arms of our own forging, and our clothes of our own cutting out and sewing.' Plato was by chance upon the next shelf, and observing those that spoke to be in the ragged plight mentioned a while ago; their jades lean and foundered, their weapons of rotten wood, their armour rusty, and nothing but rags underneath; he laughed loud, and in his pleasant way swore, by G— he believed them.

Now, the Moderns had not proceeded in their late negotiation with secrecy enough to escape the notice of the enemy. For those advocates who had begun the quarrel by setting first on foot the dispute of precedency, talked so loud of coming to a battle, that Temple happened to overhear them, and gave immediate intelligence to the Ancients, who thereupon drew up their scattered troops together, resolving to act upon the defensive; upon which several of the Moderns fled over to their party, and among the rest Temple himself. This Temple, having been educated and long conversed among the Ancients, was, of all the Moderns, their greatest favourite, and became their greatest champion.

Things were at this crisis, when a material accident fell out. For, upon the highest corner of a large window, there dwelt a certain spider, swollen up to the first magnitude by the destruction of infinite numbers of flies, whose spoils lay scattered before the gates of his palace, like human bones before the cave of some giant. The avenues to his castle were guarded with turnpikes and palisadoes, all after the modern way of fortification. After you had passed several courts, you came to the centre, wherein you might behold the constable himself in his own lodgings, which had windows fronting to each avenue, and ports to sally out upon all occasions of prey or defence. In this mansion he had for some time dwelt in peace and plenty, without danger to his person by swallows from above, or to his palace by brooms from below; when it was the pleasure of fortune to conduct thither a wandering bee, to whose curiosity a broken pane in the glass had discovered itself, and in he went; where, expatiating a while, he at last happened to alight upon one of the outward walls of the spider's citadel, which, yielding to the unequal weight, sunk down to the very foundation. Thrice he endeavoured to force his passage, and thrice

* According to the modern paradox.

the centre shook. The spider within, feeling the terrible convulsion, supposed at first that nature was approaching to her final dissolution; or else that Beelzebub, with all his legions, was come to revenge the death of many thousands of his subjects, whom this enemy had slain and devoured. However, he at length valiantly resolved to issue forth, and meet his fate. Meanwhile the bee had acquitted himself of his toils, and, posted securely at some distance, was employed in cleansing his wings and disengaging them from the ragged remnants of the cobweb. By this time the spider was adventured out, when, beholding the chasms and ruins and dilapidations of his fortress, he was very near at his wit's end; he stormed and swore like a madman, and swelled till he was ready to burst. At length, casting his eye upon the bee, and wisely gathering causes from events (for they knew each other by sight), 'A plague split you,' said he, 'for a giddy son of a whore. Is it you, with a vengeance, that have made this litter here? Could you not look before you, and be d—d? Do you think I have nothing else to do (in the devil's name) but to mend and repair after your arse?'—'Good words, friend,' said the bee (having now pruned himself and being disposed to droll) 'I'll give you my hand and word to come near your kennel no more; I was never in such a confounded pickle since I was born.'—'Sirrah,' replied the spider, 'if it were not for breaking an old custom in our family never to stir abroad against an enemy, I should come and teach you better manners.'—'I pray have patience', said the bee, 'or you will spend your substance, and for aught I see, you may stand in need of it all towards the repair of your house.'—'Rogue, rogue,' replied the spider, 'yet, methinks you should have more respect to a person whom all the world allows to be so much your betters.'—'By my troth,' said the bee, 'the comparison will amount to a very good jest, and you will do me a favour to let me know the reasons that all the world is pleased to use in so hopeful a dispute.' At this the spider, having swelled himself into the size and posture of a disputant, began his argument in the true spirit of controversy with a resolution to be heartily scurrilous and angry, to urge *on* his own reasons without the least regard to the answers or objections of his opposite, and fully predetermined in his mind against all conviction.

'Not to disparage myself', said he, 'by the comparison with such a rascal, what art thou but a vagabond without house or home, without stock or inheritance? Born to no possession of your own, but a pair of wings and a drone-pipe. Your livelihood is an universal plunder upon nature; a free-booter over fields and gardens; and for the sake of stealing, will rob a nettle as readily as a violet. Whereas I am a domestic animal, furnished with a native stock within myself. This large castle (to shew my improvements in the mathematics°) is all built with my own hands, and the materials extracted altogether out of my own person.'

'I am glad', answered the bee, 'to hear you grant at least that I am come honestly by my wings and my voice; for then, it seems, I am obliged to Heaven alone for my flights and my music; and Providence would never have bestowed me two such gifts, without designing them for the noblest ends. I visit indeed all the flowers and blossoms of the field and the garden; but whatever I collect from thence enriches myself without the least injury to their beauty, their smell, or their taste. Now, for you and your skill in architecture and other mathematics, I have little to say. In that building of yours there might, for aught I know, have been labour and method enough; but, by woeful experience for us both, 'tis too plain the materials are naught, and I hope you will henceforth take warning, and consider duration and matter as well as method and art. You boast, indeed, of being obliged to no other creature but of drawing and spinning out all from yourself; that is to say, if we may judge of the liquor in the vessel by what issues out, you possess a good plentiful store of dirt and poison in your breast; and though I would by no means lessen or disparage your genuine stock of either, yet I doubt you are somewhat obliged, for an increase of both, to a little foreign assistance. Your inherent portion of dirt does not fail of acquisitions by sweepings exhaled from below; and one insect furnishes you with a share of poison to destroy another. So that, in short, the question comes all to this—Whether is the nobler being of the two, that which, by a lazy contemplation of four inches round, by an overweening pride, which feeding and engendering on itself, turns all into excrement and venom, produc[es] nothing at last but flybane and a cobweb; or that which, by an universal range, with long search, much study, true judgment, and distinction of things, brings home honey and wax.'

This dispute was managed with such eagerness, clamour, and warmth, that the two parties of books in arms below stood silent a while, waiting in suspense what would be the issue, which was not long undetermined. For the bee, grown impatient at so much loss of time, fled straight away to a bed of roses without looking for a reply, and left the spider like an orator, collected in himself, and just prepared to burst out.

It happened upon this emergency, that Æsop broke silence first. He had been of late most barbarously treated by a strange effect of the regent's humanity,° who had tore off his title-page, sorely defaced one half of his leaves, and chained him fast among a shelf of Moderns. Where, soon discovering how high the quarrel was like to proceed, he tried all his arts, and turned himself to a thousand forms. At length, in the borrowed shape of an ass,° the regent mistook him for a Modern, by which means he had time and opportunity to escape to the Ancients, just when the spider and the bee were entering into their contest, to which he gave his attention with a world of pleasure; and when it was ended, swore in the loudest key that in all his life he had never known two cases so parallel and adapt to each other, as that in the window, and this upon the shelves. 'The disputants', said he, 'have admirably managed the dispute between them, have taken in the full strength of all that is to be said on both sides, and exhausted the substance of every argument *pro* and *con*. It is but to adjust the reasonings of both to the present quarrel, then to compare and apply the labours and fruits of each, as the bee has learnedly deduced them, and we shall find the conclusions fall plain and close upon the Moderns and us. For pray, gentlemen, was ever anything so modern as the spider in his air, his turns, and his paradoxes? He argues in the behalf of you his brethren, and himself, with many boastings of his native stock and great genius; that he spins and spits wholly from himself, and scorns to own any obligation or assistance from without. Then he displays to you his great skill in architecture and improvement in the mathematics. To all this the bee, as an advocate retained by us the Ancients, thinks fit to answer—that if one may judge of the great genius or inventions of the Moderns by what they have produced, you will hardly have countenance to bear you out in boasting of either. Erect your schemes with as much method and skill as you please; yet if the materials be nothing but dirt, spun out of your own entrails (the guts of modern brains), the edifice will conclude at last in a cobweb, the duration of which, like that of other spiders' webs, may be imputed to their being forgotten, or neglected, or hid in a corner. For anything else of genuine that the Moderns may pretend to, I cannot recollect, unless it be a large vein of wrangling and satire,° much of a nature and substance with the spider's poison; which, however they pretend to spit wholly out of themselves, is improved by the same arts, by feeding upon the insects and vermin of the age. As for us, the Ancients, we are content, with the bee, to pretend to nothing of our own beyond our wings and our voice, that is to say, our flights and our language. For the rest, whatever we have got has been by infinite labour, and search, and ranging through every corner of nature; the difference is that instead of dirt and poison, we have rather chose to fill our hives with honey and wax, thus furnishing mankind with the two noblest of things, which are sweetness and light.'°

'Tis wonderful to conceive the tumult arisen among the books, upon the close of this long descant of Æsop; both parties took the hint, and heightened their animosities so on a sudden that they resolved it should come to a battle. Immediately the two main bodies withdrew under their several ensigns to the further parts of the library, and there entered into cabals and consults° upon the present emergency. The Moderns were in very warm debates upon the choice of their leaders; and nothing less than the fear impending from their enemies could have kept them from mutinies upon this occasion. The difference was greatest among the horse, where every private trooper pretended to the chief command, from Tasso and Milton to Dryden and Withers. The light-horse were commanded by Cowley and Despréaux.° There came the bowmen under their valiant leaders, Des Cartes, Gassendi, and Hobbes,° whose strength was such that they could shoot their arrows beyond the atmosphere, never to fall down again, but turn like that of Evander° into meteors; or, like the cannon-ball, into stars. Paracelsus brought a squadron of stink-pot-flingers from the snowy mountains of Rhœtia. There came a vast body of dragoons, of different nations, under the leading of Harvey, their great aga:° part armed with scythes, the weapons of death, part with lances and long knives, all steeped in poison; part shot bullets of a most malignant nature, and used white powder which infallibly killed without report. There came several bodies of heavy-armed foot, all mercenaries, under the ensigns of Guicciardine, Davila, Polydore Virgil, Buchanan, Mariana, Cambden,° and others. The engineers were commanded by Regiomontanus and Wilkins.° The rest were a confused multitude, led by Scotus, Aquinas, and Bellarmine;° of mighty bulk and stature, but without either arms, courage, or discipline. In the last place came infinite swarms of **calones*, a disorderly rout led by L'Estrange;° rogues and ragamuffins that follow the camp for nothing but the plunder, all without coats to cover them.

The army of the Ancients was much fewer in number. Homer led the horse, and Pindar the light-horse; Euclid was chief engineer; Plato and Aristotle commanded the bowmen, Herodotus and Livy the foot, Hippocrates the dragoons. The allies, led by Vossius° and Temple, brought up the rear.

All things violently tending to a decisive battle, Fame, who much frequented, and had a large apartment formerly assigned her in the regal library, fled up straight to Jupiter to whom she delivered a faithful account of all that had passed between the two parties below (for, among the gods, she always tells truth). Jove, in great concern, convokes a council in the Milky-Way. The senate assembled, he declares the occasion of convening them: a bloody battle just impendent between two mighty armies of Ancient and Modern creatures called books, wherein

* These are pamphlets, which are not bound or covered.

the celestial interest was but too deeply concerned. Momus, the patron of the Moderns, made an excellent speech in their favour, which was answered by Pallas,° the protectress of the Ancients. The assembly was divided in their affections, when Jupiter commanded the book of fate to be laid before him. Immediately were brought by Mercury three large volumes in folio containing memoirs of all things, past, present, and to come. The clasps were of silver double gilt, the covers of celestial turkey leather, and the paper such as here on earth might pass almost for vellum. Jupiter, having silently read the decree, would communicate the import to none, but presently shut up the book.

Without the doors of this assembly, there attended a vast number of light, nimble gods, menial servants to Jupiter: these are his ministering instruments in all affairs below. They travel in a caravan, more or less together, and are fastened to each other like a link of galley-slaves, by a light chain which passes from them to Jupiter's great toe; and yet, in receiving or delivering a message they may never approach above the lowest step of his throne, where he and they whisper to each other through a long hollow trunk. These deities are called by mortal men *accidents* or *events*; but the gods call them second causes.° Jupiter having delivered his message to a certain number of these divinities, they flew immediately down to the pinnacle of the regal library, and consulting a few minutes, entered unseen and disposed the parties according to their orders.

Meanwhile, Momus fearing the worst, and calling to mind an ancient prophecy which bore no very good face to his children the Moderns, bent his flight to the region of a malignant deity called Criticism. She dwelt on the top of a snowy mountain in Nova Zembla; there Momus found her extended in her den, upon the spoils of numberless volumes half devoured. At her right hand sat Ignorance, her father and husband, blind with age; at her left, Pride her mother, dressing her up in the scraps of paper herself had torn. There was Opinion her sister, light of foot, hoodwinked, and headstrong, yet giddy and perpetually turning. About her played her children, Noise and Impudence, Dulness and Vanity, Positiveness, Pedantry, and Ill-Manners. The goddess herself had claws like a cat; her head, and ears, and voice, resembled those of an ass; her teeth fallen out before, her eyes turned inward as if she looked only upon herself; her diet was the overflowing of her own gall; her spleen was so large as to stand prominent like a dug of the first rate, nor wanted excrescencies in form of teats, at which a crew of ugly monsters were greedily sucking; and what is wonderful to conceive, the bulk of spleen increased faster than the sucking could diminish it. 'Goddess,' said

Momus, 'can you sit idly here while our devout worshippers the Moderns are this minute entering into a cruel battle, and perhaps now lying under the swords of their enemies? Who then hereafter will ever sacrifice or build altars to our divinities? Haste, therefore, to the British Isle, and if possible prevent their destruction, while I make factions among the gods and gain them over to our party.'

Momus, having thus delivered himself, stayed not for an answer, but left the goddess to her own resentments. Up she rose in a rage and, as it is the form upon such occasions, began a soliloquy. ''Tis I' (said she) 'who give wisdom to infants and idiots; by me, children grow wiser than their parents; by me, beaux become politicians, and schoolboys judges of philosophy;° by me, sophisters debate and conclude upon the depths of knowledge; and coffeehouse wits, instinct by me, can correct an author's style and display his minutest errors without understanding a syllable of his matter or his language. By me, striplings spend their judgment as they do their estate, before it comes into their hands. 'Tis I who have deposed wit and knowledge from their empire over poetry, and advanced myself in their stead. And shall a few upstart Ancients dare to oppose me?—But come, my aged parents, and you my children dear, and thou my beauteous sister; let us ascend my chariot and haste to assist our devout Moderns, who are now sacrificing to us a hecatomb, as I perceive by that grateful smell which from thence reaches my nostrils.'

The goddess and her train having mounted the chariot, which was drawn by tame geese, flew over infinite regions shedding her influence in due places, till at length she arrived at her beloved island of Britain; but in hovering over its metropolis, what blessings did she not let fall upon her seminaries of Gresham and Covent Garden!° And now she reached the fatal plain of St. James's Library, at what time the two armies were upon the point to engage; where, entering with all her caravan unseen, and landing upon a case of shelves, now desert but once inhabited by a colony of virtuosos, she stayed a while to observe the posture of both armies.

But here the tender cares of a mother began to fill her thoughts and move in her breast. For, at the head of a troop of Modern bowmen, she cast her eyes upon her son Wotton, to whom the fates had assigned a very short thread; Wotton, a young hero, whom an unknown father of mortal race begot by stolen embraces with this goddess. He was the darling of his mother above all her children, and she resolved to go and comfort him. But first according to the good old custom of deities she cast about to change her shape, for fear the divinity of her countenance might dazzle his mortal sight and overcharge the rest of his senses. She therefore gathered up her person into an octavo compass: her body grew white and arid, and split in pieces with dryness; the thick turned into pasteboard, and the thin into paper, upon which her parents and children artfully strewed a black juice, or decoction of gall and soot, in form of letters; her head, and voice, and spleen, kept their primitive form, and that which before was a cover of skin did still continue so. In which guise she marched on towards the Moderns, undistinguishable in shape and dress from the divine Bentley, Wotton's dearest friend. 'Brave Wotton,' said the goddess, 'why do our troops stand idle here, to spend their present vigour and opportunity of the day? Away, let us haste to the generals and advise to give the onset immediately.' Having spoke thus, she took the ugliest of her monsters, full glutted from her spleen, and flung it invisibly into his mouth, which flying straight up into his head squeezed out his eyeballs, gave him a distorted look, and half overturned his brain. Then she privately ordered two of her beloved children, Dulness and Ill-Manners, closely to attend his person in all encounters. Having thus accoutred him she vanished in a mist, and the hero perceived it was the goddess his mother.

The destined hour of fate being now arrived, the fight began; whereof, before I dare adventure to make a particular description, I must, after the example of other authors, petition for a hundred tongues, and mouths, and hands, and pens, which would all be too little to perform so immense a work. Say, goddess, that presidest over History, who it was that first advanced in the field of battle! Paracelsus, at the head of his dragoons, observing Galen° in the adverse wing, darted his javelin with a mighty force, which the brave Ancient received upon his shield, the point breaking in the second fold. * * * * *

* * * * * * * *Hic pauca*

* * * * * * * *desunt.*°

* * * * * * * *

They bore the wounded aga on their shields to his chariot *

* * * * * * * *

Desunt * * * * * * *

nonnulla. * * * * * * *

* * * * * * * *

Then Aristotle, observing Bacon° advance with a furious mien, drew his bow to the head and let fly his arrow, which missed the valiant Modern and went hizzing over his head. But Des Cartes it hit; the steel point quickly found a defect in his head-piece; it pierced the leather and the pasteboard and went in at his right eye. The torture of the pain whirled the valiant bowman round till death, like a star of superior influence, drew him into his own vortex.°

* * * * * * * *

Ingens hiatus hic in MS. * * * * * * * * * * * * * * * *

* * * * * * * *

* * * * when Homer appeared at the head of the cavalry, mounted on a furious horse with difficulty managed by the rider himself, but which no other mortal durst approach; he rode among the enemy's ranks, and bore down all before him. Say, goddess, whom he slew first and whom he slew last! First, Gondibert° advanced against him, clad in heavy armour and mounted on a staid, sober gelding, not so famed for his speed as his docility in kneeling whenever his rider would mount or alight. He had made a vow to Pallas, that he would never leave the field till he had spoiled *Homer of his armour; madman, who had never once seen the wearer nor understood his strength! Him Homer overthrew, horse and man, to the ground, there to be trampled and choked in the dirt. Then with a long spear he slew †Denham, a stout Modern° who from his father's side derived his lineage from Apollo, but his mother was of mortal race. He fell, and bit the earth. The celestial part Apollo took and made it a star, but the terrestrial lay wallowing upon the ground. Then Homer slew Wesley° with a kick of his horse's heel; he took Perrault by mighty force out of his saddle, then hurled him at Fontenelle,° with the same blow dashing out both their brains.

On the left wing of the horse, Virgil appeared in shining armour, completely fitted to his body. He was mounted on a dapple grey steed, the slowness of whose pace was an effect of the highest mettle and vigour. He cast his eye on the adverse wing, with a desire to find an object worthy of his valour, when, behold, upon a sorrel gelding of a monstrous size appeared a foe issuing from among the thickest of the enemy's squadrons; but his speed was less than his noise, for his horse, old and lean, spent the dregs of his strength in a high trot, which though it made slow advances yet caused a loud clashing of his armour, terrible to hear. The two cavaliers had now approached within the throw of a lance, when the stranger desired a parley, and, lifting up the vizard of his helmet, a face hardly appeared from within, which after a pause was known for that of the renowned Dryden. The brave Ancient suddenly started, as one possessed with surprise and disappointment together; for the helmet was nine times too large for the head, which appeared situate far in the hinder part, even like the lady in a lobster,° or like a mouse under a canopy of

* *Vid.* Homer.

† Sir John Denham's poems are very unequal, extremely good and very indifferent; so that his detractors said he was not the real author of *Cooper's Hill*.

state, or like a shrivelled beau from within the penthouse of a modern periwig; and the voice was suited to the visage, sounding weak and remote. Dryden, in a long harangue,° soothed up the good Ancient, called him 'father', and by a large deduction of genealogies made it plainly appear that they were nearly related. Then he humbly proposed an exchange of armour, as a lasting mark of hospitality between them. Virgil consented (for the goddess Diffidence came unseen and cast a mist before his eyes), though his was of gold* and cost a hundred beeves, the other's but of rusty iron. However, this glittering armour became the Modern yet worse than his own. Then they agreed to exchange horses; but when it came to the trial, Dryden was afraid and utterly unable to mount. * * * * * * *

* * * * * * * *

* * * * * * *Alter hiatus*

* * * * * * *in MS.*

* * * * * * * *

Lucan° appeared upon a fiery horse of admirable shape, but headstrong, bearing the rider where he list over the field; he made a mighty slaughter among the enemy's horse, which destruction to stop, Blackmore,° a famous Modern (but one of the mercenaries) strenuously opposed himself and darted a javelin with a strong hand, which falling short of its mark, struck deep in the earth. Then Lucan threw a lance, but Æsculapius came unseen and turned off the point. 'Brave Modern,' said Lucan, 'I perceive some god protects you, for never did my arm so deceive me before. But what mortal can contend with a god? Therefore let us fight no longer, but present gifts to each other.' Lucan then bestowed the Modern a pair of spurs, and Blackmore gave Lucan a bridle. * * * * * * *

* * * * * * * *

Pauca de- * * * * * * *

sunt. * * * * * * *

* * * * * * * *

Creech;° but the goddess Dulness took a cloud, formed into the shape of Horace, armed and mounted, and placed it in a flying posture before him. Glad was the cavalier to begin a combat with a flying foe, and pursued the image, threatening loud, till at last it lead him to the peaceful bower of his father Ogleby,° by whom he was disarmed and assigned to his repose.

Then Pindar slew —, and —, Oldham, and — and Afra the Amazon,° light of foot. Never advancing in a direct line but wheeling with

* *Vid.* Homer

incredible agility and force, he made a terrible slaughter among the enemy's light horse. Him when Cowley° observed, his generous heart burnt within him and he advanced against the fierce Ancient, imitating his address, and pace, and career, as well as the vigour of his horse and his own skill would allow. When the two cavaliers had approached within the length of three javelins, first Cowley threw a lance, which missed Pindar, and passing into the enemy's ranks, fell ineffectual to the ground. Then Pindar darted a javelin so large and weighty that scarce a dozen cavaliers,° as cavaliers are in our degenerate days, could raise it from the ground; yet he threw it with ease, and it went by an unerring hand singing through the air; nor could the Modern have avoided present death, if he had not luckily opposed the shield that had been given him by Venus. And now both heroes drew their swords, but the Modern was so aghast and disordered that he knew not where he was; his shield dropped from his hands; thrice he fled, and thrice he could not escape. At last he turned, and lifting up his hand in the posture of a suppliant, 'Godlike Pindar,' said he, 'spare my life, and possess my horse with these arms, besides the ransom which my friends will give when they hear I am alive and your prisoner.' 'Dog!' said Pindar, 'let your ransom stay with your friends; but your carcass shall be left for the fowls of the air and the beasts of the field.' With that he raised his sword, and with a mighty stroke cleft the wretched Modern in twain, the sword pursuing the blow; and one half lay panting on the ground, to be trod in pieces by the horses' feet; the other half was borne by the frighted steed through the field. This *Venus took, washed it seven times in ambrosia, then struck it thrice with a sprig of amaranth; upon which the leather grew round and soft, and the leaves turned into feathers, and being gilded before, continued gilded still; so it became a dove, and she harnessed it to her chariot. * *
* * * * * * *Hiatus valdè de-*
* * * * * * *flendus in MS.*
* * * * * * * *

Day being far spent, and the numerous forces of the Moderns half inclining to a retreat, there issued forth from a squadron of their heavy-armed foot, a captain whose name was Bentley, in person the most deformed of all the Moderns; tall, but without shape or comeliness; large, but without strength or proportion. His armour was patched up of a thousand incoherent pieces,° and the sound of it as he marched was loud and dry, like that made by the fall of a sheet of lead which an Etesian wind° blows suddenly

The Episode of Bentley and Wotton.

* I do not approve the author's judgment in this, for I think Cowley's *Pindarics* are much preferable to his *Mistress*.

down from the roof of some steeple. His helmet was of old rusty iron, but the vizard was brass, which tainted by his breath corrupted into copperas, nor wanted gall from the same fountain; so that whenever provoked by anger or labour, an atramentous quality of most malignant nature was seen to distil from his lips. In his *right hand he grasped a flail; and (that he might never be unprovided of an *offensive* weapon) a vessel full of ordure in his left. Thus completely armed he advanced with a slow and heavy pace where the Modern chiefs were holding a consult upon the sum of things; who, as he came onwards, laughed to behold his crooked leg and hump shoulder, which his boot and armour vainly endeavouring to hide, were forced to comply with and expose. The generals made use of him for his talent of railing which, kept within government, proved frequently of great service to their cause, but at other times did more mischief than good; for at the least touch of offence, and often without any at all, he would like a wounded elephant convert it against his leaders. Such at this juncture was the disposition of Bentley: grieved to see the enemy prevail, and dissatisfied with everybody's conduct but his own. He humbly gave the Modern generals to understand that he conceived, with great submission, they were all a pack of rogues, and fools, and sons of whores, and d–mned cowards, and confounded loggerheads, and illiterate whelps, and nonsensical scoundrels; that if himself had been constituted general, those presumptuous dogs the Ancients would long before this have been beaten out of the field. †'You', said he, 'sit here idle; but when I or any other valiant Modern kill an enemy, you are sure to seize the spoil. But I will not march one foot against the foe till you all swear to me that whomever I take or kill, his arms I shall quietly possess.' Bentley having spoke thus, Scaliger,° bestowing him a sour look, 'Miscreant prater!' said he, 'eloquent only in thine own eyes, thou railest without wit, or truth, or discretion. The malignity of thy temper perverteth nature; thy learning makes thee more barbarous, thy study of humanity° more inhuman; thy converse amongst poets more grovelling, miry, and dull. All arts of civilizing others render thee rude and untractable; courts have taught thee ill manners, and polite conversation has finished thee a pedant. Besides, a greater coward burdeneth not the army. But never despond; I pass my word, whatever spoil thou takest shall certainly be thy own, though I hope that vile carcass will first become a prey to kites and worms.'

Bentley durst not reply, but half choked with spleen and rage

* The person here spoken of is famous for letting fly at everybody without distinction, and using mean and foul scurrilities.

† *Vid.* Homer. de Thersite.

withdrew, in full resolution of performing some great achievement. With him, for his aid and companion, he took his beloved Wotton; resolving by policy or surprise to attempt some neglected quarter of the Ancients' army. They began their march over carcasses of their slaughtered friends; then to the right of their own forces; then wheeled northward, till they came to Aldrovandus's tomb° which they passed on the side of the declining sun. And now they arrived, with fear, towards the enemy's out-guards, looking about if haply they might spy the quarters of the wounded, or some straggling sleepers, unarmed and remote from the rest. As when two mongrel curs, whom native greediness and domestic want provoke and join in partnership, though fearful, nightly to invade the folds of some rich grazier, they with tails depressed, and lolling tongues, creep soft and slow; meanwhile, the conscious moon, now in her zenith, on their guilty heads darts perpendicular rays; nor dare they bark, though much provoked at her refulgent visage, whether seen in puddle by reflection, or in sphere direct; but one surveys the region round, while t'other scouts the plain, if haply to discover, at distance from the flock, some carcass half devoured, the refuse of gorged wolves or ominous ravens. So marched this lovely, loving pair of friends, nor with less fear and circumspection when, at distance, they might perceive two shining suits of armour hanging upon an oak, and the owners not far off in a profound sleep. The two friends drew lots, and the pursuing of this adventure fell to Bentley; on he went, and in his van Confusion and Amaze, while Horror and Affright brought up the rear. As he came near, behold two heroes of the Ancients' army, Phalaris and Æsop, lay fast asleep. Bentley would fain have dispatched them both, and stealing close, aimed his flail at Phalaris's breast. But then the goddess Affright interposing caught the Modern in her icy arms, and dragged him from the danger she foresaw; for both the dormant heroes happened to turn at the same instant, though soundly sleeping and busy in a dream. *For Phalaris was just that minute dreaming how a most vile poetaster had lampooned him, and how he had got him roaring in his bull.° And Æsop dreamed that as he and the Ancient chiefs were lying on the ground, a wild ass broke loose, ran about, trampling and kicking and dunging in their faces. Bentley, leaving the two heroes asleep, seized on both their armours and withdrew in quest of his darling Wotton.

He in the meantime had wandered long in search of some enterprize, till at length he arrived at a small rivulet that issued from a fountain hard by, called in the language of mortal men, Helicon. Here he stopped, and

* This is according to Homer, who tells the dreams of those who were killed in their sleep.

parched with thirst resolved to allay it in this limpid stream. Thrice with profane hands he essayed to raise the water to his lips, and thrice it slipped all through his fingers. Then he stooped prone on his breast, but ere his mouth had kissed the liquid crystal, Apollo came and in the channel held his shield betwixt the Modern and the fountain, so that he drew up nothing but mud. For, although no fountain on earth can compare with the clearness of Helicon, yet there lies at bottom a thick sediment of slime and mud; for so Apollo begged of Jupiter, as a punishment to those who durst attempt to taste it with unhallowed lips, and for a lesson to all not to *draw too deep* or *far from the spring*.

At the fountain-head Wotton discerned two heroes. The one he could not distinguish but the other was soon known for Temple, general of the allies to the Ancients. His back was turned, and he was employed in drinking large draughts in his helmet from the fountain, where he had withdrawn himself to rest from the toils of the war. Wotton, observing him, with quaking knees and trembling hands spoke thus to himself:* 'O that I could kill this destroyer of our army, what renown should I purchase among the chiefs! But to issue out against him, man for man, shield against shield, and lance against lance, what Modern of us dare? For he fights like a god, and Pallas or Apollo are ever at his elbow. But, O mother! if what Fame reports be true, that I am the son of so great a goddess, grant me to hit Temple with this lance that the stroke may send him to hell, and that I may return in safety and triumph, laden with his spoils.' The first part of his prayer, the gods granted at the intercession of his mother and of Momus; but the rest, by a perverse wind sent from Fate, was scattered in the air. Then Wotton grasped his lance, and brandishing it thrice over his head, darted it with all his might, the goddess, his mother, at the same time adding strength to his arm. Away the lance went hizzing, and reached even to the belt of the averted Ancient, upon which, lightly grazing, it fell to the ground. Temple neither felt the weapon touch him, nor heard it fall; and Wotton might have escaped to his army, with the honour of having remitted his lance against so great a leader, unrevenged; but Apollo, enraged that a javelin flung by the assistance of so foul a goddess should pollute his fountain, put on the shape of ———,° and softly came to young Boyle, who then accompanied Temple. He pointed first to the lance, then to the distant Modern that flung it, and commanded the young hero to take immediate revenge. Boyle, clad in a suit of armour which had been *given him by all the gods*, immediately advanced against the trembling foe, who now fled before him. As a young lion in the Libyan plains, or Araby desert, sent by

* *Vid.* Homer.

his aged sire to hunt for prey, or health, or exercise, he scours along wishing to meet some tiger from the mountains or a furious boar; if chance a wild ass, with brayings importune, affronts his ear, the generous beast, though loathing to distain his claws with blood so vile, yet much provoked at the offensive noise which Echo, foolish nymph, like her ill-judging sex, repeats much louder and with more delight than Philomela's song, he vindicates the honour of the forest, and hunts the noisy long-eared animal. So Wotton fled, so Boyle pursued. But Wotton, heavy-armed and slow of foot, began to slack his course, when his lover Bentley appeared, returning laden with the spoils of the two sleeping Ancients. Boyle observed him well, and soon discovering the helmet and shield of Phalaris his friend, both which he had lately with his own hands new polished and gilded,° rage sparkled in his eyes, and leaving his pursuit after Wotton, he furiously rushed on against this new approacher. Fain would he be revenged on both, but both now fled different ways. And, as a woman *in a little house, that gets a painful livelihood by spinning,†if chance her geese be scattered o'er the common, she courses round the plain from side to side, compelling here and there the stragglers to the flock; they cackle loud, and flutter o'er the champaign,—so Boyle pursued, so fled this pair of friends. Finding at length their flight was vain, they bravely joined, and drew themselves in phalanx. First, Bentley threw a spear with all his force, hoping to pierce the enemy's breast; but Pallas came unseen, and in the air took off the point and clapped on one of lead, which, after a dead bang against the enemy's shield, fell blunted to the ground. Then Boyle, observing well his time, took a lance of wondrous length and sharpness; and as this pair of friends compacted stood close side to side, he wheeled him to the right, and with unusual force darted the weapon. Bentley saw his fate approach, and flanking down his arms close to his ribs, hoping to save his body, in went the point passing through arm and side, nor stopped or spent its force till it had also pierced the valiant Wotton, who, going to sustain his dying friend, shared his fate. As when a skilful cook has trussed a brace of woodcocks, he with iron skewer pierces the tender sides of both, their legs and wings close pinioned to the ribs; so was this pair of friends transfixed, till down they fell, joined in their lives, joined in their deaths; so closely joined that Charon will mistake them both for one and waft them over Styx for half his fare. Farewell, beloved loving pair!

* *Vid.* Homer.

† This is also after the manner of Homer; the woman's getting a painful livelihood by spinning, has nothing to do with the similitude, nor would be excusable without such an authority.

Few equals have you left behind. And happy and immortal shall you be, if all my wit and eloquence can make you.

And, now * * * * * *
* * * * * * * *
* * * * * * * *
* * *Desunt cætera.*

A DISCOURSE Concerning the Mechanical Operation of the SPIRIT. IN A LETTER *To a FRIEND.* A FRAGMENT.

THE BOOKSELLER'S ADVERTISEMENT.

THE following Discourse came into my hands perfect and entire. But there being several things in it which the present age would not very well bear, I kept it by me some years, resolving it should never see the light. At length, by the advice and assistance of a judicious friend, I retrenched those parts that might give most offence, and have now ventured to publish the remainder. Concerning the author I am wholly ignorant, neither can I conjecture whether it be the same with that of the two foregoing pieces, the original having been sent me at a different time, and in a different hand. The learned reader will better determine; to whose judgement I entirely submit it.

For T. H. *Esquire,*° *at his Chambers in the Academy of the* Beaux Esprits *in* New Holland.°

Sir,

IT is now a good while since I have had in my head something not only very material, but absolutely necessary to my health, that the world should be informed in. For to tell you a secret, I am able to *contain* it no longer. However, I have been perplexed for some time to resolve what would be the most proper form to send it abroad in. To which end I have three days been coursing through Westminster Hall, and St. Paul's Churchyard, and Fleet Street, to peruse titles, and I do not find any which holds so general a vogue as that of *A Letter to a Friend.* Nothing is more common than to meet with long epistles addressed to persons and places where, at first thinking, one would be apt to imagine it not altogether so necessary or convenient; such as *a Neighbour at next Door*, *a mortal Enemy*, *a perfect Stranger*, or *a Person of Quality in the Clouds*; and

This Discourse is not altogether equal to the two former, the best parts of it being omitted; whether the bookseller's account be true, that he durst not print the rest, I know not; nor indeed is it easy to determine whether he may be relied on in anything he says of this or the former treatises, only as to the time they were writ in, which however appears more from the discourses themselves than his relation.

these upon subjects in appearance the least proper for conveyance by the post; as *long schemes in philosophy*; *dark and wonderful mysteries of state*; *laborious dissertations in criticism and philosophy*; *advice to parliaments*, and the like.

Now, Sir, to proceed after the method in present wear—for let me say what I will to the contrary, I am afraid you will publish this letter, as soon as ever it comes to your hands—I desire you will be my witness to the world how careless and sudden a scribble it has been; that it was but yesterday when you and I began accidentally to fall into discourse on this matter; that I was not very well when we parted; that the post is in such haste, I have had no manner of time to digest it into order or correct the style. And if any other modern excuses for haste and negligence shall occur to you in reading, I beg you to insert them, faithfully promising they shall be thankfully acknowledged.

Pray, Sir, in your next letter to the *Iroquois Virtuosi*,° do me the favour to present my humble service to that illustrious body, and assure them I shall send an account of those phenomena, as soon as we can determine them at Gresham.

I have not had a line from the *Literati* of Tobinambou these three last ordinaries.

And now, Sir, having dispatched what I had to say of forms, or of business, let me entreat you will suffer me to proceed upon my subject, and to pardon me if I make no further use of the epistolary style till I come to conclude.

SECTION I.

'Tis recorded of Mahomet that, upon a visit he was going to pay in Paradise, he had an offer of several vehicles to conduct him upwards, as fiery chariots, winged horses, and celestial sedans; but he refused them all and would be borne to Heaven upon nothing but his *ass*. Now this inclination of Mahomet, as singular as it seems, hath been since taken up by a great number of devout Christians, and doubtless with very good reason. For, since that Arabian is known to have borrowed a moiety of his religious system from the Christian faith, it is but just he should pay reprisals to such as would challenge them; wherein the good people of England, to do them all right, have not been backward. For though there is not any other nation in the world so plentifully provided with carriages for that journey, either as to safety or ease, yet there are abundance of us who will not be satisfied with any other machine beside this of Mahomet.

For my own part I must confess to bear a very singular respect to this animal, by whom I take human nature to be most admirably held forth in all its qualities as well as operations. And therefore whatever in my small reading occurs concerning this our fellow creature, I do never fail to set it down by way of commonplace; and when I have occasion to write upon human reason, politics, eloquence, or knowledge, I lay my *memorandums* before me and insert them with a wonderful facility of application. However, among all the qualifications ascribed to this distinguished brute by ancient or modern authors I cannot remember this talent of bearing his rider to Heaven has been recorded for a part of his character, except in the two examples mentioned already. Therefore I conceive the methods of this art to be a point of useful knowledge in very few hands, and which the learned world would gladly be better informed in. This is what I have undertaken to perform in the following discourse. For, towards the operation already mentioned many peculiar properties are required both in the *rider* and the *ass* which I shall endeavour to set in as clear a light as I can.

But, because I am resolved by all means to avoid giving offence to any party whatever, I will leave off discoursing so closely to the *letter* as I have hitherto done, and go on for the future by way of allegory, though in such a manner that the judicious reader may without much straining make his applications as often as he shall think fit. Therefore, if you please, from henceforward instead of the term *ass* we shall make use of *gifted* or *enlightened teacher*; and the word *rider* we will exchange for that of *fanatic auditory*, or any other denomination of the like import. Having settled this weighty point, the great subject of inquiry before us is to examine by what methods this *teacher* arrives at his *gifts*, or *spirit*, or *light*; and by what intercourse between him and his assembly it is cultivated and supported.

In all my writings I have had constant regard to this great end, not to suit and apply them to particular occasions and circumstances of time, of place, or of person; but to calculate them for universal nature and mankind in general. And of such catholic use I esteem this present disquisition; for I do not remember any other temper of body or quality of mind, wherein all nations and ages of the world have so unanimously agreed as that of a *fanatic* strain, or tincture of *enthusiasm*; which, improved by certain persons or societies of men and by them practised upon the rest, has been able to produce revolutions of the greatest figure in history, as will soon appear to those who know anything of Arabia, Persia, India, or China, of Morocco and Peru. Farther, it has possessed as great a power in the kingdom of knowledge, where it is hard to assign one art or science which has not annexed to it some *fanatic* branch: such are the *Philosopher's Stone*, *The Grand Elixir*,* *The Planetary Worlds*,° *The Squaring of the Circle*,° *The Summum Bonum*, *Utopian Commonwealths*, with some others of less or subordinate note; which all serve for nothing else but to employ or amuse this grain of *enthusiasm*, dealt into every composition.

But if this plant has found a root in the fields of *empire* and of *knowledge*, it has fixed deeper and spread yet further upon *holy ground*. Wherein, though it hath passed under the general name of *enthusiasm* and perhaps arisen from the same original, yet hath it produced certain branches of a very different nature, however often mistaken for each other. The word in its universal acceptation may be defined, a *lifting up of the soul*, *or its faculties*, *above matter*. This description will hold good in general; but I am only to understand it as applied to *religion*, wherein there are three general ways of ejaculating the soul, or transporting it beyond the sphere of matter. The first is the immediate act of God, and is called *prophecy* or *inspiration*. The second is the immediate act of the Devil, and is termed *possession*. The third is the product of natural causes, the effect of strong imagination, spleen, violent anger, fear, grief, pain, and the like. These three have been abundantly treated on by authors and therefore shall not employ my enquiry. But the fourth method of *religious enthusiasm* or launching out the soul, as it is purely an effect of artifice and *mechanic operation*, has been sparingly handled or not at all by any writer; because, though it is an art of great antiquity, yet having been confined to few persons, it long wanted those advancements and refinements which it afterwards met with since it has grown so epidemic and fallen into so many cultivating hands.

It is, therefore, upon this *Mechanical Operation of the Spirit* that I mean to treat, as it is at present performed by our *British Workmen*. I shall deliver to the reader the result of many judicious observations upon the matter, tracing as near as I can the whole course and method of this *trade*, producing parallel instances, and relating certain discoveries that have luckily fallen in my way.

I have said that there is one branch of *religious enthusiasm* which is purely an effect of Nature whereas the part I mean to handle is wholly an effect of art which, however, is inclined to work upon certain natures and constitutions more than others. Besides, there is many an operation which in its original was purely an artifice but through a long succession of ages hath grown to be natural. Hippocrates tells us° that among our ancestors the Scythians there was a nation called *Longheads*,† which at first began, by a custom among midwives and nurses, of moulding, and

* Some writers hold them for the same, others not. † Macrocephali.

squeezing, and bracing up the heads of infants, by which means Nature, shut out at one passage, was forced to seek another, and finding room above, shot upwards in the form of a sugar-loaf; and being diverted that way for some generations, at last found it out of herself, needing no assistance from the nurse's hand. This was the original of the *Scythian Longheads* and thus did custom, from being a second nature, proceed to be a first. To all which there is something very analogous among us of this nation, who are the undoubted posterity of that refined people. For, in the age of our fathers, there arose a generation of men in this island called *Roundheads*,° whose race is now spread over three kingdoms, yet in its beginning was merely an operation of art, produced by a pair of scissors, a squeeze of the face, and a black cap. These heads thus formed into a perfect sphere in all assemblies were most exposed to the view of the female sort, which did influence their conceptions so effectually that nature at last took the hint and did it of herself; so that a *Roundhead* has been ever since as familiar a sight among us as a *Longhead* among the Scythians.

Upon these examples and others easy to produce, I desire the curious reader to distinguish first, between an effect grown from *Art* into *Nature*, and one that is natural from its beginning; secondly, between an effect wholly natural, and one which has only a natural foundation but where the superstructure is entirely artificial. For the first and the last of these I understand to come within the districts of my subject. And having obtained these allowances, they will serve to remove any objections that may be raised hereafter against what I shall advance.

The practitioners of this famous art proceed in general upon the following fundamental,° that *the corruption of the senses is the generation of the spirit*; because the *senses* in men are so many avenues to the fort of *reason*, which in this operation is wholly blocked up. All endeavours must be therefore used, either to divert, bind up, stupify, fluster, and amuse the *senses*, or else to justle them out of their stations; and while they are either absent or otherwise employed, or engaged in a civil war against each other, the spirit enters and performs its part.

Now the usual methods of managing the senses upon such conjunctures are what I shall be very particular in delivering, as far as it is lawful for me to do; but having had the honour to be initiated into the mysteries of every society, I desire to be excused from divulging any rites wherein the *profane* must have no part.

But here, before I can proceed further, a very dangerous objection must, if possible, be removed: for it is positively denied by certain critics that the *spirit* can by any means be introduced into an assembly of modern saints,° the disparity being so great in many material circumstances, between the primitive way of inspiration and that which is practised in the present age. This they pretend to prove from the second chapter of the *Acts*° where, comparing both, it appears first, that *the apostles were gathered together with one accord, in one place*; by which is meant an universal agreement in opinion and form of worship; a harmony (say they) so far from being found between any two conventicles among us that it is in vain to expect it between any two heads in the same. Secondly, the *spirit* instructed the apostles in the gift of speaking several languages, a knowledge so remote from our dealers in this art that they neither understand propriety of words or phrases in their own. Lastly (say these objectors) the modern artists do utterly exclude all approaches of the *spirit*, and bar up its ancient way of entering, by covering themselves so close and so industriously a-top. For they will needs have it as a point clearly gained that the *Cloven Tongues* never sat upon the apostles' heads while their hats were on.°

Now, the force of these objections seems to consist in the different acceptation of the word *spirit*, which, if it be understood for a supernatural assistance approaching from without, the objectors have reason and their assertions may be allowed; but the *spirit* we treat of here proceeding entirely from within, the argument of these adversaries is wholly eluded. And upon the same account, our modern artificers find it an expedient of absolute necessity to cover their heads as close as they can, in order to prevent perspiration, than which nothing is observed to be a greater spender of Mechanic Light, as we may perhaps further show in convenient place.

To proceed therefore upon the phenomenon of *Spiritual Mechanism*, it is here to be noted that in forming and working up the *spirit*, the assembly has a considerable share as well as the preacher. The method of this *arcanum* is as follows. They violently strain their eyeballs inward, half closing the lids; then, as they sit, they are in a perpetual motion of *see-saw* making long hums at proper periods and continuing the sound at equal height, choosing their time in those intermissions while the preacher is at ebb. Neither is this practice, in any part of it, so singular or improbable as not to be traced in distant regions from reading and observation. For first, the *Jauguis**° or enlightened saints of India see all their visions by help of an acquired straining and pressure of the eyes. Secondly, the art of *see-saw* on a beam and swinging by session upon a cord, in order to raise artificial ecstasies, hath been derived to us from our Scythian† ancestors where it is practised at this day among the women. Lastly, the

* Bernier, *Mem. de Mogol.* † Guagnini *Hist. Sarmat.*°

whole proceeding as I have here related it is performed by the natives of Ireland with a considerable improvement; and it is granted that this noble nation hath of all others admitted fewer corruptions, and degenerated least from the purity of the old Tartars. Now, it is usual for a knot of Irish, men and women, to abstract themselves from matter, bind up all their senses, grow visionary and spiritual, by influence of a short pipe of tobacco, handed round the company; each preserving the smoke in his mouth till it comes again to his turn to take it in fresh: at the same time there is a consort of a continued gentle hum, repeated and renewed by instinct as occasion requires, and they move their bodies up and down to a degree that sometimes their heads and points lie parallel to the horizon. Meanwhile you may observe their eyes turned up in the posture of one who endeavours to keep himself awake; by which, and many other symptoms among them, it manifestly appears that the reasoning faculties are all suspended and superseded, that imagination hath usurped the seat, scattering a thousand deliriums over the brain. Returning from this digression, I shall describe the methods by which the *spirit* approaches. The eyes being disposed according to art, at first you can see nothing, but after a short pause a small glimmering light begins to appear and dance before you. Then, by frequently moving your body up and down, you perceive the vapours to ascend very fast, till you are perfectly dosed and flustered like one who drinks too much in a morning. Meanwhile the preacher is also at work. He begins a loud hum which pierces you quite through; this is immediately returned by the audience, and you find yourself prompted to imitate them by a mere spontaneous impulse, without knowing what you do. The *interstitia* are duly filled up by the preacher to prevent too long a pause, under which the *spirit* would soon faint and grow languid.

This is all I am allowed to discover about the progress of the *spirit* with relation to that part which is borne by the *assembly*. But in the methods of the preacher to which I now proceed, I shall be more large and particular.

SECTION II.

You will read it very gravely remarked in the books of those illustrious and right eloquent penmen, the modern travellers, that the fundamental difference in point of religion between the wild Indians and us, lies in this; that we worship *God*, and they worship the *devil*. But there are certain critics who will by no means admit of this distinction; rather believing, that all nations whatsoever adore the *true God* because they seem to intend their devotions to some invisible power of greatest *goodness* and *ability* to help them, which perhaps will take in the brightest attributes ascribed to the divinity. Others, again, inform us that those idolators adore two *principles*, the *principle* of *good*, and that of *evil*; which indeed I am apt to look upon as the most universal notion that mankind, by the mere light of nature, ever entertained of things invisible. How this idea hath been managed by the Indians and us, and with what advantage to the understandings of either, may deserve well to be examined. To me, the difference appears little more than this that they are put oftener upon their knees by their *fears*, and we by our *desires*; that the former set them a-*praying*, and us a-*cursing*. What I applaud them for is their discretion in limiting their devotions and their deities to their several districts, nor ever suffering the liturgy of the *white* God to cross or interfere with that of the *black*. Not so with us, who pretending by the lines and measures of our reason to extend the dominion of one invisible power and contract that of the other, have discovered a gross ignorance in the natures of good and evil, and most horribly confounded the frontiers of both. After men have lifted up the throne of their divinity to the *cœlum empyræum*, adorned him with all such qualities and accomplishments as themselves seem most to value and possess: after they have sunk their *principle of evil* to the lowest centre, bound him with chains, loaded him with curses, furnished him with viler dispositions than any *rake-hell* of the town, accoutred him with tail, and horns, and huge claws, and saucer eyes; I laugh aloud to see these reasoners at the same time engaged in wise dispute about certain walks and purlieus, whether they are in the verge of God or the devil, seriously debating whether such and such influences come into men's minds from above or below, or whether certain passions and affections are guided by the evil spirit or the good.

> Dum fas atque nefas exiguo fine libidinum
> Discernunt avidi —°

Thus do men establish a fellowship of Christ with Belial, and such is the analogy they make between *Cloven Tongues* and *Cloven Feet*. Of the like nature is the disquisition before us. It hath continued these hundred years an even debate whether the deportment and the cant of our English enthusiastic preachers were *possession* or *inspiration*, and a world of argument has been drained on either side, perhaps to little purpose. For, I think it is in *life* as in *tragedy*, where it is held a conviction of great defect, both in order and invention, to interpose the assistance of preternatural power without an absolute and last necessity. However, it is a sketch of human vanity for every individual to imagine the whole universe is interessed in his meanest concern. If he hath got cleanly over a kennel, some angel unseen descended on purpose to help him by the hand; if he hath knocked his head against a post, it was the devil, for his sins, let loose from hell on purpose to *buffet* him. Who that sees a little paltry mortal, droning, and dreaming, and drivelling to a multitude, can think it agreeable to common good sense that either Heaven or Hell should be put to the trouble of influence or inspection upon what he is about? Therefore I am resolved immediately to weed this error out of mankind, by making it clear that this mystery of venting spiritual gifts is nothing but a *trade*, acquired by as much instruction and mastered by equal practice and application, as others are. This will best appear by describing and deducing the whole process of the operation, as variously as it hath fallen under my knowledge or experience.

* * * * * * * *
* * * * * * * *

* * * * * *Here the whole scheme of*
* * * * * *spiritual mechanism was de-*
* * * * * *duced and explained, with an*
* * * * * *appearance of great reading*
* * * * * *and observation; but it was*
* * * * * *thought neither safe nor con-*
* * * * * *venient to print it.*

* * * * * * * *
* * * * * * * *

Here it may not be amiss to add a few words upon the laudable practice of wearing *quilted caps*, which is not a matter of mere custom, humour, or fashion, as some would pretend, but an institution of great sagacity and use; these, when moistened with sweat, stop all perspiration, and by reverberating the heat prevent the spirit from evaporating any way but at the mouth: even as a skilful housewife, that covers her still with a wet clout for the same reason, and finds the same effect. For it is the opinion of choice *virtuosi* that the brain is only a crowd of little animals, but with teeth and claws extremely sharp, and therefore cling together in the contexture we behold, like the picture of Hobbes's *Leviathan*,° or like bees in perpendicular swarm upon a tree, or like a carrion corrupted into vermin, still preserving the shape and figure of the mother animal; that all invention is formed by the morsure of two or more of these animals upon certain capillary nerves which proceed from thence, whereof three branches spread into the tongue, and two into the right hand. They hold also, that these animals are of a constitution extremely cold; that their food is the air we attract, their excrement phlegm; and that what we vulgarly call rheums, and colds, and distillations, is nothing else but an epidemical looseness to which that little commonwealth is very subject from the climate it lies under. Further, that nothing less than a violent heat can disentangle these creatures from their hamated station of life, or give them vigour and humour to imprint the marks of their little teeth. That if the morsure be hexagonal, it produces Poetry; the circular gives Eloquence; if the bite hath been conical, the person whose nerve is so affected shall be disposed to write upon Politics; and so of the rest.

I shall now discourse briefly, by what kind of practices the voice is best governed towards the composition and improvement of the *spirit*; for, without a competent skill in tuning and toning each word and syllable and letter to their due cadence, the whole operation is incomplete, misses entirely of its effect on the hearers, and puts the workman himself to continual pains for new supplies without success. For it is to be understood, that in the language of the spirit, *cant* and *droning* supply the place of *sense* and *reason* in the language of men: because in spiritual harangues the disposition of the words according to the art of grammar hath not the least use, but the skill and influence wholly lie in the choice and cadence of the syllables;° even as a discreet *composer*, who in setting a song, changes the words and order so often that he is forced to make it *nonsense* before he can make it *music*. For this reason, it hath been held by some that the Art of Canting is ever in greatest perfection when managed by *ignorance*; which is thought to be enigmatically meant by Plutarch° when he tells us that the best musical instruments were made from the bones of an *ass*. And the profounder critics upon that passage are of opinion, the word in its genuine signification means no other than a jaw-bone, though some rather think it to have been the *os sacrum*; but in so nice a case I shall not take upon me to decide. The curious are at liberty to *pick* from it whatever they please.

The first ingredient towards the Art of Canting is a competent share of *inward light*; that is to say, a large memory plentifully fraught with theological polysyllables and mysterious texts from holy writ, applied and digested by those methods and mechanical operations already related: the bearers of this *light* resembling lanterns compact of leaves from old Geneva Bibles; which invention, Sir H[u]mphrey Edw[i]n,° during his mayoralty, of happy memory, highly approved and advanced, affirming the Scripture to be now fulfilled where it says, *Thy word is a lantern to my feet, and a light to my paths.*°

Now, the Art of *Canting*° consists in skilfully adapting the voice to whatever words the spirit delivers, that each may strike the ears of the audience with its most significant cadence. The force or energy of this eloquence is not to be found, as among ancient orators, in the disposition of words to a sentence or the turning of long periods, but agreeable to the modern refinements in music, is taken up wholly in dwelling and dilating upon syllables and letters. Thus it is frequent for a single *vowel* to draw sighs from a multitude, and for a whole assembly of saints to sob to the music of one solitary *liquid*. But these are trifles, when even sounds inarticulate are observed to produce as forcible effects. A master workman shall *blow his nose so powerfully* as to pierce the hearts of his people, who are disposed to receive the *excrements* of his brain with the same reverence as the *issue* of it. Hawking, spitting, and belching, the defects of other men's rhetoric, are the flowers and figures and ornaments of his. For, the *spirit* being the same in all, it is of no import through what vehicle it is conveyed.

It is a point of too much difficulty to draw the principles of this famous art within the compass of certain adequate rules. However, perhaps I may one day oblige the world with my critical essay upon the Art of *Canting*,° *philosophically*, *physically*, *and musically considered.*

But, among all improvements of the *spirit* wherein the voice hath borne a part, there is none to be compared with that of *conveying the sound through the nose*, which under the denomination of *snuffling** hath passed with so great applause in the world. The originals of this institution are very dark, but having been initiated into the mystery of it, and leave being given me to publish it to the world, I shall deliver as direct a relation as I can.

This art, like many other famous inventions, owed its birth or at least improvement and perfection, to an effect of chance, but was established upon solid reasons and hath flourished in this island ever since with great lustre. All agree that it first appeared upon the decay and discouragement of *bagpipes*, which having long suffered under the mortal hatred of the *brethren*, tottered for a time, and at last fell with *monarchy*. The story is thus related.

As yet *snuffling* was not, when the following adventure happened to a *Banbury saint*.° Upon a certain day, while he was far engaged among the tabernacles of the *wicked*, he felt the outward man put into odd commotions, and strangely pricked forward by the inward; an effect very usual among the modern inspired. For, some think that the *spirit* is apt to feed on the *flesh*, like hungry wines upon raw beef. Others rather believe there is a perpetual game at *leap-frog* between both, and sometimes the *flesh* is uppermost, and sometimes the *spirit*; adding that the former,

* The *snuffling* of men who have lost their noses by lewd courses is said to have given rise to that tone, which our dissenters did too much affect. W. WOTTON.

while it is in the state of a *rider*, wears huge Rippon spurs,° and when it comes to the turn of being *bearer*, is wonderfully headstrong and hard-mouthed. However it came about, the *saint* felt his *vessel* full *extended* in every part (a very natural effect of strong *inspiration*), and the place and time falling out so unluckily that he could not have the convenience of evacuating upwards by repetition, prayer, or lecture,° he was forced to open an inferior vent. In short, he wrestled with the flesh so long that he at length subdued it, coming off with honourable wounds, all *before*. The surgeon had now cured the parts primarily affected, but the disease, driven from its post, flew up into his head; and, as a skilful general, valiantly attacked in his trenches and beaten from the field, by flying marches withdraws to the capital city, breaking down the bridges to prevent pursuit; so the disease, repelled from its first station, fled before the *Rod* of *Hermes*° to the upper region, there fortifying itself; but finding the foe making attacks at the *nose*, broke down the *bridge*, and retired to the *head*-quarters. Now, the naturalists observe that there is in human noses an *idiosyncrasy*, by virtue of which the more the passage is obstructed, the more our speech delights to go through, as the music of a flageolet is made by the *stops*. By this method the twang of the nose becomes perfectly to resemble the *snuffle* of a bagpipe,° and is found to be equally attractive of British ears; whereof the saint had sudden experience by practising his new faculty with wonderful success in the operation of the *spirit*. For, in a short time, no doctrine passed for sound and orthodox unless it were delivered through the nose. Straight, every pastor copied after this original, and those who could not otherwise arrive to a perfection, spirited by a noble zeal, made use of the same experiment to acquire it. So that I think it may be truly affirmed, the *saints* owe their empire to the *snuffling* of one animal as Darius did his to the *neighing* of another, and both stratagems were performed by the same art; for we read how the *Persian beast* acquired his faculty by *covering a mare* the day before.*°

I should now have done, if I were not convinced that whatever I have yet advanced upon this subject is liable to great exception. For allowing all I have said to be true, it may still be justly objected that there is, in the commonwealth of *artificial enthusiasm*, some real foundation for art to work upon in the temper and complexion of individuals, which other mortals seem to want. Observe but the gesture, the motion, and the countenance, of some choice professors though in their most familiar actions, you will find them of a different race from the rest of human creatures. Remark your commonest pretender to a light *within*, how

* Herodot.

dark, and dirty, and gloomy he is *without*; as lanterns which, the more light they bear in their bodies, cast out so much the more soot and smoke and fuliginous matter to adhere to the sides. Listen but to their ordinary talk, and look on the mouth that delivers it; you will imagine you are hearing some ancient oracle, and your understanding will be *equally* informed. Upon these and the like reasons, certain objectors pretend to put it beyond all doubt that there must be a sort of preternatural *spirit* possessing the heads of the modern saints; and some will have it to be the *heat* of zeal working upon the *dregs* of ignorance, as other *spirits* are produced from *lees* by the force of fire. Some again think that when our earthly tabernacles are disordered and desolate, shaken and out of repair, the *spirit* delights to dwell within them, as houses are said to be haunted when they are forsaken and gone to decay.

To set this matter in as fair a light as possible, I shall here very briefly deduce the history of *Fanaticism* from the most early ages to the present. And if we are able to fix upon any one material or fundamental point wherein the chief professors have universally agreed, I think we may reasonably lay hold on that and assign it for the great seed or principle of the *spirit*.

The most early traces we meet with of *fanatics* in ancient story° are among the Egyptians, who instituted those rites, known in Greece by the names of *Orgia*,° *Panegyres*,° and *Dionysia*,° whether introduced there by Orpheus° or Melampus° we shall not dispute at present, nor in all likelihood at any time for the future.* These feasts were celebrated to the honour of Osiris, whom the Grecians called Dionysius and is the same with Bacchus, which has betrayed some superficial readers to imagine that the whole business was nothing more than a set of roaring, scouring companions, overcharged with wine; but this is a scandalous mistake foisted on the world by a sort of modern authors who have too *literal* an understanding and, because antiquity is to be traced *backwards*, do therefore like Jews begin their books at the wrong end, as if learning were a sort of *conjuring*. These are the men who pretend to understand a book by scouting through the *index*,° as if a traveller should go about to describe a *palace* when he had seen nothing but the privy; or like certain fortune-tellers in North America who have a way of reading a man's destiny by peeping in his *breech*. For, at the time of instituting these mysteries there was not one vine in all Egypt,† the natives drinking nothing but *ale*; which liquor seems to have been far more ancient than wine and has the honour of owing its invention and progress not only to

* Diod. Sic. L. 1.° Plut. *de Iside et Osiride*.
† Herod. L. 2.°

the Egyptian Osiris,* but to the Grecian Bacchus, who in their famous expedition, carried the receipt of it along with them, and gave it to the nations they visited or subdued. Besides, Bacchus himself was very seldom or never drunk; for it is recorded of him that he was the first inventor of the *mitre*,† which he wore continually on his head (as the whole company of bacchanals did) to prevent vapours and the headache after hard drinking. And for this reason (say some) the *Scarlet Whore*,° when she makes the kings of the earth drunk with her cup of abomination, is always sober herself though she never balks the glass in her turn, being it seems kept upon her legs by the virtue of her *triple mitre*. Now, these feasts were instituted in imitation of the famous expedition Osiris made through the world, and of the company that attended him, whereof the bacchanalian ceremonies were so many types and symbols. From which account‡ it is manifest that the fanatic rites of these bacchanals cannot be imputed to intoxications by wine, but must needs have had a deeper foundation. What this was, we may gather large hints from certain circumstances in the course of their mysteries. For, in the first place, there was in their processions an entire *mixture and confusion of sexes*; they affected to ramble about hills and deserts. Their garlands were of *ivy* and *vine*, emblems of cleaving and clinging; or of *fir*, the parent of *turpentine*. It is added that they imitated *satyrs*, were attended by *goats* and rode upon *asses*, all companions of great skill and practice in affairs of gallantry. They bore for their ensigns certain curious figures perched upon long poles, made into the shape and size of the *virga genitalis*, with its *appurtenances*, which were so many shadows and emblems of the whole mystery; as well as trophies set up by the female conquerors. Lastly, in a certain town of Attica, the whole solemnity stripped of all its types§ was performed in *puris naturalibus*, the votaries not flying in coveys but sorted into couples. The same may be farther conjectured from the death of Orpheus, one of the institutors of these mysteries, who was torn in pieces by women because he refused to *communicate his orgies* to them;¶ which others explained by telling us he had castrated himself upon grief for the loss of his wife.

Omitting many others of less note, the next *fanatics* we meet with of any eminence, were the numerous sects of *heretics* appearing in the five first centuries of the *Christian era*, from Simon Magus and his followers to those of Eutyches.° I have collected their systems from infinite reading,

* Diod Sic. L. 1 and 3. † Id. L. 4.

‡ See the particulars in Diod. Sic. L. 1 and 3.

§ Dionysia Brauronia.°

¶ *Vide* Photium in excerptis è Conone.°

and comparing them with those of their successors in the several ages since, I find there are certain bounds set even to the irregularities of human thought, and those a great deal narrower than is commonly apprehended. For, as they all frequently interfere even in their wildest ravings, so there is one fundamental point wherein they are sure to meet, as lines in a centre, and that is the *community of women*. Great were their solicitudes in this matter, and they never failed of certain articles in their schemes of worship, on purpose to establish it.

The last *fanatics* of note were those which started up in Germany a little after the *reformation* of Luther, springing as *mushrooms* do at the *end of a harvest*; such were John of Leyden, David George, Adam Neuster,° and many others, whose visions and revelations always terminated in *leading about half a dozen sisters apiece*, and making that practice a fundamental part of their system. For human life is a continual navigation, and if we expect our *vessels* to pass with safety through the waves and tempests of this fluctuating world, it is necessary to make a good provision of the *flesh*, as seamen lay in store of *beef* for a long voyage.

Now from this brief survey of some principal sects among the *fanatics* in all ages (having omitted the Mahometans and others, who might also help to confirm the argument I am about) to which I might add several among ourselves, such as the *Family of Love*, *Sweet Singers of Israel*,° and the like, and from reflecting upon that fundamental point in their doctrines about *women*, wherein they have so unanimously agreed; I am apt to imagine that the seed or principle which has ever put men upon *visions* in things *invisible*, is of a corporeal nature; for the profounder chemists inform us that the strongest *spirits* may be extracted from *human flesh*. Besides, the spinal marrow being nothing else but a continuation of the brain, must needs create a very free communication between the superior faculties and those below: and thus the *thorn in the flesh* serves for a *spur* to the *spirit*. I think it is agreed among physicians that nothing affects the head so much as a tentiginous humour, repelled and elated to the upper region, found by daily practice to run frequently up into madness. A very eminent member of the faculty assured me that when the Quakers first appeared, he seldom was without some female patients among them for the *furor* [*Uterinus*].° Persons of a visionary devotion, either men or women, are in their complexion of all others the most amorous; for *zeal* is frequently kindled from the same spark with other fires, and from inflaming brotherly love will proceed to raise that of a gallant. If we inspect into the usual process of modern courtship, we shall find it to consist in a devout turn of the eyes, called *ogling*; an artificial form of canting and whining by rote, every interval for want of other matter made up with a shrug or a hum, a sigh or a groan; the style compact of insignificant words, incoherences, and repetition. These I take to be the most accomplished rules of address to a mistress; and where are these performed with more dexterity than by the *saints*? Nay, to bring this argument yet closer, I have been informed by certain sanguine brethren of the first class that in the height and *orgasmus* of their spiritual exercise, it has been frequent with them * * * * *; immediately after which they found the *spirit* to relax and flag of a sudden with the nerves, and they were forced to hasten to a conclusion. This may be further strengthened by observing, with wonder, how unaccountably all females are attracted by visionary or enthusiastic preachers, though never so contemptible in their *outward men*; which is usually supposed to be done upon considerations purely spiritual without any carnal regards at all. But I have reason to think the *sex* hath certain characteristics by which they form a truer judgment of human abilities and performings than we ourselves can possibly do of each other. Let that be as it will, thus much is certain that, however spiritual intrigues begin, they generally conclude like all others; they may branch upwards toward heaven but the root is in the earth. Too intense a contemplation is not the business of flesh and blood; it must by the necessary course of things, in a little time let go its hold and fall into *matter*. Lovers, for the sake of celestial converse, are but another sort of *Platonics* who pretend to see stars and heaven in ladies' eyes, and to look or think no lower; but the same *pit* is provided for both; and they seem a perfect moral to the story of that philosopher who, while his thoughts and eyes were fixed upon the *constellations*, found himself seduced by his *lower parts* into a *ditch*.°

I had somewhat more to say upon this part of the subject but the post is just going, which forces me in great haste to conclude,

Sir,

Yours, &c.

Pray, burn this letter as soon as it comes to your hands.

ADDITIONS TO *A TALE OF A TUB*°

Abstract of what follows after Sect. IX in the Manuscript.

[a] *The History of* Martin.

HOW *Jack* & *Martin* being parted, set up each for himself. How they travel'd over hills & dales, met many disasters, suffered much for the good cause, & strugled with difficultys & wants, not having where to lay their head; by all which they afterwards proved themselves to be right Father's Sons, & *Peter* to be spurious. Finding no shelter near *Peter*'s habitation, *Martin* travel'd northwards, & finding the *Thuringians* & neighbouring people disposed to change, he set up his Stage first among them; where making it his business to cry down *Peter*'s pouders, plaisters, salves, & drugs, which he had sold a long time at a dear rate, allowing *Martin* none of the profit, tho he had been often employed in recommending & putting them off; the good people willing to save their pence began to hearken to *Martin*'s speeches. How several great Lords took the hint & on the same account declared for *Martin*; particularly one, who not having enough of one Wife, wanted to marry a second, & knowing *Peter* used not to grant such licenses but at a swinging price, he struck up a bargain with *Martin* whom he found more tı actable, & who assured him he had the same power to allow such things. How most of the other Northern Lords, for their own privat ends, withdrew themselves & their Dependants from *Peters* authority & closed in with *Martin*. How *Peter*, enraged at the loss of such large Territorys, & consequently of so much revenue, thunder'd against *Martin*, and sent out the strongest & most terrible of his *Bulls* to devour him; but this having no effect, & *Martin* defending himself boldly & dexterously, *Peter* at last put forth Proclamations declaring *Martin* & all his Adherents, Rebels & Traytors, ordaining & requiring all his loving Subjects to take up Arms, and to kill burn & destroy all & every one of them, promising large rewards &c. upon which ensued bloody wars & Desolations.

How *Harry Huff* Lord of Albion, one of the greatest Bullys of those days, sent a Cartel to *Martin* to fight him on a stage, at Cudgels, Quarterstaff, Back-sword &c. Hence the origine of that genteel custom of *Prize-fighting*, so well known & practised to this day among those polite

Islanders, tho' unknown every where else. How *Martin* being a bold blustering fellow, accepted the Challenge; how they met & fought, to the great diversion of the Spectators; & after giving one another broken heads & many bloody wounds & bruises, how they both drew off victorious; in which their Exemple has been frequently imitated by great Clerks & others since that time. How *Martin*'s friends aplauded his victory; & how Lord *Harrys* friends complimented him on the same score; & particularly Lord *Peter*, who sent him a fine Feather for his Cap, to be worn by him & his Successors, as a perpetual mark of his bold defense of Lord *Peter*'s Cause. How *Harry* flushed with his pretended victory over *Martin*, began to huff *Peter* also, & at last down right quarrelled with him about a Wench. How some of Lord *Harry*'s Tennants, ever fond of changes, began to talk kindly of *Martin*, for which he mauld 'em soundly; as he did also those that adhered to *Peter*; how he turn'd some out of house & hold, others he hanged or burnt &c.

How *Harry Huff* after a deal of blustering, wenching, & bullying, died, & was succeeded by a good natured Boy, who giving way to the general bent of his Tennants, allowed *Martin*'s notions to spread every where & take deep root in Albion. How after his death the Farm fell into the hands of a Lady, who was violently in love with Lord *Peter*. How she purged the whole Country with fire & Sword, resolved not to leave the name or remembrance of *Martin*. How *Peter* triumphed, & set up shops again for selling his own pouders plaisters & salves, which were now called the only true ones, *Martins* being all declared counterfeit. How great numbers of *Martin*'s friends left the Country, & traveling up & down in foreign parts, grew acquainted with many of *Jack*'s followers, & took a liking to many of their notions & ways, which they afterwards brought back into Albion, now under another Landlady more moderate & more cunning than the former. How she endeavoured to keep friendship both with *Peter* & *Martin* & trimm'd for some time between the two, not without countenancing & assisting at the same time many of *Jack*'s followers, but finding no possibility of reconciling all the three Brothers, because each would be Master & allow no other salves pouders or plaisters to be used but his own, she discarded all three, & set up a shop for those of her own Farm, well furnished with pouders plaisters salves & all other drugs necessary, all right & true, composed according to receipts made up by Physicians & Apothecarys of her own creating, which they extracted out of *Peter*'s & *Martin*'s & *Jack*'s Receipt-books; & of this medly or hodgpodge made up a Dispensatory of their own; strictly forbiding any other to be used, & particularly *Peter*'s from which the greatest part of this new Dispensatory was stollen. How the Lady further to confirm this change, wisely imitating her Father, degraded *Peter* from the rank he pretended as eldest Brother, & set up her self in his place as head of the Family, & ever after wore her Fathers old Cap with the fine feather he had got from *Peter* for standing his friend; which has likewise been worn, with no small ostentation to this day, by all her Successors, tho declared Ennemys to *Peter*. How Lady Bess & her Physicians being told of many defects & imperfections in their new medley Dispensatory, resolve on a further alteration, & to purge it from a great deal of *Peter*'s trash that still remained in it; but were prevented by her death. How she was succeeded by a North Country Farmer, who pretended great skill in managing of Farms, tho' he cou'd never govern his own poor litle old Farm, nor yet this large new one after he got it. How this new Landlord, to shew his Valour & dexterity, fought against Enchanters, Weeds, Giants, & Windmills, & claimed great Honnour for his Victorys, tho' he oftimes beshit himself when there was no danger. How his Successor, no wiser than he, occasion'd great disorders by the new methods he took to manage his Farms. How he attempted to establish in his northern Farm the same Dispensatory used in the southern, but miscarried, because *Jack*'s pouders, pills, salves, & plaisters, were there in great vogue.

How the Author finds himself embarassed for having introduced into his History a new Sect, different from the three he had undertaken to treat of; & how his inviolable respect to the sacred number *three* obliges him to reduce these four, as he intends to doe all other things, to that number; & for that end to drop the former *Martin*, & to substitute in his place Lady *Besses* Institution, which is to pass under the name of *Martin* in the sequel of this true History. This weighty point being clear'd, the Author goes on & describes mighty quarrels & squables between *Jack* & *Martin*, how sometimes the one had the better & sometimes the other, to the great desolation of both Farms, till at last both sides concur to hang up the Landlord, who pretended to die a Martyr for *Martin*, tho he had been true to neither side, & was suspected by many to have a great affection for *Peter*.

[b] *A Digression on the nature usefulness & necessity of Wars & Quarels.*

THIS being a matter of great consequence the Author intends to treat it methodicaly & at large in a Treatise apart, & here to give only some hints of what his large Treatise contains. The State of War natural to all Creatures. War is an attempt to take by violence from others a part of what they have & we want. Every man fully sensible of his own merit, & finding it not duly regarded by others, has a natural right to take from them all that he thinks due to himself: & every creature finding its own wants more than those of others has the same right to take every thing its nature requires. Brutes much more modest in their pretensions this way than men; & mean men more than great ones. The higher one raises his pretensions this way, the more bustle he makes about them, & the more success he has, the greater Hero. Thus greater Souls in proportion to their superior merit claim a greater right to take every thing from meaner folks. This the true foundation of Grandeur & Heroism, & of the distinction of degrees among men. War therfor necessary to establish subordination, & to found Cities, States, Kingdoms, &c. as also to purge Bodys politick of gross humours. Wise Princes find it necessary to have wars abroad to keep peace at home. War, Famine, & Pestilence the usual cures for corruptions in Bodys politick. A comparaison of these three. The Author is to write a Panegyrick on each of them. The greatest part of Mankind loves War more than peace: They are but few & mean spirited that live in peace with all men. The modest & meek of all kinds always a prey to those of more noble or stronger apetites. The inclination to war universal: those that cannot or dare not make war in person, employ others to doe it for them. This maintains Bullys, Bravos, Cutthroats, Lawyers, Soldiers, &c. Most Professions would be useless if all were peaceable. Hence Brutes want neither Smiths nor Lawyers, Magistrats nor Joyners, Soldiers nor Surgeons. Brutes having but narrow appetites are incapable of carrying on or perpetuating war against their own species, or of being led out in troops & multitudes to destroy one another. These prerogatives proper to Man alone. The excellency of human nature demonstrated by the vast train of apetites, passions, wants, &c. that attend it. This matter to be more fully treated in the Author's Panegyrick on Mankind.

The History of Martin. [continued]

How *Jack* having got rid of the old Landlord & set up another to his mind, quarrel'd with *Martin* & turn'd him out of doors. How he pillaged all his shops, & abolished the whole Dispensatory. How the new Landlord laid about him, maul'd *Peter*, worry'd *Martin*, & made the whole neighborhood tremble. How *Jack*'s friends fell out among themselves, split into a thousand partys, turn'd all things topsy turvy, till every body grew weary of them, & at last the blustering Landlord dying *Jack* was kick'd out of doors, a new Landlord brought in, & *Martin* re-established. How this new Landlord let *Martin* doe what he pleased, & *Martin* agreed to every thing his pious Landlord desired, provided *Jack* might be kept low. Of several efforts *Jack* made to raise up his head, but all in vain: till at last the Landlord died & was succeeded by one who was a great friend to *Peter*, who to humble *Martin* gave *Jack* some liberty. How *Martin* grew enraged at this, called in a Foreigner & turn'd out the Landlord; in which *Jack* concurred with *Martin*, because this Landlord was entirely devoted to *Peter*, into whose arms he threw himself, & left his Country. How the new Landlord secured *Martin* in the full possession of his former rights, but would not allow him to destroy *Jack* who had always been his friend. How *Jack* got up his head in the North & put himself in possession of a whole Canton, to the great discontent of *Martin*, who finding also that some of *Jack*'s friends were allowed to live & get their bread in the south parts of the country, grew highly discontent of the new Landlord he had called in to his assistance. How this Landlord kept *Martin* in order, upon which he fell into a raging fever, & swore he would hang himself or joyn in with *Peter*, unless *Jack*'s children were all turn'd out to starve. Of several attempts made to cure *Martin* & make peace between him & *Jack*, that they might unite against *Peter*; but all made ineffectual by the great adress of a number of *Peter*'s friends, that herded among *Martin*'s, & appeared the most zealous for his interest. How *Martin* getting abroad in this mad fit, look'd so like *Peter* in his air & dress, & talk'd so like him, that many of the Neighbours could not distinguish the one from the other; especially when *Martin* went up & down strutting in *Peter*'s Armour, which he had borrowed to fight *Jack*. What remedys were used to cure *Martin*'s distemper. &c.

N.B. Some things that follow after this are not in the MS, but seem to have been written since to fill up the place of what was not thought convenient then to print. [i.e. possibly Sect. X (p. 87)]

[c] A PROJECT,

for the universal benefit of Mankind.

THE Author having laboured so long & done so much to serve & instruct the Publick, without any advantage to himself, has at last thought of a project which will tend to the great benefit of all Mankind, & produce a handsom Revenue to the Author. He intends to print by Subscription in 96. large volumes in *folio*, an exact Description of *Terra Australis incognita*, collected with great care & pains from 999. learned & pious Authors of undoubted veracity. The whole Work, illustrated with Maps and Cuts agreable to the subject, and done by the best Masters, will cost but a Guiney each volume to Subscribers, one guinea to be paid in advance, & afterwards a guinea on receiving each volume, except the last. This Work will be of great use for all men, & necessary for all familys, because it contains exact accounts of all the Provinces, Colonys & Mansions of that spacious Country, where by a general Doom all transgressors of the law are to be transported: & every one having this work may chuse out the fittest & best place for himself, there being enough for all so as every one shall be fully satisfied.

The Author supposes that one Copy of this Work will be bought at the publick Charge, or out of the Parish rates, for every Parish Church in the three Kingdoms, & in all the Dominions thereunto belonging. And that every family that can command ten pounds *per annum*, even tho' retrenched from less necessary expences, will also subscribe for one. He does not think of giving out above 9 volumes yearly; & considering the number requisite, he intends to print at least 100000. for the first Edition. He's to print Proposals against next Term, with a Specimen, & a curious Map of the Capital City, with its 12 Gates, from a known Author who took an exact survey of it in a dream. Considering the great care & pains of the Author, & the usefulness of the Work, he hopes every one will be ready, for their own good as well as his, to contribute chearfully to it, & not grudge him the profit he may have by it, especially if it comes to a 3. or 4. Edition, as he expects it will very soon.

He doubts not but it will be translated into foreign languages by most Nations of Europe as well as of Asia & Africa, being of as great use to all those Nations as to his own; for this reason he designs to procure Patents & Privileges for securing the whole benefit to himself, from all those different Princes & States, & hopes to see many millions of this great Work printed in those different Countrys & languages before his death.

After this business is pretty well establisht, he has promised to put a Friend on another Project almost as good as this; by establishing Insurance-Offices every where for securing people from shipwreck & several other accidents in their Voyage to this Country; and these Offices shall furnish, at a certain rate, Pilots well versed in the Route, & that know all the Rocks, shelves, quicksands &c. that such Pilgrims & Travelers may be exposed to. Of these he knows a great number ready instructed in most Countreys: but the whole Scheme of this matter he's to draw up at large & communicate to his Friend.

Here ends the Manuscript, there being nothing of the following piece in it. [i.e. *The Battle of the Books*]

[d] *The Kingdom of Absurdities*

In the Kingdom of Absurdities. The bells of glass, with iron clappers. The houses of gun-powder; and as they are apt to get drunk, they leave candles lighting, so that they have fires very frequently. The children always die there before their parents. There is a sort of flying insect in their jakes, which has cruel teeth, and is fond of human testicles; so that when a man goes there upon his occasions, it is forty to one but he comes away without them. Nothing is so easy as to destroy those animals; and yet ask the reason why they do it not? they say, It was their ancestors custom of old.

APPENDIX A: EXTRACTS FROM THE LITERARY CONTEXT OF *A TALE OF A TUB*

(i) *from* Thomas Vaughan, *Anthroposophia Theomagica: or, a Discourse of the Nature of Man and his State after Death; grounded on his Creator's Proto-Chimistry, and verified by a practical Examination of Principles in the Great World. By Eugenius Philalethes* [Thomas Vaughan]. Dan[iel]: *Many shall run to and fro, and Knowledge shall be increased.* Zoroaster in Oracul. [Zarathustra, *The Oracles*]. *Audi Ignis Vocem* [I have heard the voice of the Fire]. London . . . 1650.*

[The prose of Vaughan's hermetic writing, 'the most unintelligible *fustian*' as Swift's note calls it, as well as the topics, clearly fascinated him: this book is referred to several times in *A Tale of a Tub*. The extract stands here for the 'dark authors' he read and satirized.]

The Author to the Reader

I LOOK on this Life as the progress of an essence royal: The Soul but quits her court to see the country. Heaven hath in it a scene of earth; and had she bin contented with Ideas she had not travelled beyond the Map. But excellent patterns commend their Mimes: Nature that was so fair in the type, could not be a slut in the Anaglyph. This makes her ramble hither to examine the Medal by the Flask, but whiles she scans their Symmetrie, she forms it. Thus her descent speaks her Original: God in love with his own beauty, frames a Glass to view it by reflection; but the frailty of the matter excluding Eternity, the composure was subject to dissolution. Ignorance gave this release the name of Death, but properly it is the Soul's Birth, and a Charter that makes for her Liberty; she hath several ways to break up house, but her best is without a disease. This is her mystical walk, an Exit only to return. When she takes air at this door, it is without prejudice to her tenement. The Magicians tell me Anima unius entis egreditur, et aliud ingreditur. Some have examined this, and state it an Expence of Influences, as if the Soul exercised her Royalty at the eye, or had some blind Jurisdiction in the Pores. But this is to measure Magical Positions by the slight superficial strictures of the common Philosophy. It is an age of Intellectual slaveries; If they meet any thing extraordinary, they prune it commonly with distinctions, or daub it with false Glosses, till it looks like the Traditions of Aristotle. His

*Reprinted in Alan Rudrum (ed.), *The Works of Thomas Vaughan* (Oxford, 1984), pp. 50–3.

followers are so confident of his principles they seek not to understand what others speak, but to make others speak what they understand. It is in Nature, as it is in Religion; we are still hammering of old elements, but seek not the America that lies beyond them. The Apostle [Hebr.] tells us of leaving the first principles of the Doctrine of Christ, and going on to perfection: Not laying again the foundation of Repentance from dead works, and of faith towards God; of the Doctrine of Baptism, and laying on of Hands, of Resurrection, and the eternal Judgement; Then he speaks of Illumination, of Tasting of the Heavenly gift, of being partakers of the Holy Ghost, of Tasting of the good word of God, and the powers of the World to come. Now if I should question any Sect (for there is no Communion in Christendom) whither these later Intimations drive? They can but return me to the first Rudiments, or produce some empty pretence of spirit. Our Natural Philosophers are much of a Cast with Figure-flingers: these step into the prerogative of Prophets, and Antedate events in configurations, and motions. This is a consequence of as much reason, as if I saw the Suede exercising, and would finde his Designs in his postures. Friar Bacon walked in Oxford between two steeples [L. Verulam in his N.H.], but he that would have discovered his Thoughts, by his steps, had been more his Fool, then his Fellow. The Peripateticks when they define the Soul, or some Interior Principle, describe it only by outward circumstances, which every child can do, but they state nothing Essentially. Thus they dwell altogether in the Face, their Endeavours are mere Titillations, and their Acquaintance with Nature is not at the heart. Notwithstanding I acknowledge the Schoolmen ingenious: They conceive their Principles irregular, and prescribe rules for Method, though they want Matter. Their Philosophy is like a Church, that is all discipline, and no Doctrine: For bate me their prolegomena, their form of Arguing, their Reciting of Different Opinions, with several other digressions, and the substance of these Tostati will scarce amount to a Mercury. Besides, their Aristotle is a Poet in text his principles are but Fancies, and they stand more on our Concessions, than his Bottom. Hence it is that his followers, notwithstanding the Assistance of so many Ages, can fetch nothing out of him but Notions: And these indeed they use, as He sayeth Lycophron did his Epithets, Non ut Condimentis, sed ut Cibis [Arist. Rhet.]; Their Compositions are a meer Tympany of Terms. It is better than a Fight in Quixot, to observe what Duels, and Digladiations they have about Him. One will make him speak Sense, another Non-sense, and a third both, Aquinas palps him gently, Scotus makes him winch, and he is taught like an Ape to shew several tricks. If we look on his adversaries, the least amongst them hath foiled him, but Telesius knocked him in the head, and Campanella hath quite discomposed him. But as that bald haunter of the circus had his skull so steeled with use, it shivered all the tiles were thrown at it, so this Aristotle thrives by scuffles, and the world cries him up, when truth cries him down. The Peripateticks look on God, as they do on Carpenters, who build with stone and Timber, without any infusion of life. But the world, which is God's building, is full of Spirit, quick, and living. This Spirit is the cause of multiplication, of several perpetual productions of minerals, vegetables, and creatures engendered by putrefaction: All which are manifest, infallible Arguments of life. Besides, the Texture of the universe clearly discovers its animation. The Earth which is the visible natural Basis of it, represents the gross, carnal parts. The Element of Water answers to the Blood, for in it the Pulse of the Great world beats; this most men call the Flux and Reflux, but they know not the true cause of it. The air is the outward refreshing spirit, where this vast creature breathes, though invisibly, yet not altogether insensibly. The Interstellar skies are his vital, æthereal waters, and the stars his animal sensual fire. Thou wilt tell me perhaps, this is new Philosophy and that of Aristotle is old. It is indeed, but in the same sense as Religion is at Rome. It is not the primitive Truth of the Creation, not the Ancient, real Theosophy of the Hebrews and Egyptians, but a certain preternatural upstart, a vomit of Aristotle, which his followers with so much diligence lick up, and swallow. I present thee not here with any clamorous opposition of their Patron, but a positive express of principles as I find them in Nature. I may say of them as Moses said of the Fiat: These are the Generations of the Heavens, and of the Earth, in the day that the Lord God made the heavens and the Earth. They are things extra Intellectum, sensible practical Truths, not mere Vagaries and Rambles of the Brain. I would not have you look on my Endeavours as a design of Captivity: I intend not the Conquest, but the Exercise of thy Reason, not that thou shouldst sweare Allegiance to my Dictates, but compare my Conclusions with Nature, and examine their Correspondency. Be pleased to consider, that Obstinacy enslaves the Soul, and clips the wings which God gave her for flight, and Discovery. If thou wilt not quit thy Aristotle, let not any prejudice hinder thy further search; Great is their Number who perhaps had attained to perfection, had they not already thought themselves perfect. This is my Advice, but how welcome to thee I know not. If thou wilt kick and fling, I shall say with the Cardinal, etiam Asinus meus recalcitrat: for I value no man's Censure. It is an Age wherein Truth is near a Miscarriage, and it is enough for me that I have appeared thus far for it, in a Day of Necessity.

(ii) *from* Charles Perrault, *Le Siècle de Louis le Grand*, 1687 [trans.].*

[Read on 26 January NS 1687 at the meeting of the French Academy convened to celebrate Louis XIV's recovery from the operation on his fistula.]

The Age of *Lewis* the Great

ANTIQUITY 'tis own'd, does well deserve
Profound Respect, yet not to be adored.
The *Ancients* I with unbent Knees behold,
For they, tho' great, were Men as well as we,
And justly one may venture to compare
The Age of *Lewis*, to *Augustus's* Days.
What Time more Conquering Chiefs did ere produce?
What Time more Rampiers forc'd by brave Assault?
Or when did Victory 'ere urge her Steeds
With speed more rapid thro' the glorious Course? 10
Would we at last throw off the specious Veil,
Which Prejudice has cast before our Eyes,
Errors traditionary cease to praise,
Thro' our own Opticks view the homely Scene;
Plainly we might perceive the Ages past
No title to our Adoration claim,
And that with them for Skill in Lib'ral Arts
Without the least presumption we may vie . . . .

(iii) *from* Bernard Le Bovier de Fontenelle, *Digression sur les Anciens et Modernes*, 1688 [trans.].†

A DISCOURSE Concerning the ANCIENTS and MODERNS. Translated from the French of M. FONTENELLE.

THE whole dispute for pre-eminence between the Ancients and Moderns being well understood, has this short issue, *viz.* to know

*Perrault, *Characters and Criticisms, upon the Ancient and Modern Orators, Poets, Painters . . . Together with a Poem (in Blank Verse) Intitled: The Age of Lewis the Great. Made English from the French original* . . . London: Printed and Sold by John Nutt . . . 1705, pp. 181–211 [lines 1–18].

†*Conversations with a Lady, on the Plurality of the Worlds. Written in French by Mons. Fontenelle . . . Translated by Mr. Glanville. The fourth edition. To which is added, A Discourse concerning the Ancients and Moderns. Written by the same Author: and translated by Mr. Hughes.* London, 1719.

whether the trees which formerly grew in our fields were larger than those of the present time. If they were, Homer, Plato, Demosthenes, cannot possibly be equalled in these later ages; but if otherwise, they can.

Let us explain this paradox. If the Ancients had more wit or capacity than the Moderns, their brains must have been better formed, of stronger or of more delicate fibres, and filled with more animal spirits. But what could be the cause of this? Their trees then must have been larger and more beautiful: for if Nature at that time was younger and more vigorous, plants, as well as human brains, must have shared of this youth and vigour.

Let the adorers of the Ancients take care what they say, when they tell us, *they* are the sources of good taste and reason, and the luminaries destined to give light to all mankind: that nobody has wit or judgement, but in proportion to his veneration for them; that Nature has exhausted herself in producing those great originals: for, in truth, they make them of a species different from us, and philosophy does by no means agree with all those fine expressions. Nature has between her hands a kind of clay, which is always the same, which she forms and reforms into a thousand shapes, and of which she makes men, and beasts, and plants: and 'tis ridiculous to fancy that she composed Plato, Demosthenes, or Homer of a finer mold, or better prepared, than the philosophers, orators, and poets of the present time. For, though our minds are immaterial, I regard here only their Union with the brain, which is material, and which, according to its various dispositions, produces all the difference between them . . .

If I were to draw a picture of Nature, I would represent her like Justice, with a balance in her hand, to signify that she employs it in dividing to her sons their several portions; and that for the most she makes pretty near an equal weight in what she distributes to mankind; happiness, capacity, the advantages and disadvantages of their different conditions; the facilities and difficulties which regards matters of wit and learning.

By virtue of those compensations we may hope the ages to come will admire us to an extravagance, in amends for the little regard which is paid us in our own age. Future critics will perhaps study hard to find out in our writings beauties we never designed: on the other hand, faults which are not to be defended, and which the author himself would now give up, may meet with advocates of an invincible courage. Heaven knows with what scorn, in comparison of us, they will treat the great wits and geniuses of their own time, who possibly may be Americans. Thus, it seems, that prejudice sinks us in one age, to raise us in another. We are now the sacrifice; and then the divinity. A sport diverting enough to be looked upon by impartial observers! I might extend the prophecy much further. The time has been when the Latins were the Moderns; and then the complaint was of the infatuation the world had for the Greeks, who were Ancients to them. The distance of time between those competitors disappears to us, who are at so much a greater distance. They are both ancients to us; and we make no difficulty of preferring ordinarily the Latins to the Greeks because there is no hurt done, in a victory of the Ancients over the Ancients. But it would be of the most terrible consequence, if it were a victory of the Moderns over the Ancients. Let us have patience, and by a long succession of ages, we shall become, as it were, contemporaries with the Greeks and Latins. And when we are thus all Ancients, it is easy to forsee that there will be no scruple in giving us, in many things, the preference. The best works of Sophocles, Euripides, Aristophanes, will scarcely stand before the *Cinna*, *Horace*, *Ariane*, the *Misanthrope*, and many other tragedies and comedies written at a good time; for, indeed, to speak impartially, it must be owned that good time has been past for some years. I do not think *Theagenes* and *Charliclea*, *Clitophon* and *Leucippe* will ever be compared to the *Cyrus*, *Astræa*, *Zayde*, or the *Princess of Cleves*. The same may be said of the newer kinds of writing, as letters of love and gallantry, tales, opera's and the like; each of which kinds has furnished us with some excellent author, to whom antiquity has nothing to set in opposition, and who will not perhaps be surpassed by posterity. If we were only to instance in songs (a sort of writings which perhaps may be lost, and to which nobody pays much regard), it is certain we have a prodigious Number of them, full of wit and spirit; and such as I will venture to say, if they had been known to Anacreon, he would have sung oftner than his own. We see, by a great variety of poetical writings, that the versification is capable at present of as much dignity, and at the same time of more justness and exactness than ever. I have designed to avoid entering into particulars; therefore I will not undertake to display at large our riches. But I am convinced we are in the condition of some wealthy lords, who do not keep always an exact register of their goods, and have more possessions than they think of . . .

(iv) *from* Sir William Temple, 'An Essay upon the Ancient and Modern Learning', printed in *Miscellanea. The Second Part* (1690).*

*Reprinted in S. H. Monk (ed.), *Five Miscellaneous Essays by Sir William Temple* (Ann Arbor, Mich., 1963), pp. 37–71.

WHOEVER converses much among the old books will be something hard to please among the new; yet these must have their part too in the leisure of an idle man, and have many of them their beauties as well as their defaults. . . .

Two pieces that have lately pleased me . . . are, one in English upon the Antediluvian World; and another in French upon the Plurality of Worlds; one writ by a divine [Thomas Burnet], and the other by a gentleman [Fontenelle], but both very finely in their several kinds, and upon their several subjects, which would have made very poor work in common hands: I was so pleased with the last (I mean the fashion of it rather than the matter, which is old and beaten) that I enquired for what else I could of the same hand, till I met with a small piece concerning poesy which gave me the same exception to both these authors, whom I should otherwise have been very partial to. For the first could not end his learned treatise without a panegyric of modern learning and knowledge in comparison of the ancient, and the other falls so grossly into the censure of the old poetry, and preference of the new, that I could not read either of these strains without some indignation, which no quality among men is so apt to raise in me as sufficiency, the worst composition out of the pride and ignorance of mankind. But these two being not the only persons of the age that defend these opinions, it may be worth examining how far either reason or experience can be allowed to plead or determine in their favour.

The force of all that I have met with upon this subject, either in talk or writings is, first, as to knowledge, that we must have more than the ancients, because we have the advantage both of theirs and our own, which is commonly illustrated by the similitude of a dwarf's standing upon a giant's shoulders, and seeing more or farther than he. Next as to wit or genius, that nature being still the same, these must be much at a rate in all ages, at least in the same climates, as the growth and size of plants and animals commonly are; and if both these are allowed, they think the cause is gained. But I cannot tell why we should conclude that the ancient writers had not as much advantage from the knowledge of others that were ancient to them, as we have from those that are ancient to us . . . .

[*The ancients may have had more original books than the modern world, even though printing has multiplied copies. Books are not necessary for learning anyway, as is shown by ancient Mexico and Peru. In the East, partly using writing but also relying on oral tradition, colleges of priests seem to have been the conservers of knowledge, and formed the reservoirs of learning, which were the sources for Orpheus, Homer, Lycurgus, Pythagoras, Plato and other Greek sages.*]

Now to judge whether the ancients or moderns can be probably thought to have made the greatest progress in the search and discoveries of the vast region of truth and nature, it will be worth enquiring, what guides have been used, and what labours employed, by the one and the other, in these noble travels and pursuits.

The modern scholars have their usual recourse to the universities of their countries; some few it may be to those of their neighbours, and this in quest of books, rather than men, for their guides . . . And who are these dead guides we seek in our journey? They are at best but some few authors that remain among us, of a great many that wrote in Greek or Latin, from the age of Hippocrates to that of Marcus Antoninus, which reaches not much above six hundred years: before that time I know none, besides some poets, some fables, and some few epistles; and since that time, I know very few that can pretend to be authors rather than transcribers or commentators of the ancient learning. Now to consider at what sources our ancients drew their water and with what unwearied pains: 'tis evident, Thales and Pythagoras were the two founders of the Grecian philosophy; the first gave beginning to the Ionic sect, and the other to the Italic; out of which, all the others celebrated in Greece or Rome were derived or composed. Thales was the first of the Sophi, or wise men famous in Greece, and is said to have learned his astronomy, geometry, astrology, theology, in his travels from his country Miletius to Ægypt, Phœnicia, Crete, and Delphos; Pythagoras was the father of philosophers, and of the virtues, having in modesty chosen the name of a lover of wisdom, rather than of wise; and having first introduced the names of the four cardinal virtues, and given them the place and rank they have held ever since in the world. Of these two mighty men remain no writings at all, for those golden verses that go under the name of Pythagoras are generally rejected as spurious, like many other fragments of Sybils, or old poets, and some entire poems that run with ancient names: nor is it agreed, whether he ever left any thing written to his scholars or contemporaries, or whether all that learned of him did it not by the ear and memory, and all that remained of him for some succeeding ages were not by tradition. . . .

As there were guides to those that we call ancients, so there were others that were guides to them, in whose search they travelled far and laboured long.

There is nothing more agreed than that all the learning of the Greeks was deduced originally from Ægypt or Phœnicia; but whether theirs might not have flourished to that degree it did by the commerce of the Æthiopians, Chaldeans, Arabians, and Indians, is not so evident (though I am very apt to believe it) and to most of these regions some of the Grecians travelled in search of those golden mines of learning and knowledge . . . I shall only trace those of Pythagoras, who seems of all others to have gone the farthest upon this design, and to have brought home the greatest treasures. . . .

[*The ancient accounts of the Indian Brahmins show the kind of men Pythagoras visited. From the Brahmins he (like several other Greeks) probably drew most of his natural and moral philosophy, just as the Egyptians did their own learning (and as the Brahmins had originally from the Chinese). But modern knowledge may not be able to claim any advantage from this, since human advance comes from the native genius of individual men; the achievements of the ancients may indeed inhibit modern spirit and effort. A modern dwarf is a dwarf still, even though standing on a giant's shoulders, and will weakly see less, if shorter-sighted, less alert, or dazzled with the height. Science and the arts have risen and declined at different times in different parts of the world, though the trend of transmission has been from East to West; the restoration of learning and knowledge has made great progress in western Europe since the decay that followed the complex fall of Rome, but that does not mean the moderns have outgrown all that was ancient.*]

But what are the sciences wherein we pretend to excel? I know of no new philosophers that have made entries upon that noble stage for fifteen hundred years past, unless Descartes and Hobbes should pretend to it; of whom I shall make no critique here, but only say, that, by what appears of learned men's opinions in this age, they have by no means eclipsed the lustre of Plato, Aristotle, Epicurus, or others of the ancients. For grammar or rhetoric, no man ever disputed it with them; nor for poetry, that ever I heard of, besides the new French author I have mentioned, and against whose opinion there could, I think, never have been given stronger evidence than by his own poems, printed together with that treatise.

There is nothing new in astronomy to vie with the ancients, unless it be the Copernican system; nor in physic, unless Harvey's circulation of the blood. But whether either of these be modern discoveries, or derived from old fountains, is disputed, nay it is so too whether they are true or no; for though reason may seem to favour them more than the contrary opinions, yet sense can very hardly allow them; and, to satisfy mankind, both these must concur. But if they are true, yet these two great discoveries have made no change in the conclusions of astronomy, nor in the practice of physic, and so have been of little use to the world, though perhaps of much honour to the authors . . .

The greatest invention that I know of in later ages has been that of the loadstone, and consequently the greatest improvement has been made in the art of navigation . . . However, 'tis to this we owe the discovery and commerce of so many vast countries which were very little, if at all, known to the ancients, and the experimental proof of this terrestrial globe, which was before only speculation, but has since been surrounded by the fortune and boldness of several navigators. From this great, though fortuitous invention, and the consequences thereof, it must be allowed that geography is mightily advanced in these latter ages . . .

It were too great a mortification to think that the same fate has happened to us, even in our modern learning, as if the growth of that, as well as of natural bodies, had some short periods beyond which it could not reach, and after which it must begin to decay. It falls in one country or one age, and rises again in others, but never beyond a certain pitch . . . There is a certain degree of capacity in the greatest vessel, and, when 'tis full, if you pour in still, it must run out some way or other, and the more it runs out on one side, the less runs out at the other: so the greatest memory, after a certain degree, as it learns or retains more of some things or words, loses and forgets as much of others. The largest and deepest reach of thought, the more it pursues some certain subjects, the more it neglects others . . .

But what would we have, unless it be other natures and beings than God Almighty has given us? The height of our statures may be six or seven feet, and we would have it sixteen; the length of our age may reach to a hundred years, and we would have it a thousand. We are born to grovel upon the earth, and we would fain soar up to the skies . . .

But God be thanked, [man's] pride is greater than his ignorance, and what he wants in knowledge, he supplies by sufficiency. When he has looked about him as far as he can, he concludes there is no more to be seen; when he is at the end of his line, he is at the bottom of the ocean; when he has shot his best, he is sure, none ever did nor ever can shoot better or beyond it. His own reason is the certain measure of truth, his own knowledge, of what is possible in nature; though his mind and his thoughts change every seven years, as well as his strength and his features; nay, though his opinions change every week or every day, yet he is sure, or at least confident, that his present thoughts and conclusions are just and true, and cannot be deceived: and, among all the miseries to which mankind is born and subjected in the whole course of his life, he has this one felicity to comfort and support him, that in all ages, in all things, every man is always in the right. A boy at fifteen is wiser than his father at forty, the meanest subject than his prince or governors; and the modern scholars, because they have, for a hundred years past, learned their lesson pretty well, are much more knowing than the ancients their masters . . .

But let it be so, and proved by good reasons, is it so by experience too? Have the studies, the writings, the productions of Gresham College, or the late Academies of Paris, outshined or eclipsed the Lycæum of Plato, the Academy of Aristotle, the Stoa of Zeno, the Garden of Epicurus? Has Harvey outdone Hippocrates; or Wilkins, Archimedes? Are d'Avila's and Strada's histories beyond those of Herodotus and Livy? Are Sleyden's commentaries beyond those of Cæsar? The flights of Boileau above those of Virgil? If all this must be allowed, I will then yield *Gondibert* to have excelled Homer, as is pretended; and the modern French poetry, all that of the ancients. And yet, I think, it may be as reasonably said, that the plays in Moorfields are beyond the Olympic games; a Welsh or Irish harp excels those of Orpheus and Arion; the pyramid in London, those of Memphis; and the French conquests in Flanders are greater than those of Alexander and Cæsar, as their operas and panegyrics would make us believe.

But the consideration of poetry ought to be a subject by itself. For the books we have in prose, do any of the modern we converse with appear of such a spirit and force, as if they would live longer than the ancient have done? If our wit and eloquence, our knowledge or inventions, would deserve it; yet our languages would not: there is no hope of their lasting long, nor of anything in them; they change every hundred years so as to be hardly known for the same, or anything of the former styles to be endured by the later; so as they can no more last like the ancients, than excellent carvings in wood, like those in marble or brass . . .

[*The most esteemed modern languages (Italian, Spanish, French) are imperfect copies of an excellent original (Latin), framed by the thoughts and uses of the noblest nation on record; Greek offering the only contest.*]

It may perhaps be further affirmed, in favour of the ancients, that the oldest books we have are still in their kind the best. The two most ancient that I know of in prose, among those we call profane authors, are Æsop's *Fables* and Phalaris's *Epistles*, both living near the same time, which was that of Cyrus and Pythagoras. As the first has been agreed by all ages since for the greatest master in his kind, and all others of that sort have been but imitations of his original, so I think the *Epistles* of Phalaris to have more race, more spirit, more force of wit and genius, than any others I have ever seen, either ancient or modern. I know several learned men (or that usually pass for such, under the name of critics) have not esteemed them genuine, and Politian, with some others, have attributed them to Lucian: but I think he must have little skill in painting, that cannot find out this to be an original; such diversity of passions, upon such variety of actions and passages of life and government, such freedom of thought, such boldness of expression, such bounty to his friends, such scorn of his enemies, such honour of learned men, such esteem of good, such knowledge of life, such contempt of death, with such fierceness of nature and cruelty of revenge, could never be represented but by him that possessed them; and I esteem Lucian to have been no more capable of writing than of acting what Phalaris did. In all one writ, you find the scholar or the sophist; and in all the other, the tyrant and the commander.

The next to these, in time, are Herodotus, Thucydides, Hippocrates, Plato, Xenophon, and Aristotle; of whom I shall say no more, than, what I think is allowed by all, that they are in their several kinds inimitable. So are Cæsar, Sallust, and Cicero, in theirs, who are the ancientest of the Latin (I speak still of prose) unless it be some little of old Cato upon rustic affairs . . .

The great wits among the moderns have been, in my opinion, and in their several kinds, of the Italian, Boccace, Machiavel, and Padre Paolo; among the Spaniards, Cervantes (who writ *Don Quixot*) and Guevara; among the French, Rabelais and Montaigne; among the English, Sir Philip Sidney, Bacon, and Selden: I mention nothing of what is written upon the subject of divinity, wherein the Spanish and English pens have been most conversant, and most excelled. The modern French are Voiture, Rochefoucault's *Memoirs*, Bussy's *Amours de Gaul*, with several other little relations or memoirs that have run this age, which are very pleasant and entertaining, and seem to have refined the French language to a degree that cannot be well exceeded. I doubt it may have happened there as it does in all works, that the more they are filed and polished, the less they have of weight and of strength; and as that language has much more fineness and smoothness at this time, so I take it to have had much more force, spirit, and compass in Montaigne's age . . .

[*Among the accidents that have hindered the advancement of learning in modern Europe may be mentioned: venemous disputes about religious matters, the want or decay of royal or princely patronage, avarice and greed, the pedantry of 'the sufficient among scholars' which has attracted scorn to all.*]

An ingenious Spaniard at Brussels would needs have it that the history of Don Quixot had ruined the Spanish monarchy; for, before that time, love and valour were all romance among them; every young cavalier that entered the scene dedicated the services of his life to his honour first, and then to his mistress. They lived and died in this romantic vein; and the old Duke of Alva, in his last Portugal expedition, had a young mistress, to whom the glory of that achievement was devoted, by which he hoped to value himself, instead of those qualities he had lost with his youth. After *Don Quixot* appeared, and with that inimitable wit and humour turned all this romantic honour and love into ridicule, the Spaniards, he said, began to grow ashamed of both, and to laugh at fighting and loving, or at least otherwise than to pursue their fortune, or satisfy their lust; and the consequences of this, both upon their bodies and their minds, this Spaniard would needs have pass for a great cause of the ruin of Spain, or of its greatness and power.

Whatever effect the ridicule of knight-errantry might have had upon that monarchy, I believe that of pedantry has had a very ill one upon the commonwealth of learning; and I wish the vein of ridiculing all that is serious and good, all honour and virtue, as well as learning and piety, may have no worse effects on any other state: 'tis the itch of our age and climate, and has overrun both the court and the stage; enters a House of Lords and Commons as boldly as a coffee-house, debates of Council as well as private conversation; and I have known in my life more than one or two ministers of state that would rather have said a witty thing than done a wise one; and made the company laugh, rather than the kingdom rejoice. But this is enough to excuse the imperfections of learning in our age, and to censure the sufficiency of some of the learned: and this small piece of justice I have done the ancients, will not, I hope, be taken, any more than 'tis meant, for any injury to the moderns.

I shall conclude with a saying of Alphonsus (surnamed the Wise) King of Arragon:

'That among so many things as are by men possessed or pursued in the course of their lives, all the rest are baubles, besides old wood to burn, old wine to drink, old friends to converse with, and old books to read.'

(v) *from* William Wotton, BD, *Reflections upon Ancient and Modern Learning* (1694; 2nd edn., with additions, 1697).

[The Dedication may be compared in tone and substance with Swift's Dedication of *A Tale* to Lord Somers. Wotton also shows the connection of the

Ancients and Moderns controversy with religious controversy. Like his friend Bentley, who had in 1692 given the first course of Boyle Lectures (founded to defend religion against its enemies), Wotton sought to derive arguments against unbelief from the new scientific discoveries of Newton, and from the consensus politics of the Revolution Settlement.]

The Epistle Dedicatory

To The

Right Honourable

DANIEL

Earl of Nottingham,

Baron Finch of Daventry.

May it please Your Lordship,

Since I am upon many accounts obliged to lay the studies and labours of my life at your lordship's feet, it will not, I hope, be thought presumption in me to make this following address, which on my part is an act of duty. I could not omit so fair an opportunity of declaring how sensible I am of the honour of being under your lordship's patronage. The pleasure of telling the world that one is raised by men who are truly great and good, works too powerfully to be smothered in the breast of him that feels it; especially since a man is rarely censured for showing it, but is rather commended for gratifying such an inclination, when he thankfully publishes to whom he is indebted for all the comforts and felicities of his life.

But your lordship has another right to these papers, which is equal to that of their being mine: the matter itself directs me to your lordship as the proper patron of the cause, as well as of its advocate. Those that enquire whether there is such a spirit now in the world as animated the greatest examples of antiquity must seek for living instances, as well as abstracted arguments; and those they must take care to produce to the best advantage, if they expect to convince the world that they have found what they sought for.

This therefore being the subject of this following enquiry, it seemed necessary to urge the strongest arguments first, and to prepossess the world in favour of my cause by this Dedication. For those that consider that the virtues which make up a great character, such as magnanimity, capacity for the highest employments, depth of judgment, sagacity, elocution, and fidelity, are united in as eminent a degree in your lordship, as they are found asunder in the true characters of the ancient worthies; that all this is rendered yet more illustrious by your exemplary piety and concern for the Church of England, and your zeal for the rights and honour of the English monarchy; and last of all, that these virtues do so constantly descend from father to son in your lordship's family, that its collateral branches are esteemed public blessings to their age and country, will readily confess that the world does still improve, and will go no further than your lordship to silence all that shall be so hardy as to dispute it.

Justice therefore, as well as gratitude, oblige me to present these papers to your lordship: though, since I have taken the freedom in several particulars to dissent from a gentleman whose writings have been very kindly received in the world, I am bound to declare that the principal reason which induced me to make this address was, not to interest your lordship in my small disputes, but to let the world see that I have a right to subscribe myself,

May it please your lordship,
Your Lordship's
Most Obliged,
And Most Dutiful
Servant and Chaplain,

Preface

THE Argument of these following papers seems, in a great measure, to be so very remote from that Holy Profession and from those studies to which I am, in a more particular manner, obliged to dedicate myself, that it may, perhaps, be expected I should give some account of the reasons which engaged me to set about it.

In the first place, therefore, I imagined that if the several boundaries of *Ancient and Modern Learning* were once impartially stated, men would better know what were still unfinished, and what were, in a manner, perfect; and consequently, what deserved the greatest application upon the score of its being imperfect: which might be a good inducement to set those men who, having a great genius, find also in themselves an inclination to promote learning, upon subjects wherein they might probably meet with success answerable to their endeavours: by which means, knowledge in all its parts might at last be completed . . .

To read Greek and Latin with ease is a thing not soon learned; those languages are too much out of the common road; and the turn which the

Greeks and Latins gave to all their thoughts cannot be resembled by what we ordinarily meet with in modern languages; which makes them tedious till mastered by us. So that constant reading of the most perfect modern books, which does not go jointly on with the ancients, in their turns, will, by bringing the ancients into disuse, cause the learning of the men of the next generation to sink; by reason that they, not drawing from those springs from whence these excellent moderns drew, whom they only propose to follow, nor taking those measures which these men took, must, for want of that foundation which these their modern guides first carefully laid, fail in no long compass of time.

Yet, on the other hand, if men who are unacquainted with these things should find everything to be commended because it is *oldest*, not because it is *best*; and afterwards should perceive that in many material and very curious parts of learning the Ancients were, comparatively speaking, grossly ignorant, it would make them suspect that in all other things also they were equally deficient . . .

But I had another and a more powerful reason to move me to consider this subject; and that was that I did believe it might be very subservient to Religion itself. Among all the hypotheses of those who would destroy our most Holy Faith, none is so plausible as that of the *eternity of the world*. The fabulous histories of the Egyptians, Chaldæans and Chinese seem to countenance that assertion. The seeming easiness of solving all difficulties that occur, by pretending that sweeping floods, or general and successive invasions of barbarous enemies, may have by turns destroyed all the records of the world, till within these last five or six thousand years, makes it very desirable to those whose interest it is that the Christian Religion should be but an empty form of words, and yet cannot swallow the Epicurean whimsies of chance and accident. Now, the notion of the Eternity of Mankind through infinite successive generations of men cannot be at once more effectually and more popularly confuted, than by showing how the world has gone on from age to age improving; and consequently, that it is at present much more knowing than it ever was since the earliest times to which history can carry us . . .

Besides these, I had a third reason to engage me to this undertaking; which was, the pleasure and usefulness of those studies to which it necessarily led me: for discoveries are most talked of in the mechanical philosophy which has been but lately revived in the world. Its professors have drawn into it the whole knowledge of nature, which, in an age wherein Natural Religion is denied by many, and Revealed Religion by very many more, ought to be so far known at least, as that the invisible things of the Godhead may be clearly proved by the things that are seen in the world. Wherefore I thought it might be labour exceedingly well spent, if, whilst I enquired into what was anciently known and what is a new discovery, I should at the same time furnish my mind with new occasions of admiring the boundless wisdom and bounty of that Almighty and Beneficient Essence, in and by whom alone this whole universe, with all its parts, live, and move, and have their being.

I had also a fresh inducement to this search, when I found to how excellent purpose my most learned and worthy friend, Dr. Bentley had, in his late incomparable discourses against atheism, shown what admirable use may be made of an accurate search into nature, thereby to lead us directly up to its Author, so as to leave the unbelieving world without excuse . . .

Chapter 1. General Reflections upon the state of the question:

. . . Soon after the restoration of King Charles II, upon the institution of the Royal Society the comparative excellency of the Old and New Philosophy was eagerly debated in England. But the disputes then managed between [Henry] Stubbe and [Joseph] Glanvill were rather particular, relating to the Royal Society, than general, relating to knowledge in its utmost extent. In France this controversy has been taken up more at large: the French were not satisfied to argue the point in philosophy and mathematics, but even in poetry and oratory too; where the ancients had the general opinion of the learned on their side. Monsieur de Fontenelle, the celebrated author of a book, *Concerning the Plurality of Worlds*, begun the dispute about six years ago, in a little discourse annexed to his Pastorals [*see* above p. 152]. He is something shy in declaring his mind; at least in arraigning the Ancients, whose reputations were already established; though it is plain he would be understood to give the Moderns the preference in poetry and oratory, as well as in philosophy and mathematics. His book being received in France with great applause, it was opposed in England by Sir William Temple, who in the *Second Part* of his *Miscellanea*, has printed an *Essay* upon the same subject. Had Monsieur de Fontenelle's discourse passed unquestioned, it would have been very strange, since there never was a new notion started in the world, but some were found who did as eagerly contradict it.

The hypothesis which Sir William Temple appears for is received by so great a number of learned men, that those who oppose it ought to bring much more than a positive affirmation, otherwise they cannot expect that the world should give judgment in their favour. The question now to be asked has formerly been enquired into by few, besides those who have chiefly valued oratory, poesie, and all that which the French call the *belles lettres*; that is to say, all those arts of eloquence wherein the Ancients are of all hands agreed to have been truly excellent. So that Monsieur de Fontenelle took the wrong course to have his paradox be believed; for he asserts all, and proves little; he makes no induction of particulars, and rarely enters into the merits of the cause: he declares that he thinks love of ease to be the reigning principle amongst mankind; for which reason, perhaps, he was loth to put himself to the trouble of being too minute. It was no wonder therefore if those to whom his proposition appeared entirely new condemned him of *sufficiency, the worst composition out of the pride and ignorance of mankind*...

Chapter 7. General reflections relating to the following chapters: with an account of Sir William Temple's hypothesis of the History of Learning:

... This is a short account of the history of learning, as Sir William Temple has deduced it from its most ancient beginnings. The exceptions which may be made against it are many, and yet more against the conclusions which he draws from it. For, though it be certain that the Egyptians had the grounds and elements of most parts of real learning among them earlier than the Greeks, yet that is no argument why the Grecians should not go beyond their teachers, or why the Moderns might not outdo them both.

Before I examine Sir William Temple's scheme, step by step, I shall offer, as the geometers do, some few things as *postulata*, which are so very plain that they will be assented to as soon as they are proposed. 1. That all men who make a mystery of matters of learning, and industriously oblige their scholars to conceal their dictates, give the world great reason to suspect that their knowledge is all juggling and trick. 2. That he that has only a moral persuasion of the truth of any proposition which is capable of natural evidence cannot so properly be esteemed the inventor, or the discoverer rather, of that proposition, as another man who, though he lived many ages after, brings such evidences of its certainty as are sufficient to convince all competent judges; especially when his reasonings are founded upon observations and experiments drawn from, and made upon, the things themselves. 3. That no pretences to greater measures of knowledge, grounded upon accounts of long successions of learned men in any country, ought to gain belief, when set against the learning of other nations which make no such pretences, unless inventions and discoveries answerable to those advantages be produced by their advocates. 4. That we cannot judge of characters of things and persons at a great distance, when given at second-hand, unless we knew exactly how capable those persons, from whom such characters were first taken, were to pass a right judgment upon such subjects; and also the particular motives that biassed them to pass such censures. If Archimedes should, upon his own knowledge, speak with admiration of the Egyptian geometry, his judgment would be very considerable: but if he should speak respectfully of it only because Pythagoras did so before him, it might, perhaps, signify but very little. 5. That excessive commendations of any art or science whatsoever, as also of the learning of any particular men or nations, only prove that the persons who give such characters never heard of any thing or person that was more excellent in that way; and therefore that admiration may be as well supposed to proceed from their own ignorance, as from the real excellency of the persons or things; unless their respective abilities are otherwise known . . .

Chapter 28: Of the philological learning of the Moderns:

HITHERTO, in the main, I please myself, that there cannot be much said against what I have asserted, though I have all along taken care not to speak too positively, where I found that it was not an easy thing to vindicate every proposition without entering into a controversy, which would bear plausible things on both sides, and so might be run out into a multitude of words, which in matters of this kind are very tiresome . . .

. . . There are thousands of corrections and censures upon authors to be found in the annotations of modern critics, which required more fineness of thought, and happiness of invention than, perhaps, twenty such volumes as those were, upon which these very criticisms were made. For though, generally speaking, good copies are absolutely necessary; though the critic himself ought to have a perfect command of the language and particular style of his author, should have a clear idea of the way and humour of the age in which he wrote; many of which things require great sagacity, as well as great industry; yet there is a peculiar quickness in discerning what is proper to the passage then to be corrected, in distinguishing all the particular circumstances necessary to be observed, and those, perhaps, very numerous; which often raise a judicious critic as much above the author upon whom he tries his skill, as he that discerns another man's thoughts is therein greater than he that thinks . . .

Soon after learning was restored, when copies of books, by printing, were pretty well multiplied, *criticism* began; which first was exercised in setting out correct editions of ancient books; men being forced to try to mend the copies of books, which they saw were so negligently written. It soon became the fashionable learning; and after Erasmus, Budæus, Beatus Rhenanus, and Turnebus had dispersed that sort of knowledge through England, France, Germany, and the Low-Countries, which before had been kept altogether amongst the Italians, it was for about a hundred and twenty years cultivated with very great care: and if since it has been at a stand, it has not been because the parts of men are sunk, but because the subject is in a manner exhausted; or at least so far drained, that it requires more labour, and a greater force of genius, now to gather good gleanings, than formerly to bring home a plentiful harvest; and yet this age has produced men who, in the last, might have been reckoned with the Scaligers, and the Lipsius's. It is not very long since Holstenius, Bochart, and Gerhard Vossius, died; but if they will not be allowed to have been of our age, yet Isaac Vossius, Nicolas Heinsius, Frederick Gronovius, Ezekiel Spanheim, and Grævius, may come in; the two last of whom are still alive, and the others died but a few years since. . . .

In short, to conclude this argument: though philological and critical learning has been generally accused of pedantry because it has sometimes been pursued by men who seemed to value themselves upon abundance of quotations of Greek and Latin, and a vain ostentation of diffused reading, without any thing else in their writings to recommend them; yet the difficulty that there is to do any thing considerable in it, joined with the great advantages which thereby have accrued to the Commonwealth of Learning, have made this no mean head whereon to commend the great *sagacity*, as well as *industry*, of these later ages.

Chapter 30. Reflections upon the reasons of the decay of modern learning assigned by Sir William Temple.

. . . The last of Sir William Temple's reasons of the great decay of modern learning is *pedantry*. The urging of which is an evident argument that his discourse is levelled against learning, not as it stands now, but as it was fifty or sixty years ago. For the New Philosophy has introduced so great a correspondence between men of learning and men of business, which has also been increased by other accidents amongst the masters of other learned professions, that that *pedantry* which formerly was almost universal is now in a great measure disused; especially amongst the young men who are taught in the universities to laugh at that frequent citation of scraps of Latin, in common discourse, or upon arguments that do not require it; and that nauseous ostentation of reading and scholarship in public companies, which formerly was so much in fashion. Affecting to write politely in modern languages, especially the French and ours, has also not a little helped to lessen it; because it has enabled abundance of men who want academical education to talk plausibly, and some exactly, upon abundance of learned subjects. This also has made writers habitually careful to avoid those impertinences which they know would be taken notice of, and ridiculed; and it is probable that a careful perusal of the fine new French books, which of late years have been greedily sought after by the politer sort of gentlemen and scholars, may, in this particular, have done a great deal of good. By this means, and by the help also of some other concurrent causes, those who were not learned themselves, being able to maintain disputes with those that were, forced them to talk more warily, and brought them by little and little to be out of countenance at that vain thrusting of their learning into everything, which before had been but too visible.

Conclusion.

THIS seems to me to be the present state of learning, as it may be compared with what it was in former ages. Whether knowledge will improve in the next age, proportionably as it has done in this, is a question not easily decided. It depends upon a great many circumstances; which, singly, will be ineffectual, and which no man can now be assured will ever meet. There seems reason, indeed, to fear that it may decay, both because ancient learning is too much studied in modern books, and taken upon trust by modern writers, who are not enough acquainted with antiquity to correct their own mistakes; and because natural and mathematical knowledge, wherein chiefly the Moderns are to be studied as originals, begin to be neglected by the generality of those who would set up for scholars . . . though the ROYAL SOCIETY has weathered the rude attacks of such sort of adversaries as [Henry] Stubbe, who endeavoured to have it thought that studying of natural philosophy and mathematics was a ready method to introduce scepticism at least, if not atheism, into the world: yet the sly insinuations of the *men of wit*, that no great things have ever, or are ever like to be performed by the *men of Gresham*, and that every man whom they call a *virtuoso*, must needs be a *Sir Nicholas Gimcrack*: together with the public ridiculing of all those who spend their time and fortunes in seeking after what some call useless natural rarities; who dissect all animals, little as well as great; who think no part of God's workmanship below their strictest examination and nicest search: have so far taken off the edge of those who have opulent fortunes and a love to learning, that physiological studies begin to be contracted amongst physicians and mechanics. For nothing wounds so much as a jest; and when men do once become ridiculous, their labours will be slighted and they will find few imitators . . . However, be the studies of the men of the next age what they will, the writings of the learned men of the present time will be preserved; and as they have raised a nobler monument to the memory of Archimedes and Diophantus, of Hippocrates and Aristotle, of Herophilus and Galen, by improving their inventions, than had been raised for a thousand years before; so some future age, though perhaps not the next, and in a country now possibly little thought of, may do that which our great men would be glad to see done; that is to say, may raise real knowledge upon the foundations laid in this our age, to the utmost possible perfection to which it can be brought by mortal men in this imperfect state, and thereby effectually immortalize the memories of those who laid those foundations, and collected those materials which were so serviceable to them in completing the noble work.

(vi) *from* Richard Bentley, *Dissertation upon the Epistles of Phalaris, Themistocles, Socrates, Euripides, and Others; and the Fables of Aesop*, with a separate title-page in Wotton's *Reflections* (2nd edn., 1697) and [enlarged] *Dissertation upon the Epistles of Phalaris. With an Answer to the Objections of the Honourable Charles Boyle, Esquire* (1699).*

Dissertation

TO MR. WOTTON.

SIR,

I REMEMBER that, discoursing with you upon this passage of Sir W. T. (which I have here set down), I happened to say, that, with all deference to so great an authority, and under a just awe of so sharp a censure, I believed it might be even demonstrated that the *Epistles* of Phalaris are spurious, and that we have nothing now extant of Æsop's own composing. This casual declaration of my opinion, by the power of

*Bentley, *Dissertation.* Reprinted in Alexander Dyce (ed.), *The Works of Richard Bentley*, 3 vols. (London, 1836–8; reprinted A.M.S. Press, N.Y., 1966): [first], ii, pp. 130–237; [second, enlarged], i–ii, p. 129: also substantial excerpts in Guthkelch (ed.), *Battle of the Books* (1908), pp. 107–18; 158–249. Bentley, *Dissertation* [enlarged], partly reprinted in S. H. Monk, op. cit., pp. 72–97.

that long friendship that has been between us, you improved into a promise, that I would send you my reasons in writing, to be added to the new edition of your book, believing it, as I suppose, a considerable point in the controversy you are engaged in. For if it once be made out, that those writings your adversary so extols are supposititious, and of no very long standing, you have then his and his party's own confession, that some of the later pens have outdone the old ones in their kinds: and to others, that have but a mean esteem of the wit and style of those books, it will be a double prejudice against him, in your favour, that he could neither discover the true time nor the true value of his authors.

These, I imagine, were your thoughts when you engaged me to this that I am now doing. But I must take the freedom to profess, that I write without any view or regard to your controversy, which I do not make my own, nor presume to interpose in it. 'Tis a subject so nice and delicate, and of such a mixed and diffused nature, that I am content to make the best use I can of both Ancients and Moderns, without venturing with you upon the hazard of a wrong comparison, or the envy of a true one.

That *some of the oldest books are the best in their kinds*, the same person having the double glory of invention and perfection, is a thing observed even by some of the ancients [Dion. Chrysost. Orat. 33. p. 397]. But then the authors they gave this honour to are Homer and Archilochus; one the father of heroic poem, and the other of epode and trochaic. But the choice of Phalaris and Æsop, as they are now extant, for the two great inimitable originals, is a piece of criticism of a peculiar complexion, and must proceed from a singularity of palate and judgment.

To pass a censure upon all kinds of writings, to show their several excellencies and defects, and especially to assign each of them to their proper authors, was the chief province and the greatest commendation of the ancient critics. And it appears from those remains of antiquity that are left us, that they never wanted employment. For to forge and counterfeit books, and father them upon great names, has been a practice almost as old as letters. But it was then most of all in fashion, when the kings of Pergamus and Alexandria, rivalling one another in the magnificence and copiousness of their libraries, gave great rates for any treatises that carried the names of celebrated authors [Galen. in Hippoc. de Natura Hominis, Comm. 2. p. 17. ed. Basil]. Which was an invitation to the scribes and copiers of those times to enhance the price of their wares by ascribing them to men of fame and reputation, and to suppress the true names, that would have yielded less money. And now and then even an author that wrote for bread, and made a traffic of his labours, would purposely conceal himself, and personate some old writer of eminent note, giving the title and credit of his works to the dead, that himself might the better live by them. But what was then done chiefly for lucre, was afterwards done out of glory and affectation, as an exercise of style, and an ostentation of wit. In this the tribe of the Sophists are principally concerned.

It would be endless to prosecute this part, and show all the silliness and impertinency in the matter of the *Epistles*. For, take them in the whole bulk, if a great person would give me leave, I should say they are a fardle of commonplaces, without any life or spirit from action and circumstance. Do but cast your eye upon Cicero's letters, or any statesman's, as Phalaris was: what lively characters of men there! what descriptions of place! what notifications of time! what particularity of circumstances! what multiplicity of designs and events! When you return to these again, you feel, by the emptiness and deadness of them, that you converse with some dreaming pedant with his elbow on his desk; not with an active, ambitious tyrant, with his hand on his sword, commanding a million of subjects. All that takes or affects you, is a stiffness and stateliness and operoseness of style: but as that is improper and unbecoming in all epistles, so especially it is quite alien from the character of Phalaris, a man of business and despatch . . .

Dissertation [enlarged]

. . . Licinius Mucianus had reported in his history, *that when he was governor of Lycia, himself saw and read in a certain temple there a paper-epistle written from Troy by Sarpedon.* Now, if this were true, Hellanicus and his followers must be miserably out when they make Atossa invent epistles so many hundreds of years after. *But I wonder,* says Pliny, *at this paper-letter of Sarpedon's, since even in Homer's time, so long after Sarpedon, that part of Egypt which alone produces paper was nothing but sea, being afterwards produced by the mud of the Nile. Or, if paper was in use in Sarpedon's time, how came Homer to say, that in that very Lycia where Sarpedon lived, not epistles, but codicils* [lit. *writing-tablets*], *were given to Bellerophontes?* So that learned naturalist refutes the pretended letter of Sarpedon, though, with humble submission, he puts a false colour upon one part of his argument; for the epistle was not given to Bellerophontes in Lycia, but in Argos of Peloponnesus, to be carried to Lycia. However, without that needless colour, he has sufficiently confuted the credulity of Mucianus, who, though he was governor of a great province, and general of a great army, and three times consul in Claudius's and Vespasian's time, and, besides all that, a learned and inquisitive man, was miserably imposed on with a sham letter of Sarpedon's: a remarkable instance, that not only the title of *Honourable*, but even the highest quality and greatest experience, cannot always secure a man from cheats and impostures!

(vii) *from* Sir William Temple, 'Some Thoughts upon Reviewing the Essay of Ancient and Modern Learning' in J. Swift (ed.), *Miscellanea. The Third Part* (1701).

I HAVE been induced by several motives to take a further survey of the controversy arisen of late years concerning the excellence of ancient and modern learning: first, the common interest of learning in general, and particularly in our universities, and to prevent the discouragment of scholars, in all degrees, from reading the ancient authors, who must be acknowledged to have been the foundation of all modern learning, whatever the superstructures may have been; next, a just indignation at the insolence of the modern advocates, in defaming those heroes among the ancients, whose memory has been sacred and admired for so many ages; as Homer, Virgil, Pythagoras, Democritus, &c. This, I confess, gave me the same kind of horror I should have had in seeing some young barbarous Goths or Vandals breaking or defacing the admirable statues of those ancient heroes of Greece or Rome, which had so long preserved their memories honoured, and almost adored, for so many generations.

My last motive was to vindicate the credit of our nation, as others have done that of the French, from the imputation of this injustice and presumption that the modern advocates have used in this case. For which end it will be necessary to relate the whole state of this controversy.

It is by themselves confessed that, till the new philosophy had gotten ground in these parts of the world, which is about fifty or sixty years date, there were but few that ever pretended to exceed or equal the ancients; those that did were only some physicians, as Paracelsus and his disciples, who introduced new notions in physic and new methods of practice, in opposition to the Galenical; and this chiefly from chymical medicines or operations. But these were not able to maintain their pretence long, the credit of their cures, as well as their reasons, soon decaying with the novelty of them, which had given them vogue at first.

Des Cartes was the next that would be thought to excel the ancients by a new scheme or body of philosophy, which, I am apt to think, he had a mind to impose upon the world, as Nostradamus did his prophecies, only for their own amusement and without either of them believing any of it themselves: for Des Cartes, among his friends, always called his philosophy his romance; which makes it as pleasant to hear young scholars possessed with all his notions, as to see boys taking *Amadis* and the *Mirror of Knighthood* for true stories.

The next that set up for the excellency of the new learning above the old were some of Gresham College, after the institution of that society by King Charles II. These began eagerly to debate and pursue this pretence, and were followed by the French Academy, who took up the controversy more at large, and descended to many particulars: Monsieur Fontenelle gave the Academy the preference in poetry and oratory, as well as in philosophy and mathematics; and Monsieur Perrault, in painting and architecture, as well as oratory and poetry; setting up the Bishop of Meaux against Pericles and Thucydides; the Bishop of Nîmes against Isocrates; F. Bourdolone against Nicias; Balsac against Cicero; Voiture against Pliny; Boileau against Horace; and Corneille against all the ancient and famous dramatic poets.

About five or six years ago, these modern pretences were opposed in an *Essay upon Ancient and Modern Learning*: and the *Miscellanea* (whereof that essay was a part) being translated into French, the members of that academy were so concerned and ashamed that a stranger should lay such an infamy upon some of their society, as want of reverence for the ancients, and the presumption of preferring the moderns before them, that they fell into great indignation against the few criminals among them; they began to pelt them with satires and epigrams in writing, and with bitter railleries in their discourses and conversations; and led them such a life that they soon grew weary of their new-fangled opinions; which had perhaps been taken up at first only to make their court, and at second hand to flatter those who flattered their king . . .

The modern advocates, to destroy the monuments of ancient learning, first think it necessary to shew what mean contemptible men were the founders of it, and fall foul upon Pythagoras, the Seven Sages, Empedocles, and Democritus.

For Pythagoras, they are so gracious as to give him some quarter and allow him to be a wiser man than the fools among whom he lived, in an ignorant age and country; in short, they are content he should pass for a lawgiver, but by no means for a philosopher. Now the good judgment shewn in this wise censure of so great a man will easily appear to all that know him . . .

To discredit all the fountains from which Pythagoras is said to have drawn his admirable knowledge, they cannot guess to what purpose he should have gone to Delphos, nor that Apollo's priestesses there should have been famous for discovering secrets in natural or mathematical matters, or moral truths. In this they discover their deep knowledge of antiquity, taking the oracle of Delphos to have been managed by some frantic or fanatic wenches; whereas the Phythias there were only engines managed by the priests of Delphos, who, like those of Egypt, were a college or society of wise and learned men in all sorts of sciences, though the use of them was in a manner wholly applied to the honour and service of their oracle. And we may guess at the rest by the last high priest we know of at Delphos, I mean Plutarch, the best and most learned man of his age, if we may judge by the writings he has left . . .

For the Seven Sages, who are treated like the wise men of Gotham, and I doubt by such as are like acquainted with both, I shall say nothing in their defence, but direct the reader to the essay itself.

For Empedocles and Democritus, I confess, the modern advocates could not have done their cause or themselves more right than in choosing these two great men of the ancients, after Thales and Pythagoras, for the objects of their scorn; for none among them had ever so great esteem and almost veneration, as these four. The two last were the heads or founders of the Ionic and Italic sects of philosophers, and brought not only astronomy and mathematics, but natural and moral philosophy first among the Grecians, whom we may observe in Homer's time to have been as barbarous as the Thracians, governed by nothing but will and passion, violence, cruelty, and sottish superstition.

Empedocles was the glory and the boast of Sicily . . . He was an admirable poet, and thought even to have approached Homer in a poem he writ of natural philosophy, and from which Aristotle is believed to have drawn the body of his, so much followed afterwards in the world. He first invented the art of oratory, and the rules of it. He was an admirable physician, and stopped a plague at Agrigentum by the disposal of fires, which purged the air . . .

Democritus was the founder of that sect which made so much noise afterwards in the world under the name of Epicurus, who owed him both his atoms and his vacuum in his natural philosophy, and his tranquillity of mind in his morals. He spent a vast patrimony in pursuit of learning, by his travels, to learn of the Magi in Chaldæa, the priests in Egypt as far as those of Moroë, and the gymnosophists of India. He was admirable in physic, in the knowledge of natural causes and events. He left many writings in all sorts of sciences . . .

In the mean time, since the modern advocates yield, though very unwillingly, the pre-eminence of the ancients in poetry, oratory, painting, statuary, and architecture, I shall proceed to examine the account they give of those sciences wherein they affirm the moderns to excel the ancients; whereof they make the chief to be the invention of instruments; chymistry, anatomy, natural history of minerals, plants, and animals; astronomy, and optics; music; physic; natural philosophy; philology; and theology; of all which I shall take a short survey.

[Swift's connecting passage:] *Here it is supposed the knowledge of the ancients and moderns in the sciences last mentioned was to have been compared; but whether the author designed to have gone through such a work himself, or intended these papers only for hints to somebody else that desired them, is not known.*

After which the rest was to follow, written in his own hand, as before.

Though it may easily be conjectured from the wonderful productions of the ancients how great their sciences were, especially in the mathematics, which is of all other the most valuable to the use and benefit of mankind; yet we have all the testimonies besides that can be given of the height they were at among the Egyptians, from the ingenious confessions of the Greek authors, as well as from the voyages that were made into Egypt, Phœnicia, Babylon, and even the Indies, by those who are allowed for the greatest among the Greek lawgivers and philosophers; whereof so distinct an account has been given in that essay of the *Miscellanea* (already mentioned) upon ancient and modern learning. But the modern advocates can believe nothing of it, because we know none of the records or histories of those nations remaining, but what was left us by the Greeks; and conclude the infancy of the Egyptians in other sciences, because they left no account of their own history or the reigns of their kings.

I might content myself with what has been already made so plain in this matter by shewing how those ancient Eastern nations were generally without learning, except what was possessed by the priests and preserved as sacred in their colleges and temples; so that, when those came to be ruined, their learning was so too. It has been also demonstrated in the same essay, how all the traces and memorials of learning and story may be lost in a nation by the conquest of barbarous people, great plagues, and great inundations; and for instance, how little is known in Ireland of what is so generally believed, of learning having flourished there. And how little we should know, even of ancient Greece or Italy, or other parts of Europe and Asia, if the two learned languages of Greek and Latin had not been preserved and continued in credit and in use among the few pretenders to any sort of learning in those parts of the world, upon the ravages and destructions in them by the barbarous northern nations.

But, to put this matter past dispute, I shall show more particularly when and how the ancient learning decayed in those nations where it so much flourished in the height of their empires, and fell or declined with the loss of their liberties, or subjection to new conquerors . . .

There are three, which I do not conceive well how they can be brought into the number of sciences; which are chymistry, philology, and divinity.

For that part of chymistry which is conversant in discovering and extracting the virtue of metals or other minerals, or of any simples that are employed with success for health or medicine, 'tis a study that may be of much use and benefit to mankind, and is certainly the most diverting amusement to those that pursue it: but for the other part, which is applied to the transmutation of metals, and the search of the philosopher's stone, which has enchanted, not to say turned, so many brains in the latter ages; "though some men cannot comprehend, how there should have been so much smoke, for so many ages, in the world about it, without some fire," 'tis easy, I think, to conceive that there has been a great deal of fire, without producing anything but smoke. If it be a science, 'tis certainly one of the liberal ones; for the professors or followers of it have spent more money upon it than those of all other sciences together, and more than they will ever recover, without the philosopher's stone. Whether they are now any nearer than they were when they began, I do not know; nor could ever find it determined among wise and learned men whether alchemy were anything more than a wild vision or imagination of some shattered heads, or else a practice of knaves upon fools, as well as sometimes of fools upon themselves. For however Borrichus, or any others, may attribute the vast expenses of the pyramids and treasures of Solomon to the philosopher's stone, I am apt to believe none ever yet had it, except it were Midas, and his possession seems a little discredited by his ass's ears: and I wish the pursuit of many others may not fall under the same prejudice. For my own part, I confess I have always looked upon alchemy in natural philosophy to be like enthusiasm in divinity, and to have troubled the world much to the same purpose. And I should as soon fall into the study of Rosycrucian philosophy, and expect to meet a nymph or a sylph for a wife or a mistress, as with the elixir for my health, or philosopher's stone for my fortune.

It is not so difficult to comprehend how such a folly should last so long in the world, and yet without any ground in nature, or in reason, if a man considers how the pagan religion lasted for so many ages, with such general opinion and devotion, which yet all now confess to have been nothing but an illusion or a dream, with some practice of cunning priests upon the credulous and ignorant people: which seems to have been the case of this modern science; for ancient it is none, nor any at all that I know of.

For philology, I know not well what to make of it; and less, how it came into the number of sciences: if it be only criticism upon ancient authors and languages, he must be a conjurer that can make those moderns, with their comments and glossaries and annotations, more learned than the authors themselves in their own languages, as well as the subjects they treat.

I must confess that the critics are a race of scholars I am very little acquainted with, having always esteemed them but like brokers, who, having no stock of their own, set up a trade with that of other men; buying here and selling there, and commonly abusing both sides, to make out a little paltry gain, either of money or of credit for themselves, and care not at whose cost. Yet the first design of these kind of writers, after the restoration of learning in these western parts, was to be commended, and of much use and entertainment to the age. 'Tis to them we owe the editions of all the ancient authors, the best translations of many out of Greek, the restoring of the old copies, maimed with time or negligence, the correcting of others mistaken in the transcribing, the explaining places obscure, in an age so ignorant of the style and customs of the ancients; and in short, endeavouring to recover those old jewels out of the dust and rubbish wherein they had been so long lost or soiled, to restore them to their native lustre, and make them appear in their true light.

This made up the merit and value of the critics for the first hundred years, and deserved both praise and thanks of the age, and the rewards of princes, as well as the applause of common scholars, which they generally received. But since they have turned their vein to debase the credit and value of the ancients, and raise their own above those to whom they owe all the little they know; and instead of true wit, sense, or genius, to display their own proper colours of pride, envy, or detraction in what they write; to trouble themselves and the world with vain niceties and captious cavils about words and syllables in the judgment of style; about hours and days in the account of ancient actions or times; about antiquated names of persons or places, with many such worthy trifles; and all this, to find some occasion of censuring and defaming such writers as are, or have been, most esteemed in the world, raking into slight wounds where they find any, or scratching till they make some where there were none before: there is, I think, no sort of talent so despisable, as that of such common critics, who can at best pretend but to value themselves by discovering the defaults of other men, rather than any worth or merit of their own: a sort of levellers that will needs equal the best or richest of the country, not by improving their own estates, but reducing those of their neighbours, and making them appear as mean and wretched as themselves. The truth is, there has been so much written of this kind of stuff, that the world is surfeited with the same things over and over, or old common notions, new dressed and perhaps embroidered.

For divinity, wherein they give the moderns such a preference above the ancients, they might as well have made them excel in the knowledge of our common law, or of the English tongue; since our religion was as little known to the ancient sages and philosophers as our language or our laws: and I cannot but wonder, that any divine should so much debate religion or true divinity as to introduce them thus preposterously into the number of human sciences . . .

For Christianity, it came into the world, and so continued in the first age, without the least pretence of learning and knowledge, with the greatest simplicity of thought and language, as well as life and manners, holding forth nothing but piety, charity, and humility, with the belief of the Messias and of his kingdom; which appears to be the main scope of the Gospel, and of the preaching of the Apostles; and to have been almost concealed from the wise and the learned, as well as the mighty and the noble, by both which sorts it was either derided or persecuted.

The first that made any use of learning were the primitive Fathers of the second age, only to confute the idolatrous worship of the heathens and their plurality of gods; endeavouring to evince the Being of one God and immortality of the soul, out of some of their own ancient authors, both poets and philosophers, especially out of the writers of the Platonic sect and the verses of Orpheus and the Sibyls, which then passed for genuine, though they have since by the moderns been questioned, if not exploded: thus Minutius Felix, Origen, Clemens Alexandrinus, Tertullian, made use of the learning of such as were then ancient to them, and thereby became champions of the Christian faith against the gentiles by force of their own weapons.

After the third century, and, upon the rise of the Arian and other heresies in the Christian Church, their learning seems chiefly to have been employed in the defence of the several opinions professed by the Orthodox or the Arians, the Western or Eastern churches, and so to have long continued, by the frequent rise of so many heresies in the church.

And I doubt this kind of learning has been but too great, and made too much use of, upon all the divisions of Christendom, since the restoration of learning in these Western parts of the world; yet this very polemical learning has been chiefly employed to prove their several opinions to be most agreeable to those of the ancient fathers and the institutions of the primitive times; which must needs give the preference to the ancients above the moderns in divinity, since we cannot pretend to know more of what they knew and practised than themselves: and I did as little believe, that any divine in England would compare himself or his learning with those Fathers, as that any of our physicians would theirs with Hippocrates, or our mathematicians with Archimedes.

One would think that the modern advocates, after having confounded all the ancients and all that esteem them, might have been contented; but one of them, I find, will not be satisfied to condemn the rest of the world without applauding himself; and therefore, falling into a rapture upon the contemplation of his own wonderful performance, he tells us, "Hitherto in the main I please myself that there cannot be much said against what I have asserted," &c.

I wonder a divine, upon such an occasion, should not at least have had as much grace as a French lawyer in Montaigne, who, after a dull tedious argument, that had wearied the court and the company, when he went from the bar was heard muttering to himself, *Non nobis, Domine, non nobis*; but this writer, rather like the proud Spaniard, that would not have St. Lawrence's patience upon the gridiron ascribed to the grace of God, but only to the true Spanish valour, will not have his own perfections and excellencies owing to any thing else but the true force of his own modern learning: and thereupon he falls into this sweet ecstasy of joy, wherein I shall leave him till he come to himself . . .

What has been produced for the use, benefit, or pleasure of mankind, by all the airy speculations of those who have passed for the great advancers of knowledge and learning these last fifty years (which is the date of our modern pretenders) I confess I am yet to seek, and should be very glad to find. I have indeed heard of wondrous pretensions and visions of men, possessed with notions of the strange advancement of learning and sciences on foot in this age, and the progress they are like to make in the next: as, the universal medicine, which will certainly cure all that have it; the philosopher's stone, which will be found out by men that care not for riches; the transfusion of young blood into old men's veins, which will make them as gamesome as the lambs from which it is to be derived; an universal language, which may serve all men's turn, when they have forgot their own; the knowledge of one another's thoughts without the grievous trouble of speaking; the art of flying till a man happens to fall down and break his neck; double-bottomed ships, whereof none can ever be cast away besides the first that was made; the admirable virtues of that noble and necessary juice called spittle, which will come to be sold, and very cheap, in the apothecaries' shops; discoveries of new worlds in the planets, and voyages between this and that in the moon to be made as frequently as between York and London: which such poor mortals as I am, think as wild as those of Ariosto, but without half so much wit, or so much instruction; for there these modern sages may know where they may hope in time to find their lost senses, preserved in phials, with those of Orlando.

One great difference must be confessed between the ancient and modern learning: theirs led them to a sense and acknowledgment of their own ignorance, the imbecility of human understanding, the incomprehension even of things about us, as well as those above us . . . ours leads us to presumption, and vain ostentation of the little we have learned, and makes us think we do, or shall know, not only all natural, but even what we call supernatural things; all in the heavens, as well as upon earth; more than all mortal men have known before our age; and shall know in time as much as angels.

Socrates was by the Delphic oracle pronounced the wisest of all men because he professed that he knew nothing: what would the oracle have said of a man that pretends to know everything? Pliny the elder, and most learned of all the Romans whose writings are left, concludes the uncertainty and weakness of human knowledge, with "*Constat igitur inter tanta incerta, nihil esse certi; præterquam hominem, nec miserius quicquam nec superbius*" [It is clear, therefore, that besides man there is no creature more miserable or more assuming]. But, sure our modern learned, and especially the divines of that sect among whom it seems this disease is spread, and who will have the world, "to be ever improving, and that nothing is forgotten that ever was known among mankind," must themselves have forgotten that humility and charity are the virtues which run through the scope of the Gospel; and one would think they never had read, or at least never minded, the first chapter of Ecclesiastes, which is allowed to have been written, not only by the wisest of men, but even by divine inspiration; where Solomon tells us,

"The thing that has been, is that which shall be, and there is no new thing under the sun. Is there any thing whereof it may be said, See, this is new? It has been already of old time which was before us: there is no remembrance of former things, neither shall there be any remembrance of things that are to come with those that shall come after."

These, with many other passages in that admirable book, were enough, one would think, to humble and mortify the presumption of our modern sciolist[s], if their pride were not as great as their ignorance;

of if they knew the rest of the world any better than they know themselves.

(viii) *from* William King, LLD, *Some Remarks upon the Tale of a Tub* (1704).*

[The facetious King, suspected of being the author of *A Tale*, distances himself from it by a piece of self-deprecation, writing in the character of a night-soil collector.]

Gravel Lane in Old Street, 10 June 1704

. . . It may lie in the power of the meanest person to do a service or a disservice to the greatest, according as his inclination or his due respect may lead him; which is the true occasion of my writing you this letter, to show you that a person in the lowest circumstances in the world may still have a concern to do good; as I hope it is yours to do so to everybody else. Although I believe you know not me; yet I have known you from a child, and am certain you cannot forget Mr. Seyley the chimney-sweeper; any more than you can your neighbour the small-coalman at Clerkenwell, at whose music-meeting I have often performed a part in your hearing, and have seen you several times at the auction of his books, which were a curiosity that I could have wished you had been able to have purchased.

I own that I am a person, as far as my capacity and other circumstances will give me leave, desirous of my own improvement and knowledge, and therefore look into all books that may contribute towards them. It is natural for every person to look after things in their own way. The fisherman asks for *The Compleat Angler* . . . the tailor for *Gammer Gurton's Needle*.

Now, sir, I must own, that it has been my fortune to find very few that tend any way to my own employment . . .

But at last it happened that, as I was returning from my *nightly* vocation, which, beginning between eleven and twelve in the evening, generally employs me till the dawn of the succeeding morning; and being melancholy that I had not found so much gold that night as I might be supposed to have done either by my wife or my neighbours, I saw a fellow pasting up the title-pages of books at the corners of the streets; and there, among others, I saw one called *A Tale of a Tub*, which imagining to be a satire upon my profession, I ordered one of my myrmidons to attack the fellow, and not to box him, but give him two or three gentle strokes over the nostrils; till at last the fellow, being of a ready wit, as having to do with

*Reprinted in *The Original Works in Verse and Prose of Dr William King*, 3 vols. (1776), i, 213–18.

all sorts of authors, promised to go to Mr. Nutt's for one of the copies; and that, if he did not convince me that it was a more scandalous libel upon the author of that foolish Tale, than it could be upon anyone else, he would engage that I should set him astride upon one of my barrels, whenever I should meet him publishing any thing printed for the same stationer.

Sir, pardon me, if I fancy you may, by what I have said, guess at my profession: but I desire you not to fear, for I declare to you that I affect cleanliness to a nicety. I mix my ink with rose or orange-flower-water, my scrutoire is of cedar-wood, my wax is scented, and my paper lies amongst sweet bags. In short, I will use you with a thousand times more respect than the bookseller of *A Tale of a Tub* does a noble peer, under the pretence of a dedication; or than the author does his readers.

It was not five o'clock when I had performed a severe penance; for I had read over a piece of nonsense, inscribed 'To his Royal Highness Prince Posterity'; where there is so considerable an aim at nothing, and such an accomplishment of that design, that I have not in my library met any thing that equals it. I never gave over till I had read his *Tale*, his *Battle*, and his *Fragment*: I shall speak of the series and style of these three treatises hereafter. But the first remarkable story that I found was that, about the twenty-second page, concerning a fat fellow crowding to see a mountebank. I expected to have found something witty at the end: but it was all of a piece; so stuffed with curses, oaths, and imprecations, that the most profligate criminal in New[gate] prison would be ashamed to repeat it.

I must take notice of one other particular piece of nonsense, and no more; where he says, 'That the ladder is an adequate symbol of faction and of poetry. Of faction, because . . . *Hiatus in MS* . . . Of poetry, because its orators do *perorare* with a song.' The true reasons why I do not descend to more particulars is, because I think the three treatises (which, by their harmony in dirt, may be concluded to belong to one author) may be reduced to a very small compass, if the commonplaces following were but left out. But the author's first aim is to be profane; but that part I shall leave to my betters, since matters of such a nature are not to be jested with, but to be punished.

The second is, to show how great a proficient he is at hectoring and bullying, at ranting and roaring, and especially at cursing and swearing. He makes his persons of all characters full of their oaths and imprecations; nay, his very spider has his share, and, as far as in the author lies, he would transmit his impiety to things that are irrational.

His third is, to exceed all bounds of modesty. Men who are obliged by necessity to make use of uncommon expressions, yet have an art of making all appear decent; but this author, on the other side, endeavours to heighten the worst colours, and to that end he searches his ancient authors for their lewdest images, which he manages so as to make even impudence itself to blush at them.

His next is, a great affectation for everything that is nasty. When he spies any object that another person would avoid looking on, that he embraces. He takes the air upon dung-hills, in ditches, and common-shores, and at my Lord Mayor's dog-kennel. In short, almost every part has a tincture of such filthiness, as renders it unfit for the worst of uses.

By the first of these, he shows his *religion*; by the second, his *conversation*; by the third, his *manners*; and by the fourth, his *education*.

Now were the crow, who at present struts so much in the gutter, stripped of these four sorts of feathers, he would be left quite naked: he would have scarce one story, one jest, one allusion, one simile, or one quotation. And I do assure Mr. Nutt, that, if he should employ me in my own calling; I would bargain not to foul my utensils with carrying away the works of this author. Such were my sentiments upon reading these pieces; when, knowing that no sponge or fair water will clean a book, when foul ink and fouler notions have sullied the paper, I looked upon the fire as the properest place for its purgation, in which it took no long time to expire.

Now, sir, you may wonder how you may be concerned in this long story; and why I apply myself to you, in declaring my sentiments of this author. But I shall show you my reason for it, before I conclude this my too tedious epistle.

Now, sir, in the dearth of wit that is at present in the town, all people are apt to catch at anything that may afford them any diversion; and what they cannot find, they make: and so this author was bought up by all sorts of people, and every one was willing to make sense of that which had none in it originally. It was sold, not only at court, but in the city and suburbs; but, after some time, it came to have its due value put upon it: the brewer, the soap-boiler, the train-oil-man, were all affronted at it; and it afforded a long dispute at our coffee-house over the Gate, who might be the author.

A certain gentleman, that is the nearest to you of any person, was mentioned, upon supposition that the book had wit and learning in it. But, when I displayed it in its proper colours, I must do the company that justice, that there was not one but acquitted you. That matter being dispatched, everyone was at liberty of guessing. One said, he believed it was a journey-man tailor in Billeter Lane, that was an idle sort of a fellow and loved writing more than stitching, that was the author; his reason was, 'because here he is so desirous to mention "his Goose and his Garret"': but it was answered, 'that he was a member of the Society'; and so he was excused. 'But why then,' says another, 'since he makes such a *parable* upon coats, may he not be Mr. Amy the coat-seller, who is a poet and a wit?' To which it was replied, 'That that gentleman's loss had been bewailed in an elegy some years ago.'—'Why may not it be Mr. Gumly the rag-woman's husband in Turnball Street?' says another. 'He is kept by her; and, having little to do, and having been an officer in Monmouth's Army, since the defeat at Sedgemore has always been a violent Tory.' But it was urged 'that his style was harsh, rough, and unpolished; and that he did not understand one word of Latin.'—'Why then,' cries another, 'Oliver's [i.e. Oliver Cromwell's] porter had an amanuensis at Bedlam, that used to transcribe what he dictated: and may not these be some scattered notes of his master's?' To which all replied, 'that, though Oliver's porter was crazed, yet his misfortune never let him forget that he was a Christian.' One said, 'It was a surgeon's man, that had married a midwife's nurse': but, though by the style it might seem probable that two such persons had a hand in it; yet, since he could not name the persons, his fancy was rejected. 'I conjecture,' says another, 'that it may be a lawyer, that——' When, on a sudden, he was interrupted by Mr. Markland, the scrivener, 'No, rather, by the oaths, it should be an Irish evidence.' At last there stood up a sprant young man, that is secretary to our scavenger, and cries, 'What if after all it should be a parson!* for who may make more free with their trade? What if I know him, describe him, name him, and how he and his friends talk of it, admire it, are proud of it.'—'Hold, cry all the company; that function must not be mentioned without respect. We have enough of the dirty subject: we had better drink our coffee, and talk our politics.'

(ix) *from* William Wotton, *A Defence of the Reflections upon Ancient and Modern Learning, in Answer to the Objections of Sir W. Temple and Others, with observations upon The Tale of a Tub* (1705); published both separately and at the end of *Reflections* (3rd edn., 1705), pp. 411–541.†

* The clergyman here alluded to is not the real author, who was not at the time suspected, but Mr. Thomas Swift, rector of Puttenham in Surrey, whom the Dean calls his 'parson cousin', and who appears to have taken some pains to be considered as the author of the *Tale of a Tub*. [Editorial note, 1776.]

† Reprinted, at more length, in Guthkelch, pp. 314–28.

[Wotton came to believe that Temple was the author of *A Tale*.]

To Anthony Hammond, Esq;

I have now given a full answer, as I think, Sir, to all the argumentative part of Sir Temple's *Thoughts upon the Reflexions* [see above p. 173]. If we do not allow that he misunderstood the questions as I had plainly stated it, we must believe that he wilfully mistook it; and the rather, because when he was to examine the several particulars in which I apprehended that the preference was to be given to the moderns, he drops the question. It is done decently indeed, and there is a *Hiatus in Manuscripto*, as the publisher of the *Tale of a Tub* expresses it, that so we may suppose the comparison was intended to be made, and only by accident left imperfect . . . This method of answering of books, and of publishing such answers, is very dissatisfactory. Just where the pinch of the question lay, there the copy fails, and where there was more room for flourishing, there Sir W. Temple was as copious as one would wish. To use his own words, *This is very wonderful, if it be not a Jest*; and I take it for granted, Dr. Swift had express orders to print these fragments of an answer.

This way of printing bits of books that in their nature are intended for continued discourses, and are not loose apophthegms, occasional thoughts, or incoherent sentences, is what I have seen few instances of; none more remarkable than this, and one more which may be supposed to imitate this, *The Tale of a Tub*, of which a brother of Dr. Swift's is publicly reported to have been the editor at least, if not the author. In which though Dr. Bentley and myself are coarsely treated, yet I believe I may safely answer for us both, that we should not have taken any manner of notice of it, if upon this occasion I had not been obliged to say something in answer to what has been seriously said against us.

For, believe me, sir, what concerns us, is much the innocentest part of the book, tending chiefly to make men laugh for half an hour, after which it leaves no farther effects behind it. When men are jested upon for what is in itself praiseworthy, the world will do them justice: and on the other hand, if they deserve it, they ought to sit down quietly under it. Our cause therefore we shall leave to the public very willingly, there being no occasion to be concerned at any man's raillery about it. But the rest of the book which does not relate to us, is of so irreligious a nature, is so crude a banter upon all that is esteemed as sacred among all sects and religions among men, that, having so fair an opportunity, I thought it might be useful to many people who pretend they see no harm in it, to lay open the mischief of the ludicrous allegory, and to show what that drives at which has been so greedily bought up and read. In one word, God and religion, truth and moral honesty, learning and industry are made a May-game, and the most serious things in the world are described as so many several scenes in a *Tale of a Tub.*

That this is the true design of that book, will appear by these particulars . . .

The next subject of our *Tale-Teller's* wit is the *Glosses* and *Interpretations of Scripture*, very many absurd ones of which kind are allowed in the most authentic books of the Church of Rome. The sparks wanted silver fringe to put upon their coats. Why, says Peter (seemingly perhaps to laugh at Dr. Bentley and his criticisms): "I have found in a certain author which shall be nameless, that the same word which in the Will is called *fringe*, does also signify a *broomstick*, and doubtless ought to have the same interpretation in this paragraph." [p. 4] This affording great diversion to one of the brothers: "You speak, says Peter, very irreverently of a *Mystery*, which doubtless was very useful and significant, but ought not to be overcuriously pried into or nicely reasoned upon." [p. 42] The author, one would think, copies from Mr. Toland, who always raises a laugh at the word Mystery, the word and thing whereof he is known to believe to be no more than a Tale of a Tub . . .

But I expect, sir, that you should tell me, that the *Tale-teller* falls here only upon the ridiculous inventions of popery; that the Church of Rome intended by these things to gull silly superstitious people; and to rook them of their money; that the world had been but too long in slavery; that our ancestors gloriously redeemed us from that yoke; that the Church of Rome therefore ought to be exposed, and that he deserves well of mankind that does expose it.

All this, sir, I own to be true: but then I would not so shoot at an enemy, as to hurt myself at the same time. The foundation of the doctrines of the Church of England is right, and came from God: upon this the Popes, and Councils called and confirmed by them, have built, as St. Paul speaks, *hay and stubble*, perishable and slight materials, which when they are once consumed, that the foundation may appear, then we shall see what is faulty and what is not. But our *Tale-teller* strikes at the very root. 'Tis all with him a farce, and all a ladle, as a very facetious Poet says upon another occasion. The Father, and the WILL, and *his son Martin*, are part of the *Tale*, as well as *Peter* and *Jack*, and are all ushered in with the common old-wives introduction, *Once upon a time* [p. 34]. And the main *body of the Will* we are told consisted in *certain admirable Rules about the wearing of* their coats [p. 34]. So that let *Peter* be mad one way, and *Jack* another, and let *Martin* be sober, and spend his time with patience and phlegm in picking the embroidery off his coat never so carefully . . . Yet still this is all part of a *Tale of a Tub*, it does but enhance the *Teller's* guilt, and shows at the bottom his contemptible opinion of everything which is called Christianity.

For pray, sir, take notice that it is not saying he personates none but papists or fanatics, that will excuse him; for in other places, where he speaks in his own person, and imitates none but himself, he discovers an equal mixture of lewdness and irreligion. Would any Christian compare a *Mountebank's-Stage*, a *Pulpit*, and a *Ladder* together? A *Mountebank* is a professed cheat, who turns it off when he is pressed, with the common jest, *Men must live*; and with this man the preacher of the Word of God is compared, and the pulpit in which he preaches, is called *an Edifice* (or castle) *in the Air* [p. 25). This is not said by *Peter*, or *Jack*, but by the author himself, who after he has gravely told us that he has had poxes ill cured by trusting to bawds and surgeons, reflects with "unspeakable comfort, upon his having past a long life with a *Conscience void of offence towards God and towards man*" [p. 33] . . .

. . . His whole VIIIth Section concerning the *Aeolists*, in which he banters inspiration, is such a mixture of impiety and immodesty, that I should have as little regard to you, sir, as this author has had to the public, if I should barely repeat after him what is there. And it is somewhat surprizing that the citation out of Irenaeus, in the title-page, which seems to be all gibberish, should be a form of initiation used anciently by the Marcosian heretics . . . So great a delight has this unhappy writer to play with what some part or other of mankind have always esteemed as Sacred!

And therefore when he falls upon *Jack*, he deals as freely with him, and wounds Christianity through his sides as much as he had done before through *Peter's* . . . And because he could not of a sudden recollect *an authentic phrase*, for the necessities of nature, he would use no other [p. 93]: can anything be prophaner than this? Things compared, always show the esteem or scorn of the comparer . . . The agreement of our Dissenters and the Papists, in that which Bishop Stillingfleet called the *Fanaticism of the Church of Rome*, is ludicrously described for several pages together by *Jack's* likeness to *Peter*, and their being often mistaken for each other, and their frequent meeting when they least intended it [p. 97]: in this, singly taken, there might possibly be little harm, if one did not see from what principle the whole proceeded.

This 'tis which makes the difference between the sharp and virulent books written in this age against any sect of Christians, and those which were written about the beginning of the Reformation between the several contending parties then in Europe. For though the rage and spite with which men treated one another was as keen and as picquant then as it is now, yet the inclination of mankind was not then irreligious, and so their writings had little other effect but to increase men's hatred against any one particular sect, whilst Christianity, as such, was not hereby at all undermined. But now the Common Enemy appears barefaced, and strikes in with some one or other sect of Christians, to wound the whole by that means. And this is the case of this book, which is one of the profanest banters upon the religion of Jesus Christ, as such, that ever yet appeared. In the *Tale*, in the *Digressions*, in the *Fragment*, the same spirit runs through, but rather most in the *Fragment*, in which all extraordinary inspirations are the subjects of his scorn and mockery, whilst the Protestant Dissenters are, to outward appearance, the most directly levelled at. The Bookseller indeed in his Advertisement prefixed to the *Fragment*, pretends to be *wholly ignorant of the author, and he says, he cannot conjecture whether it be the same with that of the two foregoing pieces, the original having been sent him at a different time, and in a different hand.* It may be so; but the style, and turn, and spirit of this *Fragment*, and of the *Tale* being the same, nobody, I believe, has doubted of their being written by the same author. If the authors are different, so much the worse, because it shows there are more men in the world acted by the same spirit. But be the author one or more, the mask is more plainly taken off in the *Fragment* . . . Enthusiasm with him is an universal deception which has run through all sciences in all kingdoms, and everything has some *Fanatic Branch annexed to it* [p. 128]; among which he reckons the *Summum Bonum*, or *an Enquiry after Happiness* . . . Can anything be more blasphemous than his *game at leap-frog between the Flesh and Spirit*? [p. 136: Romans 7]. This affects the doctrine of St. Paul, and not the private interpretations of this or that particular Sect; and this too is described in the language of the stews, which with now and then a Scripture-expression, compose this writer's style . . . And in his account of Fanaticism, he tells us, *That the Thorn in the Flesh, serves for a Spur to the Spirit* [p. 140]. Is not this to ridicule St. Paul's own description of his own temptation; in which the Apostle manifestly alludes to a passage in the Prophet *Ezekiel* [2 Cor. 12; Ezek. 28: 24].

What would men say in any country in the world but this, to see their religion so vilely treated from the press? I remember to have seen a French translation of the learned Dr. Prideaux (the present worthy Dean of Norwich's) *Life of Mahomet*, printed in France, I think at Paris, in the

Advertisement before which, the translator tells the public that he did not translate the *Letter to the Deists*, thereto annexed in English, because, says he, our Government suffers no such people, and there is no need of antidotes where there is no poison. Be this true or false in France, it matters not to our present purpose; but it shows that no man dares publicly play with Religion in that country. How much do the Mahometans reverence the *Alcoran*? Dares any man among them openly despite their Prophet, or ridicule the words of his Law? How strictly do the Banians, and the others Sects of the Gentile East-Indians worship their Pagods, and respect their temples? This, sir, you well know, is not superstition nor bigotry. It is of the essence of Religion, that the utmost regard should be paid to the Name and Words of God, both which upon the slightest, and the most ridiculous occasions, are played upon by common oaths, and idle allusions to Scripture expressions, in this whole book. I do not carry my charge too far.

For admitting that this writer intended to make himself and his readers sport, by exercising his wit and mirth upon a couple of pedants, as he esteems Dr. Bentley and myself; yet since the *Tale* may thus be explained, and since to your knowledge and mine, sir, it has been thus interpreted by unconcerned readers, the mischief which it does is equally great to mankind. Besides, even that excuse will not serve in the *Fragment*, which is levelled at no particular man that I can find whatsoever. Dr. King, late of Christ-Church, was so sensible of this, that when by reason of the personalities (as the French call them) in the book, it was laid at his door, he took care immediately to print such *Remarks* upon it, as effectually cleared him from the imputation of having writ it: he therein did like a Christian; and he that is one, would be very uneasy under the character of being none. And this is what Mr. [Thomas] Swift is yet under greater Obligations to do, because of his profession. The world besides will think it odd, that a man should in a dedication play upon that great man, to whom he is more obliged than to any other man now living; for it was at Sir William Temple's request, that my Lord Somers, then Lord-Keeper of the Great Seal of England, gave Mr. Swift a very good benefice in one of the most delicious parts of one of the pleasantest counties of England. It is publicly reported that he wrote this book: It is a story, which you know, sir, I neither made, nor spread; for it has been long as public as it can well be. The injury done to Religion, that any of its ministers should lie under the imputation of writing such a burlesque upon it, will be irreparable, if the person so charged does not do *it* and *himself* justice. I say *himself*, for in my own conscience I acquit him from composing it. The author, I believe, is dead, and it is probable that it was writ in the Year 1697, when it is said to have been written . . .

And now, sir, I heartily ask your pardon for troubling you with so long a letter. You know the true reasons and inducements of my writing the *Reflexions* at first; I cannot think it needed any apology then, and so I do not write this letter as an Apology now . . .

SIR,

May 21. *Your most Obliged and*
1705. *Faithful Servant,*

W. Wotton.

FINIS.

APPENDIX B: THOMAS SWIFT AND *A TALE OF A TUB*

THE Revd Thomas Swift (1665–1752) was Jonathan Swift's first cousin and almost his exact contemporary. For perhaps twenty years their lives seem to have run the same course: both were left fatherless in infancy; they attended Kilkenny School together and then Trinity College, Dublin. The Revolution in Ireland sent them to England: Jonathan to Moor Park, Thomas to Oxford, where they both took the degree of Master of Arts in 1692. Each took holy orders and then resided, perhaps alternating, at or near Moor Park for the rest of the decade. Clearly Sir William Temple represented to both cousins their likeliest avenue to preferment, which came to Thomas in 1694 at Puttenham, only four miles away in Surrey, while Jonathan, after the brief residence at Kilroot near Belfast, remained as Temple's literary assistant until his death in 1699.

Two letters from Jonathan to Thomas testify to some degree of friendship in 1692 and 1693, and a common interest in literary composition (*Correspondence*, i. 6 and 13). If, as several early sources affirm, the first drafts or sketches of what became *A Tale of a Tub* were composed at Trinity College, Dublin, then the likelihood that Thomas Swift saw them and even advised his cousin over a period of years must be regarded as fairly strong. Similarly, the full extent of Jonathan's literary involvement with Temple in the 1690s must have been difficult to screen from the neighbouring Rector of Puttenham. These probabilities stand independently of the evidence which has accumulated since 1705 that Thomas Swift claimed, after its publication, some share in writing *A Tale of a Tub*.

Briefly, this evidence proceeds from the following sources. In William Wotton's *A Defence of the Reflections* . . . (see p. 185), both Swift cousins are mentioned, and distinguished, Jonathan as *Dr* and Thomas as *Mr.* Twice Wotton refers to the report, 'as public as it can well be', that Thomas Swift was the 'Editor at least, if not the Author' of *A Tale of a Tub*, but goes on to add, '*in my own Conscience* I acquit him from composing it' since he believed that Temple was in fact its author. Five years later, just before publication of the fifth edition of *A Tale*, a pamphlet entitled *A Complete Key to the Tale of a Tub* (Teerink 1004) and published by the notorious Edmund Curll, explicitly assigned the authorship of *A Tale* jointly to Jonathan and Thomas Swift, whom it further identified, and circumstantially accounted for the divided authorship, finally listing the responsibility of each (see p. 198, below).

A Complete Key constituted a serious challenge. Jonathan Swift on 29 June 1710 told his London publisher (see p. 200) that he suspected his cousin Thomas of being 'at the bottom of this'. He then issues the challenge which was printed, in similar terms, as a postscript to the *Apology* that accompanied the fifth edition of *A Tale* in 1710 (see p. 10): 'and tell him, "if he can explain some things, you will, if he pleases, set his name to the next edition."'

That Jonathan was correct in his conjecture we now know for certain. Two annotated copies of *A Tale* associated with Thomas Swift's claim were known in the eighteenth and nineteenth centuries; both were seen by John Nichols (*TLS*, 30 September 1926, p. 654). One appears to have contained the matter of *A Complete Key* in the margins in Thomas Swift's autograph; the other belonged to Lady Betty Germain, who testified in a note at the beginning that Thomas Swift had himself written in this copy, and the respective sections were assigned to either cousin in the margins.

The various reports of these volumes (Guthkelch, p. xvii and note 1) are difficult to reconcile. However, any doubts are resolved by the crucial discovery, by R. M. Adams and D. D. Eddy, of the most vital piece of evidence (see p. xxv, above; Adams 1967). This is a copy of the first edition of *A Tale*, now in Cornell University Library, which has been annotated by Thomas Swift in his own hand. The marginal annotations in this volume, as well as similar but not identical annotations (in another hand) in a copy of the third edition at Columbia University Library, provided the source almost word for word of the 'Clavis' section of *A Complete Key*. Edmund Curll's note in his own copy of this *Key*, 'Given me by Ralph Noden, Esq.', scarcely affects the ascription to Thomas Swift of the *Key*, which Adams clearly demonstrates. Even the first four pages of the pamphlet, 'The Occasion of Writing *A Tale*', have links with the marginal annotations. An expansion of the latter gives a text that might lead one reasonably to infer that Thomas Swift provided the matter in the first instance.

This may be shown by considering the matter in the margins of the Cornell first edition. Near the beginning, in 'The Bookseller to the Reader' (p. 13), Thomas Swift has drawn a pointing hand, and has underlined, amended, and annotated the second paragraph to read unambiguously that *he*, being the author, concludes that the manuscript is lost, having lent it to a person 'since dead [*deleted*]' and being never in Possession of it after: So that, whether the Work received his last Hand ["which it never did"], or, whether he intended to fill up the defective Places, is like to remain a Secret.' He then comments [contractions expanded]: 'Excepting the words blotted out the rest are exactly true. Vide the Advertisement of the Bookseller before the Fragment'. One accordingly turns to a similar piece of underlining and commenting, accompanied by two pointing hands, on the 'Bookseller's Advertisement' to the last piece in the volume, *The Mechanical Operation of the Spirit* (p. 165). The penultimate sentence has been underlined and the concluding words glossed in the lower margin thus: 'in a *Different Hand*, because the One was my hand, & I suppose the other my cozens'. On an interleaf belonging at this point Thomas Swift has written, 'Whoever put this Book into the Press however he might have the Conscience to make a Penny of It, yet had withall the Modesty not to own It, as the Reader may well perceive by this Advertisement & by that to the Reader which follows the Dedication to Lord Somers.' And on the blank verso of the title-page to *The Mechanical Operation* is written the longest and most significant of his comments:

Whoever reads this Book may plainly see by this & the other part of the Bookseller to the Reader which follows the Dedication, & says thus [As to the Author I can give no manner of satisfaction, however I am credibly informed that this Publication is without his knowledge; for He concludes the Copy is lost having lent it to a Person, and being never in possession of it after] that this Fragment & the Tale of the Tub belong to the same hand; & any One of judgment may perceive that they are of a different stile from the Battle of the Books the Dedication the Preface & the Digressions which are indeed of a much more refined fancy as I must freely acknowledge: tho' I do find Dashes of His & mine mingled which makes the style so much the harder to be distinguished. I do remember that I ranged the Armies of the Antients & Moderns in the Battle of the Bookes, assigning which should be the Horse & which the Foot, but It being seven years agoe I do remember the less of the particulars.

This quite categorical statement establishes the extent of Thomas Swift's claim, and a number of useful facts apart. He does not claim the preliminary sections or the Digressions, or the *Battle* (beyond some details). He does claim the *Tale* proper and the *Fragment*, which he places from recollection in the body of the *Tale* between sections X and XI. And he appeals to the reader to discriminate on the grounds of style between the two groups, at the same time conceding that the former is of 'a much more refined fancy, as I must freely acknowledge'. Then he must be referring to his own group in admitting to 'find Dashes of His & mine mingled which makes the style so much the harder to be distinguished'. What starts out as a bold appeal to the reader who may 'plainly see', ends rather lamely with exceptions and an admission that 'It being seven years agoe I do remember the less of the particulars'. If these marginalia were set down in, or soon after, May 1704 then 'seven years agoe' points to 1697 (see p. 104).

Thomas Swift's annotations may be readily evaluated. Two similar sets of annotations are available for comparison. Wotton published his consecutively in the text of his *Defence of the Reflections* (partly reprinted in Guthkelch, pp. 315–28). Jonathan Swift selected some of these in making up a set of annotations of his own, which were then printed in the fifth edition of *A Tale*, 1710, and separately in 1711 (Teerink 222 and Teerink 223; see p. xxviii). Believing that Temple wrote *A Tale*, and asserting that Thomas Swift was held to be the editor at least, Wotton levelled his charges of irreligion at Thomas, not Jonathan Swift. Wotton's explication is confined to the *Tale* and the *Fragment*; given their tendentious aim, the learned explanations are what one might expect from an earnest clergyman reading a new book of divinity. Obvious points are elucidated. Much the same may be said of Thomas Swift's notes, though more numerous and detailed, many of which simply give the gist of passage after passage, in the manner of the printed side-notes of seventeenth-century texts. Indeed it appears, from their placing in the margins, aligned with the relevant bit of text yet grammatically continuous through several separated notes, that they may first have been written out *en bloc* and then transcribed into the margins of the book. Insights that might prove Thomas's authorship turn out to be very few. 'By this Gold Lace I intended to sett forth the Processions & vain Pomp of the R C Religion but He has inserted it here in a wrong place' (see p. 39) is almost the sole example. A reminiscence is attached to the mention of Vaughan's *Anima Magica Abscondita*: 'When the Author was a Youth He had this book of Eug: Philalethes bestowed Him by a R. Priest with the Character [of] a very learned Piece, but found it [to] be onely a mad grave Banter.' Compare with this the note written by Jonathan Swift at the same point (p. 91). It is perhaps correct to say that Thomas Swift remembered enough from 1697 not to go wrong.

And yet he has gone demonstrably wrong here and there. Comparing his notes with Jonathan Swift's notes (to the 5th edn. of *A Tale*, 1710), we can find contrary explanations of the same text. In such a case, who is right? The very first note to Section II (p. 34), the opening chapter of the allegory proper which Thomas unequivocally claimed, may serve as an example. Wotton's 'note' on the three sons identifies them with 'Popery, the Church of England and our Protestant Dissenters'; then his next 'note' says that the coats are 'the Garments of the Israelites'. These were then excerpted by Jonathan from Wotton's *Defence*. Upon them Jonathan Swift wryly comments in *his* note, 'An Error (with submission) of the learned Commentator, for by the Coats are meant the Doctrines and Faith of Christianity, by the Wisdom of the Divine Founder fitted to all Times, Places and Circumstances', and he appends the mock editorial signature 'Lambin.' Thomas Swift gets it wrong. He says 'these Coats are the 3 Religions C of England of Rome & Presby:'. He has not even caught (as Wotton had) the subtle distinction between the sons and their coats, which is fundamental to the fairly obvious mechanics of the allegory.

The revealing comparison, however, is with the notes printed as a body by Jonathan Swift. Not only are they infinitely better written, but fuller and more informative, and annotate a host of points on which Thomas Swift remains silent. One is driven to the conclusion that for Jonathan the book is a familiar and living thing, but for his 'parson cousin' an inflexible and indistinct memory, so that his only resort was to paraphrase the text before him.

The familiar and quite legitimate argument against Thomas Swift's authorship of even part of *A Tale* is that he was, on the evidence of his surviving work, simply unequal to the achievement. If one looks first at the acknowledged work of the two cousins, one arguably the greatest English prose stylist of his time, the other the author of one turgid published sermon, *Noah's Dove* (1710), some scepticism is no doubt justified. Even on these disproportionate terms some direct comparisons may be made. Both men have left a description of the occasion of writing *The Battle of the Books*, a work allowed by Thomas to Jonathan, whose succinct account of the quarrel between the Ancients and the Moderns precedes *The Battle* and is called 'The Bookseller to the Reader' (see p. 104). In the blank space which follows the printing of this in his copy of the first edition, now at Cornell, Thomas thought it necessary to set down in his own words an alternative account:

> Sir William Temple being a great admirer of the Antients & expressing it much in a Treatise He published, was answered by One Mr Wootten then Chaplain to my Lord Guernsey, who I suppose did it out of no other design than that of raising his own Character, & making his Book be taken the more notice of, by the Eminence of the Person it opposed, the Author of this Treatise having Love & Honour for Sir Will: Temple writt these few pages to lash Mr Wootten.

The total effect of Thomas's sentences is muddy. There is no poise in the phrases; the development of thought is by jerks. Jonathan Swift automatically shaped everything he wrote, no matter what the occasion; Thomas, like most people, did not.

The awkward and obscure expression of *Noah's Dove* has till now been the principal exhibit in the case against Thomas's claim to have written *A Tale*. But there is at Harvard University, in the Houghton Library (MS. Eng. 218.14), some unpublished testimony specifically on this point. In the course of annotating an interleaved copy of his *Remarks on . . . Swift*, the Earl of Orrery has underlined this passage (on p. 304) in his discussion of *A Tale*: 'sometimes not a syllable of it was his work, it was the work of *one of his uncle's sons*, a clergyman'. On the interleaf opposite, in a clerk's hand, is this long note:

The Character of the Reverend Mr. Thomas Swift, Cousin German of the Dean of St. Patrick's In a Letter from Dean[e] Swift Esqr.

The Son of *Thomas Swift* by a daughter of *Sir William Davenant*. He and Doctor *Swift* are much of the same age: both were educated at Kilkenny School. It is certain that Thomas Swift is a man of abilities, but Wit and Humour are not his talent, as may be judged from his Sermon [i.e. *Noah's Dove*] occasioned by the peace, and dedicated to my Lord Oxford, in which, without the least Genius for Wit and Humour, he seemed in his dedication, and sermon to be eternally aiming at both. He was led into that mistake by the great encouragement which was given by that ministry to all sorts of genius. I have several letters by me from *Thomas Swift* written from the year 1690 to 1700. They are honest, plain, good sense. Yet I confess they sometimes squint a little at Wit and Humour. The style of them is neither base nor elegant. The phrases are not ill chosen, but they have a cast of rusticity. In short, let Thomas Swift be what he will, he never was capable of writing three lines in the Tale of a Tub.

NB This last paragraph was in answer to a letter from the Earl of Orrery, wherein he had told him, of a report that had reached him, that a Cousin of Doctor Swift's had been the real Author of the Tale of a Tub. A performance which although never owned by the Dean of St. Patrick's was certainly his own, as [Jonathan Swift's housekeeper] Mrs. Whiteway has assured Lady Orrery.

Earlier, at the commencement of Letter XXIII on p. 300, where *A Tale* is introduced, Orrery has inscribed the interleaf in his own hand, 'An Extract of a Letter from Deane Swift Esq. in answer to one wherein I had exprest the general surmizes, that Swift was not Author of the Tale of a Tub'. The extract follows in a clerk's hand:

There is no doubt but that he was Author of the Tale of the Tub. He never owned it: but as he one day made his Relation Mrs. Whiteway read it to him, he made use of This expression. 'Good God! what a flow of imagination had I, when I wrote this.' And another time in the Battle of the Books 'Well, I think I was revenged on those pinioned Woodcocks Wooton and Bentley, for attacking my two favourites Boyle and Temple.'

He shewed it to Mr. Waring his chamber fellow at the College in his own handwriting.

Enough is known now about this contentious matter to make possible some firm conclusions. Thomas Swift's claim cannot be dismissed out of hand. That the Swift cousins conferred, even over an *ur*-text of *A Tale*, seems likely. Ideas or 'hints' Thomas may well have contributed. In the seven years before publication it appears that he did not even see the work. Considering Jonathan Swift's extreme sensitivity to any charge of plagiarism, it is at least a fair supposition that the 1704 volume is entirely Jonathan's, while some broad and some specific influences may be seen at work in the final text, and Section I of *The Mechanical Operation* may preserve segments by Thomas turned to the satirist's own use. There is, moreover, personal testimony in Thomas Swift's lifetime that *he* was not capable of writing *A Tale of a Tub*.

(i) from *A Complete Key to the Tale of A Tub; with some Account of the Authors, The Occasion and Design of Writing it, and Mr. Wotton's Remarks examined. London,* Printed for Edmund Curll, 1710.*

To The Reader

As these Notes *were communicated to me purely for my own Use, so had I never the least Intention of making 'em publick: But finding what various Opinions are entertain'd of the* Authors, *and Misrepresentations of the* Work *to which they belong, insomuch that Mr.* Wotton *has added to his* Reflections upon Learning *some severe Remarks, in which he represents the* Book *as a design'd Satyr upon the* Church of England, *and even to ridicule the Doctrine of the* Trinity; *upon which score these Papers now appear, plainly to demonstrate, that the true Intent and Aim of the* Authors *was not to ridicule all Religion, but to assert and defend the Purity of our Church's Doctrine, which Mr.* Wotton *and his Party would insinuate they have aspers'd, and to display the Innovations of* Rome *and Fanatical Hypocrisy in their proper Colours.*

[Signed 'E. Curll' in his copy of the *Complete Key*, British Library, C. 28 b. 11.]

Some Annotations and Explanatory Notes upon *The Tale of a Tub.*

The Occasion of Writing it.

A Preface of the *Bookseller* to the *Reader* before †*the Battle of the Books* shews the Cause and Design of the whole Work, which was perform'd

**A Complete Key*, reprinted in more detail in Guthkelch, pp. 325–42.

†Generally (and not without sufficient Reason) said to be Dr. *Jonathan* and *Thomas Swift*; but since they don't think fit publickly to own it, wherever I mention their Names, 'tis not upon any other Affirmation than as they are the *Reputed Authors*.

by *a couple of young Clergymen in the Year 1697. who having been Domestick Chaplains to Sir *William Temple*, thought themselves oblig'd to take up his Quarrel in Relation to the Controversy then in Dispute between him and Mr. *Wotton* concerning *Ancient* and *Modern* Learning.

The †one of 'em began a *Defence* of Sir *William* under the Title of *A Tale of a Tub*, under which he intended to couch the General History of Christianity; shewing the Rise of all the Remarkable Errors of the *Roman Church* in the same order they enter'd, and how the Reformation endeavoured to root 'em out again, with the different Temper of *Luther* from *Calvin* (and those more violent Spirits) in the way of his Reforming: His aim is to Ridicule the stubborn Errors of the *Romish Church*, and the Humours of the *Fanatick Party*, and to shew that their Superstition has somewhat very fantastical in it, which is common to both of 'em, notwithstanding the Abhorrence they seem to have for one another.

The Author intended to have it very regular, and withal so particular, that he thought not to pass by the Rise of any one single Error or its Reformation: He design'd at last to shew the Purity of the Christian Church in the primitive Times, and consequently how weakly Mr. *Wotton* pass'd his Judgment, and partially in preferring the *Modern* Divinity before the *Ancient*, with the Confutation of whose Book he intended to conclude. But when he had not yet gone half way, his ‡Companion borrowing the *Manuscript* to peruse, carried it with him to *Ireland*, and having kept it seven Years, at last publish'd it imperfect; for indeed he was not able to carry it on after the intended Method: because *Divinity* (tho it chanc'd to be his Profession) had been the least of his Study; However he added to it the *Battle of the Books*, wherein he effectually pursues the main Design of lashing Mr. *Wotton*, and having added a jocose Epistle Dedicatory to my Lord *Sommers*, and another to Prince *Posterity*, with a pleasant Preface, and interlarded with one *Digression* concerning *Criticks*, and another in the *Modern* kind, a *Third* in Praise of *Digressions*, and a Fourth in praise of *Madness* (with which he was not unacquainted) concludes the Book with a *Fragment* which the first Author made, and intended should have come in about the middle of the *Tale*, as a Preliminary to *Jack*'s Character.

Having thus shewn the Reasons of the little Order observ'd in the Book, and the Imperfectness of the *Tale*, 'tis so submitted to the Reader's Censure.

**Pag.* 225 [of the 1st edn., p.104, above, of this edition].
†*Thomas Swift.*
‡Dr. *Jonathan Swift.*

Thomas Swift is Grandson to Sir *William D'avenant*, *Jonathan Swift* is Cousin German to *Thomas Swift* both Retainers to Sir *William Temple.*

The two Gentlemen as before hinted being the reputed Authors of the *Work*, the several Parts of the Book are thus attributed to 'em, *viz.*

The Dedication to my Lord *Sommers*, the Preface, Epistle to Prince *Posterity*, the four Digressions, *viz.* 1. Concerning *Criticks.* 2. In the Modern kind. 3. In Praise of *Digressions*. 4. In Praise of *Madness* and *the Battle of the Books* are assign'd to Dr. *Jonathan Swift*; and the *Tale of a Tub*, and the *Fragment* containing a Mechanical Account of the *Operation of the Spirit*, to *Thomas Swift* . . .

[Followed by the *Clavis* [Key], i.e. line by line notes.]

(ii) Letters of Jonathan Swift and Benjamin Tooke, relating to the fifth edition (1710) of *A Tale of a Tub.**

SWIFT TO BENJAMIN TOOKE

Dublin, June 29, 1710.

Sir,

I was in the country when I received your letter with the Apology inclosed in it; and I had neither health nor humour to finish that business. But the blame rests with you, that if you thought it time, you did not print it when you had it. I have just now your last, with the complete Key. I believe it is so perfect a Grubstreet piece, it will be forgotten in a week. But it is strange that there can be no satisfaction against a bookseller for publishing names in so bold a manner. I wish some lawyer could advise you how I might have satisfaction: for at this rate, there is no book, however vile, which may not be fastened on me. I cannot but think that little Parson-cousin of mine is at the bottom of this; for, having lent him a copy of some part of, &c. and he shewing it, after I was gone for Ireland, and the thing abroad, he affected to talk suspiciously, as if he had some share in it. If he should happen to be in town, and you light on him, I think you ought to tell him gravely, 'That, if he be the author, he should set his name to the &c.' and railly him a little upon it: and tell him, 'if he can explain some things, you will, if he pleases, set his name to the next edition.' I should be glad to see how far the foolish impudence of a dunce

**Letters of Swift and Tooke*, first printed by Deane Swift in 1765; reprinted in Guthkelch, pp. 349–50: *Correspondence*, i, 165–70. The manuscripts of these letters are lost.

could go. Well; I will send you the thing, now I am in town, as soon as possible. But, I dare say, you have neither printed the rest, nor finished the cuts; only are glad to lay the fault on me. I shall, at the end, take a little contemptible notice of the thing you sent me; and I dare say it will do you more good than hurt. If you are in such haste, how came you to forget the Miscellanies? I would not have you think of Steele for a publisher [i.e. editor]; he is too busy. I will, one of these days, send you some hints, which I would have in a preface, and you may get some friend to dress them up. I have thoughts of some other work one of these years: and I hope to see you ere it be long; since it is likely to be a new world, and since I have the merit of suffering by not complying with the old. Yours, &c.

Benjamin Tooke to Swift

London, July 10, 1710.

Sir,

Inclosed I have sent the Key, and think it would be much more proper to add the notes at the bottom of the respective pages they refer to, than printing them at the end by themselves. As to the cuts, Sir Andrew Fountain has had them from the time they were designed, with an intent of altering them. But he is now gone into Norfolk, and will not return till Michaelmas; so that, I think, they must be laid aside; for, unless they are very well done, it is better they were quite let alone. As to the Apology, I was not so careless but that I took a copy of it before I sent it to you; so that I could have printed it easily, but that you sent me word not to go on till you had altered something in it. As to that cousin of yours which you speak of, I neither know him, nor ever heard of him till the Key mentioned him. It was very indifferent to me which I proceeded on first, the Tale, or the Miscellanies: but, when you went away, you told me there were three or four things should be sent over out of Ireland, which you had not here; which, I think is a very reasonable excuse for myself in all these affairs. What I beg of you at present is, that you would return the Apology and this Key, with directions as to the placing it: although I am entirely of opinion to put it at the bottom of each page; yet shall submit. If this be not done soon, I cannot promise but some rascal or other will do it for us both; since you see the liberty that is already taken. I think too much time has already been lost in the Miscellanies; therefore hasten that: and which-ever is in the most forwardness, I would begin on first. All here depend on an entire alteration. I am, &c.

EXPLANATORY NOTES

ABBREVIATIONS

Correspondence	Sir H. Williams (ed.), *The Correspondence of Jonathan Swift* (see p. xxiii).
*ODEP*³	*The Oxford Dictionary of English Proverbs*, 3rd edn., revised by F. P. Wilson (Oxford, 1970).
SL	George Faulkner's *Sale Catalogue* of Swift's Library, 1745; reprinted in Sir H. Williams, *Dean Swift's Library* (Cambridge, 1932).
Teerink	H. Teerink, revised by A. H. Scouten, *A Bibliography of the Writings of Jonathan Swift* (see p. xxiii).

A TALE OF A TUB

1. *Diu multumque desideratum.* 'Deeply desired for a long time.'

Basima eacabasa . . . camelanthi. Iren. Lib.*1.* C.*18.* Based on 'certain Hebrew words', mumbo-jumbo used by the Marcosian heretics, 'the more thoroughly to bewilder those who are being initiated' according to the second-century father, Irenaeus, attacking Gnosticism in his work *A Refutation and Overthrowing of Knowledge falsely so called*, commonly entitled *Adversus Haereses*; Swift made an abstract of Irenaeus in 1697 (Guthkelch, p. lvi).

Juvatque novos . . . tempora Musæ. 'It is a delight to gather fresh flowers and to seek a noble garland for my head from a source which the Muses never before used to deck the brow of any man': Lucretius. *De Rerum Natura*, i. 928–31.

Terra Australis incognita. 'The unknown southern land [near Australia].'

treatises written expressly against it. William King, *Some Remarks on the Tale of a Tub* (1704) see p. 182; William Wotton, *Observations upon the Tale of a Tub*; see p. 186 for the text of the *Observations* [part].

2. *a late discourse.* [? Francis Gastrell], *The Principles of Deism truly represented and set in a clear Light, in two Dialogues between a Sceptic and a Deist* (1708).

3. *nondum tibi defuit hostis.* 'You have never yet been in want of an enemy': Lucan, *De Bello Civili*, i. 29.

the weightiest men in the weightiest stations. Traditionally taken to refer to Dr John Sharp, Archbishop of York.

another book . . . Letter of Enthusiasm. Anthony Ashley Cooper, 3rd Earl of Shaftesbury, *A Letter concerning Enthusiasm* (1708).

the tritest maxim in the world. The worst is the best corrupted.

4. *L'Estrange.* Sir Roger L'Estrange.

Dryden . . . in one of his prefaces. The lengthy *Discourse concerning the Original and Progress of Satire* (1693); reprinted in G. Watson (ed.), *Dryden's Critical Essays*, ii (1963).

the number Three . . . a dangerous meaning. Some shadow-boxing by Swift, to defend himself from charges of meddling with the doctrine of the Trinity; *four* was the 'perfect number', cabbalistically powerful as the *tetragrammaton*, the four letter word for God, such as JeHoVaH.

Eachard . . . the Contempt of the Clergy. The Revd John Eachard (d. 1697), *The Grounds and Occasions of the Contempt of the Clergy and Religion Enquired into* (1670), provoked several violent replies, answered by Eachard the following year.

5. *Marvell's Answer . . . Orrery's Remarks.* Samuel Parker (later Bishop of Oxford), *A Discourse of Ecclesiastical Polity* (1670), strongly attacked toleration; it was part of the occasion of Andrew Marvell's answer to attacks on Nonconformists, *The Rehearsal Transpros'd*, i and ii (1672 and 1673) . . . The 'Remarks' on Bentley's *Dissertation* on Phalaris were by Charles Boyle; see p. xv.

one . . . first . . . as from an unknown hand. Dr William King's *Remarks.*

person of a graver character. The Revd William Wotton.

a certain great man. Sir William Temple.

6. *Porsenna's case, idem trecenti juravimus.* 'Three hundred of us have sworn the same oath': Lucius Annaeus Florus (second century AD), *Epitome* [of the Wars in Roman History to Augustus], i. 10. 6. This is Gaius Mucius Scaevola's answer to the Etruscan Porsenna, whom he had failed to murder and before whom as a captive he thrust his hand in the fire to show his contempt for pain.

another antagonist. Richard Bentley.

a Letter of . . . Buckingham. George Villiers (1628–87), 2nd Duke of Buckingham, 'To Mr. Clifford on his Humane-Reason'.

Peter's banter . . . his Alsatia phrase. Swift assigns the currency of one of his most hated, cant words to a district between Fleet Street and the Thames, where a legal sanctuary for debtors and criminals was abolished in 1697.

7. *Combat des Livres.* [*Battle of the Books*] François de Callières, *Histoire Poëtique de la Guerre nouvellement déclarée entre les Anciens et les Modernes* [*Poetical Account of the War newly declared between the Ancients and the Moderns*] (1688).

the answerer and his friend. Wotton and Bentley.

8. *Minnellius or Farnaby.* Jan Minell (*c.*1625–83), Dutch scholar and editor of

Latin school texts; Thomas Farnaby (*c.*1577–1647), grammarian and schoolmaster.

optat . . . piger. Using an older editorial lack of punctuation, Swift makes the classical commonplace *optat ephippia bos, piger optat arare caballus* read 'The lazy ox longs for the horse's trappings, [the horse yearns to plough]' (Horace, *Epistles*, I. xiv. 43).

that the author is dead. Wotton in his *Observations* hinted at Temple as the author of the *Tale*: see p. 190.

the publishers. The editors; the modern *publisher* was indicated by 'bookseller'.

put it into the bookseller's preface. See note to p. 1 (1).

9. the bullies in White-Friars. See note to p. 6 (4).

a farce and a ladle . . . impedimenta literarum. 'What should be great you turn to farce: | I wish the Ladle in your A[rse].' Matthew Prior, *The Ladle* [reminiscent of Swift's poem *Baucis and Philemon*] (1703), 139–40 . . . 'Pieces of literary baggage'.

10. *some explanatory notes.* The first four editions of *A Tale* have a series of marginal notes, all part of the joking and certainly placed there by Swift. A further series of footnotes was added in the fifth edition of 1710 (see p. 201), and also separately printed as a set in *An Apology for the Tale of a Tub. With Explanatory Notes by W. W[o]tt[o]n, B.D. and Others* (1711), for the convenience of owners of earlier editions. Swift was also certainly responsible for this second series of notes, which offers a 'commentary' on *A Tale*, and (using material from Wotton's hostile criticism of the book) satirizes the critic as 'the learned commentator' (see p. 34, n. †).

a prostitute bookseller . . . a foolish paper. A Complete Key to the Tale of a Tub: with some Account of the Authors, and the Occasion and Design of writing it, and Mr. Wotton's Remarks examined (1710), published by Edmund Curll; reprinted in Guthkelch, 329–48 (see pp. 198, 200).

The gentleman who gave the copy. 'Ralph Noden, Esq; of the Middle Temple': Curll's manuscript note in a copy of the *Key* in the British Library C. 28. b. 11).

11. *a maxim . . . title to the first.* Perhaps Themistocles after the defeat of Xerxes.

12. *your enemies . . . brought to light.* Somers was impeached in 1701 but acquitted.

a late reign. King William III died 8 March 1702.

13. *formerly used to tedious harangues.* In the Commons, when he was a Crown law officer; and in the Lords, when he presided as Lord Chancellor.

in his preface. p. 18.

Boccalini . . . Troiano Boccalini (1556–1613), some of whose journalistic pieces, *Ragguaglia di Parnaso*, appeared as *Advertisements from Parnassus . . . Newly done into English, and adapted to the present Times by N.N.*, 3 vols. (1704), part of a spate of free paraphrases and adaptations that occupied Grub Street at this period.

14. *Marcosian Heretics*. From Marcus, second-century Gnostic teacher.

the person. Time, Posterity's 'tutor'.

15. *maitre de palais*. i.e. *maire du palais*: see *Glossary*.

Moloch. In the Old Testament, a divinity who required the sacrifice of children by fire (Jeremiah 32: 35).

16. *the laurel*. Renown in poetry, or the royal office of poet laureate.

posted fresh upon all gates and corners of streets. Books were advertised by pasting up their title-pages.

memorial of them . . . to be found. Phrases reminiscent of the Bible: cf. Deuteronomy 22: 26; Psalm 9: 6.

there is a large cloud near the horizon . . . and topography of them. Striking reminiscences of Shakespeare's *Antony and Cleopatra*, IV. xii. 1–10.

17. *Dryden, whose translation of Virgil*. Dryden's folio appeared in July 1697; with its subscriptions, dedications, engravings, it was a publisher's 'event', enough to attract Swift's satire; he also had political and religious animosities to fuel his bad feeling towards the old poet.

B[en]tl[e]y . . . Wo[o]tt[o]n. Richard Bentley and William Wotton are obvious members of this group, because of their anti-Temple writing in the Ancients v. Moderns controversy (see pp. xiv–xv): Bentley's 'near a thousand pages' is his enlarged *Dissertation* (1699) on Phalaris; Wotton's 'good sizeable volume' is his *Reflections* (1697): see pp. 169 and 162.

a friend of your governor. Sir William Temple, who reveres the Ancients.

18. *a Grand Committee*. In Parliament, a committee of the whole House, or one of the four standing committees of the Commons.

Hobbes's Leviathan. Thomas Hobbes, *Leviathan: or, The Matter, Form and Power of a Common-Wealth, Ecclesiastical and Civil*, was first printed in 1651; it expounded a theory of society rooted in materialism, and its anti-traditional doctrine that all laws are framed by man made Hobbes one of the most controversial thinkers of the age.

given to rotation. Discussed in the London political club, The Rota, which met in the 1650s.

the ship in danger . . . its old antitype, the Commonwealth. An antitype is what is shadowed forth or represented by a symbol or *type*; the image is from printing, or impressing with a die.

19. *the Spelling School*. Swift was a stickler for what he understood as the propriety of spelling.

insigne . . . alio. 'Something extraordinary, new, [. . .] unspoken by another voice': Horace, *Odes*, III. xxv. 7–8.

20. *fixed this mercury.* An alchemical phrase, to render mercury solid by combination with some other substance; *mercury* is also a sparkling wit.

the very newest . . . refiners. The Moderns; *refiners* has also an alchemical meaning, but is wider; cf. Temple, 'Of Poetry', '. . . reasoners upon government . . . refiners in politics . . . refined luxurists'.

21. *The tax upon paper.* A sales tax of £17.10*s.* per cent on the value of paper, vellum, and parchment, imposed in 1697.

Leicester-Fields. Now Leicester Square in London.

22. *the first monarch of this island . . . thistles in their stead.* James VI of Scotland by the Union of the Crowns became the first king of 'Great Britain'. He was attacked for appointing Scotsmen to English offices and dignities. The Scottish Order of the Thistle was revived by Queen Anne in 1703.

23. *all pork . . . *Plutarch.* Plutarch, *Life of Titus Quinctius Flamininus*, gives an early version of a common story. A parsimonious host wishes to make an impression; a rich meal is served in which each course has the same base, pork; but however delicately flavoured, the guest finally realizes that it is 'all pork'.

24. *Vide Xenophon.* Xenophon (*c.*428–*c.*354 BC) was formerly credited with a pamphlet, *The Constitution of Athens* (*c.*431).

C[l]eon . . . Hyperbolus. Cleon and Hyperbolus, two Athenian demogogues, referred to by Aristophanes, *Clouds*, 549–51.

all are gone astray . . . not one. Psalm 14:3.

Astræa. The goddess of Justice who lived on earth in the Golden Age.

splendida bilis. 'Glittering [black] bile'; Horace, *Satires*, II. iii. 141; the ancients supposed it to be a cause of madness.

Covent Garden. Theatre and fashionable red-light district in London.

White-Hall. A London royal palace, centre of the Court and Government offices; the buildings were burned down 4 January 1698.

Inns of Court . . . city. In London: one of the lawyers' centres . . . the financial and commercial district.

25. *A Panegyric upon the World . . . A Modest Defence . . .* Two of 'the Author's' treatises; see p. 1.

Evadere . . . labor est. Virgil, *Aeneid*, vi. 128–9: the translation is from Dryden's *Virgil.*

edifices in the air. Intellectual systems.

Socrates . . . in a basket. In Aristophanes, *Clouds*.

26. *the ladder.* The last standing place of those about to be hanged ('turned off'): often used for addressing the crowd of spectators.

senes . . . recedant. 'So that when they are old, they may withdraw into untroubled leisure': Horace, *Satires*, I. i. 31.

27. *sylva Caledonia.* The Caledonian forest: the austere Calvinist Kirk of Scotland, like many of the 'dissenting' groups in England, emphasized preaching.

the only uncovered vessel . . . human ears. Puritans kept their hats on in church as a protest against ritual. Their emphasis on the individuality of Christian witness made prominent use of the text '. . . [Saul of Tarsus] is a chosen vessel unto me . . .' (Acts 9: 15). English religious and political dissidents in the earlier seventeenth century were sometimes punished by mutilating their ears.

publication of these speeches. From 1698 to 1719 Paul Lorraine, the Ordinary [chaplain] of Newgate prison, organized a lucrative flow of 'last dying speeches and confessions', published in folio sheets.

28. *Corpoream quoque . . . impellere sensus.* 'For we must confess that voice and sound also are corporeal since they can affect our senses'; Lucretius, *De Rerum Natura*, iv. 526–7; the translation offered in the footnote is Thomas Creech's (1682).

our modern saints. 'Saint' and 'sanctified' in New Testament use are applied to the elect under the New Covenant, i.e. members of the Christian Church: e.g. 1 Corinthians 1: 2; sixteenth- and seventeenth-century 'covenanted' groups applied the term to themselves, and the ironical use that Swift employs became common among their Anglican opponents.

29. *perorare with a song.* Conclude with the psalm customarily sung at the gallows.

Grub-Street. North of London Wall; symbolically the centre of all literary hacks and catch-penny writers. Swift was its great topologist and toponymist.

Gresham. Gresham College in Broad Street, a City foundation, was the meeting place of the Royal Society from 1660 until 1710.

30. *prodigals . . . their husks and their harlots.* The Royal Society's empty investigations as 'husks', which formed the diet of the prodigal son after he had wasted his substance on the 'harlots' of riotous living (Luke 15): the latter part of the allusion is relevant at this time in the aftermath of Jeremy Collier's *Short View of the Immorality and Profaneness of the Stage* (1698).

31. *Pythagoras, Æsop, Socrates.* All traditionally ugly men.

History of Reynard the Fox. A group of beast stories which from medieval times were loaded with political and social satire.

Tom Thumb . . . Dr. Faustus . . . Whittington and his Cat . . . the Wise Men of Gotham. All chap-book subjects: *The Hind and Panther*—Dryden's allegorical poem, published 1687, defending the Roman Catholic Church to which he had been converted; *Tommy Potts*—a broadside ballad, *The*

Lovers' Quarrel, about fair Rosamund of Scotland, whose love was won by 'the Valour of Tommy Potts'. The critique assigned to each title mocks a different 'corruption' of learning.

The paragraph on *Dr. Faustus* is appropriately one of the places where joking about alchemy surfaces in the book. *Artephius*—the half-legendary author of a hermetic text, *Clavis Majoris Sapientiae* [The Key to the Greater Wisdom], who is supposed to have reached his great age by taking his own elixir: *adeptus*—adept, the alchemical code-word for an initiate in the study; *reincrudation*—chemical reduction, but also given mystical meaning; *via humida*—the humid or watery path, a chemical process involving water or a liquid; *the male* and *female dragon*—symbolic terms in alchemy for sulphur and mercury, using favourite sexual and organic analogies.

The paragraph on *Dick Whittington* calls to mind the traditional rabbinical study of the Talmud ('doctrine'); this collection of texts sets out the Jewish law as it crystallized, after centuries of oral transmission, into the Hebrew Mishnah ('learning'), finally codified at the end of the second century AD by rabbi Juda Ha-Nasi, accompanied by the Aramaic *Gemarah* ('commentary').

The paragraph on *The Wise Men of Gotham* flirts with the Ancients and Moderns controversy (see p. xiii).

32. *meal-tubs*. A meal-tub, named in evidence as the hiding-place of treasonable papers, gave its name to one of the factitious 'conspiracies' of 1679, peripheral to the main Popish Plot.

33. *conscience void of offence* [*towards God and towards Men*]. Acts 24: 16.

Dryden . . . a multiplicity of godfathers. Dryden in his translation of Virgil dedicated the *Eclogues*, the *Georgics* and the *Aeneid* to three separate noblemen, and the hundred full-page engravings each bore the name and the arms of a top-rate subscriber, including Temple's sister, Martha, Lady Giffard.

34. *Garments of the Israelites*. Deuteronomy 8: 4.

Lambin. Denys Lambin, French scholar (1516–72), ed. Cicero's works (Strasburg, 1581) (*SL* 402) and ed. Plautus (Paris, 1576) (*SL* 593).

the first seven years. i.e. seven centuries of the Christian era.

35. *Locket's*. Adam Locket's fashionable eating-house at Charing Cross.

36. *Jupiter Capitolinus*. In 390 BC the sacred geese in the Roman temple of Jupiter on the Capitol gave the alarm as a party of invading Gauls silently entered the citadel.

Hell. Where the tailor throws his scraps of cloth.

deus minorum gentium. 'A god of the lesser nations' (the *goyim*).

that creature. A louse, 'cracked' as the renovating tailor smoothed a seam.

primum mobile. 'The first moving heaven' (in the medieval cosmography).

37. *ex traduce.* 'Transmitted by propagation'; theologians disputed whether the soul was derived from the parents like the body (traduction), or whether a new soul was created at each birth.

in them we live . . . being. Acts 17: 28.

all in all. Corinthians 15: 28.

all in every part. 'Anaxagoras . . . asserts that there is in everything a mixture of everything': Lucretius, *De Rerum Natura*, i. 874.

vein and race. Two words used excessively by Sir William Temple; *race* is an adaptation of a French word, which '. . . applied to wines, in its primitive sense, means the flavour of the soil' (Johnson, 'Life of Thomson', who notes Temple's use of the term in 'An Essay upon the Ancient and Modern Learning').

38. *shoulder-knots.* A French mode which became fashionable in the 1670s.

ruelles. A lady at this time admitted visitors of a morning to the ruelle, or space between her bed and the wall; hence, a levee, or a boudoir generally.

sculler. A boat propelled by one man, thus cheaper and less fashionable than oars, i.e. a boat with two rowers.

the Rose. A tavern at the Drury Lane (theatre) end of Russell Street.

temper. Compromise, adjustment.

39. *jure paterno.* 'By paternal law'; cf. the *jure divino* ('by divine law') by which the exiled James II was still said to be king.

40. *altum silentium.* 'Deep silence': Virgil, *Aeneid*, x, 63.

circumstantial. Unimportant.

aliquo . . . adhærere. 'In some manner inhere in the essence.'

Aristotelis . . . Interpretatione. There is no specific work by Aristotle called *Dialectica* (Logic); this represents some college collection of pieces translated into Latin: *De Interpretatione* is a straightforward piece, probably by Aristotle, on the relation of thought to language.

conceditur . . . negatur. A formula of scholastic disputation: 'I agree. But, if the same thing be affirmed of the nuncupatory, I deny it.'.

41. *a codicil annexed.* The Apocrypha.

written by a dog-keeper. Tobit 5: 16; 11: 4.

42. *Edinburgh streets in a morning.* In the apartments of Edinburgh's multi-storeyed 'lands', after 10 p.m. the filth collected by each householder was by custom emptied from the windows into the street, nominally to be collected at 7 a.m. the next morning by the inadequate force of street cleaners.

Momus . . . Hybris . . . Zoilus . . . Tigellius. For *Momus*, 'the patron of the Moderns', and the descent of criticism, see p. 115 above and ibid., n. (1).

Hybris, in Greek 'insolence, violence coming from pride in strength', hence pride personified; *Zoilus*, fourth-century BC. Cynic philosopher of Amphipolis, notorious for his bad-tempered attacks on Homer; *Tigellius* was an ungenerous critic of Horace (*Satires*, I. ii. 3); for *Perrault* see p. 18 and ibid., n. (5), and p. 152

As Hercules most generously did. Hercules, mortally sick by the poison on the shirt of Nessus which his credulous wife Deianira had given him to regain his love, committed suicide on Mt. Oeta and was elevated to heaven by Jupiter.

45. *the proper employment of a . . . critic.* There follows a parody of the exploits and labours of Hercules: he killed Cacus, a fire-breathing monster living on the Palatine Hill; he killed the Hydra; cleaned out the Augean stables; and exterminated the carnivorous birds of prey that infested the shores of Lake Stymphalis in Arcadia.

46. *noble moderns . . . volumes I turn . . . over . . .* 'For yourselves, turn over the Greek models in your hands night and day': Horace, *Epistle to the Pisos* [*Art of Poetry*], 269.

Pausanias is of opinion. Greek geographer *c.*AD 150; the reference is to his *Description of Greece*, ii. 38.

47. *Herodotus. c.*480–*c.*425 BC: *Histories*, iv. 191.

Ctesias yet refines. A Greek from Coridos (*fl.* late fifth century BC), a doctor at the Persian court; Swift cites a work on India as found in a compilation of extracts from Greek and Latin prose works, the *Bibliotheca* of Photius, ninth-century patriarch of Constantinople, of which work he possessed an edition (Rouen, 1653) in folio, *SL* 104.

our Scythian ancestors. Temple, *Introduction to the History of England*, believed they came from Norway and were the ancestors of the Scots.

Diodorus . . . ventures. Apparently not. Guthkelch, 99 n., suggests that 'Dio (dorus)' is a mistake for 'Dic (aearchus)' (Greek miscellaneous writer, *fl.* *c.*300 BC), fr. 60, who mentions a plant on Pelion the shade of which, when it flowered, killed those who slept under it.

Lucretius gives exactly the same relation. 'And on the great peaks of Helicon there is a tree which generally kills men by the foul smell of the blossom': vi. 786–7. The verse translation at n. § is by Creech. Swift probably substituted *retro* ('on the back-side') for Lucretius's *tetro* ('foul') intentionally.

Ctesias . . . these remarkable words. See note to p. 45 (2).

48. *Terence makes . . . mention . . . malevoli.* Prologues to his comedies *Andria*, *Heautontimorumenos*, and *Adelphi* . . . 'spiteful people'.

like Themistocles and his company. Plutarch, *Themistocles*, 2: 'When, therefore, he was laughed at, long after, in company where free scope was given to raillery . . . he was obliged to answer . . . : " 'Tis true I never learned how to tune a harp, or play upon a lute, but I know how to raise a small and inconsiderable city [Athens] to glory and greatness" ' (trans. J. and W. Langhorne).

composition of a man. 'Nine tailors made a man': proverbial (*ODEP*³, 567).

49. *sine mercurio*. Without mercury: cf. p. 20 and ibid., n. (1).

Terra Australis Incognita. See p. 1, below and ibid., n. (4).

51. *sovereign remedy for the worms*. . . This paragraph (with p. 109) calls to mind contemporary patent medicine advertisements.

repeating poets. Who give readings of their own verse.

office of insurance . . . damage by fire. Indulgences were issued to protect against Hell Fire, just as the recently founded insurance offices (e.g. the Friendly Society itself) issued insurance policies to cover damage by fire.

52. *powder pimperlim-pimp*. *Poudre de perlimpinpin*; a quack medicine, thence an ironical phrase for the magic ingredient, the universal remedy.

53 *bulls of Colchos*. Before he could carry off the Golden Fleece from Colchis, Jason had to yoke a pair of fire-breathing bulls to sow the dragon's teeth.

the metal of their feet . . . sunk into common lead. A papal bull takes its name from the *bulla* or lead seal, depicting SS Peter and Paul with the Pope's name, attached to the bottom of the document.

Varias inducere plumas . . . Atrum desinit in piscem. 'To insert many coloured feathers' . . . 'turns into a black fish': Horace, *Epistle to the Pisos* [*Ars Poetica*], 2–4, laughs at the licence of imagination in a painting of a grotesque figure made up of a human head, horse's neck, feathered limbs, and fish's tail. The less formal papal *brief* (letter) was sealed in red wax with the Pope's personal seal depicting St Peter fishing.

appetitus sensibilis. Or *sensitivus*: in Thomas Aquinas's system the natural 'appetite' or inclination towards a particular form of behaviour with which all sensitive life is endued; in addition, man possesses a rational or intellectual 'appetite', the will.

pulveris exigui jactu. '*By the scattering of a little dust* these passionate turmoils, these fierce contests [of bees] are borne down and quieted': Virgil, *Georgics*, iv. 87.

54. *bull-beggars*. The connection of this word for spectres or bug-bears with papal bulls was common.

the north-west. Cf. p. 26.

most humble | man's man. The opening formula of a bull named the Pope as *servus servorum dei*, 'servant of the servants of God'.

tax cameræ apostolicæ. The apostolic *Camera* was the papal treasury, and the 'tax' was the fee for engrossing and expediting a papal writing.

verè adepti. 'Truly adepts, initiates'; this phrase introduces more alchemical references: *arcana*, 'the operation', sons of [the] art'.

58. *Chinese waggons*. '... where Chineses drive | With sails and wind their canie waggons light': Milton, *Paradise Lost*, iii. 438–9.

59. *Quemvis perferre laborem ... vigilare serenas*. Addressing Gaius Memmius, Lucretius says that '[the delight I hope to draw from our enjoyable friendship] persuades me to endure many labours and makes me keep awake through the nights of stillness': *De Rerum Natura*, i. 141–2.

a very strange, new, and important discovery ... A satirical mishandling of a maxim of classical critical theory: Horace, *Epistle to the Pisos* [*Ars Poetica*], 343–4: 'He gains every vote who mixes the pleasant and profitable, delighting and instructing the reader at the same time.'

60. *fastidiosity, amorphy, and oscitation*. Fastidiousness, shapelessness, and yawning; the first and second of these pedantic word-forms seem to have been used first by Swift (*OED*).

whether there have been ever any ancients or no. Bentley had 'annihilated' Phalaris as a letter-writer, as well as Aesop: but there is also the paradox that the Moderns are the true Ancients; see note to p. 110.

O. Brazile. Or *Hy-Brazil*: an imaginary island to the west of Ireland.

Painters' Wives Island. The earliest mention of this in print seems to be Walter Ralegh, *History of the World* (1614), i, cap. 23, sect. 4: 'while the fellow drew that map, his wife sitting by, desired him to put in one country for her ...'

balneo Mariæ ... Q.S. A *bain-marie* or kitchen steamer ... *quantum sufficit* ('as much as is needed': in cooking or medicine).

sordes ... caput mortuum. 'Dregs ... the residue after distillation' (pictographically represented in alchemical texts by a skull).

Catholic. Universally applicable or effective (medical and Rosicrucian).

medullas, excerpta quædams, florilegias. Marrows or piths, certain extracts, anthologies (collections of flowers, garlands), all in Swift's opinion examples of the Moderns' superficial drive to acquire knowledge without labour, thinking, or serious study. The 'reader's digest' was a characteristic of two contemporary developments, a popular audience and a literary market.

61. *Homerus omnes* ... 'Homer covered all human topics in his poem': Xenophon (*c*.427–*c*.354 BC), *Symposium*, iv. 6.

cabalist. Specifically, a student of the cabbala ('what is received'), the mystical tradition of interpreting the Jewish Scriptures; this has a strong likeness to Gnostic teaching: more generally, one skilled in secret meaning.

opus magnum. The 'great work' in alchemy, the transmutation of base metals into gold.

Sendivogius, Behmen, or Anthroposophia Theomagica. Michael Sędjiwój (b. Poland 1566, d. Silesia 1636), alchemist and metallurgist, author of an often-printed alchemical treatise, *De Lapide Philosophorum* [*On the Philosophers' Stone*], 1604, as well as a dialogue on mercury and a tractate on sulphur; his hermetic teaching was influenced by Paracelsus. Jacob Boehme (1575–1625), German theologian, mystic, and prophet; all his writings were made available in English in the mid-seventeenth century. Thomas Vaughan, *Anthroposophia Theomagica* (1650); see p. 149.

the answer to it writ by the learned Dr. Henry More. Henry More (1614–87), the Cambridge Platonist, published two replies to Vaughan (1650).

sphæra pyroplastica. 'Fire-globe' or 'sphere of fire', a term peculiar to Thomas Vaughan in his recipe for the universal medicine, and related to the mysterious 'third principle' of Boehme.

vix crederem . . . vocem. 'I should find it difficult to believe that this author ever heard of fire': cf. preceding note.

62. *these last three years.* Wotton's *Reflections* first appeared in 1694.

political wagering. In 1708 an Act was passed penalizing laying bets on the outcome of events relating to the war with France.

63. *proceed critics and wits by reading nothing else.* See p. 71.

64. *zeal . . . the most significant word.* The biblical word was of some standing as a pejorative characterization of religious feeling held to be too unrestrained and probably hypocritical: cf. Ben Jonson's Puritan, Zeal-of-the-Land Busy, in *Bartholomew Fair* (1614).

68. *Exchange-women.* The Royal Exchange on the north of Cornhill and the New Exchange in the Strand both had shops, mostly kept by women.

the fox's arguments. When he had lost his tail, in Aesop's fable.

Dutch Jack. Jack of Leyden (Jan Bockleszoon or Beukelsz) became leader of the Anabaptists who took over Münster; the bishop regained the city in 1535 and Jack was put to death by torture.

the sect of Æolists. See Section VIII, p. 72, and note (2).

69. *—Mellaeo . . . Lepore.* Lucretius, *De Rerum Natura*, i. 934: *Mellaeo* should be *Melleo* (honeyed), which would be a false quantity; Lucretius wrote *Musaeo*: 'touching all with the Muse's charm'.

70. *get a thorough insight into the index.* A common accusation against Bentley: see note to p. 120 (3).

the wise man's rule, of regarding the end. Solon's unwelcome advice to Croesus.

like Hercules's oxen by tracing them backwards. The monster Cacus stole some of the cattle of Geryon from Hercules (see note to p. 45), dragging them backwards into his cave to avoid detection.

not at this present . . . matter left in nature to furnish . . . a volume. Cf. '. . . in every part of natural and mathematical knowledge . . . the next Age will not find much work of this kind to do' (Wotton, *Reflections upon Ancient and Modern Learning*, 1697 (p. 416).

71. *Ctesiæ fragm.* . . . A fragment of Ctesias quoted by Photius (see note to p. 47 (2)).

sed quorum . . . pertingentia. 'But whose genitals were gross and reached to their ankles.'

72. *everlasting chains . . . in a library.* See p. 108 and ibid., n. (1).

The learned Æolists. This section operates in very dangerous territory for Swift and his contemporary readers. See Wotton, *Observations*. p. 188 above. The rhetoric of Swift's own religious expression is public, controlled, reticent; the language of those he attacks, who delighted in extemporary preaching and praying, is personal, emotional, open.

Quod procul . . . gubernans. 'May the Fortune that governs things avert this from us': Lucretius, *De Rerum Natura*, v. 107.

73. *anima mundi.* Thomas Vaughan, *Anthroposophia Theomagica* (quoted by Guthkelch, 150 n. 3), dilates on the 'World Soul', identifying it as 'etherial Nature', a middle Spirit, by means of which man is made subject to the influence of the stars, and 'partly disposed of by the *celestial harmony*'; elsewhere he identifies it as the 'universal spirit of Nature'.

forma informans. 'The *form* which imparts form', one of the 'distinctions' of a term in the Aristotelian dualism of form and matter employed by the Schoolmen.

the breath of our nostrils. Genesis 2: 7.

three distinct animas. The traditional scholastic threefold division of the vital principle into vegetative (life), sensitive (feeling), rational (reason).

cabalist Bumbastus . . . the four cardinal points. For *cabalist*, see note to p. 61 (3); for *Paracelsus*, see note to p. 114 (5). Made from the four elements, man the *microcosm* had a correspondence with the four cardinal points of the compass of the *macrocosm*, the face with the east, the posteriors with the west.

74. *learning puffeth men up.* 1 Corinthians 8: 1.

the choicest . . . belches . . . through that vehicle. Swift in common with other contemporary satirists plays on the 'twang of the nose' said to be characteristic of popular preaching: see *The Mechanical Operation of the Spirit*, pp. 131ff.

latria. 'divine worship' (Greek).

omnium deorum . . . celebrant. 'They worship the North Wind more than all other gods': Pausanias, *Description of Greece*, VIII. xxxvi. 6.

75. Σκοτία. Gr. 'darkness, gloom'; also *Scotia*, 'Scotland'.

Pancirollus. Guido Pancirolli (1523–99), *Rerum Memorabilium jam olim deperditarum libri II* (1599); i, arts and discoveries of the ancients now lost; ii, inventions of the moderns (*SL* 457).

ex adytis and penetralibus. 'From the inner shrines and sanctuaries': Virgil, *Aeneid*, ii. 297.

77. *Laplanders . . . buy their winds . . . from the same merchants . . . retail them . . . to customers much alike*. They 'buy' them from dishonest *shamans* and sell them to merchants (i.e. Puritans and Nonconformists, or perhaps the credulous): 'This, that we have reported concerning the Laplanders, is by Olaus Magnus, and justly, related of the Finlanders, who . . . sell winds to those merchants that traffic with them' (John Scheffer, *History of Lapland* (Oxford, 1674), xi. 58).

Delphos. An erroneous form of *Delphi* used in English by Temple (see p. 156), for which he was rebuked by Bentley. The oracle of Apollo answered through the Pythia, a woman in a state of possession.

78. *A certain great prince*. Henry IV of France (1553–1610), assassinated by a Catholic fanatic.

79. *corpora quaeque*. A Lucretian phrase, 'any bodies'; iv. 1065.

Idque petit . . . gestique coire. 'And the body seeks that object by which the mind is wounded in love. He tends to that by which he is struck and desires to unite with it': Lucretius, *De Rerum Natura*, iv. 1048 and 1055.

[*Cunnus*]*teterrima belli* | *Causa* ——. '[A cunt], most dreadful cause of war': Horace, *Satires*, I. iii. 107.

a mighty king. Louis XIV.

dragoon. The dragonnades in the Cevennes against the Protestant *camisards*, a French 'enthusiastic' sect.

80. *academy of modern Bedlam*. Bedlam (originally the priory of Bethlehem), a mental hospital for 150 patients, in 1675 moved into a new building in Moorfields near London Wall, not far from where the Royal Society met (see note to p. 116 (2).

Apollonius. Of Tyana, *fl*. at the beginning of the Christian era, a sage who held Pythagorean doctrines and was credited with miraculous powers.

clinamina. Lucretius (ii. 292) used *clinamen* ('inclination') to render Epicurus's *parenklisis*, the deviation from the straight path which allowed atoms to collide by chance and create the matter of the world.

Cartesius . . . his romantic system . . . vortex. See p. 114 and ibid., n. (3), and p. 117 and ibid., n. (4).

81. *our hackney-coachmen . . . Est quod gaudeas . . . viderere*. The joke springs from two letters written in May and December 54 BC by Cicero to his young friend C. Trebatius Testa, whom he was recommending to Julius Caesar for employment in the invasion of Britain. (1) '. . . enter a [caveat] for

yourself against the tricks of those charioteers in Britain . . .'; (2) 'You have good reason to rejoice in having arrived [in Gaul] where you can appear as a knowledgeable man! Had you gone to Britain as well, I dare say there would have been no greater expert than you in the whole vast island'; Cicero, *Letters to Friends*, vii. 6 and 10.

82. *to cut the feather.* To split hairs, to make a fine distinction.

Jack of Leyden. See note to p. 67 (3).

84. *the films and images that fly off . . . from the superficies of things.* Lucretius, *De Rerum Natura*, iv. 30–2: '. . . *What we call "images" of things*, a sort of outer skin perpetually peeling off the surface of objects and flying about this way and that through the air . . .'

85. *one man . . . leaps into a gulf.* Marcus Curtius to save Rome leaped fully armed, on horseback, into the chasm that had opened in the Forum.

another . . . unluckily timing it . . . Empedocles. fl. 450 BC, philosopher and mystagogue, said to have perished on entering the crater of Mt. Etna, either to show he was a god, or out of curiosity.

the elder Brutus. Lucius Junius Brutus, traditional founder of the Roman republic; he was said to have feigned stupidity to avoid the vengeance of the Tarquin kings.

ingenium par negotiis. 'A character equal to its duties': Tacitus, *Annals*, vi. 39 and xvi. 18.

Sir E[dwar]d S[eymou]r . . . Leading Tory MPs.

Bedlam. see p. 80 and ibid., n. (1); the following passage will remind the reader of the Academy of Lagado in *Gulliver's Travels*, Book III. iv, and also of Swift's poem *The Legion Club.*

threepence in his pocket. The traditional share of the (shilling) coach-hire for each of a party of four lawyers from the Inns of Court to Westminster Hall.

86. *ecce cornuta erat ejus facies.* Exodus 34: 29, 30.

the society of Warwick Lane. The Royal College of Physicians stood in Warwick Lane from 1674 to 1825.

87. *the orator of the place.* The guide.

88. *Will's . . . Gresham College . . . Moorfields . . . Scotland Yard . . . Westminster Hall . . . Guildhall.* Will's coffee-house was the resort of the wits and poets . . . The Royal Society met in Gresham College, Broad Street . . . Bedlam was in Moorfields . . . There was a barracks in Scotland Yard, 'where gentlemen soldiers lie basking in the sun, like so many swine upon a warm dunghill' (Ned Ward, *The London Spy*, ed. A. L. Hayward [1927], p. 172) . . . The law courts met in Westminster Hall . . . The Lord Mayor and aldermen of the City of London meet in Guildhall, north of Cheapside.

the famous Troglodyte philosopher. Probably one of the series of covert (and ambivalent) references in *A Tale of a Tub* to Francis Bacon, who earns this sobriquet by his image of the *Idols of the Cave* in *The New Organum*, I. liii–lviii: 'The *Idols of the Cave* take their rise in the particular constitution, mental or bodily, of each individual . . .' They include 'certain particular sciences and speculations' to which men become attached, 'either because they fancy themselves the authors and inventors thereof [folly embossed], or because they have bestowed the greatest pains upon them and become habituated to them [folly inlaid] . . .' The whole passage is relevant to Swift's satire.

89. *Dr. Bl[ackmo]re*, Richard Blackmore, see p. 119, n. (3).

L[estran]ge. Sir Roger L'Estrange.

rectifier of saddles. 'Set the saddle on the right horse': lay the blame on those who deserve it; proverbial from 1607 (*ODEP*³, 690).

furniture of an ass. See note to p. 113 (1).

90. *the Rosicrucians*. The secret society of the Rosicrucians, one of the interests of Thomas Vaughan (see pp. (64 (4), 149), is supposed to have been founded by Christian Rosenkreuz in the fifteenth century, to preserve a system of occult wisdom allowing the attainment of knowledge into all the secrets and mysteries of Nature. The brotherhood were required to conceal their membership and their hermetic knowledge.

91. *Bythus and Sigè*. Bythus, Sigè (depth, silence, two of the primary 'aeons' or religious principles), and Acamoth (representing the Hebrew word for wisdom) come from the account of the teaching of Valentinian the Gnostic, in Irenaeus, *Adverus Haereses* (see note to p. 1 (2)), I. iv. 2.

à cujus lacrymis . . . timore mobilis. 'From the tears of the Demiurge proceeds the damp substance, from his laughter the bright, from his sorrow the solid, from his fear the mobile': Irenaeus, see above.

Anima Magica Abscondita. Thomas Vaughan (see note to p. 61 (5)), *Anima Magica Abscondita: Or, A Discourse of the Universal Spirit of Nature, With his strange, abstruse, miraculous Ascent and Descent . . .* (1650).

92. *reduce all things into types*. See note to p. 18 (4): typological or symbolic reading of the Scriptures, and relating this typology to politics and historical events, are characteristics of some Christian groups, such as seventeenth-century 'Puritans' or the modern Jehovah's Witnesses.

93. *a passage near the bottom*. Guthkelch, 191, suggests Revelation 22: 11: 'he which is filthy, let him be filthy still', omitted in some manuscripts.

94. *It was ordained*. A passage mocking the Calvinistic emphasis on predestination.

95. *Vide Don Quixote*. Part I, chap. xviii; silver was used in nasal prosthesis.

an ancient temple of Gothic structure. Stonehenge, 'Gothic' because it was judged rude and barbarous, supposedly built by the Druids.

96. *a strange kind of speech*. See note to p. 74 (2).

the Spanish accomplishment of braying. Don Quixote, Part II, chapters xxv and xxvii; the adventure of the alderman braying to recover a lost ass.

the stinging of the tarantula. Those bitten by the tarantula spider were believed to be afflicted with hysterical dancing (tarantism), which could be calmed by music.

feared no colours. 'Feared no enemy', from 'colours' meaning 'flags'; 'colours' may also mean embellishments of style, rhetorical ornaments.

leap . . . into the water. Total immersion in adult baptism.

pilgrim's salve. An ointment made from pork fat and isinglass.

a-groaning, like the famous board. Elm boards made to groan in this way, by virtue of their fibrous structure, were exhibited as prodigies.

98. *Effugiet . . . Proteus.* 'But Proteus, the rascal, will still escape from these bonds': Horace, *Satires*, II. 71.

artes perditae. 'Lost arts': see note to p. 75 (2).

slitting of one ear *in a stag . . .* A remark of Aristotle's in *Historia Animalium*, vi. 29 (578[b]).

99. *improve the growth of ears.* The cropped hair of male Puritans (Roundheads) gave prominence to the ears.

100. *six senses . . . *Including Scaliger's.* J. C. Scaliger, *De Subtilitate* (1537), p. 358; cf. Robert Burton, *The Anatomy of Melancholy* (1628), Pt. I. sect. 1, memb. 1, subsect. 6: '. . . to which you may add Scaliger's sixth sense of titillation, if you please'.

oscitancy. See note to p. 60 (1).

101. *that noble Jesuit.* Father Pierre-Joseph d'Orleans (*fl.* 1688–1734) SJ, *Histoire de M. Constance* (1690), 'Avertissement'.

102. *to write upon nothing.* Cf. Rochester's poem 'Upon Nothing' (*c.*1680) and, later, Henry Fielding, 'Essay on Nothing' (1743).

ut plenus vitæ conviva. 'Like a dinner guest full of life': Lucretius, *De Rerum Natura*, iii. 938.

a very polite nation in Greece. The people of Troezen; Pausanias, ii. 31. 5.

THE BATTLE OF THE BOOKS

104. *Bookseller.* The publisher; but the sentences were probably written by Swift.

Books in St. James's Library. The royal library, inadequately housed in St James's Palace.

105 *Vide Ephem. de Mary Clarke; opt. edit.* 'Vincent Wing's' sheet almanac printed by Mary Clark; it contained the annual calendar [ephemerides], prognostications, and other material, and was embellished with a set of eight verses: 'War begets Poverty, | Poverty Peace: | Peace maketh Riches flow, | (Fate ne'er doth cease:) | Riches produceth Pride, | Pride is war's

ground, | . . .' Swift's jocular reference parodies 'modern' pedantic citation and specifies the 'best edition'.

in the Republic of Dogs . . . A satirical version of Hobbes's political philosophy; see note to p. 18 (2).

106. *especially towards the East.* Referring to Temple's notions of traditional and unrecorded wisdom in Egypt, India, and the east.

107. *representatives, for passengers to gaze at.* Books were advertised by pasting up copies of their title-pages in the street.

a certain spirit, which they call brutum hominis. Guthkelch, 222, cites Thomas Vaughan's *Anthroposophia Theomagica* (1650), p. 58, quoting Paracelsus, as Swift's source for this phrase.

108. *to bind them to the peace with strong iron chains.* Swift's main joke refers to the books in chained libraries, but he also utilizes the magistrates' sentence of 'binding over to keep the peace'.

the works of Scotus. John Duns Scotus (?1265–1308), the 'Subtle Doctor', contributed to the already dominant Aristotelianism of European theology.

the guardian . . . chiefly renowned for his humanity. Richard Bentley, Keeper of the Royal Library; Boyle in the preface to his edition of Phalaris's *Epistles* sarcastically complained of Bentley's refusal of sufficient access to a manuscript, 'pro singulari sua humanitate' ('with that courtesy which distinguishes him'); Bentley, in replying, chose to take this as meaning 'out of his singular humanity', i.e. care of readers. *Humanity* could also mean classical literature and civilization.

two of the Ancient chiefs. Phalaris and Aesop.

109. *a strange confusion of place among all the books in the library.* Bentley argued that the royal library was so disorganized when he took it over in 1693, that he could not safely allow public access to it.

the Seven Wise Masters. 'The seven sages' of Greece was a collective description, also as 'the seven wise men', of any seven of a group of sages of the sixth century BC, including Solon and Thales. 'The Seven Wise Masters', however, or 'The Seven Sages of Rome', is the title of various medieval collections of stories nested in a tale concerning a young prince and his seven teachers. See p. 174 above.

Withers. George Wither or Withers (1588–1667), poet and writer of Puritan pamphlets in verse, commonly at this time cited as a hack rhymester, as in Dryden's *Essay on Dramatic Poesy* (1668); Swift yokes him with Dryden, and contrasts Dryden with the great poet Virgil, whose *Aeneid* Dryden had translated.

light-horse, heavy-armed foot, and mercenaries. Poets, historians, and translators.

110. *the Moderns were much the more ancient of the two.* The paradox was made by,

among others, Bacon in *The Advancement of Learning*, I. v. l, '. . . These times are the ancient times, when the world is ancient. . . .'

112. *my improvements in the mathematics*. The advances in mathematics during the previous decades, together with improvements in navigation and fortification as well as the work of the Royal Society, all formed the most powerful 'modern' arguments for the superiority of the modern age.

the regent's humanity. Bentley; see note to p. 108 (3).

113. *the borrowed shape of an ass*. In his *Dissertation*, Bentley quoted the Greek proverb, 'Leucon carries one thing, and his ass quite another', in relation to Boyle's mistaken view of the authorship of 'Phalaris's' *Epistles*. Boyle chose to say that Bentley distinguished between the Greek text and the ass who edited it.

a large vein of wrangling and satire. Temple's 'Essay': '. . . the vein of ridiculing all that is serious and good, all honour and virtue, as well as learning and piety . . . is the itch of the age and climate, and has over-run both the court and the stage . . .' (p. 161).

sweetness and light. A phrase taken up by Matthew Arnold in *Culture and Anarchy* (1869).

114. *consults*. '. . . the great consult [of Satan and his followers] began': Milton, *Paradise Lost*, I. 798.

Despréaux. Nicholas Boileau (1636–1711), known as Despréaux, was one of the chief French supporters of the Ancients; here as one of the leading Modern poets, along with Abraham Cowley (see note to p. 120 (1)).

the bowmen . . . Des Cartes, Gassendi, and Hobbes. Philosophers . . . Swift names as their leaders three of the leading Moderns in this field, united in Swift's eyes by 'sufficiency', belief in the uniqueness and novelty of their arguments. Each of them, too, elaborates a mathematico-physical framework for their ideas. Temple in his 'Essay' knows 'of no philosophers that have made entries upon that noble stage for fifteen hundred years past, unless Descartes and Hobbes should pretend to it'. See p. 157.

that [*arrow*] *of Evander*. In the *Aeneid*; although attention is drawn to king Evander's 'noble quiver of Lycian arrows' (viii. 166), it was during the archery contest (v. 485–544) that the arrow of *Acestis* 'caught fire, defined its track with flames and vanished into thin air, as shooting stars . . .'.

Paracelsus . . . Harvey, their great aga. Theophrastus Bombast von Hohenheim (1493–1541), Swiss alchemist and physician, took the name Paracelsus [the equal of Celsus, the principal Roman writer on medicine]; he struck out against medical dogma drawn from the traditional study of the writings of Aristotle and Galen . . . William Harvey (1578–1657) demonstrated the circulation of the blood; Temple reasonably enough in his 'Essay' says that this had at that date made no change 'in the practice of physic', but it had far-reaching theoretical implications. Harvey is given the title of a Turkish commander-in-chief.

Guicciardine, Davila, Polydore Virgil, Buchanan, Mariana, Cambden. Francisco Guicciardini (1483–1540), Florentine author of *Historia d'Italia* 1521; English 1579); Enrico Davila, *Historia della Guerre Civili di Francia* (1630); Polydore Vergil (1470–1555), an Italian who became naturalized and wrote a history of England (1534); George Buchanan (1506–82), Scottish humanist, the author of a *History of Scotland* in Latin (1582); Juan de Mariana (1537–1627), author of *Historia d'España* (1601); William Camden (1551–1623), historian and antiquary, author of the compilation *Britannia* (in Latin, 1586; translated into English from 1610).

engineers . . . Regiomontanus and Wilkins. Mathematicians . . . Johann Muller (1436–76) of Königsberg; John Wilkins (1614–72), one of the founders of the Royal Society, later Bishop of Chester; in his 'Thoughts on Reviewing the Essay', Temple sneers at Wilkins's *The Discovery of a World in the Moon . . . that . . . there may be another habitable World in the Planet* (1638–40) and at his *Essay towards a Real Character and Philosophic [universal] Language* (1668). Swift jokes about the latter ideal in *Gulliver's Travels*, 'Voyage to Laputa', chapter V.

Bellarmine. Cardinal Roberto Bellarmino (1542–1621), Roman Catholic apologist, who is linked with two of the great Schoolmen.

calones . . . led by L'Estrange. Roman grooms or lower servants . . . Sir Roger L'Estrange (1616–1704), translator of, among other things, *The Fables of Aesop and Others* (1692); see p. xiiif. above.

Vossius. Isaac Vossius (1618–89), Dutch scholar and canon of Windsor; Swift read his work on classical prosody, *De Sibyllinis*, in 1698 and owned a copy of it (*SL* 434).

115. *Momus, the patron of the Moderns . . . Pallas.* Momus, in mythology a son of primeval Night, became the personification of carping criticism; contrasted with Pallas Athena, daughter of Zeus and tutelary goddess of Athens.

second causes. See *Glossary*.

116. *schoolboys judges of philosophy.* See Temple, 'Essay', p. 159 above.

seminaries of Gresham and Covent Garden. In London, the Royal Society met at Gresham College in Broad Street until 1710; Covent Garden, the area of the theatre, of Will's coffee-house and others, and of the Rose Tavern (see Glossary), was the 'college' of the wits.

117. *Paracelsus . . . Galen.* The 'chemical' medicine of Paracelsus, Val Belmont and others, emphasizing observation and experiment, scorned the medical tradition founded on the precepts of the ancient Greek physician, Galen (see note to p. 114 (5)).

Hic pauca desunt . . . Swift parodies the formulae by which scholars indicated incomplete manuscripts: 'Here a little is missing', 'Not a little wanting', 'A large hiatus in the manuscript', 'A hiatus greatly to be mourned'.

Bacon. Mentioned by Temple in his 'Essay' as one of the 'great wits among the moderns'; he is significantly not wounded.

Des Cartes . . . his own vortex. See note to p. 114 (3); Descartes' mathematico-physical picture of the universe involved a theory of *vortices*, which attracted hostile theological criticism as materialistic.

118. *Gondibert.* Sir William Davenant (1606–68) projected a heroic poem set in medieval Lombardy; this was published at some length, but unfinished, in 1651. 'Are . . . the flights of Boileau above those of Virgil? If . . . this must be allowed, I will then yield Gondibert to have exceeded Homer, as is pretended . . .' (Temple, 'Essay'; see p. 159).

Denham, a stout Modern . . . Sir John Denham (1615–69) was best known for a blank-verse play, *The Sophy* (1642), and for his innovatory topographical poem, *Cooper's Hill* (1642).

Wesley. Samuel Wesley (1662–1736) the elder, rector of Epworth in Lincolnshire and father of John and Charles. His extensive verse writings, especially *The Life of our Blessed Lord and Saviour Jesus Christ: an heroic poem* (1693) and *History of the Old and New Testament in Verse* (1701–4), attracted scorn.

Perrault . . . Fontenelle. Charles Perrault (1628–1703), French poet and writer of fairy-tales, reformer of the French Academy, whose poem in praise of the Moderns, *Le Siècle de Louis le Grand* (1687), initiated the controversy in France (see p. 152) . . . Bernard Le Bovier, Sieur de Fontenelle (1657–1757), secretary of the French Academy of Sciences and author of several works on the side of the Moderns, principally *Nouveaux Dialogues des Morts* (1683) and *Digression sur les Anciens et les Modernes* (1688): see p. 152.

the lady in a lobster. A small, bony structure in a lobster's stomach.

119. *Dryden, in a long harangue.* Dryden published his translation of *The Works of Virgil* in 1697; a particularly long dedication to the Marquis of Normanby was prefixed to the *Aeneis*, dealing with epic poetry and the translation itself.

Lucan. Marcus Annaeus Lucanus (39–65), author of the unfinished epic poem *Pharsalia; De Bello Civili* [*On the Civil War*] in ten books.

Blackmore. Sir Richard Blackmore (*c.*1650–1729), poet and physician-in-ordinary to William III and Queen Anne; his long philosophical, heroic and epic poems, such as *King Arthur* (1697), provoked satirical scorn at 'Blackmore's endless line', but Aesculapius, the god of medicine, takes a charitable view of his practice as a doctor.

Creech. Thomas Creech (1659–1700), translator: his version of *Lucretius* (1682) is quoted in *A Tale of a Tub*, and was followed by his *Horace* (1684).

Ogleby. John Ogleby or Ogilby (1600–76) translated *Aesop* into verse (1650); his *Virgil* (1649; with plates, 1654) and *Homer* (1660–5) were lavishly printed and illustrated; the *Virgil* plates were reused in Dryden's volume.

Oldham . . . and Afra the Amazon. Both John Oldham (1653–83), a notable satirist, and Mrs Afra Behn (1640–89), novelist and dramatist, tried their hands (as did Swift himself) at the fashionable, complicated Pindaric odes.

120. *Cowley*. Abraham Cowley (1618–67) had a very high reputation as a poet in his own day; he introduced the fashion for Pindaric odes in English; he published a collection of love poems, *The Mistress* (1647), which gains him here the protection of Venus.

scarce a dozen cavaliers . . . '. . . a giant stone . . . this, scarce twice six chosen men, of such build as earth now produces, could lift on their shoulders . . .' (*Aeneid*, xii. 896ff.), an epic formula, also in Homer; several others are buried here and there in Swift's text, forming an important layer in the satire.

a thousand incoherent pieces. Critics scorned Bentley's habit of stitching together numerous quotations from classical texts, which they claimed he drew not from wide reading but from dictionaries and lexicons: cf. *A Tale of a Tub*, p. 69 above.

an Etesian wind. Regular winds [Greek, 'yearly'].

121. *Scaliger*. Joseph Justus Scaliger (1540–1609), a classical scholar whose bad manners are noticed in Boyle's *Examination*, but defended by Bentley in his *Dissertation*.

thy study of humanity. See note to p. 108 (3).

122. *Aldrovandus's tomb*. Ulisse Aldrovandi (1522–1605), a Bolognese naturalist, who spent his life on his compilations, his *tomb*.

roaring in his bull. Perillus invented the brazen bull for Phalaris, tyrant of Acragas in Sicily, in the early sixth century BC, and was himself the first victim of the device.

123. ————. Francis Atterbury.

124. *new polished and gilded*. Boyle's editing of Phalaris's *Epistles* (1695).

THE MECHANICAL OPERATION OF THE SPIRIT

126. *T. H. Esquire*. Possibly Thomas Hobbes, a theorist of 'motion' (see note to p. 114 (3)).

New Holland. Australia: by the mid-seventeenth century, Dutch seamen voyaging from the Dutch East Indies had sailed down the west coast of the as yet unexplored continent.

127. *Iroquois Virtuosi . . . Gresham . . . the Literati of Tobinambou*. In 1687, Charles Perrault read his modern poem lauding *Le Siècle de Louis le Grand* to the French Academy (see p. 152), provoking several epigrams by Boileau; Sir

William Temple reprinted one of them in his 'Thoughts upon Reviewing the Essay of Ancient and Modern Learning' (see p. 154); it concludes: 'Where can anyone have said such a shameful thing? Among the Huron Indians? Among the Topinambous?' 'No! In Paris.' 'In the mad-house then?' 'No! In the Louvre, at a full meeting of the French Academy.' The Topinambous were a tribe of Brazilian Indians. The Royal Society was meeting at this time in Gresham College, Broad Street.

129. *The Planetary Worlds.* The plurality of inhabited worlds was an old speculation given new life by sixteenth- and seventeenth-century discoveries in optics and astronomy: see note to p. 114 (7), and cf. Fontenelle, *Entretiens sur la pluralité des mondes habités* (1686).

The Squaring of the Circle. An impossible problem solved, as he believed, by Thomas Hobbes.

Hippocrates tells us. De Aere, Aquis, et Locis, 35, 36, but in his mention of the [long-heads] he says nothing of the Scythians (see note to p. 47 (3).

130. *Roundheads.* See note to p. 99.

the following fundamental. The Aristotelian antithesis of 'corruption' and 'generation' was a scholastic commonplace and the source of many jokes: e.g. 'the corruption of pipes is the generation of stoppers' (Swift, *Polite Conversation*, Dialogue II).

131. *modern saints.* See note to p. 28 (2).

the second chapter of the Acts. i.e. Acts of the Apostles, dealing with the day of Pentecost, when the Holy Spirit appeared to the Apostles as cloven tongues of fire, and they spoke with 'other tongues'.

while their hats were on. See note to p. 27 (2).

Jauguis. Yogis (*Suite des Memoires du Sieur Bernier, sur L'Empire du Grand Mogol*, Paris, 1671, 57, 60–1: Swift owned a two-volume set of Bernier's *Voyages*, Amsterdam, 1699 [*SL* 65]). *Yoga* is union with the supreme spirit.

Guagnini ... Alexander Guagninus, *Sarmatiae* [Poland and south-east Russia] *Descriptio* (1578), 'Moschoviae Descriptio' *sub* 'Mulierum conditio' ['the condition of women'].

133. *Dum fas ... avidi—.* 'When furious with passion they distinguish right and wrong by the narrow line their desire marks out': Horace, *Odes*, I. viii. 10, 11.

134. *the picture of Hobbes's Leviathan.* At the top of the engraved title-page of the first edition of Hobbes, *Leviathan* (1651), a crowned figure holding a sword and a crozier rises behind a view of hills and a city; the torso and arms are made up of diminutive figures.

135. *the choice and cadence of the syllables.* An important critical principle for Swift.

enigmatically meant by Plutarch. Convivium VII Sapientium, 5.

Sir H[u]mphrey Edw[i]n. A presbyterian Lord Mayor, 1697–8; see p. 101.

Thy word . . . paths. Psalm 119: 105.

Canting. See p. 1.

136. *a Banbury saint.* Banbury, Oxfordshire, was famous for the zeal of its Puritans, who in 1602 demolished the famous cross there.

137. *Rippon spurs.* Ripon in the West Riding of Yorkshire was the centre of a celebrated equestrian accessories industry, including saddlery and the proverbial 'right Ripon spurs'.

lecture. An exposition of a scripture passage, often held in mid-week, not part of the Sunday services.

the Rod of Hermes. The winged *caduceus*, herald's staff (or magic wand) of Mercury, messenger of the gods.

the snuffle of a bagpipe. 'Bagpipe' glimmers throughout this passage to represent the Scottish Kirk; see also note to p. 27 (1).

as Darius did . . . the day before. Darius conspires with six other Persian noblemen to kill Smerdis, the usurper; when they have done so, the assassins agree that he should be king whose horse neighs first after sunrise. Darius' groom arranges the previous night for his master's stallion to cover a mare, and the next morning, on encountering the mare, Darius' horse neighs (Herodotus, *Histories*, iii, 85–6).

138–9. *The most early traces we meet with of fanatics in ancient story* . . . i.e. history. The references in this dense paragraph on ancient ecstatic religion, amusing as many of them are individually, may be so congested as to have driven the whole piece out of *A Tale* proper. The passage may also be one of the links between *A Tale* and Tolland's deist volume, *Christianity not Mysterious* (1696), which sets out to attack religious 'mysteries' as profitable ecclesiastical shams. The following are a few suggestions for elucidating it: *Orgia*—secret rites, e.g. the Eleusinian Mysteries; *Panegyres*—an assembly of a whole nation; *Dionysia*—festival (orgia) of Dionysus, a Thracian god of an ecstatic religion; *Orpheus*—to whom is attributed in Greek mythology the foundation of the mystic religion of Orphism, involving Demeter and Dionysus; *Melampus*—a Greek prophet who used the voices of birds and reptiles, which he (like Orpheus) understood, for divination; *Diod. Sic. L.1.*—Diodorus Siculus [*World History*], i (Egypt), 97, 286;—*scouting through the index*—see note to p. 120 (3) (1); *Herod. L.2*—Herodotus, *Histories*, ii. 77, 'they drink a wine made from barley'; *the Scarlet Whore*—Revelation 17, identified by the sectaries with the Pope and mitred bishops.

139. *Dionysia Brauronia.* Brauron, on the east coast of Attica, was the centre of a quinquennial festival of Dionysus.

Vide *Photium* . . . Photius, *Bibliotheca*, iii, preserves fifty stories from Greek mythology by Conon, *fl.* 90 BC.

Simon Magus . . . Eutyches. Simon the Magician (or the Revealer) was a name to which many stories in early Christian legend were attracted;

Irenaeus, *Adversus Haereses*, I. xxiii, identifies him with the Simon of Acts 8: 9–24 and further names him as the original Gnostic teacher. . . . Eutyches was a fifth-century heresiarch, archimandrite of Constantinople, who taught that Christ possessed only a divine essence; this in turn implied the deification of human nature.

140. *John of Leyden, David George, Adam Neuster.* For the Dutch-born Anabaptist, Jan Bockleszoon, see note to p. 167 (3); David George or Joris (1501–56), another Dutch Anabaptist, founded the 'Familists' or Family of Love; Adam Neuster (d. 1576) was a German Socinian theologian, i.e. he denied the divinity of Christ.

Family of Love, Sweet Singers of Israel. By using these generic names, Swift introduces into his catalogue of 'enthusiasts' the Anabaptist or 're-baptized' groups that proliferated in England in the middle decades of the seventeenth century. He gives an undeserved prominence to these extreme groups, provocatively associating them with quietists like the Quakers.

furor [*Uterinus*]. 'Mania of the uterus': nymphomania: see G. S. Rousseau, 'Nymphomania, Bienville, and the Rise of Erotic Sensibility' in Boucé (ed.), *Sex and Sexuality in Eighteenth-Century Britain* (1982).

141. *that philosopher . . . into a ditch.* An ancient jest sometimes attributed to Thales: see Diogenes Laertius, I, i, 8, 34; and Plato, *Theaetetus*, 174A.

ADDITIONS TO *A TALE OF A TUB*

142. [a] *The History of Martin* and *A Digression on Wars and Quarrels* and [b] *A Project, For the universal improvement of Mankind* were first printed in *Miscellaneous Works, Comical and Diverting*: by *T*[he] *R*[everend] *J*(onathan) *S*[wift] *D*[ean] *O*[f] [St] *P*[atrick's] *I*[n] *I*[reland]. *In Two Parts*: *I The Tale of a Tub*; *with the Fragment* & *The Battle of the Books* [the 1711 piracy: Teerink 224]; *with considerable Additions, & explanatory Notes, never before printed. II Miscellanies in Prose and Verse* [part of 1711 vol.: Teerink 2], *by the supposed Author of the first Part* (London [properly, The Hague], *printed by order of the Society de propagando*, &c. [1720]). The book was published by Thomas Johnson, a Scottish printer working in The Hague, who seems to have had good contacts with the trade in London, and was well respected.

'A general Table or Index of the whole work' was constructed of material said to have been derived from 'a manuscript' and which had been sent to the publisher, together with a letter printed in the 'Booksellers Advertisement' (Guthkelch, 293–7). An attempt was made to fit the unpublished pieces into the sequence of the Table, which is of course a summary of the printed work. The manuscript seems to have been the substance of *A Tale* before it was joined with *The Battle of the Books* to 'make a four shilling book'. The 1720 volume must be regarded *prima facie* as more or less accurately reporting the manuscript, and this is supported by the several other indications that link the material with Swift's other works (see p. xvii).

GLOSSARY

adust, burned up with heat (also a medical term).
afflatus (literally) breathing upon; inspiration.
alamode, in the fashion.
amarant (*Amaranth; amarathine*) unfading (flower).
ambages, circuitous, roundabout ways.
an, if (an archaic word surviving only in dialect and proverb: 'ifs and ans').
anatomy, skeleton.
anima, air exhaled and inhaled, the breath of life.
animal rationale, rational animal.
animus (literally) wind; the rational and feeling soul, as opposed to *anima*, physical life.
antitype, the impression corresponding to the die; in typological interpretation, what is shadowed forth or indicated by the 'type' or symbol.
approves, shows, affirms.
arcanum, a mystery or hermetic secret.
argent, silver.
arrect, pricked up.
ars poetica, poetic art (as *The Art of Poetry*, the common title of a poem by Horace).
atramentous, black as ink.

bagnio (literally) baths or a bathing establishment; notoriously, a brothel.
bait, to stop for rest and refreshment.
basso relievo (bas-relief); low-relief carving, in which the figures are raised only a little from the background.
bedlam, a bedlamite, inmate of the St Mary of Bethlehem Hospital for the insane in London (see note to p. 80 (1)), or any mad person.
beeves, oxen, cattle; *pl.* of 'beef'.
bere, barley.
birth-day night, celebration for a royal birthday, royal reception.
bolus, a large pill.
boutade, a sudden motion, like a kick from a horse's hind legs.
briguing, intriguing, conspiring, from F *briguer.*
bulks, frameworks projecting from the fronts of buildings in a street, stalls, used for sleeping rough.

cabal *vb.* & *n.*, to intrigue; the intrigue itself; a small clique of intriguers.
calendae, calends: the first day of the month.
case (physical) condition; *in case*, in good condition.
cast a nativity, frame a horoscope for prediction.
chair, sedan-chair, a common mode of transport in London.
chapman, purchaser.
character, a cabbalistic sign or symbol.
cheapen, bargain to reduce the price.
choler, bile: one of the four humours; hot and dry, yellow.
christiana religio absoluta et simplex, the Christian religion, complete, all of a piece.
clap, venereal disease, usually gonorrhoea.
classis, kind, division; it was also a

Puritan word for the ministers of a district.

clyster-pipes, enemas.

cockle, the weed corn cockle (*Agrostemma githago*), whose seeds had to be sifted out of the seed corn; the task gave rise to several proverbs.

coelum empyreum, the highest heaven.

coif, close-fitting cap.

coil, uproar, fuss.

common-place, a passage or text of general application; often collected in 'common-place books'.

commons, daily fare.

complaisance, courtesy.

complexion, character, temperament.

congee, bow, originally at taking leave (*congé*).

conjurer, a person with occult powers; a fortune-teller.

control, to overrule.

conversed, an old form of *conversant*.

copia vera, true copy.

copperas, green vitriol or ferrous sulphate, used in making ink.

copy-hold, an English tenure of land, bound by the custom of the manor, less absolute than 'freehold'.

cully, a simpleton, gull.

cum appendice, with an appendix.

cum grano salis, with a grain of salt, sceptically.

deshabille, informal or leisure dress.

desiderata, things that are desired (to fill up blanks).

desunt nonnulla, not a few [words] are missing.

devoted, consecrated, doomed.

dispensible, subject to dispensation, able to be allowed; a royal 'dispensing power' was claimed by Charles II and James II, to set aside laws in special cases.

disploding, discharging or bursting out explosively.

distress, seizure of goods for the payment of a debt.

districts, limits, bounds; scope.

division, the disposition of material in a discourse, preliminary classification (in rhetoric and scholastic logic).

drawing room (royal) reception.

duo sunt genera, there are two kinds.

elogy (elogies), characterization(s); since these were usually favourable, the word became confused with *eulogy* and lost its separate existence.

enormous, out of the ordinary, abnormal: a Latinism.

every fit, every now and again.

exantlation, drawing or pumping out, as water from a well (L *exantlare*).

ex cathedra, from the bishop's chair, infallibly.

expatiating, wandering, roaming about.

exploded, clapped or hissed off the stage (L *explaudere*).

ex post facto (a law) made to punish a crime after it has been committed; retrospective.

expostulate the case, argue through, discuss, enlarge on.

fact, crime (in legal parlance).

fade, wan, commonplace.

fee-simple, absolute heritable possession.

figures, emblems; types (q.v.).

flight-shot, long-distance shot in archery.

flirted at, jeered at, bantered.

fonde, foundation, (financial) support.

free-thinkers, unbelievers, atheists.
fresh and fasting, medicinal direction found in patent medicine advertisements.
fugitive, volatile (in chemistry).

garnish, money extorted by a gaoler in return for better treatment, particularly, allowing light manacles, or freedom of movement within the prison.
gasconnade, vainglorious boasting or fiction, from the reputed character of the inhabitants of Gascony in south-west France.
goose, tailor's smoothing-iron, with a goose-neck handle.
grand monde, the great world.
Grands Titres, Noble Titles.
groat, fourpence; i.e. a small sum, in proverbial use.

hamated, hooked (L *hamatus*).
hic multa desiderantur, a great deal is missing here.
hieroglyph, secret character or hermetic symbol.
hobby-horses, obsessions.
horsed for discipline, placed piggy-back to be flogged on the posteriors by a schoolmaster.

impar, uneqal to the task.
in capite, in chief, holding land directly from the Crown.
inclusivè, inclusively, comprehensively (L *adv.* used in scholastic disputation).
Index expurgatorius, the list of books which Roman Catholics are forbidden to read, reviewed annually by the cardinals of the Congregation of the Index.
individuation, in Scholastic philosophy, the process leading to individual existence as distinct from the species (*OED*).
in foro conscientiae, in the court of conscience.
innuendo, an explanation in parenthesis (legal and scholastic use).
in petto, secretly (It., literally 'in the breast').
instinct, animated, impelled
interessed, concerned (archaic even in Swift's day).
in terminis, in the exact words.
interstitia, intervals.

jakes, a privy.
jure ecclesiae, by the law of the Church.

King's Bench, the highest court of common law in England.

lantern, a case for carrying a light, with transparent side(s) sometimes made of oiled paper.
last, a model of the foot on which a shoemaker or cobbler places the footwear on which he works.
levee, a (royal) morning reception, literally at the rising of the patron.
lover, affectionate friend, well-wisher.

maire du palais, the chief royal officer of the ancient Frankish kingdom [*mayor of the palace*]; turned the Merovingian kings into puppets, until (eighth century) Charles Martel seized the crown.
mangé votre bled en herbe, (having) eaten your corn in the blade; i.e. lived on your capital.
marish, obsolete form of 'marsh'.
medium, average.
meum et tuum, mine and thine.

mobile, *mobile vulgus* ('the volatile crowd'), the mob.
morsure, biting.
multa absurda sequerentur, many absurdities would follow.
mutatis mutandis, the necessary changes being made.

needle, not only the tailor's needle, but also the magnetic needle of the compass.
nemine contradicente, no one speaking against; unanimously.
nostrum, patent (or quack) medicine.
nuncupatory, oral.

olios, stews, cf. *olla podrida.*
opus magnum, great work; in alchemy, changing base metal to gold.
ordinaries, public eating-houses where a meal was regularly offered at a fixed price, as a *five-penny ordinary.*
os sacrum, 'the sacred bone'; a triangular structure at the base of the vertebrae, of which it is a continuation. A Jewish tradition explains its 'sacredness' as, resistant to decay, it will be the growth-point at the resurrection of the 'new body'.
oscitancy, negligence, sluggishness.

pale, an area within certain bounds, subject to a specific jurisdiction; cf. the effective English jurisdiction round Dublin established in 1547.
pandect, originally, Justinian's compendium of Roman law; hence any body of laws and, more generally, a complete digest of any subject.
parts, talents.
party, part, constituent.
pennyworth, bargain.
pericranies, brains (from L *pericrania*).
perorare, to bring a speech to an end, to conclude.
philologer, lover of letters or learning.
philomath, a lover of learning, especially a student of mathematics or natural philosophy; frequently, an astrologer.
phlebotomy, opening a vein to bleed a patient.
physic, medicine.
plate, precious metal, usually silver.
plight (good) condition.
points, laces for fastening together parts of the dress.
porringer, a small basin or bowl.
postulatum (postulata) thing(s) demanded or taken for granted before an argument starts.
prerogative, the royal pre-eminent right, theoretically subject to no restriction, particularly the claim to be able to be outside the common law, also to make peace and war etc.
pretend, claim. *Pretender,* Claimant.
primordium, first principle.
professors, professionals (of any science, art, or activity).
projector, promoter; for Swift always in a bad sense, a cheat, a speculator.
propriety (proprieties), property; an older form favoured by Swift.
prototype, an original type (q.v.).
puris naturalibus, in a state of nature; naked.
purlieus, outlying districts, perhaps disreputable.
put (country) bumpkin, 'buffer'.

quartum principium, fourth principle, or element.
quinta essentia, the 'fifth essence' drawn from the four elements (earth, air, fire, water); in ancient

and medieval philosophy it was the substance of the heavenly bodies.
quit, requite, repay.
quoad magis et minus, as far as, more or less.

ra[i]lly, to banter, to treat with good-humoured ridicule.
rationis capax, capable of reason.
receipt, recipe, prescription.
reinfunds, pours in again.
relievo, a work of art in relief, i.e. parts of it raised from a plane surface.
resent, feel deeply, take badly. *Resentments*, feelings of indignation.
Rose, tavern in Russell Street, Covent Garden, frequented by men of fashion and play-goers.
rubs, disagreeable experiences.

sack-posset, a drink made of hot curdled milk, white wine (cf. F. *sec*), and perhaps spices.
salivation, the contemporary treatment by mercury of veneral disease; it stimulated the flow of saliva.
sans consequence, without repercussions; unimportant.
save-all, a holder that allows the candle to be burned to the last.
scandalum magnatum, libelling magnates (peers).
scantling, a sample or specimen.
schools, universities, from the places of disputation which formed a main part of the academic programme in Swift's day.
second cause, in Aristotelian metaphysics, there was a fourfold account of causality: (1) *material cause*, the stuff out of which a thing is made; (2) *formal cause*, the essence of that thing; (3) *efficient cause*, the impetus or effect by which a thing is produced; (4) *final cause*, the aim or idea of the change.
serve the king, enlist as a soldier.
shadows, symbols, types (q.v.), foreshadowings, prefigurations.
sheet, broadside, or folded to a four-page pamphlet.
si mihi credis, if you will believe me.
smatter, talk ignorantly, prate.
snap-dragon, a Christmas game in which raisins are snatched from a bowl of burning brandy and eaten as they flame.
sophisters, at Trinity College, Dublin, third- or fourth-year students.
spargefaction, sprinkling.
sparkish, smart or elegant, likely to please a *spark* or dandy.
specie, kind, sort.
spleen, melancholy, ill humour, peevishness, depression; all thought to come from a disorder in that organ.
sponging-house, a baillif's house, in which he held debtors before their committal to prison.
stews, brothels, or in general the red-light district.
story, history.
stroll, to wander as a vagabond or prostitute.
sub dio, in the open air.
summity, summit (an obsolete form).
summum bonum, the supreme good.
surtout, an overcoat.

tabby, see *water tabby*.
table-book, a pocket- or memorandum-book.
taking off, distracting or diverting; also, putting to death.
tell, count.
tentiginous humour, an inclination to lust (from L. *tentigo*, an erection).

terms of art, technical expressions.
tertio modo, in the third way.
toilets, the morning ceremony of dressing.
totidem syllabis, in so many syllables.
totidem verbis, in so many words.
totis viribus, with all [our] strength.
trait, a touch or stroke.
truckling, subservient, obsequious.
turned head, opposite of *turned tail.*
turnpikes, spiked barriers across a road.
twelve-penny gallery, the cheapest (and uppermost) range of theatre seats, traditionally occupied by footmen.

uncontrollable, unalterable, independent.
undertaker, promoter of a speculative [for Swift, usually fraudulent] business enterprise; contractor.
use, interest, hence *usury*.

vamped, refurbished, patched.
vapours, hysterics.
virga genitalis, phallus.
virtuoso (usually) antiquary, scientific dilettante [from It., 'one specially skilled']; *pl. virtuoso[es]*; or *virtuosi*; also *adj.*
vizard, visor (of a helmet); also, mask.

water tabby, wavy or water-silk.

yard, a straight piece of wood, a stick; (nautical) the spar at right angles to the mast which extends the sail; a tailor's measure; the erect penis.

z[oun]ds, God's wounds!

INDEX

In this select Index, page numbers in roman refer to Swift's text, and those distinguished thus, 141°, also refer to relevant notes; numbers in *italics* refer to editorial matter and to the Appendices.

THE WORLD'S CLASSICS

A Select List

JANE AUSTEN: Emma
Edited by James Kinsley and David Lodge

Mansfield Park
Edited by James Kinsley and John Lucas

Northanger Abbey, Lady Susan, The Watsons, *and* Sanditon
Edited by John Davie

Persuasion
Edited by John Davie

Pride and Prejudice
Edited by James Kinsley and Frank Bradbrook

Sense and Sensibility
Edited by James Kinsley and Claire Lamont

ROBERT BAGE: Hermsprong
Edited with an introduction by Peter Faulkner

WILLIAM BECKFORD: Vathek
Edited by Roger Lonsdale

JAMES BOSWELL: Life of Johnson
The Hill/Powell edition, revised by David Fleeman
With an introduction by Pat Rogers

JOHN BUNYAN: The Pilgrim's Progress
Edited by N. H. Keeble

FANNY BURNEY: Camilla
Edited by Edward A. Bloom and Lilian D. Bloom

Evelina
Edited by Edward A. Bloom

JOHN CLELAND: Memoirs of a Woman of Pleasure (Fanny Hill)
Edited with an introduction by Peter Sabor

DANIEL DEFOE: Moll Flanders
Edited by G. A. Starr

Robinson Crusoe
Edited by J. Donald Crowley

Roxana
Edited by Jane Jack

MARIA EDGEWORTH: Castle Rackrent
Edited by George Watson

JOHN EVELYN: Diary
Selected and edited by John Bowle

HENRY FIELDING: Joseph Andrews *and* Shamela
Edited by Douglas Brooks-Davies

OLIVER GOLDSMITH: The Vicar of Wakefield
Edited by Arthur Friedman

MATTHEW LEWIS: The Monk
Edited by Howard Anderson

ANN RADCLIFFE:
The Italian
Edited by Frederick Garber

The Mysteries of Udolpho
Edited by Bonamy Dobrée

SIR WALTER SCOTT: The Heart of Midlothian
Edited by Clare Lamont

Redgauntlet
Edited by Kathryn Sutherland

Waverley
Edited by Claire Lamont

SIR PHILIP SIDNEY:
The Countess of Pembroke's Arcadia (The Old Arcadia)
Edited with an introduction by Katherine Duncan-Jones

TOBIAS SMOLLETT: The Expedition of Humphry Clinker
Edited by Lewis M. Knapp
Revised by Paul-Gabriel Boucé

The Last Chronicle of Barset
Edited by Stephen Gill

Orley Farm
Edited by David Skilton

Phineas Finn
Edited by Jacques Berthoud

Phineas Redux
Edited by John C. Whale
Introduction by F. S. L. Lyons

The Prime Minister
Edited by Jennifer Uglow
With an introduction by John McCormick

The Small House at Allington
Edited by James R. Kincaid

The Warden
Edited by David Skilton

The Way We Live Now
Edited by John Sutherland